PEACE, LOVE, AND FANGS

Twice Bitten: Book Five

CRYSTAL-RAIN LOVE

ISBN: 9798756729108

DEDICATION AND ACKNOWLEDGEMENTS

Huge thanks to Christle Gray, Greg Bennett, and TL Macon for always listening and always giving me the push I need.

Thanks to Manuela Serra for such gorgeous and inspiring cover art.

Thank you to all the readers who've left reviews or sent personal messages to brighten my day. It's been a rough year. Y'all help more than you'll ever know. I appreciate you all.

Thank you to Danielle Muething for bringing Danni to life so wonderfully in audio.

CHAPTER ONE

"Danni London Keller!"

The steady hum of voices, clinking bottles, and other bar noises ceased as all eyes turned toward the short, thick-waisted blonde woman standing ten feet from the booth I currently sat in. Only the song on the jukebox broke the silence, but I didn't think anyone was listening to it anymore. My mother's light eyes burned through me, pinning me in place.

"Of course she just had to screech my full name," I muttered as I stood from the booth, Rider right beside me.

My mother didn't waste any time storming toward us, nor did Rider waste any stepping in front of me. I grabbed his arm, gave a little squeeze to let him know I was good. I could handle my mother. He got the message and moved aside, but stayed close.

"Mom," I said by way of greeting once my mother stopped in front of me. The shady-looking man she'd brought with her stood at her side. He had dark hair thinning at the top, a sharp nose, and shrewd little eyes that burrowed into me before shifting over to Rider. He swallowed hard as he took in my boyfriend, wilting a little under Rider's hard gaze. Rider was a beautiful man, but he didn't exactly give off friendly vibes, especially when he went into protective mode. My mother's presence was one of numerous things guaranteed to bring out his protective instincts.

"Where is your sister?" my mother asked, not bothering with pleasantries. "I know you know something and you're going to tell me right this moment, young lady."

Rider's body tensed, his head dipped slightly to the side. I recognized the movement and knew someone was communicating with him telepathically. He looked over at the bar to where Daniel sat with Lana, the dragon shifter's attention focused on me. Their eyes met, Rider nodded, gave my back a gentle parting touch, and moved toward the door at the back of the room which led to his office. Clearly, something requiring his immediate attention had just come up and Daniel had been left in charge of handling whatever shitfest was about to go down between me and my mother.

"Is she dead?" my mother asked, clamping her hand around my forearm hard enough her nails almost penetrated my flesh. "Tell me what you know!"

I shook my mother's hand off and turned my head in a subtle side-to-side movement, locking eyes with Daniel as he stood from the bar, ready to intervene if need be. "You're making a scene."

"My daughter is missing. I'll make all the scenes I want. I'll make an entire production!"

"Calm down." The song finished playing on the jukebox, adding to the silence. "Let's take this somewhere private."

"Let's take this to wherever you're hiding Shana." Her nostrils flared as she stepped close enough I could feel the heat radiating from her body. "I am done playing games with you and these thugs. I want my daughter and I want her now."

A low growl came from my left. My mother jerked back as Kutya crept to my side. His head lowered, lips peeled back. I hadn't even realized Rider's new dog had stayed behind. He usually went wherever Rider went.

"Get control of that beast!"

"He isn't a beast," I said, scratching between the Doberman-shepherd mix's ears as he maintained the warning growl at my side. "My friends aren't thugs either, and I'm not a little girl you can yell at and boss around anymore. I'm also not my sister's keeper."

Her eyes narrowed. "You know where she is. You know her husband's body was found, or what was left of it."

I winced. I knew Kevin had been murdered and his body had been found, but Rider hadn't shared details about the where or how of his disposal. From the sound of it, it wasn't pretty.

"Just tell me if Shana was with him. Tell me what happened to her. Tell me what you did to her!"

"What I did to her?" Okay, so maybe Shana was lying in a coma-like state in a room in one of the bar's sublevels, and maybe I was part of the reason for that, but my mother had no clue about that or any reason to think I would harm my sister. I grabbed her by the arm and pulled her across the room, giving her skeevy-looking acquaintance who had yet to utter a word no choice but to follow as my mother tried in vain to pry my fingers off her bicep.

"Unhand me! I will not have this disrespect," she sputtered as I dragged her to the front door. Rome held it open as I stepped through, my mother in tow, along with her companion and now Daniel and Ginger.

I didn't release my grip on her arm until we were all outside and away from the entrance. "Just what exactly are you implying I did to my own sister, and who the hell is this guy?"

"Nick Pacitti," he introduced himself. "I'm looking for your sister."

I studied the man, taking in the day's worth of stubble

covering his round cheeks and the cheap suit that stretched a little too snug over his midsection. A bulge beneath the jacket indicated a gun holstered at his hip. He hadn't flashed a badge, so I figured he wasn't a cop. "Private dick, Dick?"

"It's Nick," he said, and fished out a business card from his pocket. "Pacitti Private Investigations."

I glanced at the card but didn't take it. I returned my attention to my mother. She stood still as a stone, except for her chest. It rose and fell forcefully with each angry breath.

"Kevin White's remains were found and two men who worked private security for him have gone missing, along with your sister," the man said. "We have reason to believe you know their whereabouts."

"I haven't seen Shana since she went back to Kevin shortly after their wedding," I told him, "and I don't know anything about anyone who worked security for her husband. I barely knew Kevin, let alone his employees."

This wasn't entirely true. I'd killed a man named Jamal who worked security for Shana's husband. He'd offed Kevin after being seduced by my sister, but I really had no clue anyone else Kevin had employed had gone missing. I was pretty sure, however, the other missing security guard was probably dead, a consequence of knowing too much. Shana had gone a little psycho after being turned. Maybe she'd killed the guy just to drink fresh blood, or because he'd annoyed her. It was hard to say what had happened in the short time between her turning and the spell that had been worked which now left her comatose.

"You know something," my mother snapped. "She was perfectly happy all the way up to her wedding, then you said something, did something, to cause her to leave her reception with you. You hid her here with this gangster you've taken up with."

"You spoke with her while she was here," I reminded her. "She told you she was here of her own free will."

"Maybe she was forced to say that!"

"Why would she be forced to say that? What reason would I have to kidnap my sister from her wedding reception? She had doubts, and she needed time to work through them. Once she did, she went back to Kevin. You know she did. You spoke with her."

"She was changed after you got through with her."

Well, that was kind of true. However, my mother had no clue just how changed she was. "I don't know what to tell you, Mom."

"You can start by telling me what the two of you got into it about. Your boyfriend said the two of you got into an argument and he hadn't seen her since."

Crap. I forgot Rider had told my mother that. I'd been a little busy with other life or death matters when I'd discovered Kevin's body had been found. I still hadn't entirely caught my breath from those events. Now I was stuck facing off with my mother and having to make up an argument off the top of my head.

"Well?" She tapped her foot, waiting.

"I don't remember."

"Oh, that's convenient." She turned toward Pacitti. "I want you to stick to her like glue. She knows what happened to her sister. She's always been jealous of her."

"I'm not jealous of Shana. She doesn't have anything I want," I said, and for the first time in my life I meant it. "Except for a mother's love, maybe, but you know what… I'm over needing that too."

I heard my mother gasp as I turned away, but I didn't react to it, sure it was the sound of indignation. She'd have to actually give a damn about me in order to be hurt, and she'd only ever given a damn about Shana.

Daniel squeezed my shoulder as we made our way back into the bar, but didn't say anything. The normal sounds of the bar greeted us, everyone inside having found other sources of amusement after we'd moved the show outside. We barely had time to enjoy the normalcy before the door opened behind us and Pacitti stepped inside.

Rome glanced down at the man, then over at us, raising an eyebrow in silent question. His meaty hand clamped on the shorter man's shoulder, holding him in place, before the detective could fully step to us.

"Watch the hands, Goliath!" Pacitti squared his shoulders. "I have every right to be in this establishment, and I'm meaner than I look."

"Don't toss him out… yet," I said, closing the distance. "Look, Dick, I know my mother hired you to find my sister and I appreciate that you have a job to do, but you're wasting your time with me. I haven't seen her and have no clue where she's at. In case you didn't figure it out from that little exchange we had outside, we aren't close. My family is a little dysfunctional."

"What family isn't?" he said. "And it's Nick."

"Sure, Dick. I'll be sure to tell Shana to call my mother if I hear from her."

"That's kind of you, but if you don't mind, I'll just hang around to see if she shows up." He shrugged out of Rome's hold and took a step forward, putting himself directly eye to eye with me. "And I'll follow you until you slip because I have this gut, you see, and this gut is telling me you know exactly where your sister is. This gut is telling me you're going to eventually give me exactly what I need."

I looked down at his rounded belly. "You might want to listen a little closer to that gut. I'm pretty sure it's telling you what you need is to lay off the beers and snack cakes."

His eyes narrowed. "Where's your sister?"

Where the hell was this guy's toothbrush? I stepped back, distancing myself from the halitosis burning my corneas. "Look, Dick, I'd love to hand Shana over, but I'm afraid that's impossible. I just got back into town and haven't seen her since before I left, which was weeks ago. I just heard her husband's body was found, and that is all I know. I don't even know where his body was found, how it was found, or how he was killed. I have nothing useful to give you, so why don't you do us both a favor and go look for Shana somewhere else?"

"You know, you don't seem very concerned about a missing sister whose husband was just found murdered."

"I have to be honest with you, Dick. If the situation were reversed and I was the one missing, neither my sister nor mother would even notice. Sue me if I can't muster more emotion than they'd spare for me. Now, I think I've given you more than enough of my time. You can leave."

"Lucky for me, it's a free country, and this is a public place. I think I'll order a beer and do a little people-watching."

"Unlucky for you, my boyfriend owns this establishment and you've gotten on my nerves." I looked up at Rome and nodded. The big guy immediately grabbed the private detective by the shoulder again.

Pacitti managed to wriggle out of Rome's meaty fingers before the hulking guard could get a firm grip and turned toward him, craning his head back to look up at him. "Grab me one more time, you oversized jackass, and I'm going to have to get physical."

Rome blinked, unbothered. "Are you really threatening me, little pot-bellied man? I shit things bigger than you."

"He does," Daniel said. "Don't ask me how I know."

"Thank you both for that image," I muttered. "Now, please, see Dick out."

"It's Nick," the red-faced investigator growled.

"Later, Dick." I gave him a little finger wave as Rome grabbed the back of his collar and hefted him off his feet.

"See ya, Dick." Daniel waved goodbye.

"Toodles, prick." Ginger blew him a kiss.

"Have a nice flight, Dick." Rome opened the door and literally tossed the man outside before returning to his post.

"Is it just me, or did that guy seem really shady?" I asked. "Was I unnecessarily mean to him?"

"No, he seemed like a greasy little rat to me," Ginger said.

"Always trust your gut instincts," Daniel told me, "and considering your go-to move on men who annoy you is to pulverize their balls, you were kinder to him than most."

"Yeah, you're losing your touch," Ginger said before grinning at me. "Don't tell me you're going soft. I still have Danni the Teste Slayer keychains on backorder."

I rolled my eyes and looked around the bar, searching for Kutya. I noted Daniel also scanned the room, no doubt looking for Lana to continue the cozy conversation they'd been having, but the anaconda shifter was no longer at the bar. "You and Lana seem to be getting along well."

"We have history," he said, still scanning the room.

Something I didn't want to put a name to flared deep in my chest. Lana had helped us out a lot in West Virginia. If not for her, we all might have ended up spider food. Not only was she a pretty awesome fighter, she was a nice person, as far as I knew. The fact she was a blonde bombshell, prettier than even my "perfect" sister, enhanced by the fact she didn't seem self-absorbed like Shana, shouldn't bother me at all. Rider had shown no interest in her, and if Daniel did.... Well, I shouldn't have any issues with that. I really shouldn't. So why the hell was it bothering me that he might be scanning the bar for her?

"I'm going to go find Kutya," I told them. "He must have gone off to look for Rider."

"No doubt," Ginger said. "That dog is his shadow."

I parted from my bodyguards and moved toward the back of the bar, carefully avoiding the servers balancing trays of bar food and alcoholic beverages.

I'd just stepped through the door to the narrow hallway that ran between the public business part of The Midnight Rider and the secret business part that filled the back of the building and the sublevels when I collided with a cute woman about my size with ebony curls and green monolid eyes.

"Jadyn! I heard you were working here now. Sorry, I didn't see you." I looked toward the door she'd just come through, the one that led to the secret part of Rider's building, and couldn't imagine why someone would come out of that door unless they were part of his security staff, which Jadyn wasn't, or visiting his private quarters.

"I was just coming from downstairs," Jadyn said, seeming to know where my thoughts had gone. "Rider let Christian and I stay in a room down there while we were hiding out and now he lets me use the room for studying before my shift."

"Studying?"

She nodded, all bright-eyed, then frowned. "Rider is paying my way through veterinary school as a wedding gift for me and Christian. He didn't tell you?"

Now it was my turn to frown. I'd missed so much. "No, but most of our communication while I was away was of the life or death variety. I heard about the wedding. I'm sorry. I should have led with a congratulations."

"It's fine." She waved my apology away. "You were in a pretty deep mess in West Virginia. Christian filled me in. I'm so happy you're all here, and safe."

"I'm happy you and Christian have joined the team." I smiled genuinely. "And I'm glad Rider thought of such a perfect wedding gift. Your ability to communicate with animals will make you the best vet they could ever have. Speaking of animals, I was looking for Kutya."

Jadyn inhaled deep and looked up as if in deep thought, then grinned. "He's bounding up the stairs now, and he needs a potty break."

I cast out my own senses. "And Rider's with him. Of course."

"Those two adore each other, even if one denies it." She chuckled and moved toward the door I'd just come from. "Work calls. Maybe we can talk more later."

I gave her a nod and an automatic smile, her own smile pretty darn infectious, as we parted, each going through a door leading to a different section of the building. The door leading to the sublevels opened as the door I'd come through closed behind me, and Kutya barreled through, Rider close behind him. I watched the dog run right to the garage door and start pawing at it.

"Stop that, Kutya. You'll scratch the door."

"Jadyn said he's really got to go potty."

Rider frowned at me. "He doesn't *go potty*. He's a man."

"Whatever." I fought a grin as I rolled my eyes. "He's got to go."

Rider walked over to the set of hooks that had been installed while I'd been away and grabbed a black leash. He held it out to me with a grin while Kutya spun in circles in front of him.

"Sure, I'll walk him," I said. "And you bag the poop."

Rider groaned. "It's beneath my station."

"Oh, whatever. He's your dog. The poop is your responsibility."

He looked down at the dog, sighed, and halted the spinning canine long enough to clip the leash onto the ring on his collar, which was black and studded with metal bones. "Let's go."

I walked over to the door as Rider placed his palm over the access panel next to it. There was a click as the bolt unlocked, then Rider pushed the door open and Kutya took off like a horse fresh out the gate at the Kentucky Derby, but Rider pulled back on the leash. "Whoa. We're going, we're going."

Rider closed the door behind us, then walked over to the front of the garage to place his palm over yet another access panel and open that door. Kutya pulled against the leash as we waited for the garage door to roll up. As soon as it cleared enough we could walk out into the cool night air, we allowed Kutya to lead the way. He beelined it over to a large dumpster, hiked a leg up, and emptied his bladder.

"Geez, he really did have to go," I observed, and tried

not to think of my last encounter with a dumpster, but it proved too difficult and I shuddered at the memory.

"Remind you of that time you rolled around in spoiled milk and baby crap?"

"Smartass."

Rider chuckled. "You love me anyway."

"Very true."

"Good." He grew serious as Kutya finished what had to be the world's longest pee stream and we strolled down the alley. "Now, what was the deal with your mother and the shifty-looking toad with her?"

"She thinks I know where Shana is, or worse, did something to her. The toad is the private detective she hired to follow me until I reveal all my secrets."

"That's going to be a problem. Your secrets are the paranormal community's secrets." Rider scratched behind his ear, thinking. "Grissom just got bumped to detective and is handling that case. He's supposed to be handling your mother, but she's proving to be a major pain."

"Rome tossed the guy out."

"Yeah, but keeping him from following you isn't going to be as easy as keeping him out of the bar. If you must go out, be mindful of any shifting, feeding, or other paranormal activity you and Daniel do outside The Midnight Rider. I'll contact Grissom to make sure he knows about this rodent and if he becomes too much of a risk to our community… we'll have to retire him."

I blinked. "You want to kill the guy?"

"I'm hoping there's another choice to be made, but if you can't persuade him to back off…" He shrugged one shoulder. "You need to stay alert anyway. I received word there could be an incubus in the area."

Goosebumps broke out on my arms. "Your brother?"

"I haven't been able to break Trixell yet. For all we know, he's still toasting his ass in Hell, but I wouldn't put anything by the sneaky fucker. There's no such thing as a good incubus though and they aren't above poaching from others. Your succubus side makes you pretty appetizing to incubi, so while I look into this thing, I want you to stay inside. If you want to work, you can work security inside the bar. You are not going out unless necessary and unless you have me or Daniel with you, at minimum."

Ah, home sweet home, I thought. It seemed some things hadn't changed much while I was gone.

"I know what you're thinking and I am loosening my grip, Danni. You know the old me wouldn't let you go out, period, not when there's the possibility of an incubus in the area, and you know—"

I kissed him, cutting off what I was sure would be a long spiel. "I know, and I know I said I would trust your gut more and trust that you're protecting me, not controlling me. I'm working on it, but these knee-jerk reactions of mine are a bitch. I guess they're a habit, like the bossy way you say things."

His lips twitched. "Oops."

We stared at each other for a moment, both fighting grins. Then he dipped his head to kiss me, but a whiff of something absolutely revolting blew us each back a foot before our lips could meet. I held my hand over my nose as we turned to see Kutya straightening up from a shaky-legged squat, a large mound of poop in his wake. He looked at us with what appeared to be an actual smile, his tongue lolling out, eyes bright. I was pretty sure he was proud of himself, and I guess I would be too if I'd just broken a Guinness World Record, but damn.

Without a word, Rider gave the leash a tug and herded us back toward the building.

"You have to clean that up," I told him, my hand still covering my nose.

"Sorry. Didn't bring a shovel." He looked down at Kutya, who practically skipped with joy between us, and shook his head.

Hank, one of Rider's more muscle-bound security staff, stepped out of the garage and jogged toward us. His nose wrinkled in disgust, his shifter-nose no doubt able to pick up the smell of what Kutya had left in the alley easily, but the smell didn't stop him. "Hey, Boss. Another report just came in."

"Shit," Rider muttered as he plucked a baggie from the little bag-holder attached to Kutya's leash and handed it to the tank of a man. "Kutya's mess needs to be cleaned up. Grab a shovel if the bag doesn't work. There'll be extra in your paycheck."

Hank stared open-mouthed as Rider urged me and Kutya along, then looked between the little bag in his hand and the smoldering pile down the alley. The way his shoulders slumped as he accepted his fate and jogged toward the small mountain pulled at my heartstrings.

"Aww, you can't make him—"

"You're welcome to do it for him."

"Nope. You said you'd pay him extra. It's all good."

Rider's eyes gleamed with silent laughter as we entered the garage. "Daniel's going to take you to your appointment with Eliza and then I want the two of you to come right back here."

"Sonofabitch!" Hank bellowed from the alley. "That's a Rome-sized turd!"

Rider laughed as I stopped and looked back toward the alley, befuddled. "Why does everyone seem to know the size of Rome's poop?"

Rider laughed harder and smiled wide, but didn't say anything. Men. I would never understand them or their concept of humor.

CHAPTER TWO

"What behind us has you so interested?" I asked Daniel, turning to look through the back window of his truck, but Kutya stood in the truck bed, blocking a lot of my view.

"We've had a tail since we left the bar," he explained. "Your ratty new friend."

"Pastrami?"

Daniel frowned. "Spaghetti?"

I dug around through my memory. "I honestly can't remember the guy's name."

"Me neither, but now I'm kind of hungry."

"My session shouldn't last long and I know he said he wants us to come straight back, but Rider won't mind if we dip through a drive-thru on the way back to the bar."

He glanced at me. "I can wait until you turn in for the day."

"Daniel, you don't have to skip eating just because I can't eat a lot of foods yet. I appreciate the thought though."

His mouth curved up at the corners. "So if I go through Dunkin' and grab a dozen chocolate frosted cake donuts?"

"I'll drag you into their kitchen, fry up your balls and serve 'em up as Munchkins."

He barked out a laugh. "You'd have to do a lot of carving to get me to Munchkin-sized."

I scrunched my nose, earning another laugh. "Anyway, you can grab a burger, taco, or whatever you want, but please have a heart and skip the sweet stuff."

"Deal." He glanced at the side mirror and took a hard last-minute turn into an alley.

"Hey, watch it!" I turned toward the back. "Kutya's in the back of the truck."

"He was lying down. He's all right." The dog in question stood up, looked through the rear window and barked at the dragon shifter. "I had to lose our tail before the weasel follows us to Eliza's house. You know she's not much of a fighter, physically or verbally. I don't want the creep harassing her."

"Good point." I glanced back, not seeing any cars following us. "I think you lost him."

"For now," Daniel muttered. "I have a feeling he won't give up easily."

Daniel's maneuver appeared to have worked. We were the only vehicle in motion when we turned onto Eliza's street. Daniel parked along the curb in front of the small gray brick house.

Kutya jumped out of the truck bed, landing on his feet before we'd managed to get ours on the ground. We joined him on the sidewalk, where he promptly trotted over to Daniel and raised his leg.

"Hey, you sonofa—"

I laughed as Daniel jumped back, narrowly avoiding the stream of urine that had been aimed at his ankle. "Well, I suppose now you'll be more careful not to take any more hard turns while Kutya's in the back."

"Remind me again *why* we have this dog with us."

"Because he can't be cooped up inside all day and night, so I figured we'd bring him with us when we go places and Rider can't get away from The Midnight Rider."

"If I'm going to have to haul that fleabag around, I guess I'll need to upgrade to an extended cab." He shot us both a dark look before leading the way to Eliza's front door.

I admired the yellow, pink, and white flower bushes running along the front of the house as Daniel knocked. Eliza was always quick to answer her door with a warm smile and welcoming energy, so I was surprised when Daniel knocked a second time. My stomach started to feel a little queasy.

"Something's wrong," Daniel said. His nostrils flared. "I don't sense her. Do you?"

Scanning using my supernatural senses wasn't second nature to me, especially when sensing for someone other than Rider, but I could do it if I focused. I took a breath, cleared my mind, and reached out with my senses, sort of like casting a net, but didn't sense Eliza inside the small house. I took my cell phone out of my pocket and checked for messages. "I don't sense her, and it isn't like her to just skip out on a session. Even when we did them by phone while I was away, she was always right on time. She didn't send me any messages about needing to reschedule either."

"Call her."

I nodded and pressed the button to dial her number. We locked concerned eyes as Eliza's cell phone rang from within the house. A second later, Daniel disappeared in a shower of rainbow-colored sparkles and opened the door from the inside. "She can forgive us for trespassing later," he said, gesturing for me to follow him.

Kutya and I stepped inside and I closed the door before taking a quick look around Eliza's living room. I'd never actually spent any time in the living room and I'd never seen any of the other rooms, always going directly to her office for our sessions. The living room walls were a pale blue. A large painting of a pastel hummingbird in flight hung above a white couch with pink and blue roses.

A gorgeous cherry blossom bonsai tree rested in the center of the glass coffee table and a record player stood where most people would have a television set. Next to the record player was a pretty impressive record collection, which consisted mostly of 60's and 70's artists.

"Call the phone again."

I pressed the button, and we both followed the sound of the ringing into a bedroom. I ended the call so the ringing would stop and picked up the cell phone, which had been left charging on the oak nightstand. It was locked, but I could see bubbles showing missed calls, including mine. Heavy brown light-blocking curtains were drawn, but my eyes were good enough to make out the dark green walls with framed prints of animals and nature scenes, and the thick sunflower comforter and pale yellow sheets on the unmade bed.

"Does Eliza strike you as the type of person who'd leave her bed unmade?" I asked.

"She carries a mouse on her shoulder," Daniel answered, scanning the room. "I doubt she's a neat-freak, but I know where you're going. I don't see any signs of struggle indicating she was snatched while getting in or out of bed. I don't smell any blood or traces of intruders. Of course, a person's scent only stays behind for so long."

"Her phone is locked, but I can see a lot of missed calls going back to three nights ago."

"That doesn't sound good." Daniel ducked to look under the bed.

"I don't think she's hiding under the bed, Daniel."

"I know that." He gave me a mildly perturbed look and walked over to the closet. "There are a lot of clothes in here. There are some empty hangers, but I can't really tell if anything's missing without knowing what all she actually owns. I see a suitcase, but without knowing how many she has, I can't say if this one being here means anything or not. She could have easily packed a small duffel and went somewhere."

"Without telling Rider? Eliza may be a bit of a free spirit, but she's responsible when it comes to her job, and she wouldn't just go somewhere and not tell Rider."

"We just got back into town. Maybe she went somewhere and told him while we were gone. Maybe she's just not back yet."

"And she left her cell phone here?" I arched an eyebrow. "Besides, Rider reminded me of my appointment, remember? She clearly didn't tell him anything."

"Yeah." Daniel closed the closet and scanned the room again, hands on hips. "This is strange. Let's check the office."

Closest to the door, I led the way to the office. The moment I opened the door, Kutya let out a growl and bounded past me, dashing head-first into the wall next to one of Eliza's bookcases.

"That dog clearly wasn't the brightest pup in the litter."

"Don't insult him just because he tried to pee on you," I said and watched as Kutya backed up, shook his head, and barked at the wall. "That's where the mouse hole is. He probably just chased the poor thing in there. Kutya, stop it! Leave it be."

The dog whined and looked back at me with a sad look that said, *but hoooooman, I wants to eats the nugget.*

"Leave it." Kutya let out a sound resembling a frustrated sigh, walked over to Eliza's desk, and plopped down in front before resting his head on his large paws. "See. He's smart. He understands."

"Good, then train him not to piss on me." Daniel walked over to the desk and opened a drawer.

"Should we be going through Eliza's office? She's a counselor. We could be snooping into other vampires' personal business."

"If she's missing, we need to look for anything that'll help us find her. She has file cabinets back here. I'm sure anything personal about her clients is locked up. I'm just checking the desk."

"I guess that's all right then." I gave Kutya a scratch between the ears and walked behind the desk to join Daniel. I saw the light to Eliza's monitor was on and moved the mouse. An image of Jimi Hendrix popped up, along with a password request. "Crap."

"You didn't expect it to be that easy, did you?" Daniel asked, pausing in his rifling to glance at the monitor. "If it comes down to it, Rider's tech team can crack it. Maybe we should call him."

I dialed Rider.

"You miss me already?"

I bit my lip to avoid the ridiculously goofy smile I felt wanting to break free, sure to invite an eye roll, maybe even a gag reflex, from Daniel. "I do, but I actually need to tell you about something."

"What's wrong?" All traces of amusement fled Rider's tone. I could practically see him drop everything he was doing to straighten up, stiff as a rod, completely focused.

"Nothing's wrong with me, but Daniel and I are in Eliza's house and she's not here."

"You have a scheduled appointment with her."

"Yes, I know," I said dryly. "That's why I'm here. Her cell phone was on her nightstand and I can see she's missed some calls the past couple of days, but there are no obvious signs of abduction or violence. Her bed's unmade, but I'm not sure that's a big deal. We're checking her desk now. Did she tell you anything about going anywhere?"

"She left town shortly after you left for assignment at Gruff's, but she's been back at least a week now."

"Where did she go? We still had our weekly sessions by phone, and she never said anything about being away."

"She doesn't always ask for time off when she leaves town because, for the most part, her job can be done by phone or through the internet," Rider explained. "She always advises when she'll be away, but I don't pry into her plans because she's never given me trouble and she's so kind by nature she's never drawn any negative attention. I know she likes camping and anything nature related."

"You don't say," I murmured, thinking of her décor as I watched Daniel tapping away at Eliza's keyboard. "Well, I'm worried about her. Why would she leave her phone?"

"I could see her taking a technology break while off on one of her nature excursions, but not without notifying me. She's usually very reliable."

"Can you use your vampire master radar or whatever to locate her?"

"That works for you because I'm your sire." He grew quiet as I sensed him thinking. "And it doesn't look like she's checked her phone in three days?"

I looked at the phone in my hand. "Nope."

"Shit. Yeah, that doesn't sound like she just ran out to the store, and it's unusual for her to miss an appointment or not notify me of time she'll be away or unavailable. Bring the phone to my tech team. Leave the computer. They can remote in to it if need be. I'm notifying them now."

"Ha! I'm in," Daniel said, eyes focused on Eliza's monitor.

"Daniel just got into her computer. We'll take a quick look and bring the phone in."

"Danni, she's a counselor. You can't just go looking through all her files. My tech team will know what to look through and what to bypass. Bring the phone. I'm going to have Grissom check out her place too, so don't disturb anything."

"All right. We're on our way." I disconnected from Rider and moved to Daniel's side to see he'd figured out Eliza's password. "How did you do that?"

"The power of deduction. Her password was WOODSTOCK69. Big surprise, huh?"

"Astonishing." I was pretty sure Eliza had probably been at the original Woodstock.

"Rider tell you he doesn't want you snooping through

her computer?"

"Yep."

"Hmm. Well, he didn't tell me not to." Daniel opened the internet browser and went right to Eliza's email account, which we could easily access because she'd stored her password. "I don't want to dig into her files unless necessary because we could invade clients' privacy, but a general glance at her personal email shouldn't… What's this?" Daniel clicked on a confirmation email dated over a month ago.

"Lovefest," I read over his shoulder.

"Sounds like an orgy."

I rolled my eyes. "Could you see Eliza in an orgy?"

"I can see any woman in an orgy if I close my eyes and wish hard enough."

"Ew." I swatted the back of his head before reading the whole email. "A festival of peace, love, and community with free-minded inhabitants of… oh brother. Eliza was definitely one of the original hippies. This sounds right up her alley, and took place while we were at Gruff's, but Rider said she'd been back from wherever she'd gone to about a week, so this is old."

Daniel clicked back to the inbox and scrolled down the email list. "That appears to be the most recent thing she had planned. I didn't find anything else interesting in her desk."

"I guess we'll just take the phone to the tech team, like Rider said, and let them handle it." I sighed and tried to remember it didn't matter if I was part of the investigation or not. The important thing was finding Eliza and making sure she was safe. I turned toward the barely audible sound of tiny feet scurrying and saw a little nose and pair of whiskers twitching from within the hole in the wall next to Eliza's bookcase, and perked up. "We'll also take the mouse."

"We'll what now?"

"Eliza always has that mouse with her. I bet it knows

more about her than Rider's tech team will find on the computer or phone, and Jadyn can talk to animals. Hell, she communicated with the dragon soul inside you. She can question a mouse."

"All right," Daniel said, then shut down the computer and stood. "But Jadyn does all the questioning. The last time you interrogated a rodent, you stabbed it in the testicle."

"Your friend is back," Daniel said as he parked his truck and cut the engine.

I followed his line of sight to see Pacitti parked along the curb across from the lot outside The Midnight Rider. He shoved a handful of pork rinds into his mouth as he watched us from within an old Ford Crown Victoria that had seen better days. The investigator stuck his hand out the window while rubbing his fingers together to rid himself of pork rind crumbs, then gifted us with a pudgy middle finger.

"I guess he doesn't appreciate how we ditched him earlier."

"Yeah," Daniel said. "That was the impression I got too."

We unbuckled and exited the truck. I carefully held the teapot I'd used to transport the mouse, having to get creative since apparently Eliza didn't believe any animal should ever be caged. I understood given her free spirit and in most cases would agree, but capturing the little critter so used to freedom had been an adventure. Luring the mouse out had only taken food since Eliza hadn't been around to feed it in a few days, but Kutya had gotten excited, the mouse had tried to flee back to its haven in the wall, and chaos had ensued.

"Don't you bother this mouse anymore," I ordered Kutya as he stood looking up at the teapot in my hands, ears perked. I closed the door with my hip and rounded the truck to meet up with Daniel. "Let me do all the talking about the mouse, all right?"

He glared down at the teapot as we walked toward the building. "Danni, I'm supposed to be a badass fire-breathing giant beast of a security expert who beats information out of criminals and psychopaths. Believe me, I have no intention of telling people I'm on board with sweet-talking information out of a freaking mouse, especially not one that bit me where a man should never be bit."

"Oh, it wasn't so bad. Her teeth are tiny, and if you didn't want to get bit there, you shouldn't have blocked access to her shelter with your crotch."

"You told me to block the hole and sitting in front of it was the fastest way I could think of. How was I supposed to know the little demon was going to bite me in the nuts?"

"She's not a demon, and hello, she's a girl. A guy was in her way and she had a clear path to his balls. With all the time you've spent with me, surely by now you should know to guard those when going up against a girl."

"I'd love to argue with you, but you're right. I guess I didn't realize your evil desire to castrate all mankind could spread to animals." He grinned roguishly. "And I should have known not to give her such a big target."

I rolled my eyes. "I'll never understand why men brag so much about the size of their testicles when it merely takes the tiniest flick at one of the delicate things to turn you into crying babies."

Daniel opened his mouth to respond, then frowned as he took a moment to process. By the time we'd reached the front of the bar, the only comeback he'd managed was "Nuh uh."

I smiled sweetly at him and batted my eyelashes. "Would you care for a demonstration? I promise I'll just give you one good flick, nothing more."

I realized my mistake the moment his shoulders tensed,

and we stood before the entrance staring awkwardly at each other. I'd accidentally gone from innocent joking to flirtatious teasing. Once upon a time, Daniel would have taken the bait and hit me back with commentary on how I couldn't keep my hands off his balls. We'd laugh and go about our day, but that was before a demon had lured me into a dream realm, and even though he had yet to admit it, had lured Daniel in with me. Now we just stared at each other, both knowing a line had been crossed inside that realm, neither wanting to speak of it, and apparently neither doing a good job of ignoring the fact it had happened.

Kutya barked and pawed at the door, thankfully giving us the push we needed to break eye contact. Without a word, Daniel held the front door open for me and we stepped inside The Midnight Rider. Posted at the front, still on door duty, Rome gave the teapot a curious glance, but said nothing as we passed him.

I looked around the room, noting who was on duty, and saw Jadyn. At the moment, she appeared busy taking orders from a group at one of the tables on the left side of the bar, so I decided to check in with her later.

"Let's check in with Rider first," Daniel suggested.

"Sure." I opened my senses and located Rider in his office. I led the way toward the back of the bar. Kutya took off running as we pushed through the back door, slid to a stop in front of the office, and started pawing at the closed door.

We picked up the pace before Kutya could scratch up the door. I twisted the knob and Kutya pushed through, barreling into the room. The big dog went around the desk and came to an abrupt stop next to where Rider sat in his leather chair. Rider gave the dog a head pat and a chin scratch without taking his eyes off the teapot in my hands. "Lay down," he ordered, and Kutya obeyed the command, merrily taking up his post in the plush dog bed Rider kept in the office.

"Your tea sounds frantic," Rider said dryly, still eyeing the pot.

Daniel bit his lip, but didn't say anything, and followed suit as I took a seat in one of the two chairs before Rider's desk and set the teapot on top. "This is the mouse Eliza carries around on her shoulder," I explained. "I thought I'd take care of it while she's ... wherever she is."

"Eliza has never kept a pet in her life," Rider told me. "It goes against her nature to take away an animal's freedom. That thing will be fine if you put it back where you got it."

"It was hungry. She may let the poor thing roam freely in her house, but I'm positive it was hand-fed by her. I'm going to care for it until she returns. I'd be glad to do so at Eliza's house."

Rider's eyes narrowed as he slowly turned his head from side to side. "You know that's not going to happen, and I can tell you're not telling me something. Spill it."

Ugh, I could never get anything past him. "You're not cheating and reading my mind, are you?"

"Don't have to. You haven't been able to look me straight in the eye since you walked in here and Daniel's vibrating, so whatever you're going to tell or ask me has got to be good."

I glared over at Daniel and he looked away, lips twitching. I noticed the vibrating Rider mentioned in the way his shoulders shook.

I guess I was just going to have to come out and say it. "I want to question the mouse."

Rider sat stone still, staring straight ahead of me. Just when I'd begun to think he'd gone catatonic, he blinked and repeated what I'd said very carefully, as if he thought he might have misheard. "You want to question the mouse?"

I felt my cheeks go warm, but straightened my shoulders. I didn't care how silly it sounded. I knew my idea was good. "Eliza always has this mouse with her. I know she talks to it. It has to know everything that happens in that house. If someone did somehow abduct her from inside the house, the mouse might have even seen who, and you have someone employed here who can communicate with animals."

"So you actually want Jadyn to communicate with the mouse and see if it knows anything about what happened to Eliza?"

"Yes."

"Thank goodness," he said, the tension in his shoulders loosening as he leaned forward and reached for his phone. "The last time you questioned a rodent, you stabbed it in the testicle."

Daniel lost it, doubling over in laughter, which only caused Rider's mischievous grin to grow as he hit a button on the phone and told Tony to send Jadyn to his office.

"Don't you have a phone to take to the Bat Cave?" I asked, not bothering to hide my irritation.

"Yeah, I better get the phone to the tech nerds and get out of your way," Daniel said between hearty guffaws as he stood and turned for the door. "Your rodent interrogations can get messy."

I swatted at him, but he swerved out of my reach and ducked out the door, leaving me with a highly amused vampire. "My idea is good."

"Your idea is smart," Rider agreed. "Grissom wouldn't have thought of it."

"Then what's so funny, and you better not utter the words Danni the Teste Slayer."

Rider's eyes shone with amusement, but a light knock on the door saved him from having to respond. "Come in, Jadyn."

Jadyn entered the room, her gaze immediately zeroing in on the teapot and the noise that increased from inside it since she'd entered. "Oh dear. Someone is upset."

"Two someones," Rider said. The corner of his mouth curved up as he winked at me. "But we're hoping you can see if the mouse can help us find our friend."

CHAPTER THREE

Jadyn took the seat Daniel had abandoned and carefully lifted the lid of the teapot before tipping it over so the mouse could crawl out into her open palm.

"Don't you dare," she told Kutya in a firm voice as he sat up, legs braced to take a flying leap at the fussing mouse. I couldn't communicate with animals like she could, but I was pretty sure the little fur ball was cussing out me, Rider, Kutya, and the horses we rode in on. "You lie there and behave like a good boy."

Jadyn waited until Kutya did as told despite the beautiful big guy looking thoroughly put out about it, then turned her attention to the mouse. "Yes, yes, I know you're upset. Take a breath, little friend, and I will help you." Jadyn listened intently as the mouse chattered away, nodding her head at what I assumed to be the appropriate times. The mouse glanced at me a few times as it squeaked on, and I got the impression I wasn't its favorite person. Not by a long shot.

"I am so sorry for that. I know Danni didn't mean any harm," Jadyn told the mouse after it wrapped up an exceptionally long spiel. "Her friend is missing. She is concerned and is hoping you will help her."

The mouse gave me a long appraising look, its little eyelids narrowing until its beady black eyes became mere slits, did the mouse equivalent of a *humph* sound and started off on another long squeaky tangent. Rider's eyes sparkled with amusement as he watched.

Only you could thoroughly piss off a mouse, he spoke into my mind. I glared at him in response and ignored his silent chuckling as I settled back in my chair, unable to do anything until Jadyn translated for us.

Jadyn listened intently and asked questions whenever the mouse took a pause. I tried to follow along, obviously not able to understand the squeaky chitter-chatter, but thinking maybe I'd get the general sense of what was being said. From where I sat, the mouse still seemed irate, with very little chance of calming down.

Daniel knocked once and slipped into the room, immediately zeroing in on Jadyn and the mouse. His golden eyebrows rose as he walked over to the couch that ran along the wall next to the door and sat down. *That is one pissed off mouse*, he spoke into my mind. *You following any of this?*

You're closer to the animal species than I am, I responded in the same way. *Sounds like jibber-jabber to me.*

Same, and just because I hold a dragon soul inside me and shift into one doesn't mean I can communicate with animals. Dragons aren't really that similar to animals like rodents and dogs and such either. Like gargoyles, they're kind of their own separate thing.

I studied him, from his rainbow-colored hair to the hoop in his nostril that looked silver to me, but I knew was really imortium, some kind of gorgeous multi-colored gem. *Interesting. The world you come from sounds so amazing.*

He grunted, never taking his eyes off the mouse. *It was, then it wasn't. Maybe it'll get back there someday.*

I watched him close enough to notice his shoulders sank, sorrow filled his eyes, and regret rolled off of him in waves. I knew he thought of her. Salia. His beloved, whose death haunted his every memory of Imortia. I wanted to reach out to him, hold his hand or simply rest mine on his shoulder, anything to let him know he wasn't alone and he was loved. Loved? Where had that come from?

I gave my head a little shake, redirected my full attention back to the squeaky conversation happening between Jadyn and the mouse, but didn't miss the fact Rider's eyes were on me.

"All right, guys." Jadyn removed a shelled peanut from her coin pocket and handed it to the mouse, who snatched it greedily and immediately started doing its best impression of a wood chipper on the thing. "I got as much information as I could once our little friend here vented enough to work with me."

"I knew that mouse was pissed off," Daniel said as he leaned forward, rested his elbows on his knees. "Still no reason for it to bite me. It give us any leads?"

"Maybe. It's a little hard explaining how I communicate with animals. Although I often speak aloud to them because speaking is how I'm used to communicating, I think it's really my thoughts they pick up on. Apparently I do sometimes slip into their language though, or I think I do. I've been told that I sometimes growl or bark when communicating with dogs." Her cheeks filled with pink color as she looked at Rider. He grinned at her and nodded, giving me the impression he'd been the one to hear the dog sounds come from her. "They speak to me in the way they communicate with their own kind. I hear the sounds, but I get images with the vocalizations. The sounds they make do translate, but it's mostly the images that help me communicate with them, especially when they're trying to communicate something more difficult. Does that make sense, or am I just making this all even weirder?"

"No, I think I get it," I said. "It's like you get words and images, puzzle pieces you have to put together to see the complete picture."

"Yes, that's a good way of putting it."

"Were you able to decipher if the mouse saw or heard anything that helps us?" Rider asked.

"She says the house lady went away and came back different. Animals can sense our emotions, and she sensed something like worry or sadness, maybe confusion. She's not sure what it was because once she'd sense it, the house lady would get real happy, but it was a different kind of happy. The happy she felt from the woman before was calm, peaceful. She says the house lady seemed to force the happy."

"The house lady being Eliza?" Daniel asked.

Jadyn nodded. "Animals don't always know our names, and some struggle more than others."

"Forcing the happy," I said softly, processing the words. "So Eliza went somewhere and came back in a different mood from what she normally was in… but she was pushing through it, like something happened during that time, something that stayed with her after she returned, but she put on a happy front, even to herself."

"That's about what I gathered," Jadyn said, nodding her head in agreement. "I got the sense that something was bothering her, but she refused to give in to whatever it was."

"Lovefest," I said to Daniel. "She went to that Lovefest thing. Something must have happened there."

"Maybe she met someone and got her heart broken," Daniel said.

"And you really think a broken heart would cause her to just up and leave without a word, and without her phone?"

"People have done worse while nursing a broken heart," he replied.

"That's true." I turned to Rider. "Did she tell you about Lovefest? Can we send people there to look for her?"

"Let's not jump to conclusions and set off on a wild goose chase," Rider said. "She never mentioned any

Lovefest to me, but it sounds like the type of thing she'd enjoy. The woman goes to all kinds of festivals and retreats and weird hippie things. Before freaking out unnecessarily, keep in mind we're discussing the whereabouts of a woman who communes with the moon in the nude."

Daniel and I shared a *wow* look, eyebrows raised.

"Exactly," Rider said. "So the mouse didn't actually see anything to indicate she was or could now be in danger?"

Jadyn's brow furrowed in thought. "Well, our friend here did not see anyone unusual visit with Eliza, definitely didn't see her leave with anyone, but she says there was a terrible smell in the house that drew her and her mate from their dwelling just before sunrise. The smell lingered until the next sunrise and they never saw Eliza during that time or after."

"So she was taken," I said, my gut churning.

"I wouldn't rule it out," Jadyn said. "Her disappearance certainly seemed to coincide with the smell, which, if I translated correctly, was the smell of flowers over rotten eggs."

"Magic and demon-stench," Daniel growled. "The rotten eggs the mouse smelled had to be sulfur, indicating something demonic, and the flowery smell was whatever magic it used, or could be its own scent. Sometimes the sulfur scent isn't from the actual creature, but where it came from."

"You're saying a demon snatched sweet, gentle Eliza?" My chest felt hollow as I imagined the kind woman at the hands of some red-skinned, clawed entity. I'd had enough dealings with demonic entities to know they generally weren't red-skinned, clawed monsters. Many were actually quite gorgeous men and women, but that was still the image my mind conjured.

"Maybe," Daniel said. "Maybe it was just something that came through a really gnarly portal. There's also the possibility that the smell resulted from a nasty spell, but I didn't see anything in Eliza's house that indicated she practices magic."

"She doesn't," Rider said, drumming his fingers along his desktop. "She dabbles in herbal concoctions, but never magic."

"Would something herbal have left behind that smell?" I asked.

Rider's jaw was set tight as he shook his head. "Highly doubtful. The flower scent could have been from something she did, but not the rotten eggs."

"Could a witch have cast a spell on her home that left that smell?"

"If it worked a really dark spell," Daniel answered. "Twenty-four hours is a long time for the scent to linger though. If it were a spell, it would have to be a powerful one, or cast by someone much more powerful than your average witch."

The mouse let loose with another long, squeaky rant. Jadyn cringed a little. "Uh, so you recall I mentioned her mate? Turns out you kind of snatched her from her family and she's really not happy about that, especially since she wasn't able to tell them and is sure her mate is worried about her, not to mention her children. She's also pretty furious you'd intended to care for her as if she were some pathetic house animal. Her words, not mine," Jadyn quickly advised when Kutya sat up and released a clearly insulted bark.

I blinked at the dog for a moment, realizing Kutya understood what Jadyn had said on some level. Or maybe he understood the mouse. Either way, it took a moment to wrap my mind around that before I gave my head a little shake and moved on.

"All right, but in my defense, I didn't know about her family. I'd only ever seen one mouse with Eliza before, so I assumed it was this one and this was the only rodent in residence. And she came right out when I offered food, like she was starving for it, actually. Eliza had to be feeding her," I continued as Daniel stifled laughter, clearly amused

I'd managed to piss off a mouse. "It's not funny."

"It kind of is," he said, but still attempted to stop laughing.

Annoyed by his amusement and angry my good deed had been looked at as an insult, I looked right into the mouse's beady little eyes. "If you didn't need my help, if you were perfectly fine, why did you run out and scarf down the food I offered you? Huh? Ask her that," I told Jadyn.

The pretty, dark-haired guardian gave me a wary look, but did as asked. The mouse looked right at me, stood on its back legs, and released several sharp squeaks. Jadyn barked out a laugh before covering her mouth with her free hand. "Oh, that came through loud and clear."

"What did she say?"

"Um, I believe the closest translation would be... *Bitch, because I'm fat.*"

I glared at the adorable yet infuriating and highly unappreciative mouse while Daniel bent at the waist, laughing until his eyes sprung tears. Across from me, Rider's mouth curved with amusement, but his concerned gaze was somewhere distant.

"Thank you for your help, Jadyn. We'll see to it the mouse is returned safely to her family." He shook his head as if just realizing what he'd said and wondering how he'd come to the point of chauffeuring mice around the city.

"No problem." She stood and looked at the mouse in her palm. "She's not crazy about being in the teapot. She's not a pet."

Rider sighed. "I can't have a mouse running around my bar. Make sure it knows it better not run off. I'll let Kutya eat it."

Kutya's ears perked up at this, but Jadyn didn't take the bait. "I've seen what you do to animal abusers. You would never hurt this mouse."

He held Jadyn's amused stare with his own hardened gaze. When she didn't break, he softened with a grunt.

"Ask the damn thing nicely then to please not run off in my bar and draw the attention of the health department."

Jadyn chuckled softly, passed along the request, listened to the mouse's return chitter-chatter, and lowered it to the teapot where it climbed in and hung from the edge of the opening, peeking over the rim. "She requests you just leave the lid off."

Rider nodded his agreement, and Jadyn said her goodbyes to both animals with plenty of pets and scratches before leaving the office.

"I can—"

"No. You're not going back to Eliza's. If someone snatched her, who's to say they aren't still watching the house?"

The three of us stared at the mouse, watching its little nose twitch. Apparently wondering what the delay was, it let loose another of its squeaky rants, this one high-pitched enough Kutya whined and covered his ears with his paws.

"If my enemies could see me now," Rider muttered softly, "catering to a damn mouse."

I sensed Daniel's amusement, but he was smart enough not to laugh as Rider's eyes flickered gold. His power filled the air as he summoned someone. Shortly after, heavy footsteps traveled the hall, followed by a loud knock on the door, and it opened. Hank stepped in, his large black-clad frame filling the doorway. His pale gray eyes flicked over to the dog and made a quick scan over the floor. I thought I saw a flicker of fear and figured he was looking to see if he'd been called in to scoop up another of Kutya's impressive creations.

"I need you to take this to Eliza's."

Hank's gray gaze moved over to the teapot with the tiny inhabitant and he stood stone-still except for a few blinks. "That's a mouse in a teapot."

"Yes. It's Eliza's teapot," Rider told him. "Take it back to her house. Leave it anywhere."

"With the mouse?"

"With the mouse."

"You don't want me to beat on somebody or kill somethin'?" His gray eyes were full of hope as they rose to meet Rider's.

"Not tonight. Not at the moment anyway, but I'll be sure to let you know."

Hank's massive shoulders might have sagged, but it wasn't always easy to tell with him since he didn't have much of a neck. There was definitely a dip to his square chin and a droop to his bottom lip as he walked over and wrapped his sausage-fingers around the handle of the teapot, scooping the small lid into his other big palm, and stood there holding them awkwardly in his large hands.

"Is there something wrong?" Rider asked.

Hank looked at him, seeming to contemplate whether speaking was a good idea, then shook his head and started out.

"Take that out through the back," Rider said as he reached the doorway. "I don't want to risk that thing being seen in the bar."

Hank looked at the mouse, then back at Rider, and nodded before leaving.

"I think he's wondering what he did to suddenly have to scoop poop and transport mice," I said after he left, feeling a little sorry for him.

"Scoop poop?" Daniel raised his eyebrows. I nodded toward Kutya. He looked over at him and laughed.

"Hank'll be all right," Rider said. "I'll give him some heads to bust when they become available. That always puts him in a good mood."

"What is he?" I asked. "I can tell he's a shifter, but I've never been able to pinpoint what kind."

"Wererhino," Rider answered.

Holy crap. I might have sat there stunned for a moment as I pictured Hank morphing into a rhino during a fight. "Well, I guess that explains the wingspan on those shoulders."

Rider grinned, but the amusement was fleeting as he leaned forward, elbows on the desk. "Grissom's checking out Eliza's house and my techs have her phone and remote access to her computer. If there's anything to be found, they'll find it, but I really can't imagine anyone going after Eliza. She's kind to everyone and never draws much attention. The only reason I could even think of someone going after her would be to get to me, but if someone wanted to draw me out using her, they would have done it by now. They wouldn't have waited until I found out she was missing. They would have sent me a part of her."

We sat in silence, all seeming to have gone down the dark and bloody rabbit hole Rider's statement had created. I took a deep breath to calm my suddenly racing nerves before I allowed fear to get the better of me. Daniel's stomach growled loud enough to draw a yelp out of Kutya.

"You had three cheeseburgers on the way over here," I told him. "And they were all doubles."

He shrugged and rubbed his stomach. "I'm a growing dragon."

"Go grab something from the bar," Rider told him. "You and Danni will be on duty in there tonight. Between Eliza going missing and this other shit that's come up, I need a lot of the team out and it's the safest way I can possibly get her violence needs met without too much potential for a clusterfuck."

"I'll make sure she has her fun but stops short of murder or castration," Daniel promised before he grinned at me and left.

"You're starting to consider she's not off somewhere mooning the moon now, aren't you?" I asked as Rider massaged the tension out of the back of his neck.

"Damn it, yeah, I am." He leaned back in his chair with enough energy, it was more of a fall. Seeming to pick up on his mood, Kutya whined and made his way to him, licking his hand before Rider moved it to scratch the Doberman-shepherd mix between the ears. "I hope we're wrong. I didn't sire her, so I can't feel her like I feel you. I wouldn't feel it if she were dead or in pain, but she is part of my nest and can speak to me telepathically from a pretty far range. If someone had entered her home to abduct her, she should have called out to me. I would have heard."

"Unless it happened when you visited me in West Virginia."

Our eyes met, and I could see him doing the math in his head just as I was. We both cursed at the same time.

"We don't know that's what happened," he said. "Even if it did, it's not your fault, and if I hadn't brought Christian there to help you, you all could have died, so don't even think of putting this on yourself. I'm going to find her. It sucks this is going on when I have this other shit to deal with, but I will find Eliza."

"What is it exactly that you're dealing with?" I asked. "How do you know there might be an incubus in the area?"

He motioned me over as he pulled something up on his computer. I walked behind the desk, squeezed around Kutya to stand behind his chair where I could see the monitor from over his shoulder. He'd pulled up a map of the states with little red dots in North Carolina, Virginia, and Kentucky. "What am I looking at?"

"Disappearances. Each of those red dots shows where a woman with sweet blood has gone missing," he explained. "Nannette and my tech team developed this program to track disappearances of women with sweet blood in order to track when incubi are building harems. It's an imperfect system, mostly because we rely on the women in question having donated blood or having their blood tested in a lab or hospital some other way. Nannette actually used your blood to help develop it. We always knew women with what we call sweet blood had blood that smelled and tasted sweeter than other blood types, but until she had a sample she could really break down, we didn't know why that was. Turns out, your hemoglobin has less salt than other blood types, and an extra chemical similar to sugar."

"Sooo… you're saying I'm full of sugar?"

"When you want to be." He grinned. "It's not sugar, exactly, but similar enough and causes the subtle sweetness those of us with hyper-senses can pick up on. Human medical professionals don't know of it and don't even realize when they're handling it, but Nannette and my techs put their heads together and figured out how to root through blood databases to find women with sweet blood through those records. My techs then developed a program that cross-references reports of missing women with women we've identified as having sweet blood and when there's a match an alert appears in the form of a red dot on this map along with an attached file that gives us the woman's information."

I touched the monitor with my index finger and traced the line of dots across the three states.

Rider's gaze followed the path of my finger. "The first dots were in North Carolina, then Virginia—"

"Now they're here."

"*It's* here. This many women with sweet blood gone missing? Definitely sounds like an incubus building a harem, and there are more dots now than there were when I first told you I suspected an incubus in the area, which is why I want you with me or Daniel at all times. Between this, the private investigator your mother has sicced on you, and whatever is going on with Eliza because it has to be something entirely different from what caused these women to go missing, you're safest here."

I massaged his tight-set shoulders as I stared at the screen, hoping Rider would stop whoever was hunting innocent women before more of them showed up as red dots on the map. "You're positive this doesn't have anything to do with Eliza?"

"Eliza doesn't have sweet blood, and even if she did, an incubus couldn't turn her. You're a hybrid because I bit you right after Ryan did. We were close enough in age and power, and our bites went through you, changing your biology at the same time. Eliza's vampirism is set in. Any other entity's bite would do no more damage than a dog bite." He reached up, grabbed my hand, and kissed it. "Grissom should finish at Eliza's and arrive here soon. I'll keep you updated. Go on out to the bar. It's about time for shift change and it's ladies' night. The probability of some ignorant incel type showing up and getting out of line is pretty high. Go enjoy yourself, just leave any out-of-line jackasses their balls. Makes things cleaner for me legally."

I rolled my eyes. "I don't always go for the balls."

"Like I don't always drink blood." He chuckled and pulled me down for a quick kiss. "I'm glad you're back."

"Glad to be back."

Another kiss not quite as quick, and a head pat for Kutya, and I was out the door, moving down the hall toward the back entrance to the bar. My stomach churned with nerves, or maybe it was fear, as I pushed down images of Eliza having *parts* chopped off to be sent to Rider. "Stop it," I scolded myself, remembering Rider had said if that had been the plan, it would have happened already.

So what the hell was the plan? Who would want to steal sweet, gentle Eliza?

I pushed through the door to the bar and was immediately hit with the full force of the Guns N' Roses song blaring from the jukebox. The night was still pretty young, but ladies' night drew a crowd and already women were pouring in. I did a quick scan and still didn't see Lana or Ginger, but I saw Daniel working on a bacon cheeseburger and fries in a corner booth, and a redhead with a whole lot of cleavage in a too-small top trying to work on him.

I made my way over to the booth.

CHAPTER FOUR

"Hey honey," Daniel greeted me, a wide grin stretched across his face as I approached.

If I could have seen myself, I probably would have seen a vision in pasty white flesh. Instead, I made a quick scan of the room, my breath frozen in my lungs until I made sure no one had heard the fool. *Are you trying to get killed?* I asked him telepathically.

"Honey?" The redhead's hand stilled over the button she'd been about to undo, prepared to release more cleavage from her tiny top for Daniel's inspection, and glared at me. "Who are you?"

"This is my wife," Daniel answered, biting back a grin before he tossed a fry into his mouth and quickly scarfed it down. Yep, for some reason, he clearly had a death wish. "Honey, this is Veronica. Veronica was just inviting me to a threesome. I was just about to tell her all about you and upgrade to a foursome."

Yep. The man was suicidal. I looked around, half expecting Rider to be standing behind me with a rusty pair of pliers in his hand.

Veronica's icy glare thawed a bit as she looked me over. She didn't seem too impressed with the prospect of quality nookie time with me, but she cheered up after giving Daniel another once-over. "Sure, it's fine if you want your wife to watch."

"Oh, neither of us just watch," he said, then nodded across the booth. "Sit, honey. I was about to explain to Veronica about the hamsters."

"The hamsters?" Veronica asked the same time I did.

"Oh yeah, you have to have hamsters," he told the woman, who now inched away from him and withdrew a hand which I hadn't noticed before had been in an intimate location under the table. "They take the experience to a whole other level. Of course there's some risk of infection involved, but it's so worth it. You just have to be gentle enough that they don't bite when you're shoving them up your—"

"You're a freak," the woman spat before making a hasty exit from the booth.

"Takes one to know one," Daniel muttered before lifting his burger with two hands and biting out a big chunk.

I dropped into the opposite side of the booth and watched him eat until I could think of what to say. It took a few minutes and three more bites before I could, and all I came up with was, "What the hell just happened?"

Daniel swallowed the chunk of burger he was working on and wiped his hands on a napkin before he rested them on the tabletop. "She made an offer. I declined. She decided to encourage me by giving my dick some personal attention, uninvited I might add, and it pissed me off, so I decided to have some fun. Relax, Danni. If Rider did overhear, he'd understand what I was doing and why. Respect goes both ways. I'll never understand how some women think they can just grab a man by his junk, knowing damn well they wouldn't want some random man doing that to them."

I watched as Daniel grabbed the beer at his elbow by the bottleneck and took a long draw, his eyes smoldering with barely checked anger. It wasn't the first time I'd seen him appear obviously bothered by a woman's grabby hands, and while I certainly understood where he was coming from, I wondered if there was more to it. He'd been enslaved by a horrible ruler once. I had suspicions she'd wanted him to service her in more ways than just the role of a guard. I would never ask though. There were some questions you just didn't want the answers to, and some I wasn't cruel enough to ask to begin with. Instead, I grinned and shook my head. "Hamsters though? She's going to tell everyone in this bar you're a huge perv."

"Let her. She was the one inviting me to a threesome with her and her sister." He grabbed another fry. "I try not to judge people's kink, but as far as I'm concerned, fornicating with family is way too far up the gross-o-meter."

"Ew, yeah, can't argue with that. I can beat her up if you want me to."

"You're such a good friend." He winked and the anger in his eyes cooled. "You know the rules. You have to have a better reason than my irritation to bust someone's skull open all over Rider's bar."

"I hate that rule."

"I know you do." He smiled and finished his fries before scanning the room. "It's shaping up to be one of those nights. I'm sure we'll find someone for you to bounce off a wall before dawn. You might even get to use a knife."

"Yay." I looked down at my dark blue T-shirt and took in Daniel's Pink Floyd T-shirt. "I guess we need to get into our work attire. Do you need to borrow something?"

"I keep some stuff in a locker downstairs," Daniel said as he balled up the napkin he'd wiped his hands with and dropped it into the empty basket his food had came in. "Meet you back in ten? Think you can stay out of trouble that long?"

"Think you can keep from getting grabbed that long?"

"I hope so, but hard to say on ladies' night." He stood and helped me up. Not that I needed it, but he was a gentleman.

"Well, I see Veronica isn't hurting too bad over missing the pleasure of your company," I told him as I caught the redhead swapping spit with a dark-haired woman across the room.

"I sure hope that's her girlfriend and not her sister," he said before guiding me toward the back door. "And it was going to be the pleasure of *our* company, *honey*."

"Stahhhp it."

Ladies' night meant the women drank for free and the men showed up in droves, desperately seeking them. Apparently, they thought they had a better shot hooking up with one. I wasn't sure whether it was solely because they expected them to be drunker and more likely to make poor choices or because they were just cheap bastards who lacked the courtesy to pay for a drink. Either way, ladies' night usually produced some scuffles and, unfortunately, the potential for dangerous situations. Because of these issues, Rider kept taxi cabs on standby outside the bar and upped security. I wasn't sure how giving away so much free booze to the women made him money, even if it was the cheaper booze, but apparently ladies' night was lucrative. I guess that was why he ran The Midnight Rider and I just stood in a corner of it, looking for anyone unruly enough to deserve a few smacks.

"Hey."

I turned to see Lana dressed in black jeans and a form-fitting T-shirt standing next to me. I grinned. "Don't take this the wrong way, but all you need are sunglasses and you'll look just like Bouncer Barbie."

She looked over at me, taking in my clothes. "You're dressed just like I am."

"Yeah, but we wear the attire very differently. So you're on security staff here tonight too?"

"Yes. What am I in for?"

"Well, there's no giant spiders to worry about. The worst beasties we'll deal with are jackasses who like to try to take advantage of tipsy women, and tipsy women who can't keep their hands off Daniel." I tilted my head toward the other side of the room where Daniel stood. Arms crossed, jaw set tight, and dressed in the all-black required attire, he looked every inch the security staff member, but women still tried to cozy up to him. He said a few words and they moved along.

"They're human. He can handle them."

"The night is young. They get very bold after they get enough drinks in their system, and we sometimes get vamps and other paranormals in here on nights when women are easy prey." I did a quick scan using all my senses, and other than the paranormal beings on Rider's payroll, I only sensed humans. "It's pretty simple. Just keep your eyes open for anyone getting overly aggressive. Paranormals rarely start shit here. They know who the boss is and what he's capable of. Every once in a while, though, we get one with a death wish."

Lana nodded her golden head. "Got it."

We stood in companionable silence, watching the humans pour in as the minutes ticked by. An hour passed without issue and the three of us moved about the room, squashing any quarrels before they could get heated, and just making sure our presence was known. Daniel may have moved around the room to escape the women who so far were just an irritant, but hadn't done anything to warrant getting thrown out or my preference, knocked out, but I had my eye on them.

Daniel and Lana paired off to talk a bit, which for some reason made me grind my teeth. I caught a curious look from Jadyn as I did this and forced myself to focus on my job. Christian was well aware of the desire I'd had for Daniel while in Moonlight, West Virginia, thanks to my succubus side needing to be sexually sated and Rider so far away, and I wouldn't be surprised if Jadyn knew. They were married, after all. They talked about things. I didn't need her thinking I was still hot for the guy. I wasn't. Not even a little bit.

I looked up front where Rome had switched out front door duty with a boxy man of around five feet, eight inches with a mop of reddish brown hair that stopped below his ears and a wide nose. He was somewhere between chubby and muscular. You knew the muscles were there, but there was a healthy layer of flesh over them which tapered enough at the waist to give him a fit look. His eyes were a brilliant green and his skin a soft shade of peach against his black clothes, and I had no idea what the hell he was.

"Need a drink?" Tony asked as I approached the bar.

I shook my head in response to the tiger shifter, not wanting to be responsible for the bottle of blood on a packed night. I'd broken up too many fights at Gruff's over someone mistakenly grabbing someone else's bottle of beer. I wasn't about to risk setting aside a bottle of blood should I be needed to break up a fight or toss someone out and some unsuspecting tipsy human stumble upon the discovery of vampires in their midst. "Who's the guy on the door?"

"Marty," he answered as he filled a chilled mug from the tap.

"Haven't seen him before."

"There have been changes since you were in West Virginia," Tony said, and didn't elaborate further, for which I was glad. Knowing Rider had lost people during that time was bad enough. I didn't need the names to add to the horrible ache in my heart, and I was thankful for every familiar face I'd seen since returning. The tiger shifter slid the mugs of fresh-poured brew down the bar to their waiting guzzlers, grabbed a bag of pretzels and stepped away without so much as a "later" as was his way. I would bet a month's pay Tony had never gotten detention for talking. I, on the other hand, had gotten into all sorts of trouble for talking.

"Bitch!" an angry male voice snarled.

I turned toward it to see Lana forcibly removing a man of average build from a booth of women who didn't seem pleased with his presence. He took a swing at Lana, who easily ducked the blow and grabbed him by the throat before twisting his arm behind his back. She kept a tight grip on the guy as she walked him right out the front door, the man cussing her out with every step.

"You're taking all my fun," I told her after she returned.

"I just don't understand the appeal of bars," she said. "Alcohol is a waste of money that makes you act stupid, and it doesn't even taste good."

"Can't say I'm a fan of bars either. The first time I drank was here, and I was attacked by an incubus." I looked around the room. "That's why Rider owns so many bars though. People are going to drink and they're going to put themselves in bad situations. At least in the bars he owns and employs paranormals to work in, there's less chance of women going home raped or turned… or not going home at all."

"But you were attacked after coming to this bar."

"And that right there tells you all you need to know about my luck, and is why I said there was less chance, not no chance." I shrugged. "Rider still saved me. I'd rather be this hybrid mess than a slave to an incubus."

"I hear that."

Lana glanced over at Daniel. The dragon shifter appeared to be busy prying a woman's hand off his shoulder as he tried to squeeze past her to talk to a man who was a little too close to a woman who didn't seem happy with the proximity. I wondered again if he'd served as more than just the queen's guard while in Imortia, but if Lana knew something about that, she wasn't offering the deets and I didn't feel it my business to ask.

I looked up front again just in time to see Aaron Grissom enter. The last time I'd seen him he'd been in uniform, but he'd been promoted to detective while I was in West Virginia chasing monsters with his brother. Now he wore a dark suit which fit his tall, lean yet muscular frame nicely and I saw the resemblance between him and his brother even better. His hair was darker, his eyes gray instead of Holden's intense amber, but the features and build were strongly matched.

Lana and I stood between him and the back door he was headed toward, so he had no choice but to stop and greet me. "Danni. I heard you had an interesting time in Moonlight recently."

"And I heard about your promotion. Detective looks good on you." I tilted my head toward Lana. "This is Lana. She had fun in Moonlight with us."

They did the customary greetings, and I was about to ask about Eliza when we heard a commotion coming from outside the bathrooms.

"I'll check that out," Lana said, and quickly headed toward the bathrooms, leaving me with Grissom.

"So Rider's in his office?" Grissom asked after Lana disappeared down the hall.

"Yes. He said you were checking out Eliza's house," I told him. "What did you find at the house? Do you have any ideas about what happened to her?"

"I need to speak with Rider first. Danni," he cut me off as I opened my mouth to press him for details. "I will check in with you after. I want to ask about Angel anyway, and it looks like you might need to take care of that."

I followed his line of sight across the bar and spotted Veronica and three other women crowding Daniel. The dragon shifter looked to be going from uncomfortable to pissed-off and in need of help.

"Yup," I said, and quickly made my way across the room as Grissom made his exit. As I neared, I noticed Daniel repeatedly declining the women's advances as they pawed at him. Veronica, clearly no longer put off by the hamster idea, squeezed a full handful of his genitals and he shoved her back before raising a warning finger. "Touch me again and woman or not, I will physically throw you out of here."

"No, he won't," I said, knowing he didn't like being rough with women, especially human women. I planted myself between him and Veronica. "He won't have to throw you out of here because the next one of you who puts your hands on this man is getting knocked the fuck out."

"Oh, it's his wife," Veronica told her group of friends, or maybe they were her sisters. Who knew? "Go find a hamster, honey," she sneered, then made the mistake of trying to push past me.

I grabbed her arm, twisted it behind her back, and used my free hand to grab a large portion of hair, drawing blood as my nails dug into her scalp. A moment later I was at the bar, the sound of her head banging face-first into the polished wood a symphony in my ears. Barstools scraped over the hardwood floor as patrons to the left and right of us fled their seats lest they get hurt as I repeatedly slammed the grabby-handed bitch's face into the bar top.

I heard a man bellow something along the lines of "Hey, that's my wife!" but I was in the zone. Hands grabbed at my shoulders, but barely connected before a man's head hit the bar, courtesy of Daniel.

Nails dug into my shoulder and I dropped Veronica, whose body had gone limp as a rag doll, and spun to deliver a solid punch to a pretty blonde's face. Suddenly, she was on her ass and not so pretty anymore.

"Anybody else wanna try me?" I asked over the den of noise.

The two remaining women who'd been crowding Daniel stood back, huddled together. They shook their heads vigorously. To my left, Daniel faced off with two men who seemed to be calculating how dangerous messing with him would be as their larger friend lay bleeding on the floor next to where I'd dropped Veronica. Lana came out of the bathroom hallway, holding a woman by her bicep and raised her eyebrows as she took in the scene. The rest of the people in the bar just watched us, waiting to see what happened next.

"If anyone puts their hands on another person in this bar, they will be kicked out or knocked out," I announced. "Unwanted sexual advances are unwanted sexual advances, whether the person giving or receiving is male or female. The rules are the same for either gender, and groping of anyone will not be tolerated. Period."

My announcement got a few cheers and applause from a group of women near the back, but most of the room remained silent. Then Kansas's "Carry On Wayward Son" came on the jukebox earning several whoops and hollers from women, including one in a Scoobynatural T-shirt, and everyone went back to what they'd been doing before Daniel and I had given them a floorshow.

I checked Veronica for a pulse, found one, and hoisted her up off the floor as Daniel picked his guy up in a fireman's carry. One glare at Veronica's three mates was all it took for the untouched two to usher the one whose nose I'd broken toward the front door. Daniel's own hard glare did similar work on the two men who'd been contemplating whether or not to defend their busted-up friend.

Daniel carried his guy, and I dragged Veronica, not wanting to show off my vampiric strength by tossing her over my shoulder, right out the front door where we unceremoniously handed them over to their group and told them in no uncertain terms they weren't welcome back.

I looked up the street to see Pacitti still parked in the same place. His bushy eyebrows rose a fraction, and he raised his cell phone, I presumed to snap off a picture of me. I raised my middle finger in his direction in case he wanted to take another.

"Thanks," Daniel said as we watched the uninjured members of the obnoxious group maneuver the injured and unconscious members of their party down the sidewalk toward the parking lot. "I didn't want to have to get physical with them."

"I know, but no one would have blamed you if you did. Was that her husband you slammed into the bar top?"

"Who the hell knows?" he muttered. "The whole damn bunch was crazy."

He reached over and pushed my middle finger down. I saw blood on his hand and grabbed it.

"Danni!" He jerked his hand away and glanced back at where Pacitti sat, watching. "What the hell are you doing?"

Realizing I'd been about to lick the blood off his knuckles, my mouth fell open and heat climbed my cheeks. What was I, a starving out of control newb? "I'm s-sorry," I finally sputtered. "I didn't realize I was that thirsty." And I shouldn't have been. I'd drank from Rider within the past twenty-four hours. And I didn't feel thirsty, because I wasn't, so why the hell had I just been about to absent-mindedly lick blood straight off of Daniel?

"It's fine." He shot another look toward the private eye and prodded me back toward the entrance to the bar. "Maybe grab a drink, though."

"Yeah."

We stepped through the entrance and the new guy working the post at the front gave me a curious once-over.

"Hi, I'm Danni," I introduced myself.

His eyes widened a little, and he repositioned himself to subtly guard his crotch. "They told me about you."

I'm sure they did, I thought as Daniel snickered next to me. "I only stab bad guys. You're Marty?"

He nodded.

I again tried to sense what he was. He didn't have the same feel as an Imortian or any shapeshifter I'd ever come across. He definitely didn't put out vampire vibes, and he didn't have the same feel to him as the new server, Hazel, who Rider had told me was a fae, whatever exactly that was. He didn't seem like any of those beings, but he was something. I moved aside as a couple moved past us to exit the bar and lowered my voice. "What's your flavor, Marty?"

He seemed puzzled for a moment, then slowly lifted one of his meaty arms and licked the skin. "Salt?"

Daniel made a small choking sound, which I ignored as I blinked at the big lug in front of me, wondering if he was messing with me. "No. I mean, what *are* you?"

"Oh." He straightened his black shirt with the small The Midnight Rider logo over the breast and puffed his chest out. "I'm a bouncer."

"No, I mean—" I waved my hand dismissively. "You know what? It doesn't matter."

I stepped away, Daniel at my side, and shook my head. "He's not the sharpest knife in the block, is he?"

"Well, he's a troll. They're not particularly known for their comprehension of rocket science."

I came to a dead stop and stared at Daniel. "Did you say troll?"

"Yes. Marty is a troll."

"What the hell is a troll?"

"Marty."

I gave Daniel my best annoyed face, earning a broad smile in return, and looked back at the big guy on door duty. He sure didn't look like any troll I'd seen in storybooks, although I guess his build and the broad nose kind of fit. "Vampires, witches, wolves, rhinos, dragons, tigers, snakes, fae, and now trolls… Is Rider starting some sort of paranormal circus or what?"

"My guess would be strengthening his fortress. What trolls lack in smarts, they make up for in the ability to clobber. And you know Imortians kick ass."

"And vampires," I said, picking up on his playful boast. "Especially hybrids."

"Eh, I suppose. You're good with balls anyway." His chuckle died a quick death as the unintentional double entendre sunk in and we stood there in awkward silence. Finally, he glanced toward the hall leading to the bathrooms and raised his blood-smeared hands. "I'm going to go wash up."

I averted my gaze by checking my own hands and found them clean enough. The bar top had been wiped down and disinfected. Lana was on the other side of the room, keeping a watchful eye on the crowd, and everything seemed normal.

I walked over to the bar and flagged Tony down for a very bloody mary, our code for bottled blood. I still wasn't what I'd consider thirsty, but after the close call with Daniel, I wasn't taking any chances. Things had calmed down enough for me to take a break. I hoped.

"Everything all right?"

I turned to see Jadyn holding an empty tray, having just finished delivering to a table. She shot a look in the direction Daniel had gone, then back at me, and I knew she sensed the awkwardness between Daniel and me and had her own suspicions as to its cause.

"Everything's fine," I said and forced a smile.

Grissom entered the bar from the back door, and I excused myself. Bottled blood in hand, I met the tall werewolf in the middle of the room and pointed out a booth in the back. "Join me on my break?"

He nodded, and we walked over to the booth. A well-heated glare at a couple about to snatch it up before us quickly sent them looking elsewhere for somewhere to sit.

Grissom chuckled as we slid into opposite sides of the booth. "That glare would work wonders in my job."

"You seem to do well with your own tricks," I told him, and waited until he'd ordered a drink from a passing server and loosened his tie to continue. "What do you think happened to Eliza?"

CHAPTER FIVE

"I did a thorough search of her house and saw no signs of forced entry or anything that suggested violence occurred inside the residence," the werewolf told me. "In human cases of abduction I would question the neighbors, but with Eliza being a vampire, I'd rather not put her on her human neighbors' radar. You remember meeting my partner before I was promoted? Amelia?"

"The psychic?"

He nodded. "Her shift ends in a few hours and she'll take a walk through the house to see if she picks up anything. Rider's tech team is doing all the tech work for me and, so far, haven't found anything suspicious or indicative that she was having issues with anyone."

I thought about what he said. "If Rider's tech team is doing the tech part of the job for you and you're waiting for Amelia's shift to end before she helps you out, you're doing this without the department knowing."

The new fae server delivered Grissom's drink in an icy cold mug. He waited for her to leave, took a drink, and replied. "There's a few of us in the department, which I'm sure Rider has probably told you a little about. We work together to handle, as well as cover up, any cases that fall into the department's hands, usually by unsuspecting humans reporting crimes against individuals they mistakenly think are humans too. When the paranormal community makes a report, it goes directly through one of us, and we do our best to make sure the department never sees or hears about any of it."

"It must be hard doing your job and working paranormal cases on the side, hiding this whole community's existence, all while protecting your own secrets from the very people you work with and are supervised by."

He shrugged. "It has its sticky situations, no doubt, but with the help of witches, fae, psychics, and others with the necessary skills, we make it work. Rider is very helpful. His tech team does a lot of the work for us, as do his security staff. As you're well aware, we don't simply arrest the criminals of our nature."

I nodded. Having been the judge, jury, and executioner myself, I knew exactly what happened to the abductors, murderers, and rapists Rider caught. Not even the human ones made it out of his interrogation room alive. "So you found nothing at all of interest in her house?"

"Nothing that screams abduction."

I took a long draw from my bottle and scanned the room. Daniel had returned from the bathroom and I noticed women weren't quite as determined as they had been to invade his personal space as he walked the room, keeping his eye out for trouble. Lana stood with her arms crossed over her chest, feet firmly planted. The pose and hard set of her jaw all but screamed *Don't fuck with me*, but the few men who didn't seem to notice were given a look that sent them headed right back to whatever corner of the bar they'd come from before attempting to hit on her.

"You think I've determined there to be no case and I'm just going to walk away from this."

I set the bottle on the table and met his gaze. "You said nothing pointed to abduction."

"I said nothing screams abduction, which in our world doesn't always mean anything. Rider filled me in on your, uh…" His lips twitched.

"Yes, I had Jadyn question a mouse. It was our best lead, even if it was ridiculous."

"I didn't say it was ridiculous." He laughed. "It was a really smart idea, actually, but, I mean, it's still funny. I definitely won't be suggesting the concept of interviewing rodent witnesses to anyone in the department."

"You won't be telling them you're investigating the disappearance of a vampire either."

"Exactly." He stopped chuckling long enough for another drink of beer, then got serious. "The smell that coincided with her disappearance is definitely something I'll be looking into. The first thought that pops into any of our heads at even the mention of sulfur is demons. Demons, however, are generally violent. They don't just walk in to someone's house and take them without some sort of scuffle."

"Everyone tells me Eliza would never harm a fly and from what I know of her, she does seem very gentle."

"No one's so gentle they'll just let a demon take them off to Satan knows where, unless, of course, they aren't aware of what the demon is, or it's not a full demon. You're a hybrid so you understand there are paranormal beings that don't always fit one category."

"Yes, but I'd assume if someone could leave that smell, they'd be a pretty strong demon." Like the demonic entity that had harassed my friends and me in Moonlight. I'd smelled sulfur when it invaded my dreams.

"That's usually the case," Grissom agreed. "Nothing is ever one hundred percent guaranteed in our world. Most vampires can't survive the sun without special sunscreen, but there have been cases of some who can. Usually, they're hybrids, but you get the point. There are werewolves who are controlled by the moon, and some who only shift forms when they want to. There are some shifters who can shift partially. Others have to fully take on the animal's form."

I took another glance around the room to make sure things were still calm enough that Daniel, Lana, and, if necessary, Marty, could handle things without me. So far, it seemed like our previous display of what happens to those who don't follow the rules was keeping patrons in line. "I get what you're saying. Our community has a lot of variables."

"Right, and demons are part of our community in a way."

"Like the thugs nobody wants in the neighborhood, but we all live here and have to deal with it."

"Pretty much." He took a drink. "I don't see your basic demon peacefully entering a residence and abducting a woman, no matter how sweet and gentle that woman is. No one simply walks away with a demon. There are, however, more seductive demonic entities."

"Like incubi." I sighed. I knew all too well how seductive incubi could be given one had led my ass out of the bar and right into a whole new type of existence where I couldn't even have a cupcake.

He nodded. "Incubi, succubi, sirens… More kinds than that. However, with Eliza being a vampire, she wouldn't be likely prey for an incubus. Succubi wouldn't want her, but there is the possibility she could have been caught in a siren's snare."

I paused with my bottle halfway to my mouth. "Siren's snare? What is that?"

"What do you know about sirens?"

I turned the bottle up and depleted it before passing it to Jadyn as she moved past our table. "I know they're like a type of succubi, but they sing. I've heard tales of them luring fishermen to their deaths, but those were tales I heard before ever being turned, so I can't account for how factual those tales were."

"Sirens are sex demons like succubi, yes. They use their

voices to capture men. While singing, the men are totally enthralled by them, which is where the term siren's snare comes from. The men are ensnared by their song and by their image, which they can alter to make themselves appear as their prey's ultimate fantasy. Their prey actually aren't always men though. They can ensnare anyone who is attracted to women, and unlike succubi, estrogen isn't a big deal to them, and they are as capable of capturing paranormal beings as they are humans."

"And you think sirens have abducted Eliza?"

"I think it's a possibility, but not the most likely." He shrugged. "I'm spit-balling here. Rider wasn't sure what Eliza's preference was. Do you know if she is attracted to women?"

I thought about it. I knew Eliza had been rescued from a sire who forced her to have sex with other vampires, a common practice among older evil sires, from what I'd gathered from speaking to her and Nannette. I knew the vampires they'd been forced to have sex with were males and females, but I highly doubted their preference mattered when they were being forced to perform. "Eliza is my counselor. She counsels newer vampires through their adjustment to the new life we've been given, so we mostly talk about things that are specific to our survival. We don't really do a lot of girl chat, and if we did, it would probably be focused on me, the receiver of the counseling."

"She's never mentioned anything at all about having a date, or mentioned an attraction to anyone. Have you seen pictures of someone who might be a love interest?"

"I'm sure you searched her house more thoroughly than Daniel and I did," I told him. "You'd have better luck finding something like that than I would. None of our sessions involved talking about her romantic life or if she even had one. Other than a Jimi Hendrix lock screen on her computer, I've never seen any pictures of anyone she might find attractive, and for all I know, she just likes

Jimi's music."

"Okay. I won't rule out sirens, but like I said, they're unlikely."

"Why are they unlikely? And if they're unlikely, why even consider them?"

"I like to cast a wide net until I get better intel or leads and tighten it from there." He shrugged. "It's unlikely that sirens are involved though, because they tend to set multiple snares in whatever area they're in. Rider would have received reports of men missing in larger numbers than normal if this area served as siren hunting grounds."

"He's looking into missing women right now. You said they could ensnare women."

"He told me of that. Those women all have sweet blood. That's a definite sign of an incubus in the area. Incubi and sirens can work together, however incubi can't control them as well as they can succubi, so they usually stay out of each other's sandboxes. I only even thought of sirens because of the sulfur hinting at something demonic and the fact there were no signs of a fight."

"The mouse mentioned flowers too."

"Yes, which doesn't rule out a demonic entity, but could suggest magic, as could the sulfur, if the magic is dark. Right now, the only thing I know for sure is Eliza appears to be missing, and she has not checked in with Rider. I didn't see any clear signs she had packed anything, but I don't know her inventory. Leaving the phone behind is the strongest sign that she might have not left her home of her own free will."

"Has the tech team gotten into the phone yet?"

"Rider got the call while I was in his office with him. All voicemails and messages were related to her job. There were a few phone numbers without clear owners. They're digging deeper into those, but there doesn't seem like much useful on the phone. They're still checking the files on her computer, bank records, that sort of thing. It doesn't look like she's spent any money since her last trip unless she used cash, and Rider spoke with her after that trip."

"Her trip to Lovefest?"

He nodded. "Apparently, that's a typical form of entertainment for her. I'll check and see if there are any other similar events she might be attending. Of course she likes to camp and hike too. That could be done anywhere."

I thought about the Lovefest email Daniel and I had found, and what the mouse had said about her seeming different after returning from it. Maybe she really had met someone and had her heart broken, but they'd come back. Running away with a love you thought you'd lost wasn't that unthinkable. Everyone got stupid when love came into play. But how to explain the sulfur?

"I'm limited to physical evidence and what those who know her can tell me right now, but once Amelia does her walkthrough, we might have a lot more to work with. Hell, she once solved a murder case in under a minute."

"Wow. How'd she do that?"

"The deceased stuck around and told her in detail how her husband had killed her, why, and where he hid the evidence." He'd started to smile, but stopped, and I realized I'd probably blanched. "We have no reason at this point to believe Eliza has been murdered, Danni. Damn. I'm not sure why I thought it was a good idea to tell you that story."

I waved away his apology. "You didn't say anything wrong. I just wish I knew what happened to her and if she's all right."

"We'll find her. In other news…" He pulled his cell phone free of his pocket and pulled up a photo before setting it on the table and turning it toward me. "Nina Valdez, AKA Angel's mother. She's in town."

I peered at the picture of the dark-haired woman and felt my stomach twist. From what I'd been told, Angel's mother was an addict herself and had a tendency to run off with random men who all promised her a better life, only to leave her in worse shape than she'd began. Angel said her mother had given birth to her at fifteen, which would make her thirty-three years old at present, but the woman in the picture was skin and bones, with the face of a woman pushing fifty. Life had beaten the shit out of Nina Valdez.

"Yeah, she looks bad," Grissom said, reading my reaction. "How's Angel doing?"

"Pretty good," I answered. "We've had some talks about her possibly going to college. She wants to travel. I'm working on that, but so far, we only made a trip to Nothingville, West Virginia."

Grissom chuckled. "From what I heard, you found plenty of excitement there."

"Yeah, we're thinking we'd like our next trip to be more Disney World or scenic cruise, less center of Hell." I sighed. "How is Holden doing? He lost someone important to him."

"Yeah." Grissom's humor drifted away. "I knew Carrie too. Holden always said they were just friends with benefits, but he cared a lot about her, even if he didn't want to call it love. He's wounded, but he's strong. He's made it through worse shit. He'll get through this. He's already out there hunting something else."

"Tell him hi for me next time you two talk."

"Will do."

I nodded. "So, how bad is it that Nina is around?"

"It's not good," he answered, and took a drink. "Nina tends to come back to Louisville when she remembers she has a daughter and thinks she might try the mother thing again. The problem with that is she thinks being a mother includes doing drugs with your kid or using the kid to get others to be more charitable. Angel's a good kid who's been through hell. She's clean now, she's got a good situation with her current living arrangement. I know enough to know the apartment you have her in is well-watched, so I don't have to worry about any dealers coming to her, but if she runs into her mother when she's out and falls for her shit…"

"Angel's been doing great with us, and she's strong."

"Unfortunately, addiction is strong too." He finished his beer. "I'm keeping tabs on Nina the best I can. Stay alert for her while you're out, and keep a closer eye on Angel."

I nodded. "Angel's kind of like my adopted little sister now. I'll keep her safe, and given she's my donor, she already has the benefit of Rider's security. I know the two of you check in with each other by phone, but you're welcome to check in with her personally any time you want. You're pretty much her guardian angel, you know."

He blushed a little, not one to easily accept such a compliment. "More like her guard dog."

"Either way, you kept her safe out there on the street. She'd love to see you."

"I might stop by soon, but not while I'm working the disappearance of Shana White. As the lead detective on this case, it's best my association with your roommate not be known and all I need for shit to go sideways is your mother seeing me visiting her." He shook his head. "Pardon me for saying it, but your mother is a giant bur in my ass."

"That's the general consensus, believe me." I laughed, but sobered upon remembering what else was being investigated. "No one ever told me how Kevin was found or how he was killed."

Grissom stared at me until enough time passed I figured he wasn't going to tell me, but then he leaned back in his seat and let out a deep breath. "His body was a damn mess. We haven't even found all the pieces yet. Considering some of it was fished out of the Ohio and other bits found in dumpsters and Iroquois Park, there's no telling if we'll ever find it all."

My stomach turned over. "Shana said Jamal killed him for her. A human did all that?"

"Humans can be far nastier monsters than us," Grissom assured me. "In fact, they usually are. Between labs and what Amelia could get from the body, we've concluded he was forced to drink gallons of bleach. Once dead, his body was hacked to pieces and discarded all over the damn city."

My stomach took another tumble. "Why so horrific a death? The man never did anything other than just be in Shana's way after she'd been turned."

"Some people are just damn sick," Grissom answered, "and it's harder to trace bleach back to a person than it is to trace bullets if they'd just shot him. The dismembering and dumping in more than one location also helps cover them. Don't feel too bad for the guy, Danni. He was the one who hired Jamal, not Shana, and he did some dirty shit on the side, which is why he had psychos like Jamal working for him in the first place."

Given that information, I knew Grissom was right. Still, it was hard not to feel bad for someone forced to drink bleach. "So how are you handling Shana's disappearance? How are you convincing the department you're actively looking when you're not? How can they think you're handling the case correctly if I haven't been questioned yet?"

"This isn't the first case like this I've been part of, Danni, and I did question you while you were in West Virginia as well as thoroughly investigate your background, search your apartment, question your neighbors and fellow employees. I questioned you again the very night you returned from Moonlight and, as always, you gave solid answers along with a thoroughly bulletproof alibi." He winked.

"So you just tell the department anything you like, type up some fake reports, and they just accept it."

"Usually, but when they don't, I have a witch in my pocket for such problems."

I shook my head as a mirthless laugh escaped. "If only

witches could put a whammy on my mother. We had one work a spell on Kevin to keep him oblivious to Shana's turning, but she said something about such spells not working on my mother."

"Don't I know it," he muttered. "I'd love to put a spell on her and that private eyesore she's hired, but they both are immune to the type of magic needed for that. Pacitti's a damn nuisance."

"So, you're familiar with him?"

"Yeah, and I saw him posted outside when I got here. He's like a damn pit bull when he's on a case, mostly because there's usually a bookie hunting him while he's hunting whoever's capture is going to get him a nice reward. At least if he's following you, he won't be following me."

"Glad I can be of service," I said dryly.

Grissom grinned. "If he stays out of my way, it's going to be easier for me to fake investigate and put everything in place."

"You have things to put in place? That sounds like you have an actual plan."

"Of course I have a plan. You think I'm just making shit up as I go?"

I thought about it for a moment. "Well, that's pretty much how I do things."

He barked out a laugh. "I have a plan. Rider hasn't told me the entirety of what's going on with Shana, but I know enough about the situation to know she's not dead, she's being guarded here, and she may or may not ever be released. The first thing I have to do is keep anyone from focusing on you, Rider, or his organization. I have an acquaintance creating a fake credit card trail for Shana right now. There will even be some video captures of her alive, well, and completely on her own somewhere in Vegas."

My eyebrows shot up. "So if you have someone posing as my sister in another state, why am I being hounded by

Pacitti?"

"She's just started to lay the trail. Give it a little time and as soon as information can be slipped, Pacitti should be out of your hair. After we've successfully taken all suspicion away from you and Rider, I'll make it look like your sister either disappeared in Vegas or died there. Be careful until then. Pacitti's a sneaky bastard and very determined, not to mention generally in bad need of money. If he catches wind of what any of us really are, you can bet your face will be all over the tabloids and even if most humans shrug things like that off as made-up stories, you never want your face or location known to slayers."

"I've been warned." I took a quick glance around the room and noticed Daniel and Lana eyeing a man who appeared to be getting a little too close to a woman at the bar. "I guess I should get back to work and you should get out of here, so Pacitti doesn't report you've been mingling with suspects."

"I'll report that I was here to question you and Rider again, so my word cancels out his if he does. I tell you, having moral fiber is a real hindrance sometimes. It'd be so much easier to just eat the jerk."

"I'm pretty sure he'd jack up your cholesterol."

Grissom grinned and dropped some bills on the table before standing. "Be careful, Danni, and watch out for Angel."

I saluted him and watched him leave before turning toward the bar in time to see Daniel grab a fistful of shirt.

Time to get back to work.

CHAPTER SIX

"A little unimpressive for ladies' night," Daniel said as the last patron exited the building. He scooped up a handful of miniature pretzels before I took the bowl away. "Only three small brawls and not one sliced testicle."

"I'm trying to venture out," I said as I moved around the bar, picking up bowls of peanuts and pretzels. "I'm thinking less testicle stabbing, more kidney punching."

Tony grunted his appreciation of our help as he took care of the beer taps, and Daniel collected bottles and mugs that had been left behind. Lana had left after the official ladies' night hours ended and we no longer needed a fourth person working security in the bar. Marty's size was enough to keep most in line as the crowd dwindled down, and Pacitti hadn't shown his face inside the building. I wasn't sure if that was a good thing or a bad thing, but at least I hadn't had to deal with him. I'd checked in on Angel and she'd seemed fine. I hadn't tried to drink anyone's blood and the altercations we had hadn't ended in death or loss of body parts, so all in all, not a bad night.

"See you tomorrow," I called after Tony after we'd finished cleaning up the bar, Marty and the servers had gone home, and the tiger shifter took off toward the rear door. He raised his hand in farewell and emitted a grunt as he pushed through the door and disappeared. "I can just feel the love for me rolling out of that man."

"I'm pretty sure that's just gas." Daniel turned toward me. "I guess this is good night, or good morning. I never know what to call it anymore."

"I'm sorry. Guarding a vampire-hybrid must be rough with our hours."

"Nah, it's not so bad, especially when you actually sleep through the day like a good little hybrid and let me get some sleep too." He winked. "I really don't need that much. I think it's the dragon in me. They can sleep whenever and wherever, but when they need to wake up, they pop right up, instantly alert regardless of how much sleep they've gotten."

"Ah, that's good." I couldn't hold back my grin. "Better to protect all those eggs you'll eventually lay."

His eyes narrowed, but his mouth twisted, revealing his amusement before he grabbed the back of my head and pulled me to him. "Nah, I gotta protect my treasure." His lips froze on top of my head, the rest of his body following suit. Neither of us breathed for a few beats before he cleared his throat and stepped away. "It's my job. Protector of the king's castle."

My heart cracked a little as pain flitted through his eyes. He blinked, and it was gone, his face now an emotionless mask, but I'd seen enough. I was drawn back to Moonlight, to the kiss in the barn and the declaration that had come with it. To the electricity that had blazed through my body when our mouths had joined and I'd felt everything the man before me struggled to hide every day because he was in the king's castle, and Rider was definitely a king capable of slaying a dragon.

And I cared entirely too much about the dragon to risk its life. "I should go before Rider comes looking for me."

"Yeah." He nodded and stepped away. "Get some

sleep."

I watched him walk toward the front door, but before he reached it, I was suddenly overcome with dizziness and a sense that something was terribly wrong. I grabbed the bar top to steady myself and called his name.

"Danni!"

I ran toward the sound of my sister's anguished scream, barreling through the rear doors and down the stairwell. If I encountered anyone, I never saw them, my focus consumed by the horrific trauma I heard in Shana's voice as her screams filled the air. I was at her door in an instant, and a moment later I stood inside it, my heart racing as her body writhed atop the bed, the sheets a tangled mess half on the floor. Her wrists were bound to the bedrails with thick silver chains, keeping her restrained no matter how hard she pulled. A thick metal band crossed over her stomach, adding an extra layer of imprisonment. Her lips peeled back from her teeth as she screamed in fear and agony so deafening my eardrums ached with the threat of bursting.

"Shana!"

Her closed eyelids flew open, revealing the eyes of a woman looking into the face of pure horror. They found me and she sucked in a ragged breath before screaming my name with a desperation that reached right into my chest and nearly petrified my heart with fear. "It's here!"

"What?" I frantically looked around the room as I moved closer to her, seeking the enemy. "What's here?"

"The Bloom."

Time stopped. Sound vanished except for only two heartbeats. Both hearts pounded furiously, the echoes filling the small space until no air remained to breathe. Shana's intensified, the rapid booms sending a piercing jolt into my skull as I squeezed my eyes shut against the pain.

I sensed a shift in energy, a thick darkness surrounding us, and opened my eyes to see Shana's bulging from her face, her mouth open in a wide silent scream. Every part of her trembled, then time rushed forward, bringing the missing sound with it. Her scream burst free as I felt my body being sucked away, and suddenly I was inside Shana's mind, watching as an entire horde of demons fell upon her.

"The Bloom was yours." Back in my own body, I turned to see Trixell standing before me, the white-haired old witch wearing the same dark gray dress she'd worn the night she'd helped my sister try to kill me. "You could have simply sated your appetite with a single man, but in all your arrogance, you considered yourself above that which you are. You cursed your own flesh and blood with your burden, and now, because of the tricks you and your lover played, she must take all the demons of Hell into her body every season. She can't even die, no matter what they do to her body, not in the state you've suspended her in."

I gasped on a strangled sob and turned toward the mountain of rutting, screeching demons, the only silver lining of the sheer number of them was their bodies formed a wall blocking the view of what they were doing to Shana, a wall so thick not even her screams could break through.

"How do I save her?"

"Release her," the old crone ordered. "Release her and take back what is yours."

"Danni!"

I jerked and looked up toward the sound of Rider's voice.

"Release her!" Trixell screeched, drawing my attention back to her. "Release her or they will do this to her over and over and—"

"Danni! I command you to come back to me now!"

I felt a sharp pull and seemed to snap back into a body I hadn't realized I'd left. Breath filled my lungs on a gasp, my eyes opened, and I was aware of wet tears sliding down my cheeks as Rider's worried face hovered just over mine.

"What happened? Where were you just now?" Rider asked.

I realized I was on the floor of The Midnight Rider, my upper body cradled in Rider's arms as he kneeled by my side. Daniel stood just beyond him, eyes bright with alertness and concern. "I was with…" The image of Shana buried under the bodies of so many rutting demons flashed in my mind and I shoved Rider away as I scrambled to my feet. "Shana! I have to get to Shana!"

"Danni, wait!" Having risen with me, Rider grabbed me around my waist. I barely had time to register Malaika standing between us and the back door before I was lifted off my feet.

"Let me go!" I elbowed the side of Rider's head and clawed at his hands, but he only tightened his hold. "They're all over her. I have to get to Shana. We need to release her!"

"Danni, that isn't possible." He grunted as my elbow connected with his head again and growled a curse. "Damn it, stop! Your sister is safe. I don't know what that witch did, but it's a trick."

"You don't understand!" Unable to break free from the steel hold of Rider's arms, I twisted and started delivering blows to his head while kicking my legs, desperate to connect a foot or fist somewhere that would loosen his grip and gain my freedom. "Let me go! Daniel, help me!"

"Enough!" Rider roared. His power flooded out of him, taking me with it. My back hit the wall and my body stuck to it, frozen in place no matter how hard I struggled to move. Malaika gasped, and Daniel's eyes darkened, unhappy with what he'd just witnessed. He stepped forward, but stilled as Rider's glowing eyes turned toward him.

"This is not the time to test me, dragon," Rider growled in a voice I'd never heard come from him before. It shook the room and hinted at something buried deep inside him. A beast kept on a short leash because if let loose, it would destroy anything in its path. "She's in danger."

The two men stared each other down, the tension between them thick and suffocating. Finally, after what felt like hours, Daniel narrowed his eyes, but gave a firm nod before relaxing his shoulders and uncurling his fingers from the fists they'd formed.

Rider stepped toward me, but kept his glare on Daniel until he reached me. The glow in his eyes faded as he turned his head toward me and reached out to cup my face. He ran the pad of his thumbs under my eyes, wiping away the tears I'd shed at some point I couldn't remember. "I need you to let me in, Danni, so I can see what that witch did. Show me what she showed you, like you showed me the place you met with Ryan when he visited you in your sleep."

I felt his hold over me loosen enough for me to speak. "I wasn't asleep."

"You fainted. Daniel caught you before you hit the floor, summoned us, and we came running. Trixell wouldn't need you asleep. She just needed you unconscious for a minute and she managed that. Let me see why." He rested his forehead against mine. "Give the nightmare to me."

A chill ran through me at the thought of reliving what I'd seen, but if reliving it long enough to send those images to Rider was what it took for him to release his hold over me and allow me to see my sister sooner, I'd do it. I took a deep breath and recalled the horror I'd witnessed, going back to the moment I'd heard Shana's scream. Despite how badly I wanted to turn away, I forced myself to remember every sound, every visual, and every … there'd been no smell. With a growl, I gathered every bit of the terrible nightmare I could gather and sent it to Rider along the invisible wavelength we used to communicate across telepathically, the same way I'd sent him pictures of the place his brother used to bring me to in my sleep.

"Damn… I'm so sorry," he apologized in a rough whisper as he loosened his power enough for me to fall forward into his waiting arms.

Tears flowed freely as I gasped in ragged sobs, the fresh images in my mind giving birth to a fresh stream of tears, and grabbed his arms for support as he held me to him. My legs were weak, my chest full of pain.

"It wasn't real," he assured me, tightening his hold to keep me on my feet as I buried my face into the soft material covering his chest. "None of that happened. None of that *could* happen."

I wiped my eyes on his shirt and gathered my strength so I could support myself as I pulled away to look at him. Heat filled my face. "There was no smell. Everything that happened, I only saw or heard. I should have seen through it."

"It was a very good lie." He held me tight against him, tight enough I felt the subtle tremors as anger rolled through his body, burning like lava. He turned toward Malaika and allowed that anger to coat his words. "How the hell did that witch manage to get inside Danni's head with you watching her?"

I watched the pretty young witch stammer for a moment before ducking her head. "I don't know. We've kept her bound with witch's net. Her magic shouldn't have gotten past the net."

"Clearly, it did. On your watch!" The fury behind his voice cracked like a whip, causing the woman to flinch.

"Rider." I rested my hand over his heart, felt the way it pumped violently, fueled by anger. "Trixell is strong. This wasn't the first time you've had to pull me out from under someone's mind-fuckery, but it's the first time I heard you doing it, and the first time I felt the struggle. You pulled me right out when your brother screwed with me in my sleep. It wasn't as easy to pull me out from whatever the hell Trixell was doing, was it?"

The air around Rider seemed to crackle a little as he

simmered, then faded away once his eyes cooled and he gave a small nod, conceding. "There was resistance. Not as bad as when you were possessed by Ryan, but still strong."

"Ryan was my dominant sire during the Bloom, as you are my dominant sire now, so I may not yet know a ton about all this supernatural stuff, but I'm pretty sure a witch capable of magic that could resist a sire's direct command over his fledgling is powerful as hell, and Malaika has been doing pretty damn good to keep her contained at all."

Rider rolled his neck, his teeth gritted together, but I saw his mind working as he debated internally between whether to admit there probably wasn't a damn thing Malaika could have done to prevent what had happened.

"She did get through on my watch," Malaika said, her head bent forward, gaze glued to the floor. I watched her struggle not to hide her hands away inside the front pocket of her dark hoodie or shove them into her jeans pockets. She took a deep breath and forced herself to look Rider in the eyes, straightening her spine. "It won't happen again."

"It might," Rider said, "because Danni's right. The evil bitch is strong, and well acquainted with dark magic. You're also pulling twelve-hour shifts with Rihanna. She's cunning, and knew to wait before the two of you switched out to get you at a weak point. All she needed was the perfect combination of tired guard and worn-off witch's net."

"I should have known the witch's net had started to wear off."

Rider gave his head a small shake. "Not if she's been playing us from the start. She's a much older witch than you and Rihanna, and powered by dark forces. We've assumed the same amount of witch's net that would bind the two of you would be as effective on her. She could have been acting more affected than she was all this time."

Malaika frowned, causing faint grooves to appear between her perfectly groomed dark eyebrows. "If she's had the power to use her magic beyond the net, why hasn't she used it on us? If she could get in our minds, she could use that to her advantage and get free."

"Maybe she doesn't want to get free. Maybe she's right where she wants to be." Rider stared at me with an intensity that caused my stomach to take a dive, before returning his attention to Malaika. "We're doing the direct infusion now and we've doubled up the webbing. Get some rest. Danni's right. This wasn't on you. We all underestimated her."

The young witch nodded. "I can stay with Rihanna for a while, to make sure the IV is effective."

"We know what to watch for now," Rider told her. "You need rest, and you need time to check in with your family."

The mention of her family lit a spark in Malaika's caramel-colored eyes. She nodded as she stepped back, wished us a good day's rest, and left through the front door, which magically unlocked, then relocked behind her. I wasn't sure if that was her doing, or Rider's.

"I want to see Shana," I said. "I need to see her with my own eyes if there's any chance of getting any rest."

"I can stay here and stand guard outside the witch's cell," Daniel offered.

Rider gave him a narrow-eyed glare.

"I've done my homework on witches," Daniel told him. "If this one is powerful enough to work mind-magic while being bound with witch's net, a little threat of *fire* might be just what she needs to behave, at least until Rihanna's had time to ensure she really is bound this time. You really don't want to risk Danni sleeping here with a dark witch capable of creeping into her mind just a few floors below her, do you?"

Rider's jaw ticked. He pulled me against his side, one arm wrapped around me in a hold equal parts protective and possessive, and glanced toward the bar where I'd been standing before I'd blacked out. "I've assigned Lana to guard the cell. She'll be here in a few hours. You can keep watch until then," he told Daniel as he returned his dark gaze to him. "Have Hank show you the guestroom. It's not fancy, but you can rest here once Lana takes over. You'll have privacy… in that room." He glanced over at the bar again before ushering me forward, and I recalled the moment Daniel had kissed me on the top of my head, the same moment I remembered Rider had the whole bar under video surveillance.

I fought the urge to glance back at Daniel as we reached the back door, sensing the tension between the two overprotective men who both cared for me, knowing any attention I gave Daniel would fuel the ire boiling through Rider's veins.

Juan opened the garage door as we entered the hallway, and Kutya immediately barreled in to run straight to Rider. Rider paused and looked at where Kutya's leash hung on the hook next to the door. "You didn't use his leash?" he said while scratching the top of Kutya's head to calm the excited dog.

"I cannot in good conscience put a leash on that dog," Juan said.

Daniel looked at the dog and shook his head as he moved around us and disappeared through the door to the stairwell, headed toward wherever Trixell was being held below.

"Did you clean up after him?" Rider asked and grunted when Juan just gave him an *Are you fucking serious?* look back. "See you tomorrow, Juan."

The lanky werewolf saluted us and backed out of the hallway to exit through the garage. I reached down and gave Kutya a good scratch under the chin as he looked up at me, all happy and excited, with his long tongue hanging out the side of his mouth. "For a bunch of grown men who kill and maim, you're all pretty delicate about cleaning up dog crap."

"You didn't want to do it either."

"I am delicate." I batted my eyelashes.

"Yep, that's you. Danni the Delicate Teste Slayer." He made a clicking sound to get Kutya's attention and guided me toward the stairwell, the perky dog following close behind. "I guess I shouldn't have expected a wolf shifter to clean up after a dog. I can understand how that would be weird."

I could imagine so as well, enough that I got a little chuckle out of the thought, but the amusement dried up pretty quickly once we descended to the lower level and I took in the number of Rider's staff and general atmosphere. We couldn't walk ten feet without seeing a shifter or other member of staff posted in a military stance. They all appeared fresh and alert, not a surprise given I knew vampires would have made up most of the night staff, and they would have switched out with the non-vampires within the past hour to allow them time to get home before the sun fully rose.

The guards watched us in silence, subtle nods the only sign of acknowledgement. They'd clearly been given firm instruction to stay focused on the task at hand. "Where is Trixell being held?"

"In a cell on this floor."

"You have her on the same floor as my sister?" I nearly hissed.

"She can't get to your sister," Rider assured me. "She might have been able to pull that mind shit with you, but she's physically bound to the cell with plenty of guards between her and Shana. Every hall on this floor is under video surveillance as well."

The mention of video surveillance reminded me of the veiled accusation made upstairs and sent a flood of heat to my face. Assuring Rider that Daniel was just a very close friend was an immediate reflex I thankfully swallowed before I caused any more tension between the two men I cared about most in the world.

We reached Shana's room at the end of a long hallway. Two shifters stood guard outside, but Rider still had to place his palm over a scanner to the right of the door for it to unlock. We waited for the click, and Rider held the door open.

Kutya trotted ahead of us. I moved straight to the side of Shana's bed while Kutya investigated everything else, which couldn't have been very entertaining. The room was pretty sparse. Shana lie atop the bed, looking exactly as she had the last time I'd been in the room. Same position, same clothes, the clothes she'd worn the night she'd tried to kill me. I could sense life in her, but she appeared dead enough to be troubling. "She's been wearing the same clothes all this time? No one has bathed her?"

"She is suspended," Rider reminded me as he took position at the foot of the bed. "She doesn't sweat. She doesn't get dirty. She doesn't move at all. She's basically suspended in time, unaffected by the world around her, which is why what that witch showed you could never happen. She sold you a horror story, and a damn good one at that, but you have nothing to fear or be guilty of. Shana feels nothing at all."

I reached over and ran my fingers through her silky blonde hair. "You're absolutely sure she isn't lost in some mental hell?"

"I'm sure. The spell has its flaws, primarily the way it had to be performed, but Danni, you know me. No matter how I feel about your sister, do you really think I would allow any woman to suffer what that witch projected?"

I took a deep breath and shook my head. Rider could be vicious, but never without reason, and a man who'd saved nests full of women forced to do vile things wouldn't willingly put a woman through something similar. "I don't really understand the spell though. You told me she's taken on the Bloom for me. It has to affect her in some way."

"If she could feel it, she'd feel the desire and urges you felt when you went through it, but the spell prevents that. Have you ever heard of congenital analgesia?"

I shook my head.

"It's a rare medical condition that causes a person the inability to feel pain. The spell works similarly to that. She could be stabbed in the gut and not feel a thing."

"What about her mind, Rider?" I held her hand in mine. "She's not dead. What does she think is happening?"

"Nothing. Time isn't passing for her like it is for us."

I stared down at her, praying that was true. I wanted to believe Rider, and I did believe that he believed the words he was saying, but it was harder to believe that he absolutely, positively wasn't wrong and just didn't realize it. If only I could somehow go inside her mind and… "Can you get into her mind like you can mine?"

"Not while she's under the spell. Her mind is blank, Danni. There's nothing there for me to get into. All brain activity is frozen."

Man, I wanted to believe that, but the images Trixell had projected into my mind were so real despite the lack of smell. They were real enough to fill me with doubt no matter what Rider said, and no matter what he said, I knew my sister's heart was locked in a box somewhere, keeping her in the state she was in, but some part of her, some essence, had to be somewhere in order for her to be alive, even if that place was some empty void. "What about Jon?"

"Jon?"

"Jon," I repeated. "If Shana's alive, she has a spirit, and it has to be somewhere floating in the universe. Jon can float in weird places with spirits, or whatever that was he did with me while you were working the spell. Can Jon do that? Can he take me to see where Shana is?"

Rider just stood there, blinking at me, until Kutya bumped his big head into his leg. He reached down and absentmindedly scratched the dog between its ears. "I have no idea if—"

"Can you ask him? Can you just find out where he is and get him here?"

"You don't find Jon. Jon finds you."

"Well, that's just great," I muttered.

"Jon's a mystery, but he's a good guy. Seta isn't anyone you'd ever want to cross, but she's a good person. Neither of them would be any part of a spell that made someone suffer like what that witch showed you. Your sister is safe, secure, and resting peacefully."

I took a deep breath and released it slowly to calm my nerves. I was still far too upset to just let the fear go, but I did trust Rider, so I had to trust that he knew what he was talking about. Shana certainly didn't look to be suffering at all from the outside, and we were sisters. I'd like to think that if she was in some kind of hellish, otherworldly realm, I'd have some kind of an inkling about it. "All right. And you're sure Trixell can't get to her?"

"Every guard on this floor is armed with witch's net. Her cell is reinforced with it. She's bound with it, and as an added precaution after the event that just occurred, we're now giving her a small amount of it through an IV so it's inside her body. Physically, there's not the slightest thing to fear. Like most witches who practice the very dark arts, their power is primarily mental. Clearly, we underestimated her power there, but the IV should prevent her from using her mental tricks, and she wouldn't use those on your sister anyway. Your sister has no brain activity under the spell, remember? There's nothing there for her to manipulate. Honestly, your sister is the safest person in this entire building when it comes to that witch."

I studied Shana for a while longer before turning to face Rider directly. "I want to see Trixell."

"No." The word may as well have been forged steel for all my possibility of getting past it.

"Rider."

"I said no, Danni. This is one of those times you need to obey me so I can keep you alive."

I stared directly into his darkened eyes, refusing to wilt under the force of their intensity. "I thought that was what all the witch's net and the guards were for. Are Shana and I safe here or not?"

"Shana is the only truly safe person here. Everyone else is at risk, and you are in more danger than anyone in my nest. Don't forget Trixell is here because she and Ryan used your sister to lure you. She was able to get inside your head once already without laying eyes on you. I am not delivering you to her cell on a damn platter."

"If she's that dangerous to me, why is she here?"

"As dangerous as she is here, she'd be even more dangerous out of our sight." His jaw ticked. "And she's the only lead I have to finding out how to get to Ryan and end him. All the way this time."

A smart-assed quip about not fucking that up this time danced along the tip of my tongue, but I had enough human decency left in me not to let it fly. Rider had crushed his own brother's heart to save my life. There was no way I was blaming him for the fact his brother just happened to be evil enough to have planned ahead for such an inconvenience. The fact I'd even thought such a bitchy retort clued me in I was more emotional at the moment than I'd realized. "She hasn't given you anything yet. I just thought maybe if I were to work on her—"

"You've done really well in my interrogation room, babe, but this evil hag is a master of manipulation, and your strength lies in violence. Inflicting all the pain in the world on her won't do a damn thing. She's not afraid of it. Hell, she might even like it." He closed the distance between us and lifted my chin. "Speaking with her now would only rile you up, making it easier for her to get to you, so you're going to do as I say and go upstairs. You're going to get into bed, close your pretty eyes, and go to sleep, allowing yourself the rest you need to strengthen your mind because a tired mind is a lot easier to fool than a well-rested, clear one. Tell me you understand."

"I understand." I managed to say the words without growling.

"That's my good girl." He released my chin and turned for the door.

"What are you going to do?"

"I'm going to take you and Kutya to my room, tuck you in, and watch over you until you're asleep." He looked back at me. "And then I'm going to have a word with Daniel."

Great.

CHAPTER SEVEN

I opened my eyes, aware I'd slept through the entire day despite no sense of time having passed since I'd crawled into Rider's bed at sunrise. A heavy weight rested on my chest, and heat blew into my face with every exhale from Kutya's wet nose. The dog's master stood over me, dressed for the day in black pants and a black button-down shirt. His hair was wet, slicked back, and tied back at the nape in his usual style.

"You did that thing again."

Rider raised an eyebrow, doing his best impression of innocently clueless as to what I spoke of.

"I didn't fall asleep. You put a whammy on me to keep me unconscious until nightfall and unable to dream."

"I protected you from mental intrusion and ensured you received a full day's rest, yes."

Damn it. He was being controlling again, the very thing we'd argued about so much in the past, and I'd thought we'd made some headway on during our talks while I was away in Moonlight. I guess as much as a leopard couldn't change its spots, a vampire sire couldn't loosen his grip.

"I simply aided you in getting a good day's rest, Danni. We both needed it and the risk of Trixell getting to you in sleep was too great to take."

I grunted and carefully pushed the big ox of a dog off me so I could sit up. Kutya gave me a big slobbery kiss, leaving a wet streak down one side of my face before jumping off the bed and turning circles in front of the door.

"You were already taken out," Rider told the dog, who ignored him to spin faster in front of the door and added a few barks.

"You didn't sleep the entire day," I said, taking him in. He'd definitely been up for a while.

"I got as much rest as I needed. I'm not the one whose head Trixell is trying to get into. Well, not in the way she's trying to get into yours anyway." He closed his eyes, and I sensed power stir inside of him, and knew he was communicating with someone. The power drew back into him and he walked to the door, opening it to allow Kutya an exit. The dog darted out, and he closed the door, then turned toward me. "You need to drink."

I might have salivated a little as he approached, his fingers deftly undoing shirt buttons to reveal his well-toned chest. "You're trying to distract me with your sexiness."

"I'm trying to ensure you're well-fed," he said. He tossed his shirt to the floor and sat next to me on the bed. His mouth curved in a roguish grin. "The sexiness can't be helped."

"Cocky," I muttered. My fangs dropped, and I leaned forward to sink them into the smooth golden column of his throat. The first wave of powerful blood to gush over my tongue hit my system like a triple-shot of espresso and I was soon lost in the rush. Yep, the sexiness couldn't be helped, I thought while climbing into his lap, just like I couldn't help somehow losing my clothes as his intoxicating blood filled me, waking up more than just my mind. Soon he filled me in another way and what started in the bed moved to the shower.

"Still angry with me?" he asked as he held me against the glass, withdrawing until just the tip of him remained, teasing me while water rained down on us.

"No, but that'll change if you stop," I said and slid down the length of him with enough force to knock him against the opposite wall.

"Never," he growled and lost control enough to allow me to tumble into his mind and see Daniel kissing my head in the bar replaying front and center as he dug his fingers into my hips and thrust harder. "You're mine."

"Has Grissom checked in?" I asked as I laced up my black combat boots. I'd gone with dark wash jeans and a black T-shirt since I wasn't sure what was in store for me, and you could never go wrong with a basic T-shirt and jeans combo.

"Amelia did a walkthrough of Eliza's house." Rider finished buttoning up the shirt he'd removed earlier and looked at me before lowering himself onto the chaise to pull on his boots.

"And?" I prompted. He looked over to where I sat on the bed and I saw his mind working as he debated what to tell me. "Ya know, the afterglow thing only works so long. If you want to keep me in a good mood, it'd help if you didn't hide crap from me. You know, like you agreed you were going to stop doing."

"Just as you agreed you were going to listen to me." He finished putting his shoes on and stood, reaching down to help me up. "I don't want you getting caught up in whatever's happened with Eliza. We already know there's an incubus in the area. I need you focused on staying safe so I can focus on finding Eliza and all the women who've gone missing."

"So Amelia did sense something? Something did happen to Eliza. She didn't just leave?"

Rider tucked a lock of damp hair behind my ear. "She sensed something very old had been there, something dark. She didn't sense malice though. No violence. It's very baffling because as kind as Eliza is, it makes no sense she would just welcome something like that into her home, much less leave with it."

My stomach churned. The knowledge that no violence had been sensed should have made me feel better, but it had the complete opposite effect. The only thing I could think of worse than Eliza being abducted violently was Eliza willingly going somewhere with something dark and ancient. Physical wounds were easier to overcome than mental ones.

"Whatever you're thinking, stop." Rider lifted my chin, forced me to look him in the eye. "We don't know anything for sure and jumping to the worst-case scenario isn't going to help you do what I need you to do."

"Which is?"

"Focus on yourself and stay out of trouble."

"Sidelining me is babying me."

"I'm not sidelining you," he said. "I'm putting you where I need you. I'm handling the situation with the incubus in the area, as well as handling Eliza's disappearance. Grissom and Amelia are helping with that, as well as the situation with your sister. Malaika, Rihanna, and Lana are handling Trixell. I need you and Daniel to handle that damn detective your mother has sicced on us, as well as handle your donor. Grissom told me about the girl's mother being in town. There's a lot going on right now and I need everyone assigned to where they're most effective, and I need them completely focused on their own assignments. If you're going to work for me, you have to accept that. Understood?"

I took a deep breath. It was in my nature to argue, but I knew he was right. I wanted to be a real employee with real duties, and if I were to be his real employee, I needed to do as told. I still suspected he was keeping me away from the more dangerous jobs, but he wasn't wrong that Pacitti was a problem and the man was following me. I couldn't very well lead him into paranormal business. Despite the fact she was my blood donor, Angel wasn't really paranormal business. I'd take care of her and keep Pacitti away and try not to bitch about it, especially since Rider wasn't separating me from Daniel. After the little peek I'd had into his thoughts earlier, I knew he wasn't happy with the relationship we had. I didn't get a lot of peeks inside Rider's mind, but when I did, it was always because he was extremely upset, so much he couldn't block me out.

Thinking of which, I sealed up my mind. I didn't think he'd noticed my mental intrusion. Nothing like a good ol' rush of blood to your nethers to make you miss such things, but just in case, I didn't want him clued in to what I knew. "I understand. I'm just really worried about her and I want to help if I can. It beats sitting back, wondering what's happening to her."

"All signs point to her not being harmed, so try not to think about it."

"There are a lot of ways to be harmed that leave no physical trace."

"You totally missed that whole try not to think about it piece of what I just said, didn't you?" Rider pressed his lips against my forehead and held me close. I felt his arm tighten around me and knew the gesture had reminded him of the closeness Daniel and I had shared, and I recalled him saying he'd be speaking with him after tucking me in. I wanted to ask about that conversation, but knew better. "We're going to find her."

I nodded my head as I pulled away. "So, what's my schedule for tonight?"

"I have the bar covered. You're going to take care of your donor and keep Pacitti away from here. Try to relax."

"So I'm just supposed to hang out at my apartment and act like nothing's wrong?"

"You're supposed to make sure your donor's safe, keep the prying eyes of that rodent-like detective away from us as we maintain operations to find Eliza and several missing women, and stay far away from Trixell so I don't have to add you being in immediate danger to my list of shit I have to deal with today." He guided me out the door, his palm against the small of my back. "Drink from your donor, even if you don't feel thirsty. We don't need you getting out of whack. If we bring anyone in, we'll let you beat the crap out of them in interrogation to get your violence needs met, although you did pretty well on that last night. We've already dealt with one call threatening legal action this morning."

I nearly stumbled down the stairs we took to the main floor. "Someone's suing?"

"Someone's threatening to," he said as we reached the bottom. "Someone's always threatening to, especially after getting their ass handed to them in front of their friends. No worries, Danni. I have ways of changing human minds. Still, I'd rather stretch out such incidents, so I've taken you and Daniel off security duty in the bar for a while."

I sighed. "Maybe I should be restricted to interrogation. No one there tries to sue."

"Yeah, it's difficult for the dead to do that." He pulled me close. "It might not seem like it, but taking the night off from the bar, getting away from here to hang out with your donor is an important job right now. That detective and your mother, as well as your proximity to Trixell here, are major distractions, so don't feel like you're just goofing off while we work. You're staying out of harm's way and keeping that detective off our backs, allowing us to do what we need to do."

The garage door opened and Kutya bounded in, his long tongue lolling out of his mouth. He danced around in place as Rome stepped in behind him and stood in place, the end of his leash in one meaty hand.

"Oh, there's one more job I need you to do tonight."

"Dog-sitting?"

"Dog-sitting."

I accepted the leash from Rome and wrinkled my nose

as he muttered about returning after he found the shovel and took care of business, then disappeared back through the garage. "Remind me again why I'm your girlfriend."

"That thing I did with my tongue in the shower," Rider whispered in my ear.

"Oh, yeah, that's right. If I have to break out a shovel tonight, you're going to owe me several more repeats of that."

"Deal." He kissed my temple, scratched Kutya's head and moved toward the stairwell. "Have fun, but be careful. If anything happens and Pacitti sees, make sure to kill him discreetly."

"I'm not even sure if that was a joke or actual order," I told Kutya. He barked his response, and I gave his leash a gentle tug toward the bar.

I received more than a few looks as I entered the bar through the back door, the large shepherd-mix at my side, but no one complained about the dog in the bar. I noticed the look in Daniel's eyes as Kutya and I approached the booth he sat in and figured that was about to change.

"We're dog-sitting the monster?" He shoved the last giant chunk of what looked like a triple bacon cheeseburger into his gullet.

"He's not a monster." I scratched between Kutya's ears and received a goofy dog smile in return. "He's just a puppy."

Daniel swallowed with a painful-sounding gulp and wiped his hands on a napkin. "Big-ass puppy," he said and tossed the napkin into the basket his food had been in. He stood and looked down at the dog with a very serious facial expression. "Do not attempt to piss on me again. I'll piss back."

Kutya gave a sharp bark, and I swore I saw a dare in his eyes. It suddenly occurred to me that I probably hadn't been assigned the cake job I thought I'd been assigned.

"Is he still trailing us?"

"Yup," Daniel said with a quick glance in his rearview mirror. "I can see him every time Kutya moves his furry ass out of the way."

"You know, I never took you for someone who doesn't like dogs."

"I like dogs. I'm just not crazy about furry jackasses who try to piss on me." He brought the truck to a stop in one of the parking spaces near my old Taurus I hadn't driven in months.

"You didn't like my grandmother's dog either."

He put the truck in park, turned the ignition off, and stepped out. "That thing's not a dog. It's a rat."

I couldn't argue with that, so I stepped out of the vehicle and watched the street while Daniel walked to the rear to lower the tailgate. He threw his hands up when Kutya took a flying leap down from the truck bed before he could reach the gate.

I chuckled. "He's not much for patience."

"I see that." Daniel stared at the dog, hands on hips. "He breaks his fool neck, it's not on me."

I watched Pacitti ease his car past the lot and find a spot along the street to parallel park. "I can't say I'm happy this guy knows where my apartment is."

"Better he's watching you here than nosing around The Midnight Rider or tailing after Grissom." Daniel scowled as Kutya sniffed around his feet. "Raise that leg and we are going to have problems, flea-bag."

I rolled my eyes, clipped on Kutya's leash, and led him toward the building. I looked straight at Pacitti while we neared the building, noting he didn't seem the least bit concerned we knew he was there watching us. "Did he ever leave the bar or change clothes?"

"Doesn't look like it." Daniel looked in the man's direction and sniffed. "Doesn't smell like it either. Dude reeks of pork rinds, body odor, baby wipes and body spray."

"Baby wipes?"

"Yep. I'm guessing he gave himself a camping shower." Daniel mimed washing oneself with wipes.

"Gross." We entered the building and jogged up the stairs. I gave a nod to Carlos, the vampire on duty outside my door, hidden in the shadows in the corner of the hallway, inserted my key in the lock, and stepped into my apartment. I supposed it was more Angel's apartment now since I spent my days in Rider's bed, but it was nice knowing I had a place to go if his small space became too cramped, which was sometimes the case given we shared it with his need to control and my need to fight that control. And now Kutya had taken up residence there as well.

Angel stepped out of the bedroom in dark joggers and a Batman sweatshirt. Recognition flashed through her eyes as she saw us, then they brightened at the sight of Kutya. "Whoa! What kind of dog is that?"

"A German shepherd mixed with Doberman," I answered, and unclipped the leash from Kutya's collar. "He's friendly."

"Come here, big guy!" Angel plopped down to her knees and absorbed the impact of one very excited dog who ate up the attention he received.

"If he gets all excited and pisses, I'm not cleaning it up," Daniel said as he crossed over to the kitchen and opened the refrigerator door before taking a look inside.

"Hey." I walked over and leaned against the sink. "You're kind of irritable tonight."

"I'm not irritable. I'm just focused." He opened a Tupperware container and sniffed its contents before returning it to the fridge.

I remembered Rider's declaration the night before, and the hard look in his eyes when he'd said it. "I know Rider talked to you after I went to sleep this morning. Is everything all right?"

"Rider talks to me every morning. He's my boss." Daniel withdrew packages of lunch meat from the fridge and dropped them on the counter next to the bread before grabbing a paper plate from one of the overhead cabinets. "Everything's cool, Danni. Nothing to worry about."

I watched him pile ham, turkey, chicken, and roast beef onto a slice of bread, top it with cheese, mustard, ketchup, lettuce, pickles, and tomato before tossing the other bread slice on top. He noticed me watching and looked up. "I'm sorry. I don't have to eat this."

I shook my head. "It's fine. If I were really dying to eat human food, I could always munch on the lettuce."

"Yeah, like that's worth doing," he said while putting away the things he'd taken from the fridge. "I'm serious. I can wait until I'm off the clock to eat."

"No, it's fine, but I've noticed your appetite has grown a lot recently. You just downed a huge bacon cheeseburger before we headed this way. Is anything wrong?"

He shrugged and picked up the sandwich. "I'm just hungry."

I noted the breadth of his shoulders and the way his Beavis and Butthead T-shirt stretched across them. It wasn't the first time I'd seen him in the shirt, although it had seemed looser before.

"What's his name?"

I turned toward Angel, realized I hadn't told her anything about Rider's dog. "Kutya," I answered as I left Daniel in the kitchen and made my way over to her. "He's Rider's dog. He got him while we were in Moonlight."

"Oh." She frowned. "So he's not staying here?"

"No pets allowed in the building," I told her. "I'm probably pressing my luck bringing him here, but I'm watching him tonight and wanted to check in with you too."

"You need blood?"

"I should drink, yes, but that's not why I came," I said, wondering if after all the time Angel had spent with us, she knew she was more than just a blood source. She was still closed off in many ways and I never pried, figuring she'd tell me as much about her past as she was comfortable with, when she was comfortable enough to do so. I knew enough to worry though. She was a great young woman, far too good a person to fall back into the clutches of addiction. "We need to talk." I jerked my head toward the bedroom and walked that way.

Angel glanced toward the open kitchen where Daniel steadily inhaled the sandwich tower he'd created and followed me into the room. Kutya followed right along.

"Sit." I plopped down onto the bed myself and waited for Angel to sit before me and get comfortable. "Have you heard from Grissom since yesterday?"

"No." Her eyes widened. "Did something happen to him?"

"No, no." I raised my hands and patted the air in a gesture to calm down. "Sorry, I didn't mean to scare you. He's fine. I saw him last night, but he, uh, gave me some news. I'm not sure whether it's good news or bad news."

Angel's face fell. "Is it my mom or dad?"

I could almost physically see the wall she put up to steel herself against whatever I was about to say, and the fact she had to do that pulled at my heartstrings. "It's your mother."

"Is she dead or just back in town?"

"She's back here. That's all he knows right now."

I watched a myriad of emotions play through her eyes as she took this in. After a moment, she straightened her spine and nodded. "I know Grissom has told you about my past. I've been in and out of rehab a few times. I've stolen to get by. I've committed crimes, and aided my mother in doing so. I've recovered a handful of times only to go right back to that garbage heap of a life when she lost whatever guy she was with and came back here with empty promises of doing right by me. I know he's afraid I'll do that again, and I can tell you're afraid of the same thing."

"We care about you," I told her. "Addiction is strong, and I know from experience that the need for a mother's love is even stronger. It's hard to see that sometimes you have to step away from that and do what's best for you. You have to accept that even if they love you, some people just don't have the capability to love you in a way that isn't destructive."

"I know." Angel gave a firm nod. "That's why this time my sobriety is different. I didn't go into rehab because the foster care system forced me into it. I didn't fake my way through this time. I went in for me. I did it for me, just like I let go of her for me. The little girl inside me who craved a mother is long gone. I want a life with a real family that cares about me. I'm not accepting the screwed up one I was given anymore. I'm definitely not letting it destroy any hope I have for a future."

"Glad to hear it because your future is as bright as you want it to be." I covered her hand with mine. "You can have all the space you need, but I'm always available if you need to talk about anything. You're more than just blood to me."

Angel smiled and wrapped her arms around my neck in a tight hug. My heart swelled as I wrapped my arms around her. Kutya whined and nosed his face between us until he worked his way in enough to rest his head on Angel's lap, offering comfort. She chuckled, and it slowly grew into a hearty laugh. When she pulled away, tears streamed down her face and she wiped them away with her sleeves.

"What is it?"

"It just hit me I was hugging a vampire. If I told my sponsor that, she'd swear I was back on drugs."

I gave her a look which only made her laugh and soon I was laughing right along with her. "All right," I said a few minutes later, and I might have had to wipe my own eyes. "In other news, my mother has hired a pesky detective to follow me in search of my missing sister and there's a dangerous witch at the bar I'm supposed to be staying away from so what do you want to do tonight to keep me out of trouble?"

"Movie marathon?"

I shook my head on a laugh. "We've got to get you out more. I'd think after being stuck in Moonlight so long you'd be champing at the bit to go out somewhere fun."

"All three *John Wick* movies are on tonight," she said. "There's not a whole lot that tops Keanu, especially when it's badass Keanu."

"Well, I can't argue with that." As far as fictional men went, Dean Winchester would always have my heart, but I wouldn't kick John Wick out of bed. As if anyone could kick John Wick out of anywhere he wanted to be.

We moved back into the living room where Kutya got busy sniffing about and Daniel stood at the window, staring out at where I assumed Pacitti still sat in his car.

"Is it just me, or has he gotten bigger?" Angel asked, eyeing him.

"Apparently he has," I answered. "His shoulders are wider."

She nodded. "He'd probably be hot if he wasn't an idiot."

I didn't respond, knowing no good would come of admitting to any thoughts I had about Daniel's hotness. "What time does this marathon sta—"

I was interrupted by a loud pounding on the front door, followed by a voice guaranteed to make my sphincter pucker. "Danni London Keller, I know you're in there. Open this door this instant."

Daniel groaned as Angel stared at me, bug-eyed. "London?"

I rolled my eyes. "That's my mother."

Angel's gaze moved from me to the door and back again before she smiled devilishly. "This is going to require popcorn."

Three more heavy bangs on the door caused my shoulders to tense and Kutya to let out a howl.

"Open the door," Daniel said, turning toward it. "We might as well get this shit show over with."

CHAPTER EIGHT

My dread grew as I approached the door, smelling two things worse than my mother's cloying perfume: my grandmother's talcum powder and her pomchi, Terry.

I steeled my nerves and opened the door to find my mother standing outside in a light blue pantsuit with a silky white shirt and pearls. My grandmother stood, or more accurately, towered over her from behind, dressed in gray slacks and a dark purple blouse. Terry the Tiny Terror peeked out from the leather purse she held tight to her side. Pacitti stood behind both of them.

"Is it necessary to keep announcing my full name to everyone in the vicinity?" I asked as I stepped back, allowing the entrance they would forcibly demand if I hadn't.

"What's the matter with your name?" my mother asked. "You have a good name. It has class."

"What's the punk rocker doing here?" my grandmother asked, noticing Daniel by the window. He'd turned to face them, arms folded over his chest.

"Daniel's my friend, and he's not a punk rocker."

"Well, with that disheveled tutti frutti hair, he looks like the product of fornication between a parrot and a feather duster."

I shot an apologetic look Daniel's way, but he actually appeared amused. The microwave dinged, drawing our uninvited guests' attention to the open kitchen where they discovered Angel.

"Who's that?" my mother asked.

"That's my friend, Angel."

Pacitti's head swiveled toward Angel with far too much interest for my liking, while my mother and grandmother shared a look I knew all too well. They looked at each other that way any time they were faced with someone with brown skin. It was a look I wanted to smack right off their faces, but beating your elder relatives was heavily frowned upon. If Angel noticed the shared look or knew what it meant, she didn't seem bothered. She dumped the popcorn into a bowl and turned to watch the show while she munched.

"What are you doing here?" I asked, watching Pacitti out of the corner of my eye as he continued to look around, not bothering to be discreet about it. He inched his way toward my bedroom, but froze when Kutya stepped out of the room and growled low in his throat.

"What kind of beast is that?" my grandmother nearly screeched as Terry started yapping and growling from within her purse. She tightened her hold and maneuvered herself behind my mother, using her as a human shield.

"It's a dog."

"A real dog," Daniel added. "I can see how you might be confused since you've been trying to pass off that rabid hamster as one."

Her face flooded red. "How dare you!"

Daniel stepped forward, prepared to answer, but before he could, Terry the Tiny Terror jumped free of my grandmother's purse, scampered between Pacitti's legs, and jumped up to bite a curious and up-until-that-moment pretty well-behaved Kutya right on the nose.

Then all hell broke loose.

Kutya's yelp turned into a growl promising death as he lunged toward the pomchi who I imagined must have looked like a tasty little snack to him. Terry took off, losing all his bravado once Kutya bared teeth. Of course the rat-sized dog ran under my coffee table and, unable to do the same, Kutya ran through it, knocking it toward my mother and grandmother while they stood there screaming.

I scolded Kutya and chased after him, mentally calculating how long I had before the landlord was called about the ruckus and I lost my apartment. Daniel joined in, both of us trying to round up the out-of-control dogs without showing off our supernatural speed. Daniel might have been more helpful if he wasn't laughing. I had a high suspicion he was rooting for Kutya to gobble up the smaller dog.

"Stop all that screaming!" I yelled at my mother and grandmother as the dogs ran amuck, running under and into my dining table, the chairs, my bookcase, and clipped the table I kept my plants on before zooming into my bedroom.

I bit back curses as books, knick-knacks, and my Chinese evergreen fell to the floor during the chase. Terry ran under my bed, and Kutya dove underneath after him. The entire bed lifted off the floor and traveled a few inches over, knocking into my nightstand and sending the lamp there crashing to the floor before Kutya came out the other side.

"I got him!" Pacitti said from just inside the door as the small pomchi zoomed toward the living room. He stood in a half squat, arms reaching down to grab the dog, but Terry catapulted from the floor, mouth wide open, and clamped his tiny yet painfully sharp teeth right around Pacitti's unmentionables. The annoying detective screamed louder than my relatives in the other room as he turned in circles, swatting at the little dog dangling from his dangler by its teeth. "Get it off! Get it off!"

Terry stayed locked on tight, his little face contorted

into an almost demonic snarl. Behind the two, Daniel bent forward laughing his ass off, completely no help at all as Pacitti spun around and Kutya saw his opportunity.

I lunged for Kutya at the same time he lunged for Terry. The tiny terror saw the bigger dog coming in for the kill and let go, dropping to the floor. I reached for Kutya's collar and finally got hold of it … just as Kutya's teeth found purchase in whatever was left of Pacitti's genitals.

All I could think of was the impending lawsuit, the blame I would get, and the fact that Ginger could never know otherwise she'd be ordering merchandise to commemorate the moment Kutya became my sidekick in the war on all things penile.

"Kutya, let go!" I tugged at the dog's collar, realizing belatedly that was the wrong thing to do, since his teeth were firmly sunken into Pacitti's most sensitive area. "Sorry," I apologized as Pacitti released a screech guaranteed to be heard at least three blocks over. "Let go, Kutya, let go! Drop Pacitti's pecker! Drop it! Damn it, Daniel, quit laughing and help me!"

Daniel managed to get himself off the floor he'd fallen to in a fit of laughter as Kutya realized his new chew toy wasn't having a good time and opened his mouth. Pacitti fell to his knees, tears streaming down his face as he cupped his crotch and sucked in air between his teeth in an audible hiss.

Kutya darted for the door after his prey, but Daniel grabbed hold of his collar, halting him. "You've had enough fun," he told the dog, who looked up at him in complete confusion before attempting to move forward.

"I'm gonna sue," Pacitti croaked out. "I'm gonna sue the shit out of all of you."

"You might want to think about that for a moment," Daniel warned him. "You're still stuck in here with us and with one simple command, this dog will destroy whatever mush you have left in your pants."

Pacitti's eyes grew wide as he looked at the dog barely

being held back. "You wouldn't do that to a fellow man, would you?"

"I have to be honest with you, dude. I don't really think of you as much of a man."

Pacitti snarled. "I'm suing."

"Have it your way." Daniel turned Kutya toward the detective and the smaller man started to shake. "Danni, you should go now. This is going to get messy. Take Angel somewhere she can't hear the screams."

"All right, all right!" Pacitti threw his hands up in defeat, thought better of it, and clamped them back over his crotch. "No suing, but keep that damn thing away from me, and that evil rat-dog too."

"The dog goes where I go," I told him. "You want to avoid the dog? Quit harassing me."

"Hey, sweet cheeks, I'm just doing a job here."

"Fine, but don't cry when my dog decides to do a job on you."

Pacitti gulped and looked back over at the dog staring at him with its tongue lolling out its mouth. Now that all the excitement was over, Kutya looked like the overgrown, goofy pup he was, but the sheer size of him was enough to make the private dick think about his life choices. The pain-in-my-ass struggled, but eventually got up and didn't put up a fight as we ushered him back into the living room where my mother and grandmother stood together glaring daggers at us. Terry was held tight against my grandmother's ample bosom, shaking. Angel had moved to the dining table where she'd uprighted the chairs and sat munching on popcorn while watching the spectacle.

"You need to put a muzzle on that beastly mongrel," my grandmother snapped, holding her precious little rodent tighter against her chest. "It almost ate my baby."

"Your baby bit his nose!" I snapped back.

"My little angel was only defending himself!" She opened her mouth to start what I knew would be an epic defense of her precious angel who could do no wrong, but snapped it shut to watch Pacitti hobble past her to the door. "Where do you think you're going?"

Pacitti wrenched open the door and turned to face her. "I just got my junk bit into by two dogs, lady. I'm going to the emergency room to see if I still have a dick!"

"My word," my mother gasped as the door slammed behind her hired nuisance, and turned toward me. "Well, I never."

"What are you doing here?" I asked again, opting to ignore the mess of my apartment and get the answer to the question I'd asked before chaos had erupted.

"We're looking for Shana, of course," my mother answered. "You know, Shana, your sister, your flesh and blood you should be worrying about instead of hanging around with the likes of these people."

"And what the hell is that supposed to mean?" I asked, knowing perfectly well what it meant. "These people are my friends, and as far as I'm concerned, my family."

My mother's mouth hung open, her eyes glossy and wide as if struck. My grandmother, of course, only bristled in anger and indignation. "Your father ruined you with all his nonsense. You were blessed to be born into my family line, and to have women role models to teach and guide you, but you always resisted everything we taught you. Had you ever listened to us and did as told you could have landed a wealthy husband to take care of you instead of slumming around with that bar owner who had the nerve to pass himself off as a respectable business owner and this generic version of David Bowie. Had you not fought us we could have made something out of you, even if you lacked our family's beauty and—"

"Back the hell up, lady," Daniel said, still holding Kutya by the collar. He walked over to me and stood at my side, never taking his dark glare off my grandmother. "I've seen your family and I hate to break it to you, but Danni's the only true beauty in it. She's got natural beauty, a good heart, a brilliant mind, sharp wit, and despite whatever delusion you're under, she's got a great body to go with it. I'd take her over that blowup doll Shana any day, and if you can't see how gorgeous she is, that's a shame, but you can keep your opinions to yourself, you miserable old hag."

Everyone in the room gasped, including me. Unable to find my voice, I watched as a tide of red slowly climbed up my grandmother's neck, spreading until it reached the freshly touched-up roots at her hairline. My mother's mouth opened and closed, but she too had seemed to lose her ability to speak. My grandmother's arms tightened around her little dog until his little eyes bulged. Kutya whined and tugged against Daniel's hold on his collar, sensing the little mutt's discomfort. I snapped out of my speechlessness and opened my mouth to tell my grandmother to loosen her grip on the dog, but Terry took matters into his own hands, or rear, and saved himself by letting loose a boisterous fart that quickly overwhelmed us all.

"Gah!" Daniel released Kutya and sped over to the window, opening it before we all lost consciousness.

"See what you did," my grandmother snapped, holding the rather proud-looking pomchi in front of her at arm's length. "You've upset my baby's delicate constitution."

"As tight as you were squeezing him you're lucky gas was the only thing that popped out of him," I snapped back, sounding a little like a cartoon character since I'd pinched my nose closed with two fingers, "and he's just fine. The little fart-bag is always doing that."

She tucked him against her bosom again. "I don't know what we've done to deserve all this hostility."

"Seriously?" Sensing my sudden rise in anger, Kutya let out a low growl. I reached down and grabbed his collar just in case he decided to defend me. "Shana and I disappeared from her reception and you were all searching for her. Just her. She disappears again while I'm out of the state and did the thought ever cross your mind that I may have actually been missing as well? No, no it didn't. Her husband's body was found, we were both missing, and you never searched for me to make sure I was okay. You only wanted me found so you could ask about her, and once I returned, you ambushed me and practically accused me of being involved with her disappearance!" All right, so I was, but they had no reason to think that.

"I told you I wasn't and instead of believing me, you assigned some slimy private eye to follow me everywhere I go, and now look what you've done!" I released my hold on my nose, Terry's flatulence dissipated enough I no longer felt the need to gag, and swung my arm around, showing all the mess. "You barged into my home, insulted my friends, and allowed your dog to bite mine and then destroy my apartment."

"My precious little—"

"Everybody knows your precious little angel is a spoiled demonic fart-machine. That stinky gas-bag bit my dog and caused all of this mess. Period. You could at least have the decency to apologize."

My grandmother's lips flapped for a moment as words failed her. Finally, she shoved Terry back into her purse and turned toward my mother, who'd been standing in silence looking a little shell-shocked. "You see, Margaret? You see? Didn't I warn you about this one? Plain girls are always jealous and hateful, even when you try to help them. It was to be expected that she'd be jealous of Shana, but to turn on her elders who took pity and tried to help her… Well, I guess that was to be expected too." She ran her hands over her figure in a show of accentuating her well-endowed bosom as she smoothed her blouse. "It's not our fault she came out wron—"

"Oh, fuck off, Grandma!" My fists clenched at my side. I relaxed them after Kutya whined, cluing me in that my grip on his collar was too tight, but my chest still heaved with anger. My meager chest that would never be as large as the breasts belonging to every other woman in my family and I didn't give a single shit. My mother's eyes appeared glossy and something in my chest hitched, a little pang of guilt for possibly hurting her, but my grandmother's dark glare and complete lack of remorse for anything that had happened during this visit or at any point in my life kept my anger alive. "I'm not built like any of you, and if that is just too unacceptable for you, that's fine. I'm not changing myself to be loved. I've found a family who loves me just as I am, and more importantly, I've quit caring about pleasing people who never gave a damn about me. I don't need you in my life, and I have nothing to say or give to you. You won't find Shana by harassing me, so I suggest you leave. You love her so much, you should be out looking for her instead of wasting time and energy with the child you never wanted. Get the hell out of my apartment."

My mother covered her mouth with her hand and blinked. I saw wetness on her lashes. My grandmother, however, screwed her face up into an ugly mask of fury. "What did you just say to—"

"She said get the hell out," Daniel cut her off. He walked over to the door and jerked it open. "And don't forget to drag your big sagging titties out with you. Newsflash, they're not as enticing as you think they are."

My grandmother's mouth dropped open and so much red flooded her face I feared she'd have a heart attack right there in my living room. With a growl, she grabbed my mother's arm and pulled her to the door. "You'd be lucky to have a woman half as desirable as me, but I'd never sink so low," she snapped at Daniel as she walked past him and exited the apartment.

Daniel slammed the door closed behind them. "If she didn't repulse me so much, I'd lay a big wet one right on her crinkled old lips just to watch her freak the hell out. Then again, I wouldn't want to risk catching the mad cow disease I'm sure she carries."

I knew he was trying to amuse me, but I couldn't get

the sight of my mother's wet eyelashes out of my mind, or the way she'd covered her mouth as if I'd struck her. As preposterous as the thought was to me, she actually appeared hurt.

"Hey." Daniel walked over to me, stepping over the stuff that had fallen to the floor during the dog chase, and lifted my chin, forcing me to look him in the eye. "You did good. They deserved every word of that."

I backed away a step, freeing my chin, and nodded. "Hopefully Pacitti will be deterred now."

"At least until he gets his dick sewn back on." Daniel chuckled and returned my toppled coffee table to where it belonged. He picked up the remote that had fallen from it and clicked on the television, which fortunately hadn't been knocked over or damaged.

"I'm sorry you missed the first part of *John Wick*," I told Angel as she stood from the dining table and wiped her hands together.

"It's all right," she said. "You still gave me drama, action, violence, and dogs." She took the remote from Daniel, found the station playing the marathon, and set the remote on the table before she joined in to help Daniel clean up.

"You guys don't have to clean. Watch the movies. I'll get all this."

"You're getting help," Daniel said. "Deal with it."

"Yeah, what Parrot-Boy said." Angel winked at Daniel, who gave a fake glare in return.

Kutya barked, and call me crazy, but it sounded like he was saying he agreed with them. My suspicion was confirmed when he grabbed a book in his mouth and set it back on my bookshelf before turning toward me and offering a proud, goofy smile. He looked so cute I couldn't even get mad that he'd just slobbered over the tenth book in the Stephanie Plum series. Besides, that one had a lot of Ranger-time in it and it wasn't as if I'd never slobbered over Ranger myself. The man might be fictional, but he was one helluva stud.

I walked over to the big pup and dropped a gentle kiss on his big wet nose, relieved to see it didn't appear to have taken much damage from Terry's little teeth. "Thank you, big guy. How about you help me clean the bedroom?"

Kutya barked and merrily trotted his furry butt into the bedroom.

After cleaning up the apartment and getting my female live blood requirement, I'd left Angel and Daniel to finish the marathon in the living room, and secluded myself in the quiet of the bedroom. Well, quiet other than the constant sound of grunts and gunshots coming from the television in the other room as John Wick dispatched his enemies.

With Kutya snoring softly atop the bed behind me, I sat at the small desk and used the laptop I'd bought for Angel to dig around the internet. I trusted Rider to do all he could to find Eliza, and knew Grissom and Amelia were professionals who knew what they were doing, but it wasn't in my nature to just sit back and let others do all the work when someone I cared about was in possible danger, even if the others were far more capable than me. Even if I'd been specifically told to leave it alone. I'm stubborn like that.

Unfortunately, the internet wasn't the most reliable source of information on magic, demons, and other monsters. Silly humans thought my kind were all make-believe and filled the web with their musings, so what I might think was a lead could very well be someone's opening chapter of *Buffy* fanfiction. Lovefest was real though. I pulled up the website for it again, my gut saying there was something there. I just had to find it.

The bedroom door creaked open. I looked up to see Daniel step into the room, Angel dozing in his arms. "She didn't make it through the marathon?"

"She came close," he said softly. He settled Angel on

the bed and tucked her in. Kutya watched with mild interest, then shifted his weight and rested his head over Angel's legs.

"I thought you were supposed to let Rider and Grissom handle Eliza's disappearance," Daniel said as he closed in behind me and rested his hands on the back of my chair. His spicy scent enveloped me, causing a weird flutter in the pit of my stomach. I told myself I was just hungry.

"Hey, I'm just checking out Lovefest," I replied. "There's no harm in that."

His reply was a small grunt that suggested otherwise. A moment later, he reached past me and closed the laptop. "You got your blood, Angel's all right, and it appears no one in the building complained about the noise or barking. I think it's time to take the mutt for a walk and get back to The Midnight Rider."

"All right." I attached the leash to Kutya's collar and walked the big guy out of the apartment. Aware he was going out, he'd found his energy and spun in circles while we waited for Daniel to close the door behind us.

Carlos had been replaced by another vampire, one I wasn't as familiar with. All I knew about him was his name was Angelo, and he looked like the type of guy you'd expect to see selling stolen merchandise out the back of his car. "I heard you were rejected by an old lady," he said with a wide grin.

Daniel flipped him off, and the two laughed. Clearly, Daniel was more familiar with him than I was.

"So I guess Carlos heard everything and the whole nest is fully aware of tonight's events," I muttered as we walked down the stairs.

"Of course. Carlos is a huge gossip."

"Great. Ginger's going to make T-shirts to celebrate Kutya taking a bite out of Pacitti's crotch."

"Well, Danni the Teste Slayer needed a sidekick."

"Funny, I thought that was you."

He glowered at me as he held the front door to the building open. "That remark is going to require payback."

I stuck my tongue out at him and led Kutya out into the cool twilight air, and laughed, enjoying the banter. For the first time since returning from Moonlight, we'd spent time together without any awkwardness, and it felt good having that back. "Don't get your scales in a knot now, we wouldn't want you to —"

"What is it?" Daniel stepped so that he was slightly in front of me, noticing the way my retort had died on my lips, stolen with my breath as I took in the sight of the dark-haired woman standing across the street, her gaze scanning the windows running the length of the building's façade. She looked down at the cell phone in her hand, then up again. I saw the recognition in her eyes as her gaze met mine, and my stomach lurched.

"That's Nina Valdez," I told Daniel. "Angel's mother."

CHAPTER NINE

"Are you sure?" Daniel asked. "I was under the impression Angel's mother was a lot younger."

"She's thirty-three," I said, still holding the woman's gaze. "Drugs and a hard life have a way of sucking out one's youth."

"Shit," Daniel said. "That's a damn shame. She looks like she could have been a really beautiful woman."

I nodded my head in agreement. "How the hell did she find Angel this fast?"

"I'll give you a hint," Daniel said. "He's conniving, dirty, smells of eau de pork rinds and underarms, and is most likely sitting somewhere pissed off with stitches in his britches."

That sonofabitch. "You think Pacitti knows Angel's mother?"

"I think he's a lowlife who probably moves in similar circles to a lot of addicts and criminals, and he was in your apartment earlier. He saw Angel. Not much of a coincidence her mother is here now."

Nina Valdez stepped into the street, the pair of us firmly in her sights. She shoved her phone into the back pocket of jeans that appeared frayed more from age than design and squared her shoulders. The hard glint in her dark eyes told me without words she wanted her daughter and she meant business.

I turned and pushed Daniel toward the building. "Angel's come too far to have her mother screw her up now. Go get her and sneak her out the back while I deal with her mother."

"I'm your bodyguard, remember? I'm required to be with you. We'll talk to her together."

"Do you really think this woman's going to just listen to us, leave, and not come back after we're gone? Sneak Angel out. We're taking her with us."

Daniel folded his arms. "I'm not leaving you alone."

"I have Kutya, and hello, I'm half vampire, half succubus, half badass."

"That's too many halves."

"Whatever." I turned to check Nina's progress and saw she'd fully crossed the street and we didn't have much time. I turned toward Daniel again and hit him with my best pleading look. "Please, Daniel."

He released a frustrated sigh and fixed his gaze to the left of me. I turned my head that way to see a lanky shifter I'd seen around Rider's bar leaning against a building across the street. He stepped out of the shadows and nodded before looking down the street. Another shifter stepped out of an alleyway there and leaned against a light pole, his watchful eyes locked onto the woman fast approaching.

"Now that the sitters are in place," I muttered, realizing he'd conferred telepathically with the two guards Rider kept stationed outside my apartment building, "tell her to pack for a stay and make it quick. Once I get rid of Nina, I'll meet you in the alley behind the building. Give me your keys."

Daniel looked down at my open hand and laughed. "You're adorable when you're out of your mind," he said, backing up. "We'll be in the truck when you're ready. Be careful."

"I can drive very well, you know!" I called behind him.

"I'm sure you can," he called back. "Just not my truck."

How the hell are you supposed to get Angel out here to the truck and sneak past her mother if she's standing in the parking lot? I asked telepathically.

Daniel grumbled some not so sweet words back telepathically and tossed me his keys. He disappeared into the building and I turned just in time to face off with Nina. At my side, Kutya stood at full attention. Nina glanced down at the dog, swallowed, and raised her chin. "You're Danni Keller?"

"Possibly," I replied, not seeing much reason in full-out pretending I wasn't. Nina Valdez clearly knew who I was, and I was pretty sure she'd been looking at her phone earlier because a certain pork rind-eating boil on the behind of humanity had sent her my picture along with my address. "How can I help you?"

"I want to see my daughter. I was told you're harboring her."

I gave her my best confused face, complete with blinking, then raised my hand to show the leash attached to the large dog. "I only have this dog, lady, and he's a boy."

I made to move past her and she stepped in my way. "Do I have to call the police?"

I looked down at her hands peeking out from the long sleeves of the dark hoodie that hung off her thin frame and saw they trembled. Her dark eyes darted around, seeming to look for ghosts in the shadows. "Do you really want to interact with the police right now?"

"I want my daughter!" she snapped, more in desperation than anger. Kutya growled, and I grabbed his collar. Nina took a step back, eyes glued to the dog, but she wasn't done. She pulled the phone free of her back pocket, touched the screen, and held the phone out toward me to reveal a picture of Angel in my kitchen. Pacitti must have quickly snapped off a picture right after entering my apartment, his hand blocked by my grandmother's body. That slimy slug. "I know you have her. I know which apartment is yours and I'm not leaving here without her."

I blew out a breath and nudged past Nina, figuring I might as well walk Kutya while keeping the woman busy, buying Daniel time to get Angel packed and out of the apartment. "I hope Pacitti didn't charge you too much," I said, as I guided Kutya past the edge of the parking lot onto the sidewalk. He immediately moved over into a grassy area and started to sniff. "How did you come by that rodent anyway?"

"He was recommended," Nina answered, having followed me. "And he gave me a good deal."

I noticed Nina's cheeks redden, and she averted her gaze. I released a plethora of curse words in my mind, imagining what kind of deal a maggot like Pacitti would strike up with a desperate woman like Nina Valdez. I actually felt sorry for her. It was hard not to, seeing how her poor choices had taken their toll on what should have been a young, healthy body. I didn't know why she'd made the choices she'd made, or how she'd been introduced to drugs, so I wouldn't condemn her for that part of her past. However, she was the mother of a young woman I cared about, a young woman who'd made the right decisions to change her life, and I was not about to let anyone sabotage her.

"I'm going to be honest with you, Nina." I tugged on Kutya's leash and guided him down the street, walking slow while he sniffed around. I noticed the two shifters watching me moved along as well, but at a distance and mostly in shadow, never drawing Nina's attention. "I do know Angel, and I care a lot about her, which is why I'm going to tell you to go home or wherever it is you're sleeping these days. Angel is clean and sober, and she does not need a struggling addict in her life right now."

"I'm clean," Nina said.

I stopped while Kutya took interest in a patch of grass next to a large SUV, and stared at one of Nina's trembling hands. She noticed me staring and quickly hid her hands in her hoodie sleeves before shoving them in her jeans pockets.

"Angel's my daughter. She needs her mother."

"She needed her mother," I corrected her. "She needed her mother to be there to feed and clothe her, to help her with her homework, to teach her right from wrong. She needed her mother to protect her. Instead, she had a mother who left her to fend for herself."

"I left her with family."

"Oh, was that the dad who went to prison or the brother who got himself killed running the streets after turning Angel on to drugs? Or maybe one of the many cousins she was left with, all of whom were addicts or abusive?"

I saw her pockets bulge and knew she'd just tightened her hands into fists. "I came back for her. I always came back for her."

"Yes, to do drugs with her, completely destroy her life and leave her again when a new guy came along. I'm not allowing you to repeat the cycle this time."

"I don't need your permission," Nina told me. "You're handing over my daughter or I'm calling the police to report you've abducted a minor."

"Minors are children under eighteen years old."

"I know!" she snapped and took out her phone. "Think what you want of me, but the law says she's my daughter."

"The police aren't going to help you, Nina. Angel was in foster care, meaning you lost your rights." A putrid stench reached my nose, and I looked down to see Kutya sitting next to a mountain of crap, his tongue lolling out the side of his mouth as he panted and watched me with bright eyes. I stepped away from the pile before it made my eyes water. "Furthermore, I met your daughter on her eighteenth birthday. Go home, Nina, and give Angel the benefit of a life without such a negative influence. The mother card doesn't sway me. It takes more than birthing a child to be a mother. For fuck's sake, you don't even know how old she is."

Nina's mouth dropped open. She stood still for a moment, clearly stunned to realize her daughter was now an adult and she'd missed it, but instead of doing the best thing for Angel and staying out of her life, she turned and ran, running back down the street, past the parking lot and through the front of my apartment building.

"Shit!" I tugged Kutya's leash and remembered the pile of hot doo-doo still steaming down below. I quickly pulled out a baggie from the little baggie holder attached to the leash. I looked at the bag, then at the pile, then the bag again, knowing there was no way all that poop was going to fit inside. "Ah, well, it's not like it's on the sidewalk." I tossed the baggie over the pile, figuring that would have to suffice, and ran to the parking lot, fast but not so quick I'd drag Kutya. All the while, I prayed Daniel had gotten Angel packed and out the back of the building before her mother reached the door. She'd sounded strong when she'd told me she was staying clean earlier, but I cared too much about her well-being to risk her mother's influence.

Kutya and I reached the parking lot, and turned… to see Angel and Daniel sitting in the truck. I fixed the dragon shifter with the evil eye while I walked Kutya to the truck and got him loaded into the back. Daniel was still grinning when I slid into the passenger seat and dropped the keys into his outstretched hand. "It would just kill you to let me drive your truck, wouldn't it?"

"It's a possibility," he said on a laugh before inserting the keys into the ignition and starting the vehicle. "I didn't see much point waiting in the back alley when it was all clear out here."

I looked across the street at the shifter who'd been watching closest to the parking lot as I'd walked Kutya down the block. "You were coordinating with the guards the whole time."

"Of course," Daniel replied. He drove to the parking lot exit, looked both ways, and pulled out onto the street. "It's my job."

I huffed out a breath and looked over at Angel. Her eyes were droopy, and she appeared very small between us. Small and fragile. "How are you doing, kid?"

"Tired." She clutched her bag to her chest and yawned. "She didn't look good."

"No, she didn't," I agreed before shooting a dark look Daniel's way. "Fortunately, she didn't see you."

"If she had, I would have peeled out of the parking lot before she ever reached Angel," Daniel assured me.

"I'm staying clean," Angel said. "I can do it."

I reached over and took her hand in mine. "I know you can. I have faith in you, but I see no reason to make things harder for you. I'm protecting you, and I know how annoying it can be when it feels like others are overstepping in their desire to protect you…" I looked at Daniel to see a grin playing about his lips. "But I know it's sometimes necessary for those who love you to do so. I'm sorry, but I just don't think it's a good idea to interact with your mother right now. There's so many ways someone with her energy could sabotage all the progress you've made and I just don't think it's worth the risk."

"I know." Angel rested her head on my shoulder and closed her eyes. "I don't want to see her. She makes me sad."

I looked past Angel and spoke directly into Daniel's mind. *She threatened to call the police and report that I'd abducted a minor. She didn't even know Angel had turned eighteen.*

Daniel glanced my way, sharing a dark look with me before he shook his head and returned his focus to the road.

Yep, I thought. Exactly how I felt about it too.

The parking lot was mostly empty by the time we reached The Midnight Rider. I hadn't lotioned up and the sun was on the rise, so I knew I didn't have much time to give the squat man sitting in the old beater across the street a piece of my mind.

"Danni…" Daniel didn't need to say anything else, his tone warning enough, but when had I ever listened to anyone?

"Stay here. This won't take long and I highly doubt he'll attempt anything while I have Kutya with me." I gave a gentle tug on Kutya's leash and walked him across the street, Pacitti's hateful eyes on him the whole time.

He rolled his window down as I approached. "I'm reporting that beast to the authorities. You know what they do to dogs that bite, don't you?"

"Yes, but do you know what I do to assholes who report dogs for biting?" I glared at him until a strange look entered his eyes and he gulped. Feeling the hot anger in my veins, I focused on breathing, aware my eyes tended to turn red when I got really pissed and my succubus side, violent bitch that she was, decided to come out and play. "If you report my dog for that bite, I'll be forced to report my grandmother's dog. Good luck getting paid for your services then."

Pacitti glared at Kutya before shifting in his seat. He adjusted the ice pack on his groin and muttered a string of curses. "You're lucky I happen to need that money."

"You're lucky I'm choosing to play nice. I know you told Nina Valdez about Angel."

Pacitti swiveled his head to where Angel stood in the parking lot with Daniel, the dragon shifter's eyes locked on us. "Hey, I saw a kid I'd been approached about finding and did what I'd been paid to do."

"You mean what you bartered for."

Pacitti smirked, the curve of his mouth so lascivious I felt the blood I'd drank earlier threatening to spew back up. "I'm a generous man. I couldn't turn away a mother looking for her child."

"That child is eighteen, an adult, and the mother is an addict." I felt my skin warm uncomfortably, the first warning I needed to get inside soon, and reached into the car. I grabbed Pacitti by whatever Kutya and Terry had left in his drawers and ignored his ear-piercing scream. "Stay the fuck away from me, Pacitti. If you ever threaten me, my dog, or Angel again, I guarantee you a trip to the emergency room won't fix what I'll take from you."

I released his junk and left him crying in his car. Daniel's skin had grown pale, his mouth set in a grim line as I reached him. "You squeezed that man's genital mush, didn't you?"

"Yup."

Daniel shook his head and blew out a breath as we quickly moved to the front of the building toward the safety of shelter. "Wouldn't it be more humane to just kill the bastard?"

"Maybe," I replied, "but my way's more satisfying." I grinned as Daniel winced and opened the door for us.

The bar was empty except for one tall, dark, sexy, and brooding vampire standing in the center of the room, arms crossed over his chest, gaze locked onto mine. The front door clicked behind us before he spoke. "No."

"No, what?"

Rider pointed to Angel, ignoring the overexcited dog that ran to him and pawed at his leg for pets and scratches. "No."

I looked over at the young woman who'd stiffened, her brown eyes flooded with moisture. My temper rose as she bit her bottom lip to stop its trembling.

"I'll be right back." I gave Angel's slender shoulder a squeeze and marched toward Rider. "May I have a word with you, please?" I shooed Kutya away from his legs, wanting his full attention. "Daniel, can you and Angel please take Kutya to the back and feed him?"

"Sure. Is he eating Purina or Kibbles 'N Dicks?"

I gave Daniel a look that told him just how unamused I was, but he still chuckled to himself as he guided Angel through the door leading to the back and motioned for Kutya to follow. The big dog looked up at his master. Rider told him to go with Daniel, and he trotted away.

"Kibbles 'N Dicks? Tell me you didn't train my dog to eat dicks."

"I swear, everyone acts as if I'm obsessed with stabbing or maiming genitals, but you're the ones who can't seem to stop bringing it up all the time." I rolled my eyes. "Angel needs to stay here."

"Your donor has full use of your apartment and it is equipped with everything she needs, including around-the-clock security."

"Angel's mother found her. Or more accurately, Pacitti discovered her and sent her picture and my address to her mother, who now knows she lives in my apartment." I ran my fingers through my hair and fought to keep my eyes open. "Every time Angel gets clean, her mother pops back up and drags her back into the gutter. Unless your guards are going to kill a human woman whose only crime is being a shitty mother, how can I keep Angel safe in my apartment now? Her mother isn't going to give up and Angel doesn't need to deal with her right now."

"How did Pacitti discover Angel? How would he even know to contact her mother?"

I sighed and gave Rider the whole story, including everything Grissom had told me about Angel's family, the near dog fight that had turned into a crotch buffet for two, and my interaction with Pacitti outside the bar, which I knew he'd already seen thanks to the cameras he had covering the block around his building.

"Unbelievable." He pinched the bridge of his nose. "I have you watch Kutya for one night and you train him to eat dicks."

"He didn't eat Pacitti's dick. He just bit it. Sadly, I'm sure the man still has it attached and is capable of reproduction."

"Maybe not after what you just did to him." Rider shook his head. "This is a damn mess. I should just walk across the street and snap the man's neck, but as adamant as your mother is that you know where Shana is and have something to do with her disappearance, his sudden death will only fuel her theory. We're dealing with a lot of shit now, Danni. Your donor—"

"My donor is a young woman in trouble who happens to have a name. It's Angel."

"I warned you about getting attached."

"Yeah, you did." I stepped closer to him until there was no room between us. "You also once told me that you needed me with you to remind you of your humanity, to keep you from going too dark. This is your reminder. You need to help me help Angel, because when you start treating young women like nothing more than a vein you can suck juice out of, you can't have a lot of humanity left in you."

Rider stepped back, sucking in air as if he'd been punched in the gut. Metaphorically, I supposed he had, and I felt like crap for it, but I also knew I was right the moment the words left my mouth. It was a damn scary thought.

Rider ran a hand down his face, thinking. I noticed the tiredness in his eyes as the wheels turned in his head and hoped that tiredness played into his stubbornness about helping Angel. I hoped the man I loved with every breath in my body wasn't really so cold toward the innocent human.

"I wanted you out of here tonight to keep you safe from Trixell in case the witch's net couldn't hold her. There haven't been any incidents with her since we started the IV drip, but she's sneaky. I understand your concern about your don… about *Angel's* mother, but she's just a human, a human you've been drinking from, so there's a bond there. I don't want to risk Trixell discovering that and turning the girl into a weapon against you."

I felt my eyes go wide. "She could do that?"

Rider stared at me, frustration burning in his tired eyes as his jaw ticked. He closed his eyes, and I sensed his power flood the building. A moment later, the power drew back into him and he wrapped his hand around my arm. "Come on."

He led me to the back where Daniel and Angel stood watching Kutya scarf down the last of the kibble in his bowl by the door leading to the garage.

"Daniel, you'll stay here again today," Rider told him. "Angel will stay with you and Lana in the guestroom. You'll have to make do with the small space. The sofa pulls out. Watch Angel closely for any signs Trixell is screwing with her and notify me immediately if you sense anything off."

Daniel glanced at Angel, who looked between the three of us with a healthy amount if trepidation in her eyes, and nodded. "Sure."

The door to the stairwell opened and Juan entered, a glass with about four ounces of silver liquid in his hand. He handed it to Angel.

"Drink that," Rider ordered.

Angel stared at him and gulped, then looked at me. "What is it?"

"It's something that will keep the witch we have locked up here from entering your mind and possessing your body," Rider answered. "Drink it."

Angel gave me another unsure look, and I gave her an encouraging nod. "It won't hurt you," I told her, confidant in my statement. Even if Rider only saw the girl as a blood donor, he'd never give her anything that would make her blood unusable to me.

With a shaking hand, Angel raised the glass to her mouth and drank it down. "It tastes like water."

"That should keep Trixell out of her mind if she finds a way through her restraints," Rider told Daniel, "but keep an eye on her." To Juan he said, "Kutya just ate. He'll need a walk. Shovel's in the garage."

"Get some sleep," I called back to Angel as Rider laced his fingers through mine and pulled me to the staircase leading to his room. "You'll be safe here."

Once in the room, Rider kicked off his shoes and began removing his clothes. "It's time for bed."

I sensed his anger as I sat at the foot of the bed and removed my shoes and socks. A question burned in me, and I didn't want to anger him more, but curiosity got the better of me as I stood and removed my jeans. "Daniel and Lana are sharing a room?"

His naked body thrummed with energy as he turned toward me, his eyes cold and dark. "Does that bother you?"

I tried to swallow but didn't seem to have the required amount of moisture in my mouth, so I shook my head instead. "No. I just sensed some tension in their relationship. I want to make sure Angel is comfortable here."

Rider's eyes narrowed, and I got the sense he was searching me for a lie. "Don't worry about Angel," he finally said. He pulled me toward him and quickly freed me of my remaining clothes before picking me up and settling me on the bed. He loomed over me, a creature of the night looming over its prey. "I require your full attention on me, and no one else."

CHAPTER TEN

I woke slowly, dragged out of restful sleep by a powerful force, a powerful force currently parting my legs with one of his own while his tongue twirled around a nipple that quickly tightened under his sweet torture. "Mmm… what time is…"

Rider covered my mouth, sliding his devilish tongue inside to explore and cease my questioning. He entered me and started to move as the foggy clouds of drowsiness quickly parted. I sensed night had not completely fallen yet, and it occurred to me Rider had never awakened me before nightfall for sex, but as he continued to glide in and out of me while using his mouth and hands to tease and tantalize my heated flesh, I found I didn't mind at all, nor did I mind after we both climaxed together and he continued on to round two and three.

"Once more," he whispered against my lips before planting a kiss there and sitting up, taking me with him. He tilted his head, showing off the delectable column of his throat. "Drink."

My fangs automatically dropped down as he gently pressed my head until my mouth met his flesh. Warm, powerful blood poured over my tongue as he pumped inside me, his fingers firmly planted against my hips. I drank my fill and licked his wounds closed before pushing him so his back hit the mattress, filled with the need to move faster. I took over, thrusting my hips as hard and fast as I could while Rider held on, panting under me.

"Fuck, Danni," he gasped out, and raised his pelvis off the bed, filling me deeper. Lost in the sensation starting where our bodies met, spreading to overwhelm every nerve ending in my body, I rode him with all the vampiric speed I had in me and when we came I wasn't sure which was louder or more powerful, my scream or his growl.

I fell against him and rested there with my cheek against his chest, listening to his heartbeat until the sweat on our bodies cooled. "I'll never be able to walk again," I said once I regained the ability to breathe in a way that didn't resemble hyperventilation.

He chuckled under me and rose into a sitting position, bringing me with him so I straddled his lap. "That should hold us over," he murmured before kissing me. "I gotta go, babe."

"Go?" I remembered the time. "You never wake me before nightfall unless it's absolutely necessary. What's going on?"

He sighed and took my mouth in a slow, languid kiss, lifting me in the process. When our lips parted, I was settled on the bed and he stood over me. "I have to go help a friend. It's a matter of life or death, and unfortunately, I'm not able to take you with me."

"Seta," I said, instantly knowing in my gut just who the friend was. "The last time you did a favor for her, you ended up in a battle. A freaking battle, Rider. You fought an army of vampires and lycanthropes."

"I survived, as I've survived many battles, and I'm not expecting a battle this time. I can't tell you exactly where I'm going or what I'm doing, not because I don't trust you, but because it's not my secret to share, and the less you know, the safer all involved are."

"Seta's fighting something really bad, isn't she?"

Rider nodded. "I can't refuse to help. Too much is at stake."

"Yeah, like your life."

"All of our lives." He dropped a tender kiss on the top of my head. "I'm not doing anything that dangerous. It just might take a few nights. I'll be back."

"Promise."

"I swear." He cupped my chin and smiled. "After the way you just rode the breath out of me, I'll be counting down the seconds until I return."

"I should refuse to ever do that or anything with you again." I grabbed the shirt that had been discarded on the floor that morning and pulled it on before standing and folding my arms over my chest. I felt the threat of tears sting my eyes. "I don't like it. Why can't Seta find somebody else to help her get out of whatever mess she's in?"

"I'm the only one old enough and powerful enough for what's needed, and this isn't a mess she made or asked for." He pulled on black pants and grabbed a black button-down shirt that had been neatly folded and placed on the chaise. I realized then that Rider had smelled fresh from the shower when I'd been pulled out of sleep, and Kutya was nowhere around, clearly having been taken care of.

"You've been up a while, haven't you?"

He nodded as he pulled on his shirt and threaded the buttons through their respective holes. "I had plans to make, including what you'll be doing while I'm away. I don't trust Trixell, and your donor staying here is more potential trouble I don't need right now. You're going to Pigeon Forge to stay with Grey's pack." He closed his eyes and power flooded the room. "Daniel's on his way up now," he said, reopening them. "I'll fill you in together."

"On his way up?" I looked down at myself, then over at the bed that looked as if a wrestling match had taken place in it and the discarded clothes all over the floor. I cursed under my breath and grabbed a set of clean clothes from the dresser.

"Is there a problem?"

"Yes," I snapped as I carried my belongings into the bathroom. "My boyfriend's a jealous jackass who doesn't trust me and what I thought was lovemaking was really just him marking his territory."

I slammed the door behind me before he could respond and started the shower.

By the time I emerged from the bathroom, freshly showered and dressed in jeans and a dark brown sweater, Rider had made the bed and placed two duffle bags on top of it. The discarded clothes had been tossed over by the bathroom door, but I knew the scent of what we'd done still filled the small space, and the dragon shifter standing just inside the door would have no way to avoid knowing what had happened and just how recently, not with his dragon sense of smell. Kutya rested on the chaise. He looked between Rider and me and whined, apparently sensing Mommy and Daddy were in a tiff and not liking it.

I glanced at Daniel and noted he wouldn't look at me. He kept his eyes on Rider, his thumbs hooked into his pockets, and jaw firmly set. I followed suit and redirected my gaze to Rider, and found his eyes burning into mine.

"I packed for you," he told me before placing one of his folded shirts in one of the duffels. He zipped it up and turned toward Daniel. "I called you up here because I'm headed out of town on an urgent matter. You're aware of the situation here with Trixell."

Daniel folded his arms over his L.A. Guns T-shirt and nodded.

"I don't want to risk her trying something with Danni while I'm not here, so I've reached out to Grey. You're taking Danni there and keeping her out of trouble until I get back. Ginger and Rome are going with you, as well as

Danni's donor and Kutya, of course."

Daniel's eyebrow raised at this. "Are we working a job in Pigeon Forge?"

"No."

"Three guards for Danni seems excessive if we're not there to work and will be given protection by Grey's pack. You want us to take additional people when there's so much going on here?"

"Everyone has their purpose," Rider told him, with a hint of warning to his tone. "Tony can manage with the staff I'm leaving here."

I watched, my stomach in a knot as the two men stared each other down, the air between them thick with tension. Fortunately, Daniel minded his temper and didn't question Rider further.

"I've worked out the bagged blood issue with Grey. Danni has her donor for her live female blood requirement, and I'll be back soon enough. She shouldn't have to go too long without another hit of sire blood. Rome can also provide blood if necessary. Grey is being very gracious in accommodating you. Try to keep Danni from knocking down any more trees with any of his wolves."

"I'll do my best," Daniel replied, "but, honestly, I think she amused Grey the last time she did that."

"You're his guests. Behave." He looked directly at me for that last word, then picked up the duffel he'd packed for me and handed it over to Daniel. "I have to leave soon, and I want Danni out of here soon after. I had Rome grab some things for you from your apartment. He and Ginger just arrived. Go get the donor together and they'll fill you in on the plan for shaking that detective off your tail so he doesn't follow you into Grey's territory."

Daniel nodded and stepped back. "See you downstairs," he said, finally acknowledging me, and left us alone in the room.

"I made the bed up before he entered," Rider said,

turning toward me.

I didn't bother hiding my lack of appreciation for such a small breadcrumb. "He's a dragon shifter. He can smell the sex on the sheets, not to mention your body you purposely didn't shower off before meeting with him."

"Sit down, Danni."

"I don't want—"

"Sit down," he repeated, not quite a yell, but his tone sharp.

I huffed out a breath and settled next to Kutya on the chaise. The big dog whined and hunkered down, his paws over his ears, as Rider sat on the edge of the bed, facing me.

"What happened here has nothing to do with a lack of trust in you and everything to do with that dragon. You were very wrong about what you said before slamming that door. Any time we are joined together, it is lovemaking. No matter what happens between us, no matter what mood I am in, or how you feel toward me, I will only ever enter your body with love. I hope you realize that."

I nodded. "I know you love me, Rider, but you flaunted what we'd just done in Daniel's face. You did it deliberately, and you had no reason to."

"I had a reason. You were right about one thing, Danni. I am jealous." Rider bent forward and rested his elbows on his knees. "Daniel is in love with you."

"Daniel is my friend."

"He is in love with you," Rider said again. "He is in love with you and I want to kill him for that, but I can't because not only would you most likely hate me forever for killing your friend, but I need him for the very reason I want him dead."

I stared at Rider, unsure how to respond to such a statement. "I don't understand."

"A man will do anything to protect the woman he loves. If anything should happen to me, or if something should prevent me from reaching you when you are in danger, I know Daniel will give his life to save yours, and I know he will protect you from yourself if your succubus side threatens to force you into doing anything you wouldn't do while in control of your mind and body. For those reasons, and the fact I know he is your best friend, I keep him alive."

I sat stunned for a moment until Kutya's whine shook me out of it. I petted the dog, calming him. "I know I've sensed some issues between the two of you, some competitiveness, but I thought you liked Daniel. Now you're talking about killing him as if it's nothing, like he's one of your enemies."

"He is not my enemy, and I do like him in a way." Rider frowned. "I don't hate him. He's one hell of a fighter to have at my disposal, and he's honorable. I'll give him that. You can't choose who you fall for, but you can choose how you handle it. I called him here for a reason. He needed the reminder that there's a line he can never cross. You might not like the way I reminded him of the line, but the other ways of showing him would get very bloody."

"Why? Why do you feel this need to kill him if he steps over some line, and why are you even telling me this?" I asked, realizing Rider didn't have to tell me any of this.

"Because," he said, reaching out for my hand. "You were wrong about something else. I'm not your *boyfriend*, Danni. Boyfriends are fools sampling options, tasting different flavors. You are not an option to me."

I looked down at our joined hands. "If you're not my boyfriend, what are you?"

"Yours," he said, and the word came out rough. "I am yours in every possible way, Danni. Every cell, every thought, emotion, breath… every single part of me belongs to you, including the darkness inside me I've fought to keep under control. I am entirely yours, as I pray you are mine."

My eyes teared up. Damn, he made it hard to stay mad. "I'm yours," I whispered.

He held my gaze for a long stretch before speaking again. "Your presence helps me to control my darkness, but if any man tried to take you from me, there'd be no stopping the beast inside me from destroying him. That's why I've told you this, and why I did what I did. It's important you don't encourage Daniel."

I sat back on a gasp, letting go of his hand.

"I'm not accusing you of anything, Danni. It takes very little to encourage a man in love, so you need to be aware and be careful. I truly don't want to kill Daniel, but I don't think I can hold back the darkness inside me if he crosses the line with you." He rubbed the back of his neck. "The two of you are too close."

My spine instantly stiffened. "What is that supposed to mean? He's my bodyguard. He's supposed to stay close to me, or did you forget the job description you gave him?"

"There's different kinds of closeness." Rider took a deep breath, holding my gaze the entire time. "Why were you bothered about his sleeping arrangements this morning?"

"I told you I wasn't bothered."

"I know you, Danni. I know when you're bothered by something. You had an issue with Daniel and Lana sharing space. One would think *you* were jealous."

"One would think wrong," I said, careful to keep any fear out of my voice despite it flooding my veins. I had felt a twinge of something when I'd discovered the two had shared a room, and I got that same twinge whenever I saw the pair close together, but I wasn't about to label it as jealousy when I knew I was in love with Rider. It didn't matter if I had irrational reactions to the thought of Daniel and Lana together when I had no designs on the man myself.

"You were clearly bothered. What other explanation have you?"

Now it was my turn to take a deep breath and borrow a few precious seconds to come up with a reason that made sense and would assuage Rider's suspicion. I had been bothered, just like I'd been bothered when I'd seen them sitting at the bar together, whenever I thought about the fact Lana knew things about Daniel I didn't… "Did you know Daniel and Lana were in Hell together?"

"Yes."

"Do you know what happened to them there?"

"It's been my experience that most who've found themselves there don't talk about it." His eyes narrowed. "Does Daniel talk to you about it?"

I shook my head. "Not in detail. The trickster we were up against in Moonlight sicced hellhounds on us. Lana was frozen in fear. I know they went through a lot together there, and sometimes I just worry about them being around each other because of that. I kind of get a feeling sometimes that not all the feelings between them are good, or maybe they just remind each other of bad stuff." There. That wasn't entirely untrue and sure beat 'Yeah, it bothers me when Daniel is close to another woman, but no worries, I love you.'

"Maybe being around each other is good for them. Maybe they need to talk it out together." He angled his head to the side and really stared at me. "You're sure that's the only thing that bothered you?"

"Yeah, I mean, and you put Angel with them. I don't know Lana as well as I know Daniel, so that bothered me, but it was better than leaving her at my apartment with her mother hanging around." I sucked in a breath involuntarily as I sensed the sun disappear completely. Completely nightfall, energy flooded my body.

"I have to go," Rider murmured. He stood from the bed and held his hand out to me. "Still mad at me?"

I slid my hand into his and allowed him to pull me into his arms. It was kind of impossible to stay angry with a man who'd just confessed to being jealous of another man, yet was willing to assign that same man to watch over me when he couldn't because he knew the love he thought the other man felt would keep me safe. "No," I answered. "I'm worried though, and I don't like this. Promise you'll come back to me."

"Danni, I would never leave you, not even in death. I'm not going to die," he quickly added, and smiled. "I have to do this one thing and I'm coming right back."

Kutya sat up and barked before jumping down from the chaise to wedge between us.

"You'd better because if you don't I have a feeling this dog will hunt you down."

Rider scratched Kutya's head, grabbed his bag, and the three of us made our way to the garage, where Christian waited by Rider's SUV. The former angel-slash-vampire gave me a polite nod and smile.

"Christian's going with you?"

"Yes."

"Who else is going as your security detail?" I asked.

Rider stared at me, saying nothing. He didn't have to. I could read the hesitancy to answer in his eyes.

"Who else is going as your security detail?" I asked again, lending a bit of a growl to my tone.

Rider sighed. "This is highly classified, Danni. It's just me and Christian."

"Highly classified? Last I checked, FBI didn't stand for Fanged Bureau of Investigations. What's this classified nonsense?"

Rider's lips twitched. He shared a look with the equally amused Christian before the man climbed into the passenger side of the vehicle and closed the door, giving us a little privacy.

"I'm serious, Rider. This sounds dangerous, and Christian isn't a vampire anymore. Sure, he has some kind of angel juice or whatever left, but we don't know what he can handle. He's a freaking minister. You need more than just him with you."

"Christian is a guardian now, Danni. We might not know much more than that, but a guardian is pretty powerful, and he was able to protect you from the trickster that preyed on you in your dreams. We'll be all right."

"You take more than one other person with you just to see Auntie Mo. What is going on?"

"I can't tell you. I can only promise you I'll come back as soon as we're done." Rider gave Kutya another head-scratch and drew me in for a long, lingering kiss. I missed him the moment he let me go and walked to the driver's side of the SUV. He tossed his bag in, then paused with the door open, and held my gaze. "Be careful, Danni."

Then he was in the vehicle, out of the garage, and out of sight. Kutya whined mournfully at my side.

"I know, boy. I'm worried too."

Worried about Rider and whatever mess Seta had dragged him into, and worried because I got the distinct impression that last request was more than a plea to be careful of bodily harm. It was a warning that I needed to be very, very careful with Daniel if I didn't want to see my favorite dragon descaled.

CHAPTER ELEVEN

"What is witch's net made out of?" Angel asked.

"I'm not sure," I answered, looking past her to watch Daniel stare straight forward, jaw popping as he navigated the winding roads taking us toward our destination. "I just know it's used to keep witches from using their magic."

"Lana said the water Rider gave me had witch's net in it to keep some witch he has locked up from getting in my head. How would that work?"

"I'm not sure."

"You're not sure of much. Is there anything you *do* know?"

"Hey, I'm new to all this paranormal stuff myself, kid. Cut me a break."

"I'm not a kid." She turned toward Daniel. "Do you know?"

"No," he replied rather curtly.

"What's with him?" Angel whispered. "He's been a crank this whole ride."

I risked another glance Daniel's way before returning my attention back to the trees whizzing past as we sped by. Daniel had barely looked at me since being called to Rider's room, and had spoken to me even less. I knew exactly what had gotten him in such a mood, but I wasn't about to share that information with Angel. "We're all just ready to get to Pigeon Forge," I said instead. "Why don't you just listen to the music and enjoy the scenery?"

She rolled her eyes. "Classic rock is cool and all, but they've played three Van Halen songs in the last hour and this stupid station is full of erectile dysfunction commercials."

"Play whatever you want," Daniel said, throwing in the towel, and after two hours of listening to Angel complain about the station, I couldn't blame him.

"Finally," Angel said and didn't waste any time switching the radio station. "Yes! BTS!"

Daniel muttered a not-suitable-for-children string of words under his breath as Angel danced in her seat between us. I grinned and fought the urge to move to the music myself. Hey, those guys are cute and their songs are catchy. "It's all right, Daniel. Rock and roll will never die."

"The music's not bad," he replied, stringing together the longest sentence he'd spoken to me since we'd left The Midnight Rider, "but the Mexican jumping bean next to me is a bit of a nuisance."

"Hey!" Angel slugged him in the shoulder, causing him to swerve before straightening the truck out.

"What the hell? What's the matter with you?"

"That's racist!"

"What's racist?"

"You called me a Mexican jumping bean just because I'm Mexican."

Daniel blinked a few times. "You're Mexican?"

"Oh, now you want to act like you didn't know I'm Mexican."

"We met you in Kentucky. As far as I know, you're American," Daniel snapped before looking at me. "Help me out here. The kid's losing it."

"I'm not a kid."

"Angel, hon, I didn't know you were Mexican either," I

said, trying to smooth things over. "I knew you were Latina, but there's a lot of countries your family could have come from. Daniel called you a Mexican jumping bean because you were bopping all around like a Mexican jumping bean. That's just what they're called."

Angel glared at Daniel for a moment before slumping down into her seat. Daniel shook his head and blew out a breath. "Look, kid. We don't have races in the realm I come from. I mean, we do, but we don't have names for them like Asian or African or whatever because those countries don't exist in my realm. There, differences in skin color are like differences in hair or eye color and nobody really gives a shit about it. I'm sorry if I offended you somehow, but I didn't mean anything by what I said. At all."

"The realm you came from doesn't even have countries?"

"Correct."

"Why'd you leave it anyway?"

Daniel's fingers tightened around the steering wheel. I noted the way his nostrils flared as his jaw popped.

"Angel, hon, let's let Daniel focus on driving. These winding roads can be tricky."

A flash of yellow sped past us on the left and Ginger's Mustang cut in front of us. *The big toddler's gotta make a pee-pee,* she said in our minds. *We're gonna make a pit stop at the next exit.*

"Looks like we're making a pit stop," I told Angel. "Rome's gotta use the bathroom. We should probably see if Kutya needs to as well." I glanced back but didn't see the big pup. I figured he'd tuckered out of standing in the truck bed and had given in to a nap.

"Did y'all just do that mind-talking stuff?"

"Yes."

"That is so cool. And rude. I wanna do it."

"Which one of us do you want to bite and turn you?" Daniel asked.

Angel blanched.

"He's joking, Angel. Daniel can't even turn you that way."

"Can Rome do the mind-talking thing?" she asked. I nodded. "He's a human. If he can do it, why can't I?"

"Rome fights shapeshifters and vampires while dodging bullets, sharp teeth and claws," Daniel said. "Do you want to do that?"

Angel shook her head.

"Then stick to talking through your mouth and texting, kid."

We took an off ramp into a small town called Coal Valley and pulled into a gas station. Ginger parked next to one of the two gas pumps and Daniel parked at the other one.

"You need to use the restroom?" I asked Angel as we all stepped out of our vehicles to stretch our legs. The ramshackle little building had flickering neon signs advertising beer and tobacco, and had a sign indicating the outhouse was around the side.

"I'm not using the bathroom in an outhouse," she said. "That's my worst fear."

"Using an outhouse is your worst fear?"

"A snake popping up and biting me right in the hoo-ha while using one is my worst fear."

I stifled a laugh and moved to the back of the truck, where an excited Kutya awaited me. I clipped on his leash and got him down from the truck bed while Daniel pumped gas. Ginger did the same at the pump she'd parked by and Rome stood, hands on hips, looking at the building.

"I thought you had to use the bathroom," I said to him.

"I do." He scanned the area. "I think I'll wait until the next exit."

"There's not another exit for several more miles," Daniel told him.

"And the way you keep shaking those tree trunks you call legs, you're going to wear out the shocks on my 'stang," Ginger said. "Use it now or you're riding in the back of Daniel's truck with the dog."

"His big ass isn't wearing out my shocks," Daniel said. "What's the problem, man? Performance anxiety? Afraid a snake's gonna get your hoo-ha?"

"Nah, man. This place is kind of giving me a *Deliverance* vibe," Rome answered, nodding his head toward the older white man we could see staring at us from inside the small building, rifle in hand. "And I can see the outhouse from here. It's not happening."

I walked over to where Rome stood and saw the outhouse. A heavy padlocked chain was wrapped around it, and my vampire vision could just make out the Out-of-Order sign hanging from the chain. I didn't even want to think about what conditions had to be met for an outhouse to be deemed out of working order.

"I'll just go in the trees over there, man. I'll take Kutya with me and see if he's gotta go."

"Sure." I handed him the leash and watched him walk past the edge of the station, disappearing into the tree line beyond.

Other than the gas station, there didn't seem to be much around. The area was heavily wooded and, although the exit sign had indicated a restaurant nearby, it wasn't within viewing distance from the gas station. I could see lights deep in the trees, and assumed there were houses along the other side of the patch of woodland.

"This place kind of gives me the willies," Angel said. She peered at the small building where the older man's pasty white face peered back from behind the glass. "I didn't go on many family trips during my childhood, but the few I did go on, I remember the grownups telling us we'd better pee before we left because we weren't stopping in any little hick towns."

"You're traveling with vampires and a dragon," Daniel told her. He replaced the gas nozzle and closed the tank. "Whatever monsters you've heard tales about in these types of places, I'm sure we can handle them."

I sighed, knowing Daniel had no clue what types of monsters Angel's family had warned her about because he came from a world where black men and brown-skinned girls didn't have the misfortune of not feeling safe entering certain places.

Something taped to the gas pump behind him caught my attention and I pointed at it. "What's that?"

Daniel looked at the flyer. "Lovefest. Looks like it's just outside of Sevierville." His eyes narrowed as he turned toward me. "Don't even think about it."

"I'm not thinking of anything."

"Please. You're always thinking of something. Grissom is looking for Eliza. We're going to The Cloud Top to keep you safe while Rider's away and nothing more. Besides, Eliza's already been to that thing and returned from it. Rider's techs didn't find anything on her computer or in her bank account to suggest she was making a second trip."

"Yet, she's not in her home," I murmured, staring at the flyer. My gut twisted.

"Hey." Daniel walked around the truck and squeezed my shoulder. "Eliza will be all right. Grissom's good at what he does. He'll find her."

I looked down at where his warm hand rested on my shoulder, and my stomach did another nauseated little flip, remembering my discussion with Rider. I glanced over at Ginger and found her leaning back against her car, arms folded, watching us. He'd said everyone on the trip had a reason to be there, and that I needed to be careful with Daniel. Suddenly I wondered if the two people I'd thought of as friends were also spies.

I stepped back until Daniel's hand fell away from my

shoulder. "Yeah, I'm sure you're right."

The unmistakable crack of a gunshot rang out from the very trees Rome had disappeared into. I shoved Angel into the truck purely by reflex. "Lock yourself in!"

Daniel, Ginger, and I ran toward the trees. My heart was in my throat, but I forced myself to push past the fear and open my senses. I didn't smell blood as we broke through the tree line, thankfully, but I picked up on a rapidly beating heart and knew Rome was in trouble.

We came to a quick stop, spotting Rome and Kutya. Rome's back was to us, one hand in the air while holding Kutya's leash, the other appeared to be reaching down in front of him, holding on to…

"Y'all might not want to come any closer," Rome told us while staring straight ahead at the three burly men in front of him and the somewhat burly woman, all of whom pointed guns directly at Rome. "They caught me in a precarious situation and you ladies might blush… and Daniel might get jealous."

I rolled my eyes. At least Rome could joke while under gunpoint, but his rapidly beating heart belied his calm demeanor. The biggest of the three men, a near three-hundred pounder in a trucker cap, kept his shotgun pointed at Rome. The red-headed man in red plaid swung his around to point at Daniel, and the guy with the beard long enough to tuck into his bib overalls held his shotgun on me and Ginger. I supposed the woman could have taken aim at one of us, evening things out, but she couldn't seem to tear her wide-eyed gaze away from Rome's crotch. I saw tall privacy fences several feet behind them with signs warning not to trespass and figured they lived on that property.

"What's the problem here?" Daniel asked.

"Dog thief," the biggest man said, and spit.

Kutya barked at the man. I swear that dog could speak human. "Uh, if you're speaking of this dog, he's mine, and my friend didn't steal him," I told the man.

The man looked between Kutya and me before retraining his gun on Rome. "He was looking around, looking to steal. I told you to put your hands up, *boy*."

"I'm a grown-ass man, not your *boy*, Honky Kong."

"The fuck you just say to me you—"

"Everyone calm down." Daniel stepped forward until he stood alongside Rome. "We're traveling and our friend needed to use the bathroom. The outhouse at the gas station was locked, so he decided to walk the dog and go out here. From what I can tell, this isn't private property right here. Let our friend zip his pants back up and we'll just be on our way. There's no need for any violence."

"Your friend, huh?" The redhead's gaze did a slow up and down number on Daniel's frame, resting on his colorful hair before sneering. "I'm thinking this here's your boyfriend," he said with a laugh. "We got us a fruitcake here, fellas. A fruitcake with princess hair. Ain't that right, princess? You wanna give me a little smoochie smooch?" The man made kissing noises.

"I'm game if you are, sweet lips," Daniel responded deadpan, effectively silencing the redhead. His face grew redder than his hair as he swung around to look at me and Ginger. "They're homos! All of 'em. I bet those two are lesbians!"

"Well, he got one right," Ginger said, positioning herself to fight, as things were clearly going south.

"Look," I said. "We aren't looking for trouble, but if you want to start it, we'll finish it. Let our friend walk out of here and we'll let you walk out of here."

The redhead and Beardy looked at me and started laughing, clearly unthreatened, but their rotund leader wasn't amused. He pointed a chubby finger in Rome's direction. "That boy was creeping around here up to no good and his kind does that when they're stealing. He ain't goin' nowhere until I get back whatever he stole."

"Man, I didn't steal shit from y'all," Rome said, "except maybe your woman. She hasn't lifted her eyes from my dick this whole time."

The big man looked over at his wife, caught her staring, completely enraptured by Rome's package, and snatched her by the nape of her neck. "What you looking so hard at him for, woman?"

"I'm sorry!" Her eyes bugged out of her head. "I just never seen one so big before."

"What you mean? You…" The big man looked down at himself. His cheeks bloomed bright, and he snarled, then backhanded the woman across the face.

Daniel leaped forward, grabbed the shotgun out of the redhead's hands before elbowing him in the face and swinging the weapon around to ram it butt-first into the large man's eye. Beardy raised his gun toward Daniel, but Ginger clotheslined him while I took care of the redhead who'd gotten back on his feet. His nose was crooked and gushing blood, but he could still point his gun at Rome. Fortunately, I rammed headfirst into his beer belly before he could pull the trigger. The moment his body fell back onto the ground, I scooped up the gun and broke it over my knee before clubbing him in the face with it.

"Get off him! What are you doing?" I looked up from the redhead's bloody, unconscious face to see the woman pointing her gun at Daniel. "Leave my husband be!"

Daniel stood, leaving the big man's battered body on the ground where he'd pummeled him into oblivion, and faced the woman. "Seriously, lady? This man just hit you."

The woman looked between us and the three unconscious bodies on the ground. Her hands shook as tears filled her eyes. "I deserved it. I deserved it for looking at another man, that kind of man."

Her tear-filled eyes turned hard a second before she swung the gun around and took aim at Rome. Daniel's hand shot out as she pulled the trigger. Blood exploded from his hand as he shoved the gun up, effectively saving Rome from the bullet, but in doing so, took it himself. I saw the blood and bits of bone fly into the air like a gruesome fireworks display and my fangs immediately dropped as I lunged forward, and they plunged into the woman's throat before we'd hit the ground.

"Shit! Danni, stop!" Ginger pulled at me, but I clung to the woman's body, prepared to drain her despite the fact female blood was never that appetizing. I had to force myself to drink from Angel, but in the heat of vengeance, I didn't care where the blood came from, only that it ended in the source's death.

"Daniel's all right!" Ginger said, releasing me as another set of arms wrapped around my midsection. She grabbed the woman's body and pulled as I was lifted off my knees and held mid-air, effectively detached from the woman's body and the gaping wound left in her throat. "He's a shifter, remember? He can heal."

I stopped struggling against Rome's tight hold and looked over to see Daniel disappearing into rainbow sparkles and reappearing, staring at his hand. He did this a few times, then flexed his hand. "I will never understand this realm's stupid race shit," he growled. "It's skin. Skin! Who gives a fuck what color it is? Fucking ridiculous."

"I recall you once calling me a chocolate-covered hemorrhoid," Rome reminded him, still holding me in one of his muscular arms.

"And?" Daniel shook out his hand and looked at him. "Look in a mirror sometime, dude. That's not racist. That's just what you look like."

"I hate you, Puff."

Daniel placed his hand over his heart as if deeply shocked and offended. "And to think I was willing to kiss that dude for you."

Rome laughed and settled me back on my feet. "You calm now, Vampira?"

I nodded, my stomach doing a flip as I looked at the woman bleeding on the ground along with her unconscious brethren. "Ah, shit. I saw Daniel's blood, and I just lost it."

Ginger kneeled over the woman and sealed the wound with her saliva before placing her fingers over her pulse point. "She's alive, and she has a good shot at staying alive if we call in help for her."

"I bit her," I said. "She'll tell."

"You moved in way too fast for her to know what hit her," Rome said. "That said, there's still the guy at the gas station. He saw all of us and he might have cameras."

"I'll handle him," Daniel said and started back toward the gas station.

"Are you all right?" I asked Rome.

"Yeah, I'm good. I wouldn't have minded getting a piece of these jackasses myself, but y'all didn't give a man enough time to put his junk away and join the fun." He winked and tugged at Kutya's leash. "Come on, big man."

Kutya walked over to the largest man and sniffed before straddling his massive chest and hunkering down. My jaw dropped as Kutya strained, dropped a massive pile of crap atop the bib of the man's overalls, kicked some grass over it, and stepped away.

I gawked. "Did he just…"

"I am not bagging that," Rome cut me off while Ginger just shook with laughter. "Atta boy, big man. Atta boy."

We headed back toward the station, Rome and Kutya in the lead. Ginger fell in step close to my side and whispered, "Did you see Rome's dick?"

"No," I whispered back. "I wasn't looking."

She held her hands out a couple of feet wide. "No wonder that woman was stuck staring. It was kind of mesmerizing, like staring into the eye of one of those snakes that charm their prey before striking."

I cringed at the image her statement evoked. "Pretty sure the snake thing is a myth, and as for Rome's attributes, I'd rather not know, and I thought you weren't into men, except for Wilmer Valderrama."

"I'm not, but I can appreciate amazing feats of architecture."

I shook my head and quickened my pace to discourage further commentary on things I'd rather not know anything about.

Daniel stepped out of the little building as we reached the gas station and nodded at us, indicating he'd taken care of the man inside. I wasn't entirely sure what that entailed and didn't question it. Angel sat in the truck, waiting for us.

"Did you call in help for them?" Ginger asked.

"Paramedics on their way," Daniel answered gruffly. "Let's get out of here."

"What happened?" Angel asked as we got back in the truck.

"This stupid realm happened," Daniel muttered and started the truck. "Sometimes I really miss Imortia."

I stared at his hand as he navigated back onto the expressway and headed toward Pigeon Forge, remembering the emotions that had overtaken me when I'd seen the blood explode from it. For a second I'd thought I'd lost him. I imagined it would feel very similar if he went back to Imortia. I stared out the window for the rest of the trip, trying to breathe past the huge lump in my throat.

"Whoa," Angel said as we parked and stared up to see the figures emerging on the hill in front of us. She grabbed my hand.

"They're friendlier than they appear," I said, giving her hand a squeeze.

"Yeah, and Danni just beats the shit out of the ones who aren't nice," Daniel said as we stepped out of the truck. Ginger and Rome emerged from her Mustang next to us.

"Welcome back," Grey, the muscular pack leader, said as he approached us. His olive green eyes and honey-colored hair shone in the moonlight and it didn't escape my notice that Angel admired the way the dark blue T-shirt he wore stretched across his pectorals or the way his strong thighs filled out his jeans. "I have the cabin ready for you."

Daniel made the introductions and exchanged pleasantries while I got Kutya down from the truck bed.

"I don't mind the dog," Grey said, "but I hate to see any animal bound like that. My pack has been made aware of his presence and will make sure he won't stray off our land or get into any danger."

"Appreciated," I said, and unhooked Kutya's leash.

"Grab your stuff and follow me."

We did as told and followed Grey to the same cabin he'd provided Rider and me during our previous stay. A wave of nostalgia hit me as I remembered first meeting Daniel on Grey's land and my first time making love with Rider.

"Shannon's away on pack business," Grey told me as we entered the cabin, "and the females have all been warned not to cause you any trouble, not that I think any would want to try after what you did to her." He chuckled and moved on to giving a tour of the cabin since three of our party had never seen it. "Make yourselves at home," he said after finishing. "I was about to go out for a run. I can take your friend with me. I'm sure he'd enjoy stretching his legs after the drive here."

"You might want to take a Hefty bag," Daniel said. "His shits are enormous."

"He should be all right," Ginger informed him. "He pooped on a redneck a couple of hours ago."

Grey stared at her for a moment, blinked, and shook his head. "All right. Well, there's plenty of woodland here for him to use." He crouched down in front of Kutya. "Want to run with me?"

Kutya released an excited bark and trotted to the front door. I smiled at his big, goofy face. "I think that's a yes."

"He'll be all right," Grey said, moving toward the door.

"Someone will always be posted right outside if you need anything during your stay here at The Cloud Top, so don't hesitate to ask."

"There's only two bedrooms," Angel pointed out after the pack leader left with Kutya.

"You ladies can share the one with the waterfall view," Daniel said, referring to the room I'd used during the stay with Rider. "Rome and I will share the other one. After all, the guy back at the gas station pointed out we were such a happy couple anyway." He swung his arm around Rome's beefy shoulders and started to plant a kiss on his cheek.

Rome grabbed Daniel's entire face in his big hand before his lips could connect. "Put those nasty lips on this beautiful black skin and I'm gonna squeeze that big ol' rainbow head of yours until Skittles pop out."

Daniel disappeared in a burst of colorful sparkles and reappeared behind Rome. "Don't fight it, Big Sexy." He slapped Rome's ass and disappeared again.

"Did he…" Rome turned around. "Did he just…"

Daniel reappeared on the stairs and made kissing noises.

"You're dead, Puff." Rome took off after him. Ginger, Angel, and I stood in the living area, staring up, listening to all the ruckus above us as Rome chased Daniel around the second floor. "Get your rainbow ass back here! I mean it! Quit poofing, motherfucker!"

"Men," Ginger said.

"Boys," Angel corrected, and yawned. "And y'all call me a kid. At least Daniel seems in a better mood now. Don't tell him I said it, but I wouldn't want him to leave us."

"Me neither." My chest ached at the thought of a life without Daniel in it. I caught Ginger watching me with an odd look in her eye and cleared my throat. "Go get some rest. There's only one bed in that room, so you might as well take advantage of the night. Ginger and I will be squeezing in with you come morning."

"How am I supposed to sleep with that going on?" She pointed toward the ceiling just as we heard a crash.

"They'll settle down soon," I assured her, jumping as another crash sounded. "Or on second thought, Ginger and I will go wrangle them."

Ginger cracked her knuckles and started up the stairs.

CHAPTER TWELVE

"How's the ear?" I asked Daniel as he stepped out onto the porch. I'd taken my laptop out and plopped down in one of the rocking chairs after Ginger and I had finished reprimanding the children, er, Daniel and Rome.

"Fine, despite Ginger's best effort to rip it off." He rubbed the ear in question and I couldn't help but grin. Ginger had thoroughly enjoyed separating the two and dealing with their foolery.

"Did you boys clean up your mess?"

"Yes, mom." He craned his neck to see my laptop screen. "You're looking at that Lovefest site again."

"Yup."

"Danni."

"It's just a website. I'm sitting on a porch guarded by a wolf pack. There is nothing to worry about, so that tone is not necessary." I watched him, focusing on his hand as he moved over to the railing and sat on it. "It's not like I'm putting my hand over the muzzle of a gun someone is actively shooting. You scared the hell out of me, Daniel."

"What was I supposed to do, let Rome get shot?" He folded his arms. "I can heal that kind of damage easily. He can't."

"Next time, grab the barrel."

"Next time." He shook his head. "I've seen that type of unbelievable ignorance in movies. I've read about it… Actually seeing it in person at that level, though…" He shook his head again and straightened from the railing. "I gotta get out of here."

"What?" I straightened so quick the laptop slid off my lap. I grabbed it a second before it would have fallen to the floor. "You're leaving us?"

He turned, giving me a strange look. "Ginger and Rome are here. Besides, like you said, you're being guarded by a wolf pack." He swung his hand out, gesturing toward the two men posted far enough away from the cabin to give us some sense of privacy, but close enough to be available if needed. "I'll be overhead if you need me for anything. Just do the mind-talking thing."

"Oh," I said, realizing what he'd meant. "You're not leaving The Cloud Top."

"Of course not. I just need to … see someone." A strange, almost guilty look flitted through his eyes. He blinked it away and stepped off the porch.

I watched him walk away until he disappeared beyond the tree line, my gut churning. I knew he'd spent time with a few wolf packs before ending up with us. Grey's had been the most recent. He mourned the fiancée he'd lost in Imortia, but it hit me that he was still a man with needs. I really wasn't sure how long it had been since he'd left Imortia or how long he'd been with Grey's pack. It wasn't that crazy of an idea that despite seeming happy to leave with us, he might have left someone behind. Maybe not a girlfriend. I couldn't see Daniel just walking away from a girlfriend without a word about it, but a friend, maybe? A friend he had an arrangement with?

He'd been quiet and moody most of the trip, which hadn't been a surprise given Rider's way of reminding him where I slept and with who. Then he'd had the misunderstanding with Angel, followed by the horrible display of hatred and ignorance at the gas station, which had soured his mood even further. It had been a relief to see him joking with Rome, but then I'd gone and brought up what had happened at the gas station. It hadn't taken him long to split, and I feared he might want to make that split permanent.

He'd seemed so disgusted with this realm, and how long could a man stand to be around a woman he was in … even in my own mind I didn't want to say the L-word, even though I knew in my gut he'd been in the dream realm with me when the trickster had been screwing with me. I knew the kiss had happened even if he didn't want to own up to it, and I didn't want to either. It was easier to keep forcing it down whenever the memory surfaced, to tell myself it was all an illusion so neither of us would have to deal with it, but how long could that last? How long could he bear that kind of misery without having anyone to talk to about it or anywhere else to focus that longing? I stared at the path he'd taken away from me. Maybe he did have someone. While at The Cloud Top, at least.

I tried to push the thought out of my mind and focus again on what I'd been checking out on the laptop. From what I could tell, Lovefest was some sort of traveling festival similar to a Warped Tour. There were musical acts, none very popular from what I could tell. Mostly cover bands like the all-female Jimi Hendrix group, The Jimis. There was a K-Pop cover group called Bias Wrecker, and an all-girl punk rock group called Vagi Mind Trick. I chuckled at that one.

A vendor page showcased wares and food that could be purchased, a lot of vegan options, a lot of hemp. Lots and lots of crystals. Nothing on the site suggested anything dangerous or underhanded, but still my gut twisted. It wouldn't hurt to go. Maybe we'd find Eliza. Sure, Grissom was on the case, but if she was frolicking around at the festival, staying in a tent in the available camping space there, she'd be hard for him to track from Louisville. And who knew, maybe Bias Wrecker would put on a decent show?

I set the laptop aside and started to think how I would pitch the idea to the others, and just like that, my mind went right back to Daniel and wondering who he'd gone off to see, or to be accurate, who he'd walked away from me to see.

A large gray wolf loped out of the tree line, a big Doberman-shepherd mix on its tail. I watched them run up the path toward the cabin and took a deep breath to clear my mind of the troubling thoughts. If only I could clear my chest of the pain inside, a pain I shouldn't be feeling and didn't want to question why I was.

The wolf shifted into a man within the blink of an eye and stepped onto the porch. "This one's got wolf in his blood," Grey said. He leaned back against one of the columns bracketing the porch steps and grinned at the big pup licking my hand.

I gave Kutya a good scratch between his big ears and watched him curl up next to my rocking chair where he panted, his big tongue lolling out the side of his mouth. "Literally or figuratively?"

"Probably a bit of both. Dogs descend from wolves just like my people do."

I raised an eyebrow. "I was under the impression Imortians descended from magical people and the wolf thing is because of a spell."

"You're not wrong," he said, "but I was born a werewolf, just as most everyone else in my pack was. Until a handful of years ago, we'd never heard of Imortia or the people from it. We knew of The White Wolf and had been told she was the creator of our race, and that was the extent of our knowledge until a group of Imortians found a portal here and came for her help to save their realm. We knew we weren't lycanthropes, but having never heard of Imortia, we just considered ourselves Weres. Most of us still do."

"Including you?"

He held my gaze for a moment and nodded. "I've never been to Imortia, so I don't see myself coming from there. I've always known of The White Wolf, or Zaira, as she is now known to us. My people came from that wolf. We've been part wolf from birth, or became part wolf through mating magic, so although I suppose you could technically say we're Imortians, we're not like Daniel or those who came directly from the realm like he did. He had a dragon's soul forced into him through a spell that required its death. No one in my pack ever went through that."

"But Zaira did," I said, "and she created all of you."

Grey angled his head to the side, thinking. "Yes. She was the first of us. Her children became the second generation, their children the third, and so on. Each generation has carried the wolf soul, but it wasn't in the same way she carries hers. Ours is general. It doesn't come with a personality or a lost life with it. I suppose it's a fragment of the wolf soul carried by our parents … or soulmate, for those who become a werewolf through mating magic."

I blinked a few times as I processed this information. "What's this mating magic? People can become werewolves or…" I looked off into the trees where Daniel had disappeared… "other types of shifters through having sex?"

"Not through sex, no. Mating magic is an actual ritual when soulmates take what we call a moon vow. The human becomes a werewolf through the vow, and the couple can then conceive werechildren. That's how it works for wolves, anyway. I have no idea about these new Imortian shifters." He looked up at the sky. "I saw Daniel near the waterfall. I took one look at his shoulder width when you arrived and knew it wouldn't take long for him to get up there and spread his wings. I imagine he doesn't get to do so often in the city."

"He's had to shift and fly a few times in order to protect me," I advised. "He got up there some when we were in West Virginia on a job, but overall, I guess he probably doesn't fly a whole lot. You mentioned his shoulders. I thought he'd gotten bigger, but I wasn't sure."

"Daniel's very young in terms of shifter years, and I believe in Imortian years as well. From my understanding, a lot of those people can live forever, or close enough. The dragon soul inside him is getting stronger." Grey gestured toward his own body with hands that looked strong enough to crush bowling balls. "This isn't all from the gym. Shifters get big. Daniel's a *dragon*, and a first generation dragon at that. I wouldn't be surprised if he eventually gets bigger than your friend Rome, and the bigger he gets, the more he's going to need to release some energy through flying … or possibly burning shit down."

I sat in the chair, gaping, unsure what I struggled with most: the fact Daniel could eventually be hulked out like Rome, or the fact he might just live forever. I knew shifters gained mass after being turned, and I'd heard Daniel speak of immortals in Imortia before, and I knew Zaira was obviously immortal since she was still kicking after so many generations of werewolves had descended from her, but it had never really clicked that Daniel could be immortal too, that I could potentially have him in my long life forever. Somehow, I'd just never registered that. Potentially being the key word. Daniel couldn't stay in mourning forever. Eventually, he would want a partner and if I remained with Rider… Daniel was going to leave.

"I was joking about burning shit down."

I looked up to see Grey watching me. "No, sorry, I know. I was just thinking… he must be unhappy not being able to fly around whenever he wants."

Grey shrugged. "He was happy to leave with you, and he could fly every night here."

"Was he alone when you saw him earlier?"

"Of course. He's the only person on this land capable

of flying, and I imagine he probably scares the hell out of birds." Grey's mouth lifted at the corner as he straightened from the column. He started to say something else, but the large teal and purple dragon swooping down in front of the cabin caught his attention.

The dragon disappeared in a shower of rainbow sparkles and Daniel walked toward us. I could tell by the set of his jaw something was wrong.

"What is it?" Grey asked, instantly alert. Apparently, he picked up on Daniel's demeanor too.

"I spotted an old raggedy Crown Victoria winding up the mountain," Daniel said, speaking directly to me.

"It couldn't be…" I said.

"What am I missing here?" Grey asked.

"A human detective has been following Danni."

"Rider said something about that." Grey's eyes narrowed. "You think he followed you here?"

"How could he?" Kutya whined, sensing my unease, so I gave him a reassuring pat on the head. "We were so careful."

"Not careful enough," Daniel said.

"You checked for tracking devices before you left?" Grey asked.

Daniel nodded. "I just did a second check in case we missed one, but there's nothing on my truck or Ginger's Mustang."

"Maybe it wasn't him," I suggested. "From so high up in the sky, maybe it wasn't a Crown Victoria that you saw."

"I'm in full dragon form when up in the sky, Danni. I see with a dragon's eyes." He crouched down in front of Kutya. "I was thinking he has to be tracking us somehow, and he had his hands on Kutya's collar when Kutya bit him in the junk."

"Kutya bit the man in his dick?" Grey asked, shoulders shaking with laughter. I was pretty sure I saw the gleam of pride in his eyes.

"Yep," Daniel answered as he slid his fingers under

Kutya's collar and bit out a curse. A moment later, he pulled his hand free, a small black object held between two fingers. It was round and thick, but small enough it hadn't been noticed by us or seemed to have bothered Kutya at all. "I admire the determination it takes to even be able to focus on planting a bug while your dick's being used as a chew toy, but I also really, really hate this guy."

"How long until he reaches The Cloud Top?" Grey asked.

"Honestly, his clunker will probably crap out before he makes it this far up the mountain, but just in case…" Daniel jogged down from the porch, jumped up, and in a flash of sparkles, transformed into a dark red dragon and flew off.

"He takes on the actual form of the dragon that was killed in order for its soul to be forced into him, right?"

"He's first generation, so that would be right."

"Why is he a different color every time he shifts, then?"

"I've always assumed the dragon that was killed did the same, and maybe the bitch who killed it selected it because it matches Daniel's hair. Maybe all dragons change color like that." He shrugged. "I'm not Imortian, so just guessing."

"What color is Daniel's nose ring to you?"

"It's like a clear crystal that reflects different colors depending on how the light hits it," he answered, grinning.

"I hate to break it to you, Grey, but if you can see that, you *are* Imortian."

"So they tell me."

"I wish I could see it. Imortium sounds so beautiful, but it's just silver to me."

"It is beautiful, and I hear Imortia is breathtaking."

"Are you ever going to see it for yourself?"

He shook his head, his honey-colored shoulder-length hair moving with it, reminding me of a Pantene ad. "I'm needed here. There seems to always be something coming up, some new threat. Now, it's a human detective."

"I'm sorry."

"It's not your fault. Who would ever suspect a man capable of planting a tracking device on a dog while it chews his genitals? It's the last thing that would be on my mind." He chuckled. "I need to inform my scouts and take care of other matters before it gets too late. I generally don't keep the same hours as you." He winked at me, and my belly might have done a little flip. Hey, I love Rider, but Grey didn't have any trouble turning heads.

Daniel reappeared, bringing with him a powerful gust of wind as his dragon body barreled down toward the open space in front of the cabin. He did the rainbow sparkly shower thing and emerged in his own body before walking over to us. "Well, if the device survived the fall, he can track it to wherever the Chevy truck that just left town is headed. Dropped it into its truck bed."

"I know you had to fly really high up to avoid anyone noticing a dragon flying over them," I said. "Are you telling me you were able to drop that little thing from such a high altitude and still see it land in a truck bed?"

"Yes."

"Damn."

He grinned. "I did another flyover to check on Pacitti's progress, and like I figured would happen, his car was broken down on the side of the road. He's going to have to call in help, get it towed, and by the time he does all that, the tracker should lead him far from here."

"Hopefully," Grey said, "but you know sometimes people commute. That truck carrying the tracker could come back into town, and if the tracker got damaged, The Cloud Top was the last location he picked up. He's a detective. He knows how to find people, but he won't get to you here. I doubt a man who's already been through what he has at the teeth of a large dog is going to try to get through a pack of wolves." He let out a wide yawn. "Just be careful and let me know if you need anything."

"Will do," Daniel assured him.

We watched Grey walk away, noting the two men who'd been posted close to our cabin switched out with another pair of guards, this time a man and a woman. He spoke with all four, then continued on his way down the path, joined by the two departing guards.

Kutya stood and started clawing at the front door, I assumed to get to his food or water bowl. Or a comfier place to sleep. He was a bit spoiled. Daniel opened the door to let him in.

"All worn out and ready to call it a night now?" I asked.

Daniel closed the door behind Kutya and walked back over to the railing, where he sat, his thumbs shoved into his belt loops. "No, I'm good. It's been a while since I've been able to really fly without so much worry about being seen. There's so many damn airplanes in Louisville and not a lot of area like this."

Yup. Daniel wasn't happy with us. I stood, stretched, and started pacing along the porch. I'd been sitting still for too long. "It must be nice for you to be back here, spend time with friends, like the one you rushed out to meet up with." I knew he couldn't have spent very much time with whoever it was he'd left to see since Grey had seen him flying overhead all alone and clearly he'd still been on the clock, protecting me. Or maybe he was protecting the pack. The curiosity ate at me. "You never mentioned anyone from here, other than Grey, but he was out for a run with Kutya, then here with me."

Daniel peered at me. "Are you trying to ask me something?"

I chewed my bottom lip for a moment, questioning if I really wanted to know who Daniel had been with and why. In the end, curiosity won out. "I was just curious about the friend you had to see."

He frowned, appeared a little puzzled, then he blinked. "Oh. I said I had to see someone. I didn't say friend."

"Oh." I nibbled my lip some more. "Grey said to see

him if we needed anything, or the guards he leaves posted here. So, if not a friend and not Grey or…" Geez. He was going to make me straight-out ask, and I so didn't want to ask if he had a… what? A lover? Nope. Didn't want to ask that. "Does this non-friend have a name?"

"I'd have to ask Jadyn, but it's probably better I don't know it."

"Huh?" What the heck did Jadyn have to do with… *Oh.* I gave myself a mental head slap. "The dragon inside you. You just meant you were going to go fly. Why didn't you just say that?"

"It's really more than just flying sometimes. It's a communion of souls, I guess. When I'm just flying to be flying, I let him have control. In a way, it feels like giving him freedom, and some small part of his own life back." Sadness entered his eyes. "It's hard to explain."

"I think I get it, and Daniel, you don't have to feel so sad and guilty about it. Jadyn spoke with the dragon. He doesn't blame you."

"I know, but it doesn't change the fact my body is his cage."

Damn. I didn't really know what to say to that. I was half vampire and half succubus, but both were entirely different entities, entities that probably didn't have souls at all, so the way I became what I was wasn't anything like what Daniel had gone through to become a dragon shifter. "I'm sorry you were forced to take the soul of a slain dragon, and felt you had to leave Imortia, a land you loved to be somewhere you're not happy. I'm thankful, though, that I was given the chance to know you, and even long after you leave, I'll cherish every moment of our time together."

Daniel stepped in front of me, forced me to stop pacing. "Who said I was unhappy, and more importantly, who the hell said I was leaving?"

I looked up at him, trying to ignore the way the heat from his body wrapped around me while I opened and closed my mouth, fumbling for words. "You… you've said things, and I can see it sometimes. You've been unhappy lately."

"I have?"

"The men and the woman at the gas station. You seemed really upset about what happened there."

"Racist dickwads caught a good friend of mine with his pants down and were going to shoot him for no better reason than he's darker than them. That kind of shit is upsetting. It doesn't mean I'm going to leave."

"True, but you've been kind of quieter sometimes, back home. You haven't been joking as much since we returned from Moonlight."

"I'm not Jimmy Kimmel. I don't always crack jokes. It doesn't mean I'm leaving."

I started to argue that he did always crack jokes, but decided to just let that go. "You've been a little moody. You've made some comments about this realm." I shrugged. "I don't know. Sometimes it just feels like you're not happy being here."

"I came from a realm run by a dictator who threw people into Hell when they pissed her off. I might complain about the racists here and the smelly, doughy old people, and the fact Rome has clogged our toilet at least twenty times since I moved in with him, but that doesn't mean I'm leaving."

"Wait. You live with Rome? When did you move in with Rome?"

"After I was assigned as your personal guard. Rider wanted me watched, so Rome and I became roomies."

"Oh." I frowned. "I guess there's a lot I don't know."

"Clearly. Leaving this realm or this job means leaving you. I've told you before, I go where you go. I meant that, and it's not going to change." His eyes warmed. "You were afraid I was going to leave? You'd miss me?"

"Of course I'd miss you, you idiot."

He grinned, but grew serious again as his eyes grew

darker. They practically simmered with heat. "Why did you want to know the name of who I went to see?"

"Curious." I shrugged a shoulder.

"Curious, why?"

"I don't know. I just wondered…" He moved in so close to me we could have held a piece of paper between us with just our bodies. "This is dangerous, Daniel."

"What is?"

The door behind us opened and Ginger breezed through, grabbed my wrist and shouldered Daniel out of the way before pulling me off of the porch. "Come on, sweets. We're checking out that waterfall I've heard about while Daniel gets some rest."

I looked back toward the porch to see Daniel watching me, about fifty different thoughts and emotions swirling in his eyes, before he shoved a hand through his rainbow locks and went into the cabin.

"Girl, you're lucky the *NCIS* marathon I was watching went to commercial and I decided to see what you were up to," Ginger said as she pulled me along toward the waterfall. "And for the record, I'm not going out of town with you two anymore unless we pack a chastity belt. You got to get your Super-Ho power under control before you get us all killed."

CHAPTER THIRTEEN

After a rough morning of trying to sleep through nightmares of Rider perishing in battle, I woke around noon and drank a mug of warmed blood. Bagged blood was the worst, but after the close encounter with Daniel I wasn't attempting to drink from him, and despite his big and bad persona, Rome was a bit of a whiny baby when it came to giving blood. Angel was awake, but I'd drank from her recently enough that I didn't have any real need to force myself to drink from a female. I had to keep my blood diet balanced.

I'd called The Midnight Rider, hoping to reach Jadyn, but she wasn't there. She had school before her shift serving, so I'd left a message with the bartender on day shift, a shifter I didn't know well. He was pretty new and I'd never seen him tend bar before, but it made sense he'd be doing it when I called. With Tony handling operations while Rider was away, the tiger shifter would need to focus on security matters, not bartending. I wouldn't bother Tony. Even if he knew what Rider was up to, he wouldn't share that information with me, but Jadyn might know. She was married to Christian. Surely she knew something.

"You're up early."

I looked up from the laptop sitting on the table in front of me to see Daniel shuffle down the stairs in bare feet and swing into the kitchen. His REO Speedwagon T-shirt hung untucked over his faded blue jeans. I tried to ignore the way the thin fabric clung to his shoulders and the way his rainbow-colored hair, still damp from the shower I'd heard running upstairs a while ago, hung adorably over one eye.

"I could say the same for you," I told him as I watched him pour coffee into a mug and add a shot of whiskey. "You went to bed pretty late. Given we're not really here on a job, I thought you'd take the chance to sleep in."

"I did sleep in. It's noon-thirty."

"Noon-thirty isn't a time."

He walked behind me and pointed at the digital timestamp on my laptop's clock. "There's a twelve and there's a thirty, and it ain't midnight-thirty, so that makes it noon-thirty."

I shook my head as he dropped down into the chair next to mine and took a big swig from his mug. I ached to drink coffee again. I could only do it if I put blood in it, but I didn't want blood. I wanted pumpkin spice. I'm a white girl, after all. A white girl about to lose her freaking mind if she couldn't get a slice of chocolate cake soon. At least I could still wear yoga pants. Better than I could before, actually. For all its setbacks, vampirism did great things in terms of lifting and sculpting an ass.

"You're on that website again."

"Yup. I was looking for something to do while we're here."

"I suppose staying out of trouble never crossed your mind. Or catching up on your beauty sleep."

I gave him my best offended face. "You think I need beauty sleep?"

"I think you need vampire sleep. Why are you awake at this hour?"

"Why are you drinking whiskey at this hour?"

He looked at me. I looked at him. We stared at each other long enough for it to become uncomfortable.

"Fine. I had one bad dream after another, so I gave up on getting any decent sleep. Besides, you know I'm not like other vampires. I might not be at my perkiest during the day, and I might have trouble staying awake at the ass crack of dawn, but I don't always sleep the entire day. Why are you up?"

"Ginger's snoring down the hall. You'd think vampires wouldn't snore."

"I guess deviated septums are just too powerful for vampirism to cure, but I'm not complaining. At least we have clear skin and immunity to disease." I paused. "Do I snore?"

"No, but you drool a little."

My mouth dropped open, then I saw the laughter in his eyes and slugged him in the arm. "I do not!"

He let loose the laugh and took another swig of coffee, the hot temperature not seeming to bother him at all, but I guess that was just the dragon in him. He always had seemed to put out more body heat than anyone else I knew, and his blood could be used as Tabasco sauce in a pinch.

Rome came through the front door, sweating hard despite the fact it was a cool early November morning and he'd gone out running in only a sleeveless muscle shirt and track pants. He glanced at Daniel before making his way to the kitchen. "You better not have drunk all my coffee, Puff. I put the pot on for me."

"So generous of you," Daniel replied. "I left you plenty. I know you only drink it when you're clogged. You should try less meat, more vegetables."

"I eat vegetables," Rome responded while he poured himself a cup. "I had a loaded deep-fried potato with bacon, sour cream, cheese, and onions before we left last night."

"And he wonders why he can't shit," Daniel muttered.

I scrunched my nose up at both the image of what Rome had eaten the night before and the TMI about his bowel movements, or lack of movements. Thankfully, Angel chose that moment to bring Kutya in from the walk she'd taken him on and plopped down in the chair on the other side of me while Kutya trotted over to his water bowl and started lapping up the liquid like he'd spent ten days in the desert.

"We walked the trails, went to the waterfall, stared at some wolves which was kind of cool, I guess, checked out some local hotties, and now I'm bored. Can we go to Dollywood?"

"Did Kutya use the bathroom?" I asked her.

"Yup. I'm not sure what you're feeding him, but either it's way too much or it's morphing into three times its size on the way out."

I scrunched my nose again. "Did you clean up after him?"

"Hey, I didn't see any werewolves carrying bags of their poop," she said, raising her hands. "If they're not policing their poop, I'm not policing Kutya's. Besides, I'd need a crane."

I sighed and turned the laptop toward her. "You can go to Dollywood if you want, but I was thinking of going here."

Angel scrolled down the page. I'd conveniently pulled up the musical acts page, knowing if anything about the festival could pique her interest, it would be the K-Pop group. She leaned forward, suddenly enthused. "Okay, so this isn't like a for real K-Pop group, and they're all from here in America, but these guys are cute. This could be fun."

Rome stood behind Angel, coffee in hand, and looked at the screen. "I don't get y'all and this K-Pop mess. You can't even understand what they're saying."

"I can't understand half the stuff said in that rap garbage you listen to," I replied, "and what I can understand is nonsense."

"Girl, don't be dissing our culture just because your pasty white people want to bellyache over cows and pickup trucks dying in their songs. I don't get y'all's music either, but I'm not calling it garbage."

"Geese erections? Geese erections are your culture?"

His nostrils flared. "Okay, that was a crazy-ass lyric."

"My point exactly. Sugar Hill Gang was great. Run DMC, MC Lyte, Da Brat, Tupac, Nas… all good stuff, but I'll take beautifully sung lyrics in another language and cowboys mourning the loss of their favorite vehicles over songs mentioning aroused geese any day."

Rome grumbled under his breath and took a drink of coffee while he continued to check out the website. "The Jimi girls look like they might be decent," he said. "And I can always go for some festival barbecue."

I didn't bother telling him the only barbecue I'd seen mentioned was vegan. "See. We can all go and have a good time."

"Shit." Rome flattened a large hand over his gurgling stomach. "Coffee's kicking in."

"The last thing that man needs is more fried or barbecued meat," Daniel said as we watched Rome run up the stairs two steps at a time. He sounded like a rhino crashing through.

"It's vegan," I whispered.

Daniel smiled wide. "Okay, this might be fun enough to be worth it."

A few hours later, I was slathered in sunscreen and sitting in Daniel's truck, on our way to Lovefest. Angel sat between us, rambling on about what she'd learned about the upcoming BTS album online while Daniel and I had been waiting for Rome to get out of the bathroom and dragging Ginger out of bed. We'd considered leaving her to get her day sleep in since, technically, we weren't on a job, but I'd learned during our stay in Moonlight that Ginger got grouchy when left out, especially if she missed out on kicking ass. One wouldn't normally expect any ass-kicking to occur at a festival of love, but the closer we got to the festival grounds, the more my gut twisted. Then again, maybe I was just pulling negative energy off of Daniel as he sat muttering curses under his breath, annoyed by our slow progress through the line to get in.

"Come on," he growled. "Finally." The line started moving, and we rolled along behind a bright green Volkswagen Beetle, paused long enough to pay the admission fee (because contrary to popular song lyrics and sayings, love apparently did cost a thing) and crept along, following the directions given by festival workers in bright yellow vests until we eventually slid into a designated parking space in a large open field. Ginger slid her Mustang in next to us and we all got out and stretched our legs.

"Let's get some food into this one before I kill him," Ginger said, jerking her thumb over her shoulder to indicate Rome. "He wanted to stop at every place along the Parkway, then threw a hissy fit after we left the Parkway behind."

"I didn't throw a hissy fit."

"Pretty sure I saw a tear in his eye," Ginger said low enough he couldn't hear her.

"That was probably just the meat sweats," Daniel told her, rounding the truck to join our little huddle.

Ginger grinned. "Possibly. If we ever turned his big ass into one of us, I'm convinced he'd wipe out half the population in one night. He has no limits on his appetite."

"I heard that." Rome said, glaring down at her. "I'm a big man. Big men gotta eat, feed the muscles." He raised an oversized bicep and kissed the hump.

"Ugh." Ginger pushed him forward. "Let's get in there before he starts making out with his muscles."

I studied the crowd as we moved through it, taking in

the variety of people. There were older and younger, but I noticed most were women. There were quite a few who seemed to pay tribute to Woodstock in their bell bottoms and cropped peasant tops despite the cooler temperatures. Even Rome had pulled on a hoodie before venturing out. Ginger, Daniel, and I had grabbed light zippered jackets, and Angel wore a NCT-127 sweatshirt over jeans. I shook my head as I noticed a woman in a crochet bikini top. At least she'd donned a blue jean jacket, but I was pretty sure she was still going to freeze her boobs off later in the evening. I saw a willowy platinum blonde ahead of us and picked up the pace, but she turned her head to speak to a friend and my heart sank when I saw her big brown eyes and nose piercing.

"You're looking for her," Daniel said next to me.

"Is something wrong with that?"

"No, but I don't want to see you get your hopes up just to end up crushed," he replied.

"What the hell?" I heard Rome say as we reached the first set of tents and saw the huge bonfire in the center of the wide open field.

I realized then that the woman with the bikini top probably wouldn't get too cold after all. Men and women frolicked around the massive bonfire, doing some sort of weird interpretive dance to what sounded like flutes and bongos. It was like looking at what I imagined the 1960s to be in my head.

Tents and tables lined both sides of the field, stretching from where the space being used as a parking lot ended to where a stage had been erected at the other end. Vendors hawked their wares and prepared food for hungry festival-goers with bright and, I was pretty sure, substance-enhanced smiles on their faces. My gut twisted and a wave of dizziness rolled over me. I stumbled, and Daniel's hands wrapped around my shoulders the next instant.

"Are you okay?" he asked.

"Yeah, I'm fine," I assured him, and noticed Ginger

had joined him in holding onto me. Angel and Rome stared at me, concerned. I gave a dismissive wave, waving away some of the aroma of whatever I was smelling in the air in the process. I wasn't sure what patchouli smelled like, but I assumed the spicy yet floral aroma suddenly filling my nose was it. "I just got a little dizzy for a second. Must be the drugs or incense in the air."

Daniel and Ginger frowned before scenting the air. Rome and Angel looked around, searching as well.

"Smells like hippies," Daniel said, "but nothing strong enough to be bothersome."

"Drugs shouldn't have any effect on you anyway," Ginger said. "Not even if you snorted a silo of heroin."

We all stared in Ginger's direction.

"It was just an expression. I've never snorted a silo of heroin. Geez." She rolled her eyes. "Like I could even do that with my delicate little nose."

"Yeah, that's you," Rome said. "Delicate."

Ginger flipped him off. "Go find something to gnaw on."

"Gladly." He looked at me. "You all right?"

"I'm fine."

Rome rubbed his hands together and scanned the tents. "Let me see. Where to begin, where to begin…"

Ginger shook her head as we watched him walk away in search of food, then turned toward me. She released her grip on my arm. "Are you really feeling okay now?"

"Yes, I'm fine." I stepped forward then stopped short as a woman topless except for sunflower pasties skipped past us, blowing bubbles. I watched her skip (and bounce) away, leaving the pungent aroma of marijuana in her wake. "Wow. Okay."

"I think we're overdressed," Ginger said.

"Too bad," Angel and I said at the same time, neither of us having any intention of losing our shirts.

I looked over to see Daniel's reaction, but he seemed to be looking for something or someone. I tried to follow his line of sight, sure I'd see another half-naked woman, but couldn't pinpoint who or what in the crowd held his interest. "What are you looking for?"

"A big ox."

"Rome?"

"Yup. I kind of want to see his face if everything turns out vegan."

"Not everything is vegan, some is vegetarian," I said and started moving in the direction Rome had gone, although I kept my eyes peeled for Eliza. As we weaved through the people filling space between the bonfire and the tents, I noticed again how the majority of the crowd consisted of women. "Do you think it's weird there are way more women here than men? I'd think a festival that brings in half-naked women would draw in a lot of men."

"It's early. Men generally aren't the most punctual, and I'm sure people get a lot more naked after dark. The type of sleaze-bros that come to festivals to check out naked women probably wait until later when there's a better chance of finding the naked women already at least halfway drunk." Daniel's eyes narrowed as he scanned the crowd. "Hopefully, they increase security as it gets darker. I don't like this setup at all from a security standpoint."

A little smile tugged at the corners of my mouth. Daniel was probably the only man I knew who would walk into a crowd containing nearly topless women and start assessing the security rather than checking out the flesh on display. Well, maybe Rider… and I guess I could lump Rome into the not an ogler category too, I figured when we spotted him about ten feet in front of us at a vendor's tent. While he didn't appear to be interested in the security situation, the only flesh he'd seemed in search of had been pig or cow.

We reached him just in time to see him swallow a spoonful of pinto beans from a small bowl made of recycled materials and scrunch his face up in disgust. "Ugh," he said, moving the beans around in the bowl with his spoon before leaning over the vendor's table to look into the pot. "You ain't got no ham hocks in there? Some bacon, at least?"

The small sandy-haired woman serving the beans looked up at him, took a deep breath, and smoothed her red polka dot apron before adopting a pleasant smile. "We do not promote the killing of animals, sir. Our beans are flavored with nature's finest natural ingredients."

I felt the slight shaking of silent laughter in Daniel's body as he stood next to me, watching the exchange.

"Nature's finest natural ingredients, huh?" Rome shook his head and tossed the bowl into the nearby trash receptacle. "Ma'am, the finest ingredient nature gave us for seasoning beans eats shit and oinks."

Daniel's laughter became audible as the woman's jaw dropped. She stared up at Rome with her mouth gaping open, completely aghast. Hearing Daniel laughing at him, Rome turned toward us and stormed over to where we stood. "Man, what kind of place did y'all drag me to? I found a barbecue tent, and they were grilling cauliflower and calling it steak. How the hell you gonna call something a steak that ain't ever mooed a day in its life?"

Daniel bent forward, tears streaming out of his eyes as he gripped his knees.

"Laugh it up, Puff. It's all fun and games until you realize you're the closest thing to poultry I've seen here. I don't find any meat soon, I might have to shove a stick up your ass and roast you on a spit, so you just keep laughing while you can."

"You know, that's the second time I've heard someone threaten to do that to you," I told Daniel.

He straightened and wiped his eyes, still laughing. "I must be appetizing. I'm not scared, Rome. You eat me, Ginger and Danni are going to go back to The Midnight Rider and tell everyone you ate my ass, so go for it."

"Not if I just take a wing." Rome turned and pulled up short as a lanky man moving through the crowd stopped in front of him and did a weird dance move that looked like he was trying to swim up into the sky before slinking off. Rome stared after him in bewilderment for a moment before muttering a curse and started walking away. "I don't know why I let y'all bring me here. This is the whitest bunch of white mess I've ever seen."

"He might really try to cook you if we don't get a strip of bacon or something in him," I warned Daniel.

"Now, which one of us do you think would actually have better luck at cooking the other?" Daniel said.

"When will Bias Wrecker be performing?" Angel asked, already looking bored.

I looked around in search of signage or someone passing out flyers. My eyes locked with a man standing twenty feet away. He wore black pants and a dark purple long-sleeved shirt under a black vest. His hair was thick, black, and cut short, but the bangs were long enough to drape seductively over his brow. He stood in the middle of the crowd, completely alone. Focused entirely on me. I smelled the same spicy, flowery aroma I'd smelled earlier, and my vision blurred.

"Whoa." Daniel gripped one of my arms. Ginger grabbed the other. "Seriously, Danni, what's up?"

I blinked away the blurriness and looked into Daniel's concerned eyes. "What?"

"You just damn near toppled over again." He lowered his voice. "Do you need more blood?"

"No, I had Angel's just yesterday and that woman's at the gas station. I'm good until we return to The Cloud Top." I looked over at the dark-haired man, but he was gone. I shrugged out of my friends' hold. "I'm good," I assured Daniel and Ginger, before answering the question Angel had asked before the weird blurry spell. "Uh, I don't know when they'll be performing, and I haven't seen anyone handing out any programs. Maybe one of these vendors will know."

I walked over to the nearest vendor, an older snow-haired man who appeared to be selling portraits painted on location. He looked up from the blank canvas he'd just set on his easel, his eyes brightening immediately. "Hello there. Interested in sitting for a portrait?"

"No thank you, I was just…" My gaze drifted over to a large portrait on display on an easel inside the tent. In the portrait, a pretty, serene platinum blonde held a bouquet of sunflowers. One yellow bloom was tucked behind her ear as her cornflower blue eyes stared back at me. I stood in front of the easel a second later, the painting in my hands, and turned toward the older man I'd left standing just outside the tent. "When did you paint this? When did you last see my friend?"

CHAPTER FOURTEEN

"Your friend? Oh, good!" The man smiled, straightened the paintbrushes he'd been in the process of arranging, and walked over to me. "Very nice, that one. Very sensitive, kind eyes. Painting her was like painting an angel. I didn't even charge. It was a delight capturing her essence."

"Capturing her essence when?" I asked before the man could go on a lengthy spiel. He flinched a little, cluing me in to the fact I wasn't exactly exuding patience. "I'm sorry. She's kind of missing. I came here looking for her."

"Oh. Oh dear." The man worried his lip a little while, staring into the eyes he'd painted. "I saw her last when I painted that portrait about two weeks ago. I always allow my subjects to pick up their portraits when they leave the festival so they can enjoy themselves while here, not easy to do while holding a wet painting." He moved his hand in an arc, showing the other finished portraits in the tent awaiting pick-up. "She never came by. I was afraid she didn't like it."

"It's beautiful," I assured him, seeing the disappointment in his eyes, and returned the portrait to the easel. "She returned home, but disappeared again. I thought maybe she came back to the festival. You're positive you haven't seen her in a few weeks?"

"One hundred percent positive. As I said, she was a delightful subject. I wanted her to have the portrait as my gift, so I've been keeping an eye open for her." He held his hand out toward me. "I'm Hugh Wickham."

"Danni Keller." I shook his hand and waited for him to shake hands with the others and go through introductions. "Do you recall if she was with anyone when you painted her, or at any point during her time at the festival?"

His brow creased as he took a moment to think. "She was very friendly. I'd noticed her early on at the beginning of the festival. In fact, I approached her for the painting while she was dancing with a group of other women. Every time I saw her, she appeared to be mingling with new people."

"Any men?" Daniel asked.

"Yes, she got along with everyone," Hugh said.

"Did she seem romantic with any of them?" Daniel asked. "Were there any men or women who stood out as being exceptionally close to her? Anyone you think she might have left with?"

Hugh shrugged. "Every time I saw her, she was smiling and dancing. Different groups. I never saw her in any kind of romantic embraces if that's what you're asking. I saw several men approach her, women as well. She appeared so kind and inviting, such a free spirit. That type of energy draws people in naturally."

"Including you?" Daniel said, asking the question I'd wanted an answer to, but hadn't been sure how to ask without coming off accusatory.

"Pffft." Hugh gave a dismissive wave of his withered hand. "I admit being drawn to the young lady, but as an artist, I am drawn to beauty. I want to capture it, recreate it, not sully it. Despite how beautiful and full of sweetness the fair Eliza is, the girl is far too young for me. Why, I could be her grandfather."

Ginger barely suppressed a snort and turned away, hiding her struggle to hold back her laughter. I noticed Angel's lips twitch as well and shook my head. Clearly, Hugh didn't know his subject was a vampire well older than him. For all I knew, Eliza could be old enough to be *his* great-great-grandparent.

"You don't believe her to be in danger, do you?"

"All we know is she's missing," I told him, "and it's not like her to be missing. Free spirit or not, Eliza wouldn't worry friends."

"No, she didn't strike me as the type who would." He walked over to a painting of a long-haired brunette. "This young woman posed last week and hasn't returned either. She was very kind as well."

I studied the painting. The woman appeared young, with bright eyes and a smattering of freckles over her nose. "Was this another free portrait you offered, or was she a paying customer?"

"Paying customer," Hugh answered. "Pretty girl, but I don't do many free portraits. I have to survive like anyone else. I was compelled to paint your friend, but this young lady approached me."

"And she paid for the painting already?"

Hugh nodded. "I collect payment at the time of sitting, but hold the paintings until the end of the night or next day, in the case of festival goers who either stay overnight in the campground or return the following day. She never returned for it."

"Does that happen often? People paying for paintings and just not bothering to pick them up later?"

"Your friend would be the first, which is why I'd assumed maybe she wasn't impressed by it, but this young woman requested a painting and paid for it." Hugh looked out past the tent opening, scanning the crowd. "Some people stay for the whole duration of the festival so there's still a chance she may come to claim it, but I haven't seen her since I spotted her dancing around the fire just before it started to grow dark."

"You don't collect your subjects' contact information?"

"Not during events like this, unless they pay extra to have their painting shipped to their residence. Most pay in cash, as did this young woman, so I have nothing but a name and, of course, the portraits themselves, which serve as identification when being picked up."

I stared at the portraits for a moment, then scanned the rest. Other than a couple, I saw no men, only women of assorted ages. As my gaze roamed over each one, I wondered if Hugh would end up stuck with more paintings left behind. "Where's the security here?"

Hugh shrugged. "There's what you see when you enter. The folks collecting parking and entrance fees, and the ones guiding you to a parking space. There's a crew that cleans up, but I haven't really noticed any designated security since the very first night. There are a few men and women I've noticed from time to time, walking about, monitoring the crowd. I imagine they're security, but they're not in any kind of uniform. They had shirts identifying themselves as security the first night, but must have stopped wearing those. I reckon they don't want to spoil the vibe, and there really hasn't been any trouble."

"You mean to tell me that no one's gotten drunk and disorderly in a crowd this size, with women running around half naked?" Daniel asked. He shared a look with me. We both knew the effect booze had on people and had dealings with drunk men getting handsy in Gruff's and at The Midnight Rider, and those places had clear security posted.

"Not that I've noticed, but I stick to my spot here," Hugh told us, "and from what I see from here, these people just want to dance, smoke some weed, eat, and socialize. Oh, I'm sure there's some hanky-panky going on among some of 'em, but I haven't seen anything out of sorts or heard about anything bad happening. I talk to the other vendors. No one's witnessed anything to indicate security's a real issue here."

Except for two missing women, I thought, my gut twisting again. "I'd like to leave my number for you to call me if Eliza returns, or this other woman…"

"Alexis," Hugh offered the woman's name, "and I'll do that. In fact, you're free to take the portrait with you. I want Eliza to have it."

"I'll take it with me when we leave tonight, but in the meantime…" I used my cellphone to take a picture of the portrait, then sent it as a text to Daniel, Ginger, Angel, and Rome.

Hugh found a pen and handed me a sketchbook. I wrote my name and number on a blank page and thanked him for his help before stepping out of the tent. "Oh, do you know when the musical acts perform?"

"Is there a particular act you're interested in?" a deep voice asked from behind me.

I turned to see the man I'd noticed earlier. His lips turned up in the slightest hint of a smile, softening the predatory look in his dark eyes as they bore into mine from where he hovered exceedingly close to me. I felt Daniel's palm splay along the small of my back and then he stood at my side.

"Um…" I suddenly couldn't remember what he'd asked.

"Bias Wrecker," Angel answered for me. "Do you know when they go on?"

The man flicked a quick look at her before returning his gaze to me and answering. "They'll be on in about an hour. If you'd like, you can meet them."

"We can?!" Angel grabbed my arm, her short nails nearly digging into my skin in excitement.

Again, the man flicked a look her way. This time, I definitely noted his nostrils flare before he gave her a tight smile and refocused on me. He held eye contact while he reached into his vest and pulled free a card. "To the left of the stage, there's a big tree with purple blossoms as you enter the woods. You can't miss it. A small select group meets there nightly, invitation only. You have the look. Meet me there at dusk and I'll introduce you to the band."

"Thanks." Daniel plucked the card out of the man's hand.

The man's eyes flickered with anger, but he quickly schooled his features and offered another tight smile. "Yes, bring your friends, of course. Should you need anything, I am Gregori, and you are…"

"Danni," Angel said after I just stood there, holding the man's gaze, inhaling his spicy, sweet scent.

He stepped back, allowing himself enough room to bow. He grabbed my hand as he straightened and brought it to his lips. "It was a pleasure to meet you, Danni," he said before pressing his warm lips against my knuckles, sending an electric charge up my arm. "Do join us."

He released my hand, winked at Angel and nodded at Daniel while wearing a smirk, and stepped away, walking back into the crowd with his hands clasped behind his back.

"What a douche-bucket," Daniel said. "Tell me you didn't fall for that creep's bullshit?"

I shook my head and wiped the back of my hand along my jean-clad hip, not wanting anything he might have left behind to remain on my skin. "Did you smell him?"

"Wasn't my type," Daniel said dryly.

"Mine either," Ginger added. "Even if I was into men, something about him gave me the skeeves."

"I thought he was hot," Angel said.

"Stop thinking that immediately." I gave her a dark look. "Did you smell him?"

She looked at me like a few noodles had slipped out of my bowl. "No."

"He smelled sweet and spicy, like something … I don't know… herbal or magical or something. It was strong. I've gotten a few wafts of that scent since we arrived here and every time I got dizzy or my vision blurred." I ignored

Daniel's concerned look and turned toward Hugh, who'd returned to setting up his workspace. "Hugh, do you know anything about that man who just spoke to me?"

"I always assumed he was with the festival staff or the entertainment," Hugh answered. "He dresses a little uppity to be a participant, a little too fancy just to be security. I see him walking in the crowd a lot, handing cards out to young women."

"Do you ever see those women afterwards?" Daniel asked him.

Hugh twisted his mouth as he thought and shrugged. "It's hard to say. Some people stay for the whole festival, and some come in and out."

"Did you see him with Eliza at any point?" I asked, my gut churning so badly I thought I might throw up.

Hugh's brow furrowed. "I didn't, but I did notice him watching her while she sat for the portrait. I didn't think much of it because I tend to draw crowds while painting. I can't say I ever saw them speak to each other, but I got another customer to sit right after her. My attention was on my canvas."

I grabbed the card out of Daniel's hand, instantly swaying as a wave of something intoxicating rolled over me. The black foil card fluttered to the ground as Daniel grabbed me, supporting me with his body. "Danni? What the hell? You've gone white."

I watched Ginger bend and pick the card up from the grass it had fallen into while I let the dizziness leave me. "Do you feel anything?"

She looked at me, then at the card before looking back at me. "You felt something when you touched the card?"

I nodded, still leaning on Daniel for support. His body heat spilled into me and I started feeling tingly where I shouldn't be feeling tingly, so I took a deep breath, regretting it instantly as his own naturally spicy scent filled my nose. "I'm good now." I detached myself from his hold and buckled my knees. I was still shaky, but I'd rather risk falling on my ass and embarrassing myself than risk throwing myself on Daniel and embarrassing everyone.

"It's just a card," Ginger said, looking at it closer. "A black foil card with an embossed … Are those wings?"

"Yeah," Daniel said. "No text. Pretty useless business card."

"It's not a business card," Angel told us. "It's an invitation. I guess you show that to be taken backstage to meet Bias Wrecker."

"Ah, crap." I looked into her bright eyes and cursed a blue streak in my head. "Angel, I know you want to meet them, but something is wrong here. Besides, backstage is literally a big-ass field and I don't see a lot of security hanging around, so I highly doubt an invitation would be needed to meet these guys. They're not exactly BTS."

"Nobody is BTS. BTS is barely able to be on BTS's level," she said, and I supposed in her K-Pop fanatic mind she actually made sense, "but that doesn't mean these guys aren't good or don't need someone handling their private after-parties."

"I don't think they'd need a private after-party," I pointed out. "This whole place is a party."

Almost as if on cue, I heard a loud roar and we all looked toward the bonfire to see a rowdy group of men arrive, shirtless and painted in psychedelic colors. The bubble-blowing woman in pasties I'd seen before ran past us and jumped right into one's arms.

"Do these people know this is November?"

"Did you see her eyes when she went past?" Ginger replied. "I'm not sure what all drugs are in the woman's system, but I don't think girlfriend even knows this is Earth."

I glanced over at Angel and got another sinking feeling. Bringing her to the festival may have been a bad move in more ways than one. Daniel squeezed my shoulder, picking up on my worry in that way he seemed to have. "I agree something's off here, and I think that guy has something to do with it, so no one needs to follow him off into the woods at night."

"What? So I don't get to meet Bias Wrecker?"

"They're a K-Pop cover group, not the real deal," Ginger pointed out. "And they're associated with a creepy weirdo with a creepy voodoo card. Meet them and you might be meeting Satan next."

"If they're actually even associated with him," I said, going over the interaction in my mind. He'd been watching me before then, and I didn't find it a coincidence he smelled like whatever I'd been catching whiffs of since arriving at the festival. I looked around for him, but he'd disappeared. Not the easiest thing to do when you were dressed so out of sync with everyone else. He stuck out, but I got the impression he was only seen when he wanted to be seen. "He said I had the look. What look?"

"The look Bias Wrecker goes for?" Angel toed a rock with the tip of her shoe, pouting.

"No." I shook my head. "He was listening to us before he approached. He heard me ask Hugh about the musical acts and used that to approach us, but he'd already wanted to. I saw him earlier, just standing in the middle of the crowd, staring at me, and everything went blurry. I smelled him then, from completely across the field. None of you smelled anything or felt anything?"

"Other than the creeps?" Ginger shook her head. "I didn't feel or smell a thing, and I'm sure the creeps were because of the smarmy way he acted with you. He was too pretty too. It didn't fit right, if that makes any sense."

"Makes sense to me," Daniel said. "Dude looked like a douche."

I shot him a look, detecting a hint of jealousy, which wouldn't help us. "No, he looked too put together, too…" I shrugged, unable to find the right words, then I remembered the tight smile. "The façade didn't match the interior."

"Exactly." Ginger snapped her fingers and pointed.

"It's like he was something dark and dangerous, but all wrapped up in pretty paper."

"All I saw was a douchebag," Daniel muttered, taking the card from Ginger's hand to study.

"I still say he was hot," Angel said before looking up toward the stage and sighing. "Not as hot as the guys in Bias Wrecker."

"Well, he didn't set off my paranormal entity detector," Daniel said, voice low enough to keep the conversation to just us, "but if he was watching Eliza and now she's missing, we need to be watching him." He scanned the crowd, and I joined, but Gregori was nowhere to be found.

"Do you think he heard us asking about Eliza?"

"He might have," Daniel said, "but you said he was watching you before. I'm still pissed I didn't pick up on that. My dragon senses should have. The fact they didn't suggests this guy is more dangerous than he appears. He mentioned you have the look." He studied the card, thinking. "You're nowhere as sweet as you look."

"Hey." I turned toward him and frowned. "What did I do to you?"

Daniel grinned. "I'm just trying to figure out a tie between you and Eliza that could attract the same person's attention. Vampirism is the most obvious, but Ginger's a vampire too and this Gregori douchenugget didn't even look her way. Eliza's blonde and willowy. You're brunette and curvier."

I raised an eyebrow at that. "Curvier?"

Daniel made a show of craning his neck to view my backside. "Like I said, you're curvier. You both look like very sweet women though. In Eliza's case, it's actually true. You could have just fooled the dumbass."

"What?" I slugged him in the arm. "Take that back. I am sweet!"

"Then why are you abusing me?" Daniel laughed.

"No, I'm following what Daniel's saying," Ginger said.

"Danni, you do have a very sweet, innocent look. I mean, you're petite, and look at how you're dressed. Jeans, tennis shoes, and a zippered sweatshirt. Very basic. No makeup other than a little lip gloss. You have a sweet, girl-next-door vibe going on, you're not really dancing around, partying like most of the women here, you're not intoxicated, and even if Eliza is a bit of a hippie, she can't get high on anything they're selling or handing out here because she's a vampire. I can totally see that guy thinking both of you are sweet and innocent. If there's some look he's into and he had something to do with Eliza going missing, the sweet factor could be the link."

"Okay, now explain how I fooled the guy, how I'm not actually sweet."

"You're Danni the Teste Slayer. Need I say more?"

I glared at her. "You're the one who gave me that name."

"You're the one who slayed the testicles to earn it." She raised her shoulders and held her arms out as if asking who could blame her for cursing me with the moniker.

I rolled my eyes, started to point out the way Gregori had seemed irritated when Angel spoke, but realized… as young as she was, Angel didn't really look sweet. Angel had led a hard life and seen some serious shit, and the truth of that had a way of showing in a person's eyes. Shit. So despite my penchant for slicing and dicing, and knocking down trees with bitches, my friends were telling me I looked like a total sweetheart. No wonder people kept trying me.

"Saying you're not as sweet as you look isn't an insult," Daniel said.

"Yeah, it's like another superpower you have," Ginger added. "You lure prey in by looking all sweet and vulnerable… then BAM! Off with their balls."

Daniel winced. "Come on. Let's move closer to the stage. If these guys Angel wants to see are on within the hour, they should finish up before it gets dark. Let her see them and then we'll get out of here."

We moved toward the stage, and halfway to it, Rome elbowed his way past a cluster of women to meet us. He carried a cardboard food box loaded with little bags and cartons of assorted food. "What's up with the picture you sent? Was that a painting of Eliza?"

I quickly explained to him about the portrait and my idea that we'd show Eliza's portrait around to see if anyone recognized her. I also informed him what he'd missed out on with Gregori, and he frowned. "That's effed up. If there's a chance Eliza's here or that dude knows where she is, we need to find him and make him talk."

I jerked my head in Angel's direction. "We can come back, but when we're better prepared."

"You mean when you can leave me behind to be babysat," Angel said and moved ahead of us, making her way toward the stage with the stompy walk of a toddler who'd been told he couldn't take the goldfish for a walk.

"Kids," Rome muttered around a deep-fried ball of something I couldn't put a name to.

"I see you finally found something you like," Daniel said.

"I still want a rib or somethin'," Rome said with a shrug, "but I found some donuts and pie, and a booth that deep-fries okra and macaroni and stuff. I'll eat anything deep-fried. I'd eat your nuts if they were deep-fried." He punctuated his statement by popping what I now assumed was the deep-fried okra into his mouth and turned toward the stage to follow Angel.

"Remind me not to stand too close to the bonfire," Daniel whispered, and prodded me along.

I was still laughing when my cell phone vibrated from within my back pocket. I took it out, looked at the name on the screen, and sobered before thumbing the button to answer and raised the phone to my ear. "Hey, Jadyn. What the hell are Rider and Christian up to now?"

CHAPTER FIFTEEN

Jadyn's sigh was so deep I felt it in my own chest. "You severely overestimate my ability to get information out of my husband."

Now it was my turn to sigh. "He didn't tell you anything? Anything at all?"

"All I know is he's tied up in some war based on a prophecy. You're aware of what he was?"

I nodded, then realized I was speaking to her on the phone and she couldn't see me. Duh. "A vampire and an angel."

"Right. All I've been able to find out is that him being an angel that was turned into a vampire was part of some prophecy that's tied in to another prophecy that has something to do with saving the world from the ultimate evil or something. I'm not sure of the details or why he's still involved after he was cured of vampirism and gave up his angel wings, and he won't tell me anything. He says it's for my own safety and the safety of those involved."

"Yeah, I got a similar explanation as to why Rider isn't telling me shit." Daniel raised his eyebrows in question, and I shook my head in response. "He said he wouldn't be involved at all, but he discovered it on his own. Do you at least know where they're going? I know Seta is behind this."

"I would assume Baltimore since that is where Christian and his friends were before I found him again and we had to flee, but then again, he evades a lot of my questions about the vampires and others he considers his family so for all I know, maybe they fled somewhere else too."

"This is such crap. How dangerous could it be just knowing what this prophecy is?"

Jadyn was silent for a moment. When she finally spoke again, her voice carried a warning. "I'm sure you've heard of the battle that happened while you were away, and know of the losses. I was there, Danni. I saw an army of vampires, witches, and shifters you wouldn't believe. These weren't the type of shifters who work for Rider. They were rabid animals, absolute monsters, with fangs and venom. The witches made Trixell seem tame. The vampires didn't have a decent bone in their bodies, so unlike the ones you've been surrounded by. They were evil, and they were after Christian because of what he knew, what he could lead them to. I don't like not knowing what my husband is involved in any more than you do, but I understand the secrecy. Our men don't want us hunted for what we know, and they can't risk whatever they're hiding being exposed. From what I gather, they're hiding the only thing that will finally put an end to this centuries-long war."

I swallowed past the big ball that had lodged in my throat. "If Rider dies helping Seta out, I will kill her with my bare hands."

"I wouldn't make that threat," Jadyn warned me. "She's pretty lethal, and for what it's worth, she didn't ask to be part of the prophecy. None of them did. They're all trying to survive and win, to save all mankind from something really evil. Christian isn't a vampire anymore. He still has some grace, apparently, judging from what I heard about his time with you and your friends in Moonlight, but he's not a full angel. Rider is a pretty powerful vampire, but he only knows a sliver of what the prophecy entails, so I don't think they're really in the thick of anything going on. They'll make it back. Have faith, Danni."

"That would be a lot easier if I knew what they were doing, where they were. Anything."

"Ah, but then we wouldn't need faith if we already had all the answers."

"Spoken like an angel, or someone with a little angel grace of her own." I sighed. She was right. "How are things at The Midnight Rider? Is Trixell behaving?"

"I'm not really privy to the details of what happens outside of information needed for my employment here, which, as you know, is only in a serving capacity and dog whisperer." I felt her smile through the phone. "I do know that Tony cut off my access to the sublevels. He said it's a safety precaution, nothing personal. I'm now using Rider's office when I need to study. I haven't heard anything about Trixell, but security seems tighter. How's Kutya doing?"

"Oh, he's having a ball running with the pack leader."

Jadyn chuckled. "I'm glad he's fitting in."

"Hey, Jadyn…" I hesitated. It wasn't common knowledge that my sister was being held in a secret room in the sublevels. Only certain members of the security staff and others involved in the actual spell that had placed her in her current suspended state were aware, and I had no idea if Jadyn had been told about her, although I knew Christian had figured it out on his own. I did know that Rider didn't want a lot of people to know. "If anything out of the ordinary happens there at the bar, or if you hear from Christian …"

"I'll let you know. You just take care of that big pup and take care of yourself."

"Will do." We said our goodbyes, I promised to give Kutya a hug for her, and I disconnected to find Daniel watching me. "What?"

"Everything okay?"

We'd caught up to Angel and stood within the group of people clustered in front of the stage, too close to others to speak freely about prophecies and supernatural battles involving vampires, witches, and all manner of wereanimals. "Yeah. I was worried about Rider, so I tried to reach Jadyn earlier, to see if she knew anything about where he and Christian went or what exactly they're up to. Let's just say it's hard not to worry when Seta calls in favors. Her last favor ended with casualties."

"A lot of Rider's favors end with casualties too," Ginger pointed out. "It's the way of our world."

I brought up the pictures on my cell phone and opened the portrait of Eliza. "Yeah, well, let's try to prevent another. I'm going to show Eliza's picture around. If any of these people were here when she was, they might have seen her."

"I'm on Danni," Daniel told Ginger. "You watch the kid… and make sure Rome doesn't choke."

We all looked over at Rome in time to see him shove an entire ball of what must have been the deep-fried macaroni and cheese into his mouth and swallow. I wasn't entirely sure he'd bothered to chew. "I don't need you to—"

"A weird-ass douchetwat gave you a weird-ass card and invited you to meet him at some weird-ass tree at dark o'clock, and you've been having dizzy spells the whole time we've been at this weird-ass festival. I'm going wherever you go. Period. Dot. Exclamation point. End of."

"His tone could use some work," Ginger said, "but I agree with Daniel. Something is up with that guy and clearly something is up with this festival. Rider probably wouldn't want you looking into this at all, but since he didn't give us explicit instruction to stay away from this festival, we're going to let you do your Nancy Drew thing … but only if you're smart about it. Going off on your own while having dizzy spells and being watched by some creepy dude is not being smart and you know it."

"Yeah, I know, but I think it would be better for Eliza if we spread out and flashed her picture to as many people as possible."

"Not alone," Daniel said.

"Once the boy band is finished, I'm sure I can get Angel to come along with me while we show Eliza's picture," Ginger said. "Rome will come with us if his arteries don't explode first."

"Real men don't explode," Rome said, shoving in another ball of fried something-or-another.

Angel just stared up at the stage, waiting for the K-Pop group to show up. I could tell by the pinched set of her mouth she was mad, either because she felt we were treating her like a child or because she'd picked up on the fact I didn't trust her being at a festival surrounded by people with drugs to be a good thing. Maybe a mixture of both. I didn't enjoy making her feel that way, but if her being unhappy with me kept her safe, then so be it. I gave her shoulder a squeeze, told her to enjoy the show, and stepped away, Daniel right at my side.

We showed the picture to as many people as we could manage to pause in their festivities. Now that the sun was on its way down, the crowd was growing much thicker, and there were more men included in the numbers, showing Daniel had been right in his theory that they would arrive later. Most of the women were pretty drunk or high, taking away from their usefulness.

"There's still virtually no security here," Daniel said as the punk rock group that came on after Bias Wrecker had exited the stage started into their fifth song. "This is insane. With all these intoxicated people and a giant-ass bonfire in the middle of a field surrounded by trees, this is a disaster waiting to happen. I'm surprised there hasn't been a forest fire or several reported sexual assaults already."

I scanned the area, noting a lot of the vendors had started packing up when the boy band had left the stage. Hugh was already packing up his paint and brushes, which made me wonder if he hadn't seen anything bad because he retired well before things went south each night. "I had assumed the vendors stayed until the party ended, but it looks like a lot of them are leaving."

"I don't think the party ever ends here, and as for the vendors packing it up, can you blame them?" Daniel gestured toward the stage, where the lead singer of Vagi Mind Trick screeched into her microphone. "I think I preferred the K-Pop group that barely sang a lick of Korean."

"Yeah, I'm glad they were a pretty bad knockoff. It'll be less of a fight dragging Angel out of here." I looked over at where a vendor was trying to sell her last roasted ears of corn before packing it all in. "Do you need anything else to eat?"

"Nah, I'll be good until we head out. Rome doesn't know what he was missing at that barbecue grill. The cauliflower steak was pretty good."

"The cupcake stand looked really good too," I said, adding a pout, "but I'm sure Rome tried those out."

"You'll be able to eat all the cupcakes you want soon enough." Daniel slung an arm over my shoulders and led me back toward the direction of the stage. "Let's find the others. We still haven't found out anything really useful, other than a general distrust of the douchewaffle who gave you the creepo-card, and I think we're all in agreement we shouldn't follow him somewhere when we have a young human with us. Let's get Angel out of here and figure out an actual plan."

I wanted to argue, to dig my heels in and say I wasn't leaving the festival without Eliza because I knew in my gut the festival had something to do with her disappearance, but Daniel was right. I couldn't risk Angel's life in order to save Eliza's. Despite being a sweet woman who abhorred violence, when it came down to it, Eliza stood a better chance at defending herself than Angel did. I couldn't lead Angel into what might very well be a pit of vipers.

"Wait. I need to grab the painting." We cut through a throng of people covered in only body paint from the waist up and made our way to Hugh's location.

The artist looked up from the supplies he'd just finished packing and smiled. "Here to collect the painting? I was hoping you'd want it."

"Of course we want it," I assured him. "It's beautiful."

He smiled, flushing his cheeks with pink color, and walked over to the easel to grab the portrait. "I hope it finds its way to its inspiration. I saw you speaking to quite a few people. Have you discovered anything about Eliza's whereabouts?"

"Not yet," I answered. "I see you're wrapping things up for the night already. Do you usually leave before dark?"

He handed the portrait to Daniel and placed his hands on his hips. "Not always, but if I don't have anyone waiting to sit for a painting, I tend to scoot about this time. I paint better by sunlight than lantern light, and back in my day they complained about Janis Joplin screeching, but that right there…" He hooked a thumb in the stage's direction. "That's some real shrieking. I prefer when they come on last, but tonight it looks like that will be The Jimis. Those screaming Cooter Power Girls give me a headache."

"Cooter Power Girls?"

"Whatever they call themselves. I know it's got a cooter in there somewhere." He waved his hand dismissively and picked up the satchel containing his supplies. "I hope to see you again, but if not, I wish you luck finding Eliza."

I noticed the other portrait he'd been holding onto for a week still sat perched on its easel. "Still no Alexis?"

He looked over at the painting and sighed. "Still no

Alexis. I've been watching the crowd, but haven't seen her."

"Do you mind if I take a picture of the painting? I figure I can ask around about her while doing the same for Eliza."

Hugh swung his arm out toward the painting. "Be my guest. I sure hope they both just moved on to another party spot."

Me too, I thought as I took the picture, and I hoped that party spot wasn't somewhere dark and dangerous, surrounded by evil foes. "Take care, Hugh, and if you happen to see anything odd or someone else doesn't show for a pick-up, let me know. I'll be back."

Hugh frowned, but nodded. "You guys be careful now."

We assured him we would and walked back toward the direction of the stage, searching for our friends. The sky was steadily darkening, and the crowd had doubled in size, the late attendees wearing significantly fewer clothes.

"It's starting to look like Hippies Gone Wild around here," Daniel said as a man crossed paths with us. He carried a woman on his shoulders who raised her shirt, flashing her braless state. "This place is definitely going to get crazier the darker it gets."

"Maybe I should stay, go to that tree and see what that man is up to. Just imagine how many cards he's handed out."

"We haven't seen him since he handed you one," Daniel pointed out. "You could be the only one he invited today and you're not meeting him. You didn't get nearly enough day sleep. We can come back tomorrow after you've rested and drank, and we know Angel is safe back at The Cloud Top."

"But—"

"Not tonight, Danni. We're at a pretty big disadvantage here. That man didn't check off any paranormal entity boxes, but he definitely came off creepy to more than just me. You've been having dizzy spells and moments of blurred vision and we have no idea why. You're smelling something that none of us are smelling. We need to do some research and since you're obviously this man's target, we need you at your strongest if you're going anywhere near him again. We're doing this without Rider's knowledge while he's unavailable, which means we only have us. If I call Tony for backup, he will shut this thing down immediately rather than risk us fucking up and Rider killing him for allowing us to."

"But what if Eliza is wherever the man wants to lead me?"

"Judging by when she stopped answering calls on her phone, she's been missing about five nights. If she's not dead yet, we can hold off one more night." He raised his hands when I started to unleash a tirade on him. "I didn't mean for that to come out like that. I'm just saying we know the mouse smelled something possibly demonic when she disappeared from her house. If whatever took her wanted her dead, why wouldn't it do it there? It didn't kill her. It *took* her."

"Yes, and what if it's torturing her?"

"Sweetheart or not, she's still a vampire who is older than you and with age comes power. If she can't fight it off, who's to say you can? Despite her demeanor, I don't see her just taking pain and suffering. I know enough about Rider's nest to know he rescued the vampires in it from abusive sires. Eliza had no choice when it came to suffering under her sire. I can't see her willingly taking that kind of pain from someone while she actually has control of her person."

"Neither can I, which makes this even scarier. Just because whatever took her isn't her sire doesn't mean it's not powerful enough to have complete control over her."

"All the better reason to arm ourselves with more information before going in. We could end up fighting a possessed Eliza. Now ask yourself. If that happened, could you kill her?"

My mouth dropped open on a gasp. "I hadn't thought of that."

"You haven't thought of a lot. You're going entirely off of a gut feeling that this festival has something to do with her disappearance and a strong desire to rescue her. While I admire your guts and determination, I won't allow you to rush headfirst into a situation we don't know shit about." He took a deep breath and threaded his fingers through mine. "I've been trying to sense her since we got here, but I've picked up nothing. That said, I also haven't picked up whatever scent it is that you were picking up earlier. What about you?"

"There's so many people. I'm not that good at sensing, especially in crowds."

"Doesn't hurt to try, and it might help you get better at the ability. Come on." He gave my hand a squeeze.

"All right. I'll give it a try." I took a deep breath and closed my eyes. I tried to tune out the vocal noise around me, not easily done considering Vagi Mind Trick was still on stage screaming away, and cast my senses out. It was instant overload. Over a thousand heartbeats thumped away in my ears, the sound of blood gushing through veins making me feel as if I'd been pulled underwater, about to drown. My throat went dry, the knowledge of so much blood available for the taking turning me ghoulish. Down girl, I thought to myself and refocused. I wasn't sensing for blood. I was sensing for Eliza.

I tightened my hold on Daniel's hand, using the touch to keep me connected to something physical while I searched within my mind for anyone giving off any sort of non-human vibe. I sensed Daniel, but nowhere near as strongly as I should have. I felt something from inside him, a beacon, and reached out with my free hand. My fingertips glided up his chest, resting over the source of the signal, directly over his breastbone. My chest tightened in the same spot. Odd. I couldn't sense Ginger, despite knowing she was there in the crowd. I did sense something, something… old. Powerful. Dark. I inhaled, breathing it deep into my lungs and was hit with the flowery sweet, spicy scent I'd smelled earlier, and my head suddenly felt empty.

"Danni? Danni!" Something hit my cheek, and I opened my eyes to see Daniel's worried gaze hovering above me. His hand hit my cheek again. "Danni!"

I raised my hand, words failing me. It felt like cobwebs were filling space in my brain and I couldn't find words until I cleared them out of the way. I blinked several times, and that seemed to do the trick. "What happened?"

"You fainted." He lifted me up, which was when I realized he'd been bent over, having grabbed me before my body could hit the ground.

My legs were shaky, but I managed to keep upright with Daniel's support. Before I could say anything else, Ginger arrived with Angel and Rome in tow. "What happened?"

"She fainted while trying to sense Eliza."

"I've been trying to sense her, and I got nothin'" Ginger said before grabbing my arm, helping Daniel support me. "What's up, girlfriend?"

"The smell," I said. "I didn't sense Eliza. I barely sensed Daniel with him right by me. I didn't sense you, but I sensed something. Something old, something bad. Then I smelled that sweet, spicy scent again, stronger than before."

"And then it knocked you out?"

I nodded.

"Well, that's not good," Ginger said.

"We're leaving now," Daniel said, and turned me around. He prodded me forward in the direction of the parking area, one arm draped around my waist to offer support. Ginger continued to hold on to my arm.

The sun fully disappeared as we reached the cluster of vehicles and I caught the scent of flowers and spice on the cool night breeze, and knew somewhere beyond the tree line Gregori waited for me, and he wasn't going to be happy when I didn't arrive.

"Bias Wrecker wasn't really that good," Angel said as we exited the Pigeon Forge Parkway and started our ascent toward pack land, breaking the silence. "They danced like American boy bands and I don't think their Korean was even Korean. I've listened to enough K-Pop songs to know they weren't singing the Korean parts correctly."

"So you're not mad we left without venturing into the woods with Gregori?" I asked.

"No, but if Jimin and Jungkook had been there, you'd never have dragged me out." She looked over at me. "That was the closest thing to a concert I've ever been to."

I shared a look with Daniel over her head. "We need to get her to a real concert."

Daniel nodded. "Yup. Guns N' Roses is touring again."

"I want to see BTS," Angel said, "not some old guys."

"*Some old guys?*" Daniel pulled a face as if personally insulted, which, given his feelings toward older people, made sense. "How can you compare those zit-faced teenagers to the legendary Axl Rose and Slash?"

"They're not teenagers, their skin is flawless, and helllooooooo, have you seen Jimin and Jungkook?"

Daniel looked at me. "Do you believe this?"

"Hello, have you seen Jimin and Jungkook?" I batted my eyelashes.

"You're a disgrace to your realm," he muttered as we reached The Cloud Top and parked. "No one beats Axl Rose and Slash."

We got out of Daniel's truck and waited for Ginger and Rome to exit her Mustang. Rome took off ahead of us, making a beeline for the cabin.

"Headed to the kitchen?" I asked.

Ginger nodded. "I thought he was going to cry when I

told him we were headed straight here, no stops along the way. I heard a whimper every time we passed a steakhouse or burger joint."

We trekked to the cabin at a normal pace and found Grey sitting on the porch steps, Kutya lying on the ground before him. The big pup quickly got to his feet when he saw us and barreled into my legs, nearly taking me down.

"Was he a good boy?" I asked, scratching between the shepherd-mix's ears.

"We had a nice day," Grey answered as he stood and walked the few feet to meet us. "We went for a nice walk and shared a steak dinner."

"Can you hang out a while longer?" Daniel asked, and I saw something unspoken pass between him and Grey as he propped the portrait of Eliza up against the porch rail.

"As long as you need," the pack leader said, eyes shining in the moonlight.

"Good. Make sure this one doesn't leave the cabin until I get back." Daniel nodded toward me as he passed where I stood.

"Hold on. Where do you think you're going?"

Daniel let out a sigh and turned toward me. "I'm flying over the festival grounds and you're staying right here, out of harm's way."

"So it's not safe for me to be there now, but you're going back alone?"

"I'm never alone," Daniel said, "and I'm going in dragon form. My dragon senses are way sharper in that form. I can also concentrate better when I'm not keeping track of you at the same time."

"Won't you have to stay way up in the sky so people don't see you?" Angel asked. "Can you pick anything up that way?"

"As high as some of those people were, they're probably seeing dragons already." He winked at her before returning his attention to me. "I'll be careful, and I'll be quick. Once I get back, we'll all sit down and see what we can figure out about this shit and come up with a plan. If she's there, we'll find her."

He backed up a few steps, turned and jumped up once he reached wide enough space to shift shape without knocking any trees down.

"Well, he's dark blue this time," Ginger observed as Daniel took to the sky. "That should help him blend in with the night."

"So," Grey said, turning toward me. "What did I miss?"

CHAPTER SIXTEEN

Grey, Ginger, and I sat at the dining table. From where I sat, I had a clear view of Angel swimming in the infinity pool that started inside the living area of the cabin and stretched outside, and of Rome manning the grill on the back deck that ran alongside it. The man was determined to get his meat fix.

"So you think this Gregori person abducted your friend?" Grey asked, studying the painting we'd propped against the edge of the kitchen island.

"I don't know," I answered honestly, "but Lovefest was the last place we know of her going to before returning home, and apparently she'd had her portrait painted and never took it before leaving which doesn't seem like something she'd do. Eliza would never intentionally hurt someone's feelings. If someone painted her as a gift, she would take the painting."

"Unless she couldn't," Grey suggested.

"Exactly."

"The Gregori guy was definitely creepy," Ginger said, now filled in on everything I knew about Eliza's disappearance, including the information obtained from the mouse living in her home. That had gotten laughter from both of them. "But we can't be sure he had anything to do with Eliza's disappearance. Hugh saw her over a week ago and we know she was home in Louisville since then."

"And the mouse…" Grey's lips twitched "… smelled something it described as flowers over rotten eggs. You smelled something sweet and floral, but also spicy. I don't think the mouse would confuse spicy with rotten eggs."

"Yeah, I know, and I have no idea why I kept smelling it, but *only* I smelled it."

"Only you, as far as your group," Grey pointed out. "There are entities that lure prey with a scent."

"Oh, don't get started on that," Ginger said. "I'm not dealing with any more fake franky-panky bullshit."

The werewolf raised an eyebrow. "Franky-panky?"

"Frangipani," I clarified. "We had a run-in with a trickster demon recently. It passed itself off as a pontianak and lured prey with the scent of frangipani…" I waved my hand. "You know what? It's a long story. So you're saying I'm prey and that's why only I could smell the strange smell?"

"Maybe, but not necessarily." He angled his head to the side and stared at me.

"Stop staring at me unless you're going to throw out some words with it. You're creeping me out, and I've had more than enough of that for the day."

He grinned. "Sorry. I was just thinking… Do you generally pick up on scents or feelings that others don't? Do you ever see things? Get strong gut feelings?"

"The gut feelings thing rings a bell, but don't we all get those?"

"In a way, but some get them more strongly than others."

"Like Gibbs," Ginger said.

Grey turned his head in her direction. "Who?"

"Gibbs. *NCIS?* Leroy Jethro Gibbs."

"You've really developed a fixation with that show," I

told her.

"Hey, at least I'm not obsessed with the dude from the show about two dudes traveling the country to kill us."

Grey snapped his fingers and pointed at me. "*Supernatural!*"

"Yep," I said, and waited for his judgement.

"Good show."

"Really?" Ginger asked. "You too?"

"What? They're funny, and it's not like the vampires and werewolves on there are close to realistic." He grinned in response to Ginger's eye roll. "That series ending was—"

"That wasn't the series finale," I cut him off.

"Yeah, it—"

"No."

"It—"

"Uh uh." I shook my head. "They'll be back."

"They—"

"Nooooooope. That was not the series finale. Dean died all the way, and Dean doesn't die all the way, therefore that was not the series finale."

"But, they—"

"*Dean Winchester never dies all the way!*" I slammed my palm down on the table.

"Dude, you might want to let her have this before she gets upset," Ginger warned him.

"This isn't her upset?"

"No, usually when she's upset you'll find someone with missing testes in the general vicinity and she doesn't care whose testes they are, so the fact you're the pack leader won't save your ass… or your testicles."

"Good to know." Grey moved his chair away from me a little. "So, anyway, back to what I was saying. Do you get really strong gut feelings?"

"Sometimes, I guess. I mean, I've had one about this Lovefest thing since I first saw the email about it on Eliza's computer."

"And now that you've been to the festival, how strongly do you feel it has something to do with her disappearance?"

"Stronger than ever."

His eyes narrowed in thought as he studied me. "Maybe that's why you're the one smelling the mystery scent and getting the dizzy spells from it."

"Huh?"

"Wait, wait, wait." Ginger held her hands up and looked between us. "Are you saying Danni's got a little Allison Dubois in her?"

"Who?" Grey asked.

"*Medium*!"

"The psychic," I clarified when his confused expression showed he wasn't familiar with the television show or the psychic who'd inspired it. "You're suggesting I'm psychic?"

"Oh." He nodded. "Yes."

I laughed. "Sorry, but that's definitely not it."

"Being psychic isn't all winning lottery numbers and guessing what song's coming up on the radio next," he said, "and it's not always the same type of psychic ability you may have seen used by any of the witches or psychics Rider may employ. It's not always an ability someone can just turn on at will. It happens when it happens, usually to warn you of danger or help find someone in danger."

"Grey, trust me, I'm no psychic. If I had some sort of psychic warning system, I wouldn't be sitting here now because I damn sure wouldn't have walked into a bar where I'd later be attacked by a…" Oops. I allowed my voice to trail off when I couldn't come up with a quick enough change to what I was about to say.

"By an incubus?" Grey prompted. "I know what you are, Danni. I could immediately tell you weren't just a vampire the first time Rider brought you here, and when Rider asked if he could send you here this time, he told me what your other half is."

I shared a look with Ginger. "And why would he do that, considering how many times he's told me I shouldn't make the exact makeup of my hybridness known? Oh, let me guess, so you'd make sure to keep me out of trouble. And here I thought I only had three babysitters watching my every move and reporting back."

"You're under my protection while you're here, just as any wolf I send to The Midnight Rider would be under Rider's protection. That's just mutual respect among leaders, and don't worry, Danni. I gave my oath to keep your secret safe with me, as limited as the details I received of it were. I think a big part of why he told me was because of your special diet and because you're still new enough to have some hiccups. I would never send a newer member of my pack to someone else's territory unescorted by myself without warning of issues that could possibly occur. Rider simply showed me the same respect and protected you by letting me know of certain dangers to look out for."

I stewed on that information for a little, not sure why I was bothered by it. While stewing, my gaze crossed Eliza's painting, reminding me I had bigger concerns. "Okay, well, if you know I'm half vampire and half succubus, you know neither part of me is a psychic entity."

"There are psychic vampires, and psychics aren't entities. Psychic ability is a *trait*, and anyone can have it no matter their genetic makeup." He shrugged when I shot him an unconvinced look. "It's just a theory I have, and hey, it's not any more farfetched than a mouse interrogation."

"It wasn't an interrogation. It was an interview."

Ginger snorted, failing to hold back her amusement despite covering her mouth and nose with her hand, and Grey grinned. "Sorry," she said, and had the decency to flush a little pink.

"Anyway, like I said, I'm not much of a psychic if I wasn't warned not to go to the bar where an incubus was going to attack me later."

"Maybe you weren't given a psychic warning about the attack because it was meant to happen," he suggested. "Sometimes the universe puts us where we're supposed to be and sometimes it lets bad things happen to us so we can get to the good things we have in store."

"It could have given me a hint," I muttered.

"Maybe it's giving you hints now, and this time it's so you can save someone in trouble."

"Maybe. So, have any of your people been to this festival?"

"I actually never heard of it until you mentioned it," Grey answered. "We mostly stay here on pack land. When we do leave it, it's to go into town. We stay in the more touristy areas where people pay less attention to people, accustomed to people passing through. The area you said the festival was at is pretty remote, even if it's not too far from the main strip. I haven't seen or heard any advertisements for it."

"I saw one at the gas station we stopped at on our way here."

"Was it a station in a heavily populated area?" he asked.

I shook my head.

"It was in the sticks," Ginger said. "The only thing missing was a little creepy looking guy playing a banjo."

Grey seemed to consider this. "Show me the site you found."

"Sure." I jerked my head, gesturing for him to follow me, and led him to where I'd left my laptop charging on the small desk at the front window in the living area. I located the website and opened it for him.

"Thanks. Just give me a moment to look into this."

"Take your time." I glanced out the window as he took a seat at the desk and started studying the site. I looked up into the sky, looking for a dragon. Seeing none, I moved back over to the table in time to see Angel climb out of the pool and quickly wrap herself in a long terrycloth robe while Rome closed the lid on the grill and picked up a massive round platter loaded with food.

A moment later, the pair entered the cabin and Kutya's head rose from where he'd been sleeping on the couch in the living area. His nose twitched, and he jumped down to investigate the yummy new smell. "I got real food, smokin' hot," Rome announced as he carried his hefty one-platter buffet to the kitchen island and set it down carefully, managing to avoid tripping over the dog running around him. "I got pig, cow, and bird, three of the most important food groups, and I even put on some potatoes for you veggie nuts."

"All meat belongs to the same food group," Ginger told him, "and when we suggested you eat more vegetables, we were thinking of something green and leafy."

"You just can't please some people," Rome muttered. He carefully cut up some meat to drop into Kutya's bowl, then piled a plate high with pork chops and ribs for himself. Once done, he raised the plate to his nose, took a big sniff, and we all watched his eyes roll to the back of his head in a look of complete euphoria before he joined us at the table and dug in.

"I'm gonna go shower," Angel said, teeth chattering a little, and moved toward the staircase. "Try to make sure he saves me some chicken."

"I think he's pretty focused on the other animals," Ginger said, watching him eat. "Do you even chew?"

Rome just looked at her and took another big bite out of one of his pork chops.

I looked over at Grey and noted the deep frown marring his face as he navigated the website, studying it hard enough one might think he expected to be quizzed later. I could tell by the way his fingertips flew over the keyboard he was accessing other sites, doing research or sending emails. Who knew, but he was definitely looking into more than just the website itself.

He looked up, stared straight out of the window, and his body grew very still. I could see the faintest glow from his eyes for just a moment, and even though I hadn't felt a thing, I knew he'd sent a message or a calling out to his wolves, similar to how Rider communicated with his nest. Then he tapped away a bit more on the keyboard and stood up. "I need to speak with my pack for a moment. I'll be back. No one goes anywhere until I get back, and that's an order."

"Are we taking orders from him?" Rome asked around a large hunk of partially masticated meat after Grey stepped out the front door.

"While on his land? Yup," Ginger said.

"So, what's the deal with pack leaders?" I asked. "Are they way more powerful than the other wolves?"

"Grey is like the shifter version of Rider," Ginger explained. "Every wolf in his pack serves him or else. To my understanding, pack leaders usually become pack leader by killing the previous pack leader. I know Grey's pack is distanced from many of the other packs, who are way more traditional. I've heard rumors of forced breeding among some packs to keep the species from dying off. Grey isn't down with that shit. He hasn't even taken a life mate yet, which says a lot. Then again, since the Imortians came through the realm, there's probably been a lot of changes. Maybe they're more fertile than the non-Imortian shifters."

"Aren't they all Imortian though?"

"Not all shifters. I believe the non-lycan werewolves all started from an Imortian, but there have been other shifter types here long before the Imortians came. Hank's not Imortian. Neither is Tony. There's all kinds of shifters, just like there are a few different types of vampires."

"Right. Eliza gave me a little lesson on those. She said there were pranic vampires."

"Those fuckers creep me out," Rome said. "I'll take you normal bloodsuckers over those psychic freaky-deaky bastards any day. No offense."

"Some taken," I said, giving him a look before I stood and walked over to the laptop. Grey had shut down whatever sites he'd accessed. I tried to check the history, but he'd cleared that out too. Hmmm…

"What was he doing over there?"

"Well, I know he was checking out the Lovefest website, but whatever else he did will remain a mystery. He cleared the history." I looked out the window to see Grey several feet away from the cabin, his back to us as he spoke with a small group of his people. I couldn't tell what he was saying, but from the way they watched him so intently, nodding every so often, it seemed as though he were giving orders. "It's a little disconcerting."

A large rumble erupted from the dining area, and I looked over to see Rome holding his stomach. He grimaced and lifted his hulking frame from the chair. "Gotta go."

Ginger watched him jog into the downstairs bathroom, her nose wrinkled, and stood. "Nah, that right there is disconcerting. Grey was probably accessing personal email or something and just cleared out all the history as a safety precaution. I do the same thing. You never want to leave your personal biz hanging out." She picked up Rome's plate and took it to the kitchen area to clean.

I was still watching Grey from the window when Angel came back downstairs, dressed in flannel pajama bottoms and an oversized T-shirt. She paused when she caught me looking. "We're not going anywhere else tonight, are we?"

I shook my head, realizing even if I went back out, I wouldn't be taking Angel with me. "No worries. You're in for the night, unless you want to walk around. The pack land is safe. Everyone's been warned not to eat us."

"That's so not funny." She walked over to the kitchen area and grabbed a plate before selecting a piece of grilled chicken and a potato. "And it's a little too chilly out there for me. If I want to look up at the stars or something, I'll do it from the big window taking up that whole wall of our bedroom, and I'll do it from under the covers like people are supposed to."

"That's no way to enjoy nature," Ginger told her from where she stood, leaning her hip against the counter.

"I'm not a super cool vampire chick. I can freeze to death. I almost did after I climbed out of that heated pool." Angel finished prepping her food, adding salt and butter to her potato, and carried the plate over to the table.

Ginger and I joined her, even though we didn't bother with food. "You can eat if you want, Ginger. Just because I can't eat anything worth eating yet, you all don't have to go without."

"I got a quick bite while we were flashing Eliza's picture around at the festival," she replied. "I'm good. Honestly, watching Rome eat kind of kills my appetite. He actually sucks the meat off the bones. Every little scrap. I hate when people do that. Reminds me of my bloodthirsty jackass sire."

I suddenly had a flash of a vampire sucking the meat off a human thigh bone and shook my head to rid myself of the image. I decided I'd just assume she'd had a sire who'd enjoyed barbecued ribs, not of the human variety, as much as Rome did, and leave it be.

A loud grunt sounded from the bathroom, and we all pulled faces. Angel set her chicken down. "I think he needs to see a doctor."

"I think he needs to see a priest," Ginger said and crossed herself.

The front door opened. Grey and Daniel stepped in. The latter saw the platter of food and quickly went to work fixing himself a plate of meat and grabbed a baked potato. Grey helped himself to a small plate as well, after stepping over Kutya, who'd finished his meat and rolled over onto his back to snooze. We waited until they fixed their food just the way they liked it, grabbed drinks, and joined us around the table. There were only four chairs so Ginger stood, allowing Grey to take her seat.

"So, did you find out anything useful?" Grey asked as he buried the tines of his fork into his potato.

Daniel held his index finger up as he finished chewing the sizeable chunk of meat he'd bitten off the rib in his hand and swallowed. He set the rib down, wiped his hands on a napkin, and took a drink of water. "Something definitely odd is going down there. First of all, it's dark out there now and there's no police presence. Who the hell allows festivals at nights in wooded areas with great big bonfires and no police or even a firetruck in sight?"

"Yeah, that would never be allowed in Pigeon Forge," Grey agreed.

"Second, we already saw some of the people starting to get rowdy while we were there, but the freakfest part of the festival definitely gets turned up after full dark. We're talking full nudity and full-on sex."

"Like an orgy?" Grey asked, then looked over at Angel. "Is she old enough to hear this?"

"I'm eighteen!" Angel snapped. "I'm an adult."

Grey narrowed his eyes into a glare guaranteed to scare a few drops of piss out of a MMA fighter and held it until Angel muttered a shaky apology for her tone and ducked her head. Then he returned his attention to a grinning Daniel. "Like an orgy?"

"Well, not in the area we were in. There was still a lot of dancing and acting like loons around the bonfire, and there were some naked people there, mostly just topless, but deeper into the woods, there were definite orgy parties happening. I didn't see Gregori, but I got a really weird vibe."

"Was it a tingle in your dingle?" Ginger asked. "Pretty sure that always happens to skeevy guys when they watch porn."

Daniel shot her a look. "No, but your interest in my dingle tingles is noted. There was a pinkish-red haze over everything. Had it been white or gray, I would have just thought it was smoke from normal fire, but it wasn't, and it had a scent to it, like roses and sulfur."

"Like flowers and rotten eggs," I said, "like the mouse told us."

Daniel nodded. "It was heavier in the wooded areas, so thick in one spot I couldn't see through it at all."

"That has to be where Eliza is."

"Maybe," Daniel said. "At least, it's probably where we will find whoever or whatever took Eliza. All I know is I had a bad feeling flying over. I don't think we should rush into anything."

"Eliza could be in danger, and so could the other women there. How do we know the red haze you saw wasn't affecting them, making them join in orgies they wouldn't normally join in?"

"The men could be under its influence too," Daniel pointed out. "Believe me, I thought of that. I'm just saying we don't know what we could be headed into. I flew above it. What if once we're in there, it affects us too?"

"Daniel's right," Grey said, "and while you're on my land, I'm responsible for the lot of you, so that means you're only going back there with my approval."

"So that's it. You're going to prohibit us from saving our friend so you don't risk pissing off Rider?" I snapped.

"No, I'm going to go in with you and make sure you all come back out alive so I don't piss off Rider, but we're going to do it my way," he snapped back. "That means we gather some intel first and we go in at full strength. When's the last time you fed?"

I stared at him for a moment, blinking, a little surprised. Once I cleared my head, I gave him the recap of how often and from who I'd fed from recently.

"You should drink live male blood now."

Rome released a perfectly timed gasp-slash-grunt from the bathroom and I rolled my eyes. "My live male blood donor is busy trying not to die on the toilet right now."

"Didn't he already back up the upstairs toilet earlier

today?" Grey asked Daniel. "That guy needs a doctor."

"He needs a vegetable," Daniel replied, and removed a silver dagger from his boot before standing. "Just drink from me, Danni."

"No," Grey said, his gaze locked onto mine. "She can drink from me."

"She has—"

"I know what she has," Grey said, standing. "And I know what it can do, so I know what I have to do. Give me that dagger."

Daniel raised his eyebrow, but handed the dagger over. We all winced as Grey buried the blade in his thigh. Angel's fork hit her plate, then her mouth dropped open and the chunk of potato that had been inside it hit the plate too. Kutya jumped to his feet and whined, but a look from Grey kept him where he stood.

"You're sure about this?" I asked as Grey staggered back a step.

"I already put the damn dagger in my leg," Grey said from between clenched teeth. "Just drink already."

"Yeah, go on and get it done," Daniel said, "so I can tell you the rest of the bad news."

CHAPTER SEVENTEEN

"The rest of the bad news?"

"Silver dagger in my leg over here," Grey growled, motioning me closer with his hand. "Drink first, then we can talk about the bad news."

"Right. Sorry." I got up from the table and walked over to him. My face felt as if lava ran through my veins, and I knew I was blushing redder than a strawberry. It was hard not to be embarrassed when you knew a werewolf had to stab himself with a silver dagger just in case you injected him with venom that made him want to sexually assault you. At least with Rome, we didn't have to stab him unless he appeared to want to assault me. Grey, however, was a shifter and, like Daniel, could shift shape and prove himself damn hard to get under control. Unless, of course, he pinned himself with silver first.

"What the hell is wrong with you people?" Angel nearly shrieked.

I muttered a curse, noticing the fear and disbelief in her eyes as she looked between us.

"It's all right," Ginger told her. "We'll never have to do this with you because you're female, but Danni's bite can have a really bad effect on men. If necessary, the silver dagger in Grey's leg will prevent him from shifting shape and attacking her."

Angel's eyes somehow managed to grow even wider.

"The dagger's still in my leg," Grey reminded us. "And I'm a total badass and all, but the shit's silver, so it still burns like a motherfucker."

"Right. Sorry." I stepped in front of him. Ginger came around behind me, ready to pull me off of him if need be, and Daniel stood at Grey's side, a regular kitchen knife in his hand because if I did secrete venom into Grey, the silver dagger would keep him from shifting, but he'd still go for me. A stab from the kitchen knife would cause enough pain to snap his mind out of attack mode. Hopefully. Otherwise, things could go really bad, really fast.

He held his arm out; I think both of us uncomfortable with the thought of me drinking from his throat as it just seemed a lot more intimate, and I held it in both hands. I raised his wrist to my mouth, noting he didn't tremble at all, like Rome did, and lowered my fangs.

I sensed a spike of fear in the room and froze. "Angel, leave us while I drink. Go now."

Grey muttered under his breath, no doubt cursing himself out as well for being so hasty with stabbing himself with the silver dagger, but I was not going to give Angel something to have nightmares about, if I hadn't already, which I supposed was a possibility. She'd never seen me drink from anyone else.

I waited until I heard her feet patter all the way into the upstairs bedroom and the door shut behind her before I lowered my mouth and buried my fangs into Grey's wrist. While all blood had a coppery taste to it, I'd found some blood sources were more powerful than others, and some blood had tasting notes, like coffee or wine. Rider's blood was the most powerful of all, which I assumed was because of his age, strength, and the fact he was my sire. Daniel's blood also carried a strong jolt of power and was very spicy. The only other werewolf I'd drank from had been Gruff, while back in Moonlight. His blood had a hint of smoky flavor to it, almost mesquite. I expected something similar from Grey, but when his blood rolled over my tongue it hit like whiskey, and held a bit of that flavor too. It wasn't quite at the power level as Rider and Daniel's blood were, but it was still strong, far stronger of a power boost than I would have gotten from Rome's vein.

I drank a bit deeper than I would have from Rome or Angel before pulling away and licking the small wounds I'd made to help the healing process. I had to blink a few times to come up from the stupor drinking Grey's blood had caused.

"All done?" he asked.

I nodded.

He yanked the silver dagger out of his thigh, dropped it to the wooden floorboards with a clatter and no regard for the bloodstains it could cause, and shifted into his wolf form. Kutya let out a whine and walked over to the wolf. They touched noses for a moment, then Grey shifted back into his human form and rubbed Kutya's head with one of his massive hands.

Daniel picked up the dagger and walked over to the sink to run water over the blade while Ginger soaped up a rag and went to work on the blood that had transferred from it to the floorboards.

"How's the leg?" I asked, noting there was no trace of the wound left, except for the slice through Grey's jeans and the blood that had stained the fabric there.

"All good."

"I owe you a new pair of jeans."

"Nah, I'm trendier now." He winked at me. "It could be worse. I could be one of those shifters who destroys their clothes and reappears naked every time they shift. Poor assholes." He turned toward Daniel. "You were saying something about bad news?"

"Yup." Daniel dried his dagger with a dish towel and shoved it back inside his boot before straightening to lean a hip against the sink. He folded his arms, showing off muscles that had definitely grown since we'd first met. "After checking out the festival, I did a little sky patrol of the Parkway and a decent radius around The Cloud Top, just scoping things out before I returned. Pacitti's car wasn't where it clunked out, but it looks like instead of having it towed back to Louisville, it was towed to a local repair shop. I saw it in the lot of some place off the Parkway."

"Well, that's not surprising," I said. "I don't know much about cars, but that one didn't seem like something someone with a lot of money would drive, and Pacitti certainly didn't look, or for that matter, smell like a man with money. It had to be cheaper to have it towed somewhere here, or maybe he just gave up on it and left it before hitching a ride back home with a trucker and some place local was called in to tow it off the road."

"But he didn't hitch a ride with a trucker. He was there at the lot. I watched him get what looked like a travel bag out of the trunk before getting into an economy-sized rental. I followed him until he went into a cheap motel along the Parkway. The bastard is still here, and from the looks of it, still following you."

"Is this man really dangerous or just a nuisance?" Grey asked.

"He's just a nuisance for now," Daniel said, "but if he tracks Danni down, he'll make investigating possible paranormal fuckery a lot harder."

"You got rid of the tracker he used to follow us here," Ginger said, finished cleaning the floor. She threw the paper towels she'd used to dry the spot into the garbage and stood where she could look at all of us at once. "That was before we ever went to Lovefest, so he wouldn't know anything about that area. If he does happen to come here, Grey's pack has us covered."

Grey nodded. "They've been made aware already."

"I didn't mean to bring trouble to you," I said.

"Even if this man shows up here, it's not your fault," Grey assured me, "and it's not as if Rider has never helped me before. He protects my family when needed, and I protect his. Speaking of which, now that you've fed sufficiently and Daniel has returned, we need to figure out what we're up against and what we're going to do about it."

"And when," I said, "because from the sound of it, something's happening there now. We should go back tonight."

"Does she always rush headfirst into danger with half a clue and no plan whatsoever?" Grey asked Daniel.

Daniel nodded. "Pretty much, but it's not always her fault. She's kind of a magnet for trouble."

"I'm standing right here, you know."

"Yes, that's why we're being respectful and talking about you straight to your face." Daniel grinned. I stuck my tongue out at him and the grin bloomed into a smile. "Grey's right. We need a plan. We can't run in all half-cocked, and I know you didn't get much sleep at all today so even if it's night now and you have your whole vampire nighttime energy juice thing going on, you're not as strong and level-headed as you would be if you'd actually gotten a decent amount of day sleep."

"And you're emotional," Ginger pointed out. "I get it. Eliza's a sweetheart and nobody here wants to risk allowing her to suffer, but you're letting your fear of that dictate your decisions. We don't know for sure that Eliza is even there. All we know for sure is something strange is going on at that festival, and we've already decided to look into it. Now we need to figure out the smart way to do that because while we don't know for sure that Eliza is there, we do know that there is a teenager upstairs who needs you to come back safe."

I glared at her. "Low blow."

"I went there. Sue me." She shrugged.

"Since Eliza works for Rider, I assume he's looking into her disappearance," Grey said.

"He has a detective on the case, but that detective is splitting time between Eliza's disappearance, covering up the disappearance of my sister and hopefully getting Pacitti off my ass, and then doing his regular workload with the police department who of course, has no idea he's a werewolf."

Grey's eyebrows knit together. "Let me guess. Aaron Grissom?"

"Yeah. Sorry, I didn't want to presume all werewolves know each other."

"We don't, but I know Aaron and his brother. Good guys, those two. For a couple of rogues."

The toilet in the downstairs bathroom flushed and made a gurgling sound. A second later, Rome released a stream of curse words and we heard him working the plunger.

Grey shook his head and carried on. "If Aaron is working on her disappearance, he probably has information we need. I also need to know whatever Rider's tech team has found from that computer you mentioned."

"Rider's off helping a friend," I said, somehow keeping the growl that always wanted to escape me when I thought of Seta out of my voice. "Whatever it is, it's some big secret, and he left Tony in charge of everything because he'll be unreachable."

"Yes, that's his usual S.O.P., but Tony will need approval from him to share anything with me, as will Aaron." He leveled a look at me. "Rider may be unreachable to the rest of us, but as your sire, he's never unreachable to you. Even if he locks himself down so you can't track him, all you have to do is reach out through your connection and he'll hear you."

"True," Ginger said.

I studied Grey. "You know an awful lot about

vampires."

"There are a few similarities between vampire fledgling and sire, and pack and pack leader. My pack can reach me no matter what, just as you will always reach Rider, no matter how far away he is."

"She can reach him," Ginger said, "but that doesn't mean she can convince him to have Tony or Grissom hand us over the information we need. Rider sent her here to keep her out of danger while he's away."

"She can convince him," Daniel muttered, and I couldn't help but notice he sounded a little put out about it. "She can convince him to do anything."

Ginger and Grey both raised eyebrows in his direction. Maybe they noticed he sounded a little put out too. Ginger already knew Daniel had feelings that went beyond those of a normal bodyguard, but I could only imagine what Grey was thinking. Whatever he was thinking, I didn't want him thinking about it too hard. I had the distinct feeling the more people noticed something beyond protector-protectee between Daniel and me, the more Rider would want to kill him, and that was a big ol' nope for me.

"He's not going to be crazy about the idea of me going up against an unknown threat," I said.

"So make sure you tell him it's an unknown threat," Daniel said. "Tell him we're going in because lives are at stake and no one is available to take this job but us. We're here. We're in position. We have Grey going in with us, and his entire pack as our backup. Grey's already made the call to move on this."

"Yeah, and how is he going to take that?" I looked at Grey. "He sent us here for protection. This wasn't supposed to be a job."

"Grey's a leader," Ginger answered. "Just like he is. He'll respect Grey's call as a leader."

"And even if he doesn't, he's too busy to fight me on it," Grey added. "By the time we get this done with and he returns, you'll be safe. Rider and I go back a bit. He knows I wouldn't take you into any situation I didn't think you could handle."

I narrowed my eyes, smelling bullshit. "You barely know me."

"Fine, he knows I wouldn't take you into a situation I didn't feel I could confidently keep you safe in myself, and for the record, I've seen you beat the shit out of one of my wolves. I have no doubt you can hold your own in a fight."

I folded my arms and fought back a grin, mollified. "That sounds more believable. I'm glad you guys have faith in me because I still feel like I'm only going to piss him off and make him demand we return to The Midnight Rider so Tony can lock us up in some deep sublevel even we never knew existed."

"Like I said, make sure he knows we're going in against an unknown threat," Daniel said, straightening from the sink. "Make sure he knows you're going back to that festival no matter what. He knows you well enough to know you're hardheaded as hell and will run straight into danger to protect someone you care about with no regard what may happen to you. If he's truly in a situation he can't just walk away from right now, he'll make damn sure you at least get the information you need to do what you're going to do in the safest way possible."

I thought about that until my chest ached. "He'll be worried about me. I don't want him distracted while he's doing something possibly very dangerous."

"He'll be more worried if something happens and he feels your fear spike," Daniel told me. "He knows you have Ginger and me watching your back, as well as Rome. He trusts Grey and knows the man isn't going to risk dying and leaving his pack. Yeah, he'll probably be mad, definitely worried, but he's smart. He'll figure out pretty quick that you're going to go back to that festival no matter what, and he can at least give you some armor. He'll feel a lot better knowing he's done that for you."

We heard another flush, running water, and Rome rejoined us shortly after. "I'd give it at least fifteen minutes if anyone wants to go in there," he said before grabbing a plate and piling it up with ribs before plopping down at the table. He paused with a rib halfway to his mouth and looked up, sensing all of us staring at him. "What?"

"Are you seriously packing in more meat right now?" Ginger asked him. "It sounded like you just gave birth to your colon in there."

"Y'all crazy. What did I miss?" he asked before plunging his teeth into the rib meat.

"Daniel saw some weird shit going on at the festival grounds," Ginger told him, "so we're working out a plan to go back in and see if Eliza's there, or at the very least figure out what's up because we know something shady is going on and people could be in danger. Right now, we're trying to convince Danni she needs to reach out to Rider so he'll order Tony and Grissom to tell us everything they know so we have at least some intel to go off of before we swoop in to attempt to save the day."

Rome swallowed the hunk of meat he'd been working on and wiped his hands on a paper towel. "Girl, if you don't tell Rider what's happening, you can count my ass out for sure. If we go back there and something bad happens and you didn't tell him first, he's gonna kill all of us."

Daniel and Ginger nodded enthusiastically in agreement, and I looked over to see Grey doing so as well. Even Kutya nodded. I wasn't sure if he was just imitating the others or actually knew what was going on, but I tallied his nod into the vote. "Fine. I'll reach out to him, but stop nodding at me like that, and make Kutya stop doing it too. He's freaking me out."

Grey looked at the dog and Kutya instantly stopped to look up at him adoringly, and I wondered if the werewolf actually communicated with him telepathically while in human form. "Just give me some space, and a minute," I said, and walked out the front door. I took a seat in the rocking chair, ignored the pair of werewolf guards standing just outside the yard, took a deep breath full of crisp, cool mountain air, and closed my eyes.

Rider… I waited, but didn't get a response, verbal or emotional. I opened my senses to him, though, and felt his life force. Wherever he was, whatever he was doing, he was alive. *Rider… It's me. But I guess you know that. Maybe you're ignoring me. I know you're busy doing something that might be very dangerous and I don't want to bother you, so I'll be quick.*

Lovefest is here outside Sevierville, and we went today. I sensed something. There's danger there, and I think whatever it is, it has Eliza or at least knows where she is. I know you're busy and stretched thin right now. We're here. We're in place, and we have Grey's approval. I'm going back there. Grey is going with us, but we could use a little help. Grey wants to develop a plan. He needs intel, the kind of information Grissom and your tech team have been looking into. If you can okay Tony to give the order so we can have that, we can go in smarter. I know you're very busy, so if you just don't have time to reach them, I understand. We're going in though. We have to. I promise we'll be careful.

I felt something stir along our mental link as I sent my thoughts to him, a flood of emotions from rage to worry, and then just… quiet. A cold, dark quiet. And it was gone. I opened my eyes, feeling as if the line of communication between us had been snapped in half. He was gone, and he was pissed. I knew it wouldn't work. I let out a sigh and wondered how long before the order was given to lock us down or send us back to the bar with an armed guard. I looked at the thick bundles of trees surrounding the cabin and the paths leading away from it and noted not a single leaf blew. The chilly November air had frozen as if even it sensed the storm brewing and dared not make a move.

You better come back to me, I heard Rider's voice in my head clear as a bell as the wind suddenly whipped through, causing the trees to shudder. *Tell Tony 'Danni Protocol.' And tell Grey he's a dead man if anything happens to you. The others already know what I'll do to them.*

Then he was gone.

I quickly rose from the rocker and ran into the cabin. I came to a dead stop just inside the door as the others stared at me expectantly.

"What did he say?" Grey asked, standing in the same spot I'd left him. "Is he giving us the intel?"

"I…" I frowned. "I'm actually not sure. He said if anything happens to me, you're a dead man, and that the others already know this."

They all nodded and made murmurs indicating this was all general knowledge.

"He told me to tell Tony … Danni Protocol," I continued, and shrugged. "Then he broke the connection and I really don't think I should pester him by asking what that is."

"Danni *Protocol*," Daniel repeated and shook his shaggy head as he withdrew his cell phone from his pocket. "Who the hell does he think he is, Iron Man?"

"You've never heard of it?"

"Nope." Daniel hit a key and set the phone on the kitchen island with a hand gesture indicating we should all gather around it. The phone rang two times, and I heard the unmistakable sound of Tony's voice barking out a "What?" as we all surrounded the kitchen island. Daniel looked at me and pointed, telling me I was on.

"Tony, it's me, Danni."

"Ah, shit," I heard Tony mutter. "The only thing worse than seeing Daniel's number on the caller ID is finding out it's you on the other end."

"Uh, gee thanks."

"No offense, but what's the clusterfuck this time?"

I glared at Daniel, knowing that was the word he tended to use when speaking of me and various situations I'd gotten into. He fought a grin unsuccessfully. "Did it ever cross your mind that I might not be in a situation?"

I was answered by complete silence, and I was pretty

sure that wasn't going to change unless I broke it myself. "Fine, so there's a situation."

"No shit. State your clusterfuck so I can get back to the billion other things I have on my plate right now."

I took a slow, deep breath through my nose, cooling my jets before I gave in to the urge to call Tony a few choice names. Usually I seemed to amuse him, but the shifter was being a surly asshole at the moment, so in the end I decided not to poke the bear, or tiger, in this case. "Rider told me to tell you 'Danni Protocol.'"

I heard a small gasp followed by more silence. I looked up to see everyone frowning at the phone.

"Tony?"

"What did you just say?" His voice came out as a near whisper.

"Danni Protocol," I repeated. "That's all he said. He told me to tell you 'Danni Protocol.' Do you know what that means?"

"Yes," he said after another moment of silence.

"Well, what does it mean?"

More silence, a rustle of movement, and a deep sigh of defeat. "It means hell has frozen over and the universe is probably going to fuck us all up the ass with a hot poker."

CHAPTER EIGHTEEN

"Uh… could you be more specific?" Daniel asked. "Except for the hot poker up the ass thing. I'd rather not have any further details on that, if you don't mind."

"Same here," Rome said, gnawing on a pork chop. "I'm trying to eat and now you got me seeing smoking buttholes in my head. Throws a man off his appetite."

As Rome took another big bite out of his pork chop, we saw his appetite was alive and well. I shook my head and decided to get to the point. "Just tell us what it is, Tony. No jokes or cute little commentary this time. What is the Danni Protocol?"

"Give Danni everything."

We all stared at each other in stunned silence. Well, the glob of meat falling out of Rome's open maw made a little noise as it hit the floor and Kutya quickly gobbled it up. But otherwise, yeah, we were stunned stupid.

"Come again," I said. "Give me everything?"

"What do you mean by give Danni everything?" Ginger asked, leaning closer to the phone.

"Give Danni everything," Tony repeated. "That's the protocol. Whatever you want, Danni, you got it. I'm still running things while Rider's away, but you have complete access to anything you want. You want weapons, you got weapons. You want money, all you have to do is tell me cash or credit. If you want access to computer files, you got them. The tech team is at your disposal, as is any associate Rider works with." He swallowed audibly. "Please be gentle."

I rolled my eyes. "That's all? What is so end of the world about that?"

"Full access to you? Do you have any idea what you're capable of? Do I need to remind you of your greatest hits?"

"Tony, you keep talking so sweet about me like this, you're going to be my greatest hit when I get back to The Midnight Rider," I growled, and ignored Daniel's laugh. "Tell the tech team to send everything they have on Eliza and get in touch with Detective Grissom. Tell him to contact us as soon as possible with everything he has on her too."

"That's it?" he asked, sounding surprised. "That's all you want?"

I started to say yes, but got hit with a gut feeling so hard I actually wondered if Grey knew what he was talking about earlier when he'd suggested my gut had a little psychic mojo to it. "And send me everything on the missing women with sweet blood."

"Sure." I heard him tapping on a keyboard and knew he was in Rider's office. A moment later, I started hearing dings from my laptop as email alerts started coming in. Grey raised his eyebrows, asking permission, and I gave it to him with a nod. He wasted no time parking himself in the desk chair to download files. "I just sent what all is on Rider's computer, and I've sent a request to the tech team. I'll call Grissom as soon as we hang up and then run downstairs to follow up with the tech team directly. Anything else?"

"Hmmm… I think that will do it for now, Tony, but you really might want to start practicing the apology you owe me when I get back. I haven't sliced anything off a man recently and what can I say? I'm getting the itch." I pushed the button to hang up on him.

Daniel laughed as he picked the phone up and slid it into his jeans pocket. Ginger smiled approvingly, and Rome just shook his head and muttered about the evils of women around a half-chewed chunk of chicken meat.

"Has he always eaten like this?" I asked.

"Yup," Daniel answered. "You mostly only see him on duty at the bar, but his fridge is loaded with meat and he's constantly shoveling it in. The only thing he eats that isn't meat is ice cream, eggs, and potato chips."

"Ooh, we got any ice cream?" Rome asked, not bothering to swallow first.

"You don't need any dairy, you overgrown fart-bag," Daniel snapped, and grabbed a pork chop. His ass rang, and he used his free hand to take his phone out of his back pocket. "It's Grissom," he said, reading the name on the screen, and raised the phone to his ear. "Hey, man. Yeah, that's right. Yeah, give me everything."

I watched Daniel toss the pork chop back onto the platter, wipe his hand on his jeans, and walk over to the desk to grab a pen and pad of paper. Grey's brow furrowed as he studied something on the laptop screen, and Ginger peered over his shoulder, tracking what he was doing. And Rome… Rome kept on eating.

I looked over at the plate of food Angel had abandoned, complete with the chunk of potato that had fallen from her mouth when Grey had stabbed himself and felt a hitch in the area of my heart that registered guilt. As grown as she thought she was, and no matter what she'd been through on the street or in the households of pretty sucky relatives, she was still just an eighteen-year-old kid. With everyone busy gathering information or in Rome's case, stuffing their face, I moved to the cabinet to grab a clean plate, planning on loading up another for Angel, but I noticed a package of chocolate chip cookies and grabbed those instead.

"Hey, I didn't know we had cookies in there," Rome said, again not bothering to swallow first.

"I'm taking these to Angel." I grabbed a glass and opened the refrigerator, where I found an unopened carton of milk. "You should drink some water," I told him as I poured out a glass of milk to go with Angel's cookies, "and seriously, eat something green and leafy, or some beans. You need fiber and water."

"I tried to eat beans, remember? They didn't have no meat in 'em. No meat means no flavor."

I honestly couldn't disagree with him there. Anybody who knew anything at all about cooking knew you had to put a ham hock in your beans, or at least some bacon if you didn't have that. "They still would have been good for you."

"Real men eat meat."

Giving up on getting through to the big, chronically constipated lug, I finished what I was doing and carried the milk and cookies upstairs. The bedroom door was closed, so I knocked. "It's Danni. Can I come in?"

There was a pause. "Yeah. Sure."

I shoved the cookie package under my arm, freeing my hand, and turned the knob, relieved to find she hadn't locked herself in. Hopefully that meant she wasn't terrified after what she'd witnessed. I transferred the cookies back to my free hand and showed them and the glass of milk to her, presenting them as an offering. "You didn't eat all your dinner, so I brought you these. I found the cookies in the cabinet. They stocked the cabin pretty good. You should take a look around and see what all is there."

"While I'm here all alone tomorrow night while you all go back to the festival and do whatever it is you do?" She looked up from the screen she'd been focused on. She was sitting cross-legged on the bed, her cell phone in her lap. "I know the drill. Stay inside. Keep the doors and windows locked so the boogie monsters don't get me."

I set the milk and the package of cookies on the nightstand and sat on the edge of the bed. "I guess what you saw tonight was a little monsterish, huh?"

She stared at me, seeming to mull over the words in her head before she spoke them. Finally, she reached over to the nightstand and grabbed the package of cookies. I waited while she tore open the wrapper, grabbed a cookie and shoved it into her mouth. "Quality cookies," she mumbled, and swallowed. "I like the soft-baked."

"I always did too. In fact, I can't wait to eat more of them."

She looked down at the package in her hand, then back up at me. "I don't have to eat these right now."

"Eat. I hate when people feel like they have to deprive themselves because of my weak stomach. Besides, I have it on good authority I'll have centuries ahead of me to spend eating cookies once my stomach gets with the program." I smiled at her. "You know you can talk to me, right?"

She nodded.

"Are you freaked out about what happened downstairs?"

"I'm not freaked out that you drink blood," she answered. "Obviously. The werewolf dude stabbing himself in the leg with a silver dagger was a shock, but I wouldn't say it freaked me out."

"Something did. Your fear spiked so high I actually felt it. What scared you if not the blood-drinking or the way Grey stabbed himself?"

Angel popped another cookie into her mouth, and I got the sense she did so to buy herself time to think about how to respond, so I let her. As long as she wasn't running away from me or trying to escape, I could give her all the time she needed.

She chewed, swallowed, then grabbed the glass of milk off the nightstand and took a drink before replacing it. She straightened back up and took a breath, her gaze locked onto me. "Why did he need to stab himself, and why did

Daniel and Ginger crowd the two of you like that even after he did it?"

"Oh." I looked away for a moment before meeting her eyes again, knowing if I didn't meet her eyes while answering her questions, she wouldn't trust me. "My bite affects men differently than it affects women. That was all just a precaution."

"That's the same lame-ass answer I got downstairs. How does it affect them? And why is it you have to alternate live and bagged blood, and male and female?"

I sighed. "Look, you can trust me, but when it comes to the specifics of some things, I can't give you all the details. It has nothing to do with trust, and everything to do with protection. The less you know about some things, the better." Oh great. I sounded like Rider.

"If you want me to live in an apartment you have full access to and travel with you all, I need to know what I'm into. Exactly what I'm into. Ginger doesn't seem to have the issues you have, and I've heard things about you."

Great. I knew we shouldn't have let her hang around Gruff's back in West Virginia. Shifters could be such gossips. "Ginger's been a vampire longer than I have. Her stomach has settled."

"She still needs blood though, even if she can eat regular food," Angel said, "and it doesn't seem she has to put as much thought into where she gets her blood like you do. It doesn't seem very likely that new vampires would need to be so selective. It seems like it would be really hard for the species to survive if you all had to start off as such picky drinkers. Plus, I heard what Grey said. He said he knew what you had and what it could do, which was why he had to do what he had to do. You're not just a normal vampire, are you?"

Shit. I picked at a thread that had come loose from the inseam of my jeans. "No, I'm not just a normal vampire," I admitted, not seeing much else of a choice, not after what Grey had said in front of her. "But Rider is my dominant sire, so my vampire side is stronger."

"Your vampire… *side*," she said slowly, blinking a little while she stared at me. "And if you have a dominant sire, then you have a non-dominant sire, so you were… You're not just a different type of vampire. You were turned by two different entities. You're like Michael from *Underworld*."

I couldn't help but grin. Leave it to Angel to find a vampire movie to explain me. "Yes. In a way, I suppose I am like Michael. I was bitten by two different types of men and I am a rare hybrid. Actually, I'm the only hybrid of my type that Rider has ever known of, or anyone he knows has ever heard of, for that matter."

"And what type of hybrid are you?" I saw genuine anger in her eyes when I remained silent. "I let you drink from me. I think I should know what I'm feeding."

I flinched so hard I actually recoiled a little. "You're feeding *me*," I said, "and I'm the same person I've always been since you met me."

Her face flooded with pink as she looked away, but she steeled her shoulders and locked her stare on me again. "I didn't mean that to sound so hurtful. You gave me a home and you've taken care of me, but if anything happened, let's just say it wouldn't be the first time I was taken in by someone who seemed to care about me, only to have things take a really bad turn later. I need to know exactly who I'm dealing with. It's a lesson I've learned the hard way and I'm really trying to avoid making the same mistakes I've made before."

I closed my eyes and nodded. She was right. The girl had been through so much in her life already, and most of it at the hands of so-called family members who she should have been able to trust to protect her, but all she'd gotten from them was lies, abuse, and manipulation. I couldn't expect her to just put her blind faith in me. I was lucky enough she'd decided to become my blood donor in the first place. Expecting her to just take my word she could trust me without giving her any details was going too far.

"Look, I haven't lied to you. I've just kept some things from you because… well, because certain things about me sound a lot worse than they are. I don't want you to think I'm a horrible person just because of a label. I didn't ask to be what I am. I was attacked, and I was turned. But before that turn could be completed, Rider bit me in an effort to turn me into a vampire instead, a far better option than becoming what the first bastard was. I kind of got stuck at half one, half the other, but I gave my loyalty to Rider. He's my true sire, which makes my vampire side dominant."

Angel's eyes narrowed. "But your other half is still there, and there's something weird with your bite when it comes to drinking from men, but Grey said you needed live male blood, so you have to drink from men. You can't just drink from me, and you don't even like drinking from me. I notice how you hesitate before biting my wrist. I used to think it was just because you thought I was scared, but now I'm thinking there's more to it."

Of course I'd have to go and find a smarty-pants donor. "You're right. My other half has an aversion to drinking from females. That aversion is part of why I needed you as my donor. I need live female blood, live male blood, and bagged blood of both types to balance things out inside me. It keeps the side I don't want calling the shots mellowed out."

"And what side is that?" She folded her arms and hit me with a look that told me just how tired she'd grown of waiting for this information. "I have a right to know."

"Yeah, I guess you do," I agreed, "but this is information I've been warned not to make well-known. You've been with me long enough to have met a few other types of paranormal entities, but there's a ton more out there and not all are friends. Some could take advantage of me if they knew what I was."

"I thought you all kind of sensed what each other were anyway."

"I'm a hybrid, so not a lot of paranormals have been able to get a good sense of what I am. They sense the vampire in me since that's dominant, and they can tell something's off with me, but they have trouble figuring out what my other half is. We'd like to keep it that way, for safety."

"I get it. It's top secret. I won't tell, so spill it. What are you?"

I took a deep breath and made sure I was focused on the loose thread on my jeans again before answering, not really wanting to see the judgment or straight-up revulsion I feared would flash through Angel's eyes once she discovered what I truly was, and said, "I was bitten first by an incubus, so I am half succubus."

There was a moment where I only heard Angel breathing. Her heart hiccupped a little but quickly evened back out to a normal rate, so at least she wasn't scared. Of course, it was a little hard to hear it at all over the sound of my own racing heartbeat roaring in my ears. I was jittery as hell.

"So do you crawl into men's rooms at night and do the nasty on them while they sleep?"

"What?" I looked up at her. "No."

"Oh, okay." She held her hands up, palms out, as if to tell me to calm down. "I thought that's what they did. I thought succubusses were like demons that steal men's sperm and go have litters of little baby imps or something."

"Succubi," I corrected her grammar as I felt my eyes grow wide. "And no. I do not steal men's sperm. Well…"

"Well, what?" Now her eyes went wide. She snapped her fingers and pointed at me. "Your bite. You said your bite has an effect on men. You suck out their sperm with your—"

"Ew, no, no, no!" I waved my hands around, trying to

dispel the image her words had caused to violate my mind. "You saw me about to drop fang into Grey's wrist. How would I suck sperm out of… you know what, we're going to put *suck sperm* on our list of phrases to never utter again, all right?" I took a deep breath in through my nose and exhaled it slowly through my mouth, suddenly feeling the need to regather my wits. "Sometimes my succubus side tries to be dominant, and when that happens, I produce venom which can be injected into a man when I drink from him. The venom doesn't kill the man. It just makes him very horny, to the point he would automatically try to have sex with me, stopping at nothing, not even rape. If I gave in to my succubus side, I would allow it and I would…"

"You would what?" Angel prompted, leaning forward.

"Okay, so I would pretty much suck out his soul, but remember, I'm mostly vampire!"

"Holy shit." She sat back, mouth hung wide open.

"That's why I'm careful about drinking straight from men. Rider is powerful enough to handle the venom if it's there, but for others, we do like we did downstairs. Succubi hate estrogen so Ginger is always ready to grab me and basically wrap me in an estrogen cocoon, not to mention knock my ass out if needed, and Daniel was in place to stab Grey if he got all sex-crazed because stabbing him would hopefully snap him out of it."

Angel blinked a few times, then shook her head. "Okay, but why did Grey stab himself in the leg first?"

"That blade was pure silver. It would keep him from shifting shape, which could make it harder for Daniel to stop him without doing serious damage to him."

"Oh yeah, right. That makes sense." Her brow knit together. "Is the succubus thing why you and Daniel are always so …"

"So what?" My voice may have come out a little more terrified than I'd intended.

"You know."

"No, I don't know."

"I thought you two were like… friends with benefits, or something."

"What? No! There are no benefits. None." I stood and made a big X with my forearms before sweeping them wide to either side. "None. At. All. Zilch."

"Okay, okay. I was just thinking… I thought there was something there."

"Yeah, it's called friendship." I folded my arms. "Anyway, my special variety of blood diet is in place to keep succubus flare-ups from happening, so even though we're extra careful when I feed straight from a man, the venom usually isn't even there. So, are we good now? Do you feel safe again?"

"Yeah, I guess I'm super safe from whatever succubus problems you have if that side doesn't like girls, and you don't, like, sprout wings or really long fangs or anything?"

"No."

"That's good. You don't lay eggs?"

"Why the hell would I lay eggs?"

"I don't know what succubusses do!"

"Succubi."

"Suck-u-whatever." She rolled her eyes. "Okay, so … it's not that bad. I mean, it's not like you're not doing what's needed to control your powers."

"My powers?"

"Yeah, I mean, you basically have Super-Ho powers."

"Clearly, I have allowed you to spend entirely too much time with Ginger. You've started sharing the same brain cells." I pinched the bridge of my nose and huffed out a sigh. "All right, so now that we're all good here, I'm going to get back downstairs. We just received a lot of information on Eliza so I'm going to check in with the others to see what they've discovered because we're definitely going back to that Lovefest thing to see what it has to do with her disappearance."

"Oh, yeah!" Angel grabbed her phone and unlocked it.

"I got distracted by cookies and secrets, but I meant to tell you I found something weird. Do you remember how something sounded really off about that K-Pop group?"

"I remember they weren't that great."

"Right, well, I thought part of that was because they weren't pronouncing the Korean lyrics correctly, but I did some Googling into them. Outside of the Lovefest website, they barely register anywhere on the internet."

I sat back down on the bed and looked over her shoulder at the Google search that had turned up very little on Bias Wrecker. "Well, they were obviously some newly formed group of Asian-American guys trying to take advantage of BTS's world domination. Lovefest might be the only gig they've had so far."

"I hope it is because I looked into the lyrics. I had recorded them in case they were any good, so I ran what they were singing through some sites. The Korean parts not sounding right wasn't just because they weren't pronouncing those parts correctly. They weren't speaking Korean at all through a lot of it."

I frowned. "So, were they singing in Japanese or Chinese? Some groups do that."

"Some groups do that, but I don't think any groups do this." She pulled up a site with a black background and blood-red symbols. "When I sounded out what they were saying, I hit some really weird sites. According to this, Bias Wrecker was singing in some really crazy, ancient demonic language."

"Ancient, demonic … say what now?"

CHAPTER NINETEEN

"So… you're saying these K-Pop groups are out here summoning demons," Rome said around a mouthful of chocolate chip ice cream, "and you got the nerve to insult my music."

"Geese erections," I reminded him.

"One dumb lyric and you're going to beat me to death with it."

"That whole song was one dumb lyric, and I wanted to beat myself to death rather than hear it."

"And these guys are not a K-Pop group," Angel snapped. "They're a K-Pop lie! They've besmirched the sanctity of K-Pop!"

"Everyone settle down," Grey said, his tone suggesting we'd better listen. He'd given up the desk chair to Angel so she could pull up the lyrics she'd found on the laptop's bigger screen, and now stood directly behind her, arms folded, jaw locked. Daniel and Ginger flanked him, observing. I'd seen enough, so I moved to the kitchen to refill Kutya's water bowl while Rome sat at the dining table working through a mountain of ice cream.

"Whatever," Rome said. "I told y'all before that you shouldn't be listening to that music when you can't understand any of it. They could have all been calling up demons all this time and you wouldn't know it."

"I'm pretty sure Korea would have caught on that they weren't speaking Korean." Angel gave him a death glare followed by the mother of all eye rolls as she stood and walked over to the table. "This is a *fake* group. A fraud!"

"I'm just sayin' that—"

"I think you've said enough," I cut him off. "There's nothing wrong with real K-Pop, so leave Angel alone and go back to shoving food into your face until you explode."

Rome stabbed his spoon into the mound of ice cream filling the bowl before him. "Man, I'm getting tired of all the comments on the way I eat. Daniel eats a lot too, and nobody's saying anything about how much he eats. Why aren't y'all giving him any shit about eating a lot?"

"He doesn't suck every single tiny scrap of meat off the bone," Ginger said.

"He hasn't backed up our toilets," I added.

"Yeah, and they know I have to eat a lot because I'm a badass fire-breathing dragon," Daniel threw in, looking over at Rome. "And you're just a big-ass fire-farting jackass."

"Man, I've had enough of you." Rome stood from the table, and Daniel turned to face him, shoulders squared.

"Do I need to take you two idiots outside and clunk your heads together?" Grey asked, glaring at both of them.

"All you'll do is dent them," Ginger said, "just like any other set of empty cans."

Rome and Daniel turned dark looks her way. She flipped them off with a wink, and Daniel grinned. Rome, however, was truly mad. I had a feeling most of his bad mood came from his stomach and what he was filling it to capacity with.

"We've got a really fucked up situation here and I don't have time for anyone's bullshit," Grey continued. "If anyone has a tick up their ass, save it for when we find what we need to kill, then by all means, rage out on them.

Understood?"

"Yes, sir," Daniel said, fighting hard not to smile.

"Yeah," Rome said and plopped back down into his chair, the wood creaking under him.

Grey shook his head as Rome picked up the spoon and scooped up a massive glob of ice cream. "Seriously, son. Your friends are right. Eat some damn greens until you can shit without wrecking the plumbing."

Rome growled out some unsavory words under his breath as he lurched up from the chair, dumped the bowl of ice cream into the sink and took off out the front door, slamming it behind him.

"He's okay," Daniel announced. "He's just a delicate, sensitive sort of flower."

"So were you back at the gas station," Ginger told him. "Why, I even think I saw a tear in your eye when you thought those big rednecks were going to shoot him. It touched my heart."

"Huh, I'm surprised to hear that," Daniel said, smiling wide, "given how entranced you were with his junk."

"Hey, it was some pretty massive junk," Ginger said in her defense.

"Ew!" Angel covered her ears.

Grey's shoulders sagged on a deep sigh. "Suddenly it's all rushing back to me, just how delighted I was when you packed your bags and left out of here to go work for Rider. I don't know why I let him send your scaly ass back here. You bring a headache with you every damn time."

"How was any of this my fault? I told the overgrown steroid to eat a vegetable every once in a while. It's not my fault he can't shit."

"Can we just get back to the demon summoning thing?" I suggested, moving back over to the desk to rejoin the group.

"Gladly," Grey said, and sat back in the chair, folding his arms over his chest. "I've never seen anything like this. It's definitely old so I can reach out to some witches and wiccans I know and see if they can make heads or tails out of it, but as strange as the wording is, it does sound like it's calling forth some sort of being."

"Or strengthening one," Daniel suggested, pointing at the screen. "A lot of these Reddit users have mentioned that. Since we didn't actually notice any shift in the atmosphere and nothing crazy appeared on stage with them when they were singing all this, maybe they were just giving power to something already there."

"Something that was back in the woods where you saw the thickest mass of red smoke," I said before addressing Grey. "You think wiccans could actually help with this? I thought they were like the Glindas of witch stuff."

They all looked at me.

"Glinda. You know, Glinda the Good Witch."

Daniel grinned, and I might have seen a hint of a smile at the corners of Grey's mouth before he swung his head full of honey-colored hair back around. "They study the darkness enough to know how to protect against it," he advised. "They might be able to help. The real question is, is the boy band human or a bunch of demons?"

"I didn't get any kind of non-human vibe from them," Daniel said.

"They could be minions," Grey suggested.

"Minions?" Daniel's voice raised an octave.

"Dude, you have got to get a grip," Angel told him. "Grey's talking about demonic minions, not the little animated yellow guys you think are going to eat you in your sleep."

"I don't think those little movie guys are going to eat me in my sleep," Daniel mumbled. "I think my Twinkies are going to sprout eyes, come alive in my stomach, and eat their way out of me."

Grey's jaw dropped open as he blinked up at Daniel. "Are you shitting me?"

"Hey, I had a very realistic nightmare!"

Grey rubbed his forehead, no doubt feeling the

headache crank up inside his lobe, and moved on. "You're sure none of the other entertainment did any kind of demonic summoning?"

"If they did, it wasn't vocally," Daniel said. "Of course, there was a group we didn't see perform, but they were a Jimi Hendrix cover band. I can't really see anyone squeezing that stuff into a Hendrix song. The K-Pop group was able to because it was just close enough to not be noticed by anyone who doesn't speak Korean."

"I noticed it," Angel reminded him.

"You noticed it sounded off, but you didn't notice it was an entirely different language." Daniel scratched his head. "Ya know, this might just be the start of their whole plan. That group could go all over doing that. K-Pop is huge right now. I mean, it's everywhere. I poured a bowl of Apple Jacks the other day and I'm pretty sure the prize inside was an actual K-Pop dude. I mean, they're *everywhere*."

Ginger and I snorted while Angel rolled her eyes. "You're an idiot," she told him.

"I'm serious. I poured out my cereal and a little pink-haired Korean guy in skinny jeans fell out on the counter and started jopping."

Angel's lips twitched and soon her annoyed face disappeared in laughter. "You're so stupid."

"He is that," Grey agreed, "but he has a point. The Lovefest site already showed us this festival travels. It's been stopped just outside of Sevierville for a while now, but it'll be moving on soon."

"Not if we have anything to say about it," I said.

"Well, what we don't know yet is whether we need to shut down the whole festival or just this group summoning demons."

"Or one really big demon if what they're actually doing is giving it power," Daniel said.

"You mean... if they're its *minions*," Ginger said, incapable of skipping an opportunity to tease Daniel. She chuckled evilly as he shuddered, then continued. "We can't forget about that weirdo who gave Danni his card. Gregori. He didn't pass the vibe check with any of us, except maybe Angel."

"Hey."

"What? You were all googly-eyed over him," Ginger said.

"I was googly-eyed over the fact he told us he could introduce us to a cute K-Pop group, or what I thought was a cute K-Pop group."

Ginger raised an eyebrow and looked over at me before rolling her eyes, but chose to not push the issue.

"We definitely need to know why he approached Danni out of all the other women he could have approached there," Daniel said. "He was completely fixated on her, and acted all irritated when any of us interrupted his failed seduction attempt."

"Failed seduction attempt?"

"Oh, he was definitely trying to put the ol' seduction eye trance on you," Daniel said.

"It was part of what made him so creepy," Ginger said. "The man was way too confident, just oily with it." She shrugged when we all looked at her, foreheads scrunched. "Yes, I said oily. The man was greasy, slimy, *oily*, like… like a slithery snake or something."

I received a quick flash, an image of a red-eyed snake, so strong it rocked me back on my heels. I grabbed my head and gasped for breath as it left me to be replaced by a stream of women's faces and red dots that expanded into red smoke.

"Danni!"

I opened my eyes, not even recalling having closed them in the first place, and placed my hand over the one Daniel had clamped onto my bicep. "I'm fine, Daniel."

"You don't look fine. You look beyond white."

"Really? Okay, then go grab me a pumpkin spice latte." I winked to let him know I was okay, patted his hand before shrugging it off, and moved over to the desk, visions of red dots dancing in my head. "Move, Grey."

The pack leader, no doubt not used to being on the receiving end of orders, raised his eyebrows, but didn't put up a fight. The moment his ass left the chair, I dropped mine into it and went back to my email screen, opening the one with the attachment I needed.

"Yeah, I didn't know what that was so I didn't open it yet," Grey said, leaning down to watch over my shoulder.

"I'm not quite ready to say you were right about the psychic thing, but when Ginger said Gregori was snake-like, it clicked something in my brain." I opened the program Rider had shown me in his office and felt my stomach plummet. The map with red dots in North Carolina, Virginia, and Kentucky had a lot more red dots, and they'd spread into Georgia, Alabama, and Mississippi.

"What am I looking at?" Grey asked.

"This is a database that tracks the disappearances of women with sweet blood."

"Rider figured out a way to track incubi."

"Yes. The last time I saw this, there were only three states with red dots: North Carolina, Virginia, and Kentucky. The Kentucky dots were the most recent, so Rider was sure an incubus was in the area."

"But now there are missing women with sweet blood in Georgia, Alabama, and Mississippi," Ginger said. "I was working this before Rider pulled me to accompany you here. We thought an incubus was traveling linearly state to state, collecting for a harem, but this makes it look like it traveled from North Carolina to Kentucky, but then it just started up in—Check the timestamps on the first dots to appear in those bottom states."

I did as asked. "It looks like someone went missing in Alabama first, then in Georgia, then Mississippi."

"That's not really in order." She folded her arms and frowned. "This kind of destroys what we were initially thinking, but wait. Why are you pulling this up now?"

"You said that snake stuff about Gregori and I just… it sounds nuts, but I saw a red-eyed snake, women, and red dots that turned into red smoke. These are the only red dots I've seen since—" New red dots appeared, this time in Missouri. "Shit."

"Okay, now it just completely hopped over Arkansas to get to Missouri," Ginger said. "Maybe the system has a delay."

"Rider did say it was an imperfect system, and depends on the women having donated or having their blood find its way into the system some other way," I said.

"Or maybe you're looking at this the wrong way," Grey said. He placed the tip of his index finger on Missouri and followed the path of states with red dots clockwise. "Every state with red dots is touching Tennessee, and if Arkansas ends up with red dots, this state will be completely surrounded. Whether or not an incubus is behind the disappearances of these women, whatever's happening is happening around Tennessee. Why would anyone or anything go *around* a single state to hunt?"

"Because it's not," Daniel said, moving closer. "It's drawing women from surrounding states. It's in Tennessee. It's here."

"Exactly," Grey agreed. He looked at Ginger. "Whatever it was you were looking for, you were looking for it on what you thought were its hunting grounds, but it was safely tucked away here, letting its prey come to it."

Ginger's eyes narrowed as she looked between the screen and me. "And you saw these red dots when I said Gregori reminded me of a snake?"

"And you saw the red dots turn into red smoke," Daniel said, "like the red smoke I saw when I flew back over Lovefest?"

I nodded. "I've had this feeling about Lovefest since I first saw the email about it on Eliza's computer. I don't know why, and I know Eliza doesn't have sweet blood so her disappearance may not have anything to do with the disappearances of these women, but…" While I'd been speaking I'd clicked on a tab Rider hadn't shown me. It listed the names of all the women if you wanted to search by name instead of clicking on their red dot. My gaze froze on a name. Alexis Bertel. My gut clinched so hard I gulped to avoid spewing vomit. I clicked on the name. "Holy shit."

"Isn't that one of the women that Wickham guy painted?" Daniel asked.

"Alexis," I said, and fought against the bile rising in my throat as I looked into the bright eyes of the woman in the picture that had opened when I'd clicked her name. "Hugh said she requested a painting, paid for it, but never came back for it."

"Well, that could be the Eliza connection right there," Ginger said, looking over at the painting of Eliza still propped against the side of the kitchen island. "Maybe Hugh's dirty."

"Eliza doesn't have sweet blood," Grey said. "The paintings could be a coincidence, but the festival itself is definitely involved."

"Then that settles it," I said, and stood. "We're going back in."

"And doing what?" Grey asked. "We don't have enough information yet. We don't even know what the red smoke was that Daniel saw, why it was there, or how this Gregori person fits in. We're not going in guns blazing on nothing but hunches and fear."

"I'm not—"

"You are!" Grey snapped. "You're afraid your friend and these women are going to suffer the longer we take to rescue them, and I get that, but running in without knowing what we're actually up against could get us all killed and who will save them then? And as much as I hate to be the one to tell you, they could already be dead. Either way, I fully intend to help you stop this thing, whatever it is, but I'm not going to kill myself to do it. Daniel, how do you feel about doing another flyover?"

"I'm good with it."

"Go. Don't get too close. If you witness anything indicating we need to storm their castle, call us in and *wait*."

Daniel nodded, squeezed my shoulder, and exited the cabin. I watched him through the front window as he jogged down the stairs, jumped up, and turned into a large green dragon as his wings lifted him into the sky. I saw the two shifters standing guard outside the cabin turn toward it, their bodies still, and noted Grey's body was just as still. His eyes were closed. When they opened, I saw a hint of a glow.

"I've called in for supplies. We're going to research anything that is attracted to sweet blood, not limiting ourselves to incubi. That would be the most obvious guess, but you should have picked up incubus vibes if you were near one. You'd also notice if succubi were in the area. Even if an incubus was building a harem, he'd have some with him already."

"Google searches usually lead me to fanfic and *Supernatural* fan sites," I told him.

"You have Rider's tech team at your disposal. Use them. I'm having some books brought over from my place that may help, and a couple of laptops so we can all work at once. I know at least two of you will definitely need sleep once the sun rises and that one may not make it that long." He pointed at Angel, whose eyelids were drooping pretty hard. "We need to work fast and get what we can because I don't like the thought of leaving anyone in peril either, but the only thing I can think of worse than that is possibly being the only group of people to rescue them right now and not doing it because we rush in stupid and get our asses nuked before we can help anyone at all."

"Yeah, that's a good point." I ran a hand through my hair and took a deep breath to calm my nerves. Eliza needed me at my best. She needed me focused. "I'll contact the tech team and work from my laptop, using whatever information they send me."

The front door swung open and a pair of werewolves stepped in, one male, one female, both carrying boxes containing laptops, books, and notebooks. They set everything on the dining table and exited without a word, moving around Rome as he entered the cabin. Kutya took the opportunity to run out the door, all the food and water he'd put away kicking in.

Rome watched as Grey passed a laptop over to Ginger, set one out for himself and handed a book to a bleary-eyed Angel, then looked over at me just as I got through to Rider's tech team on the phone and started giving them a list of what we needed. "Okay, what did I miss?"

"We're trying to figure out what we're going to go kill." Grey passed a stack of notebooks over to him. "Get any food on those and the next thing you'll be straining to shit out will be my boot."

CHAPTER TWENTY

By the time Daniel returned to the cabin, Angel had already gone to bed and Ginger had followed not long after. I didn't know the feisty vampire's age, but I figured she wasn't too old based on the fact she started tuckering out before sunrise and would always sleep throughout the full day if allowed to. Then again, Rider preferred full day sleep when he was allowed it, but that could be because life didn't allow it that often these days, so he took it when he could get it.

Rome had also tuckered out, and currently snored from where his head rested sideways on the tabletop, half of a cold pork chop sticking out the side of his mouth. Grey had yanked the book he'd been reading out from under his head so he didn't drool on it. Kutya rested on the floor next to him, where he'd fallen asleep waiting for the pork chop he'd hoped would drop.

Grey and I sat across from each other at the dining table, each of us with a stack of books and notebooks next to our open laptops. I could tell the wolf's energy was waning, but he was determined to hang in there as long as I did, or maybe he thought I'd try to leave The Cloud Top if he took his eyes off me. Either way, I could no longer look at him without feeling a strong urge to yawn. My energy was waning too. Much longer, he wouldn't have to worry about me leaving The Cloud Top. I was going to crawl underneath the covers somewhere and zonk out.

"Well, you didn't call us in," Grey said as Daniel shut the front door behind him. "I'm assuming that means there wasn't much change from your previous flyover."

Daniel walked over to the kitchen island, picked through the cold offerings remaining on the platter of meat, and scrunched his nose up at the choices before opening the refrigerator and grabbing a carton of orange juice. I would have scolded him for not using a glass but it was late, I was tired from the near arrival of the sun, not to mention all the researching and thinking, and he drained the entire carton anyway.

"There was a shit-ton of red smoke," He said after he finished chugging down the juice and tossed the carton into the trash bin.

He picked up the platter and tossed the remaining meat into the garbage before rinsing it off at the sink. This woke Kutya, who ran over to the wastebasket and pawed at it, whining. Seeing this, Daniel finished rinsing the platter, put it in the dishwasher, and grabbed Kutya's box of kibble. The dog watched the kibbles pour into his bowl and turned a set of eyes that said 'Seriously, bro?' up to his rainbow-haired buddy and let out a heavy breath that came out sounding close to a bull's snort. As someone who deeply desired chocolate cake but kept getting offered blood instead, I felt the furry guy's pain.

Daniel walked over to the table and dropped down into the chair between Grey and I, which put him directly across from Rome. He looked at the pork chop sticking out of his sleeping friend's mouth and shook his head before continuing. "Yeah, so, there was still a lot of the red smoke when I got there and I noticed it was still heaviest in the same area, which was to the left of the stage, deep back in the woods."

"Did you see the big purple flower tree Gregori had said to meet him by?"

"Big purple flower tree?" Grey frowned at me from over his laptop. "You never mentioned a big purple flower tree."

"I told you Gregori gave me a card and told us to meet him by a tree."

"Yeah, you said he mentioned a big tree, but you never mentioned the purple flowers. That might actually be something." He started typing on the laptop. "Go on, Daniel."

"I didn't notice one, but again, a lot of area was covered in that red smoke. It was like a screen I couldn't really penetrate, so on this second time around I decided to touch ground."

"You did what?" Grey's head came up from what he'd been focused on at his laptop and I was happy I wasn't the person on the receiving end of his fiery glare.

Daniel seemed to take the evil eye in stride. He shrugged and folded his arms over his chest before slouching a little in his seat. As intimidating as the pack leader's glare was, Daniel held eye contact with him. "Look, the aerial view thing is great when you can actually see shit, and the dragon in me loves to fly so I could have just stayed up there the whole time, but I needed to see what was going on, and that red stuff was making it pretty damn hard to do that."

"You didn't know what the red stuff was," Grey growled.

"Which is why I landed far enough away from it. I'm not an idiot. I wasn't going to walk right into an area covered by it, or worse, touch that shit."

"You could have breathed it in," Grey told him.

"I could have breathed it in from flying above it," Daniel replied. "But I didn't, or maybe I did, but it didn't do anything to me. Besides, while there were a lot of people doing the whole *Girls Gone Wild* thing, there were others who weren't that far gone. I think whatever's in that smoke only affects certain people, or it affects people in different ways. Anyway, there's a campsite near there for people who travel from wherever and decide to stay close to the festival. I went there."

"Was the red smoke there too?" I asked.

"Along the edge of the site. There were less people out on the actual festival grounds when I went back the second time, and fewer cars in the lot, so people had left when it got really late. This is a good thing. It means not everyone who stays late gets trapped, which was kind of a thought I had and didn't want to say anything because I knew you'd take off running to save people if I suggested that."

"Gee, thanks for keeping things from me."

"I really wasn't. Thoughts that may lead to nothing don't count as keeping things from you, and Grey's right. We need to know what we're dealing with." He let out another yawn. "Anyway, the people at the campground were cool. There were a few small fire pits here and there and people drank beer, roasted marshmallows and played guitar and sang with each other until it got super late and they all went to bed in their tents. I noticed an offshoot of the campsite marked for vendors. I saw some tents there and trucks with attached trailers, but there were some RVs too. I'm guessing that's where Hugh and the other vendors stay, unless some of them travel all the way in to Pigeon Forge to stay at one of the motels along the Parkway. There was no red smoke in their area."

"So Hugh's okay. We can scratch him off as being part of everything."

Daniel shrugged. "I don't know. It's odd he painted two of the women who went missing and how he conveniently hasn't seen anything happen there despite working the festival every day."

"Well, he works it by painting," I reminded him. "I'm sure he could miss a lot while busy focusing on his canvas and whoever he's painting at the time."

"Yeah, that's true." Daniel released another yawn that had me yawning in response. "A lot more of the wooded area was covered in the red smog or smoke or whatever it was, so I didn't see as much going on back there, but it smelled way stronger. The stragglers out in the field where the actual festival should have been contained were your regular run-of-the-mill partiers. Some drunk, some missing more clothes than they came in with… I assume … but I didn't see anything crazy. There was no security to be found anywhere, which is just ridiculous, but it made it easier for me to sneak into the vendors' campsite area. I used my dragon senses but couldn't find those K-Pop guys. If any of the RVs or tents belonged to them, they gave off the same human vibe as anyone else, so they blended in too well for me."

"Maybe the musical acts have accommodations paid for them in town," I suggested.

"Doubt it. One of those Vagi Mind Trick girls was sitting outside one of the RVs writing in a notebook. I thought about talking to her, but honestly, that group kind of freaks me out, and she had a tattoo of a Minion on her bicep. That's a bad omen."

I grinned. "When we get Eliza back, I think you should schedule a therapy session with her. We've got to get you past this Minion-Twinkie thing."

"Sure, why not? I wish I had more to give you, but I don't. The crowd thinned out dramatically the darker it got and just as the sky started to lighten up a little, the red smoke just started disappearing and I don't know if the people I'd seen having orgies in the woods earlier left with the others or not, but there weren't any remaining there so I came back." He grabbed a book and started flipping through it. "I gather you all stayed up all night researching?"

"Yeah, and we still don't have a crystal clear picture of what is happening, but I think we have enough for me to green-light going in after we all rest properly," Grey said.

"Really?" I straightened, instantly alert despite the rising sun outside draining my energy.

"Yeah, and I'm hoping this isn't just the tiredness talking, but I think the tree thing might have given us more to go off of than anything." He turned his laptop around to show a sketch of a large tree with big purple blossoms. At first I thought they looked like roses, but as I peered closer, the centers kind of reminded me of lady parts. "This is a very rare tree. So rare, in fact, it's believed to be mythical."

"Great," Daniel said, and swung his head in my direction. "It's a cryptid. We're fighting another mythological-except-it-actually-exists creature. Wonderful. What is it this time?"

A large rumble started in Rome's stomach and blasted out of his ass before Grey could answer. We all jumped back as the smell assaulted us and fled the table. Kutya yelped and ran to the front door, pawing at the wood in desperation. I opened the door, half to let him out and half to give the smell of rotting carcass an exit as well.

Blown awake by his own flatulence, Rome sat up, picked up the pork chop that dropped from his mouth, looked at it, tossed it onto the table, wrinkled his nose, and looked at us. "What stinks?"

"You!" Daniel said, covering his nose with a dish towel. "I think you shit yourself."

Rome squirmed his ass around in the seat. "Nah, I'm good. What are y'all doing?"

The three of us looked at each other, then stared at Rome as he stretched and yawned before picking up the pork chop and sitting back in his chair as if he hadn't just dropped a nuclear bomb on us. Apparently deciding he'd had enough, Daniel stormed over to the table and slapped the pork chop out of Rome's hand a split second before it could reach his mouth. "You're on a diet, motherfucker. Water, fruit, and fiber, and if anything like that comes out of your ass again, I'm taking you to be exorcised."

"Like y'all ain't ever passed gas!"

"I think I can confidently state no one in this cabin or on this land, for that matter, has ever created a smell quite like that," Grey said, waving the air in front of him. "Let's move this to the sitting area."

We moved over to the couches in the living area, leaving the front door open to help dispel the last traces of pure funk that had escaped Rome's ass and groaned in unison when Rome decided to follow suit and sank his big frame down next to Daniel on the couch he'd just dropped onto. "If you fart again, so help me, I will punch you in the balls, then give Danni my switchblade to start in on you."

Rome raised his hands in surrender. "I'm good, man. Now, what y'all talking about? I fell asleep reading about some kind of smoke demons. Did y'all figure out anything?"

Grey shook his head and seemed to gather himself after the stinky interruption. "That tree is called a Cupid's Root. It grows near wherever the demon erects its pantry above ground."

For a moment, I just sat there staring at Grey, blinking. I looked over to see Daniel just staring at him too. As for Rome, his arm was on the arm of the couch and his hand raised to prop the side of his head on his meaty fist. His eyes were closed and I couldn't tell if he was asleep again or just resting his eyes.

"What demon?" I asked.

"Cupid."

"Cupid?"

Grey nodded. "Cupid."

I did some more blinking. Hell, maybe Rome wasn't the only one who'd fallen asleep. Maybe I was dreaming. "The demon's name is Cupid?"

"Yes, the demon's name is Cupid," Grey said. "Cupid is the demon. Cupid is not nor ever has been a cute baby in diapers with a bow and arrow that shoots love into people's hearts. Nor was he a god under his other name, Eros. Cupid has always been a very real, very evil, and very deadly demon."

"Man, I knew that Valentine's Day shit was the devil's work," Rome said, eyes still closed. "Only the devil would make a holiday that got you buyin' some girl you barely started dating a diamond and then if the diamond ain't big enough or she wanted something else or you got her the wrong kind of chocolates she slashes your tires. If that ain't the devil at work, I don't know what is."

"Actually, humans created Valentine's Day," Grey informed him.

"So it's the evil of women," Rome muttered. "Not that big of a difference."

"Hey, watch it," I said.

"Yeah, keep insulting Danni's gender and she'll slice something far more valuable than your tires," Daniel warned him.

Rome used his free hand to place a pillow over his groin, but didn't say anything else and I was back to wondering if he'd fallen asleep.

"Okay, so Cupid is a demon," I said, getting back to the subject at hand, "and because of that tree, you think that's who we're dealing with?"

"If this is the tree, then yes. It's got to be it, and it makes sense. Cupid isn't just any demon. He's an archdemon, meaning he's powerful as hell, hard to kill, and has a host of lower-level demons at his beck and call."

"Oh joy," I said. "I just love fighting hard-to-kill demons with demon armies. And what about this pantry? I'm guessing it's not full of devil's food cake."

"No. Cupid's pantry is where he keeps his food, but his food happens to be the life force of people he's captured. It should be something like a prison cell full of his prey."

Panic flared to life inside my chest. "He has Eliza."

"Possibly," Grey said as Daniel moved to sit next to me on the couch I'd chosen and held my hand, willing me the strength and calm I was suddenly at a loss for. Sitting on the loveseat across from us, Grey glanced at our hands and continued. "The good news is, according to what I pulled up on Cupid, he often keeps his captives alive for weeks, months, or even longer, depending on his use for them. He doesn't drain his prey quickly, hence the pantry. So if he has her, she could still be alive. Even better news, he can be killed. It won't be easy though."

"I figured it wouldn't be," I said. "Do normal blades and bullets work on him?"

"Not by themselves," Grey said, picking up a book he'd grabbed off the table before he'd fled Rome's flatulence. He flipped to a section inside. "Archdemons are too powerful for a simple exorcism, but if we can weaken them, we can kill them like any other demon. I'll get in touch with the local coven and see if I can borrow some wiccans when we go in. If we can get them to assemble around the vicinity we think he's in and perform the exorcism, it'll at least make it a little easier for us to do some damage. He'll be guarded by lower-level demons who should be weak enough to cut down or shoot our way through, provided we use salt bullets and salt-fired blades."

"Salt-fired blades?"

"Get the blades hot enough and salt them really well, then weld the salt to the blades with an incantation. Daniel's dragon breath should do the job."

Daniel nodded. "I can do that."

"I don't have much use for salt bullets, but as you know, I loan some of my pack out to The Moonlight Agency from time to time, and they've worked jobs like this. I know where to get them."

"What about Gregori?" Daniel asked. "Is he just a lower level demon? He gave off a weird vibe, but you know I've been around demons before. He didn't feel like a demon to me."

"There are some types of demon even you haven't been around, Daniel. If you had, you never would have made it back topside. Cupid likes it aboveground, but he needs to keep his pantry well-stocked and stay near it. I'm thinking this Gregori guy is a scout for him. He probably has a few, which explains the red dots on Rider's maps. He probably has a fetish for sweet blood, and has sent scouts out to find such women for his pantry."

"But Gregori was at the festival," I pointed out. "He wasn't out combing surrounding states for prey."

"Gregori is probably still a scout, but he's there to round up the prey once it arrives at the festival, as well as any others that happen to come on their own. You said there was a flyer at the gas station and they have a website. I don't think Cupid created the festival, but instead, just found an event that worked out well for him, so he latched on to it. But he'd need to stay hidden. That's where the festival scout comes in. Gregori wouldn't be just any kind of lower-level demon. He'd need to be able to remain in control of his lusts, and be able to blend in with humans. Also, Cupid wouldn't use someone who threw off a powerful demon scent in case his scout crossed paths with hunters. Based on what Ginger said earlier and Danni's vision once she said it, I'm thinking Gregori is probably a nalkrim."

"A what-krim?" I asked.

"A nalkrim. It's a reptilian-like demon that can take the form of a snake and inject venom into its prey. Honestly, Danni, regardless of your sweet blood, he might have approached you purely for your succubus side. Nalkrim and other types of demons have been known to mate with succubi." He flipped through the book and turned it to show me a picture of a demon with the body of a man and head of a cobra. "I came across this earlier tonight and thought it might explain Gregori, but I couldn't figure out why a nalkrim would be behind everything or why he'd pass out a card with wings on it. It made sense, though, once Cupid, a winged demon, came into play. Nalkrim tend to serve those more powerful than them, and Cupid always has an army of minions with him."

I looked over at Daniel, but noticed he didn't flinch or shudder this time. Maybe he wouldn't need therapy with Eliza after all.

"So it was Cupid's calling card," Daniel said. "Why would he bother having any type of clue at all on his card? Why even bother with the card?"

I snapped my fingers. "Is that where the idea for giving cards on Valentine's Day came from?"

"I highly doubt it," Grey said. "I'm pretty sure Valentine's Day was because of some Saint Valentine person or something. I have no idea how humans happened upon the name Cupid and depicted him as an arrow-shooting baby. I know the demon is as mischievous and arrogant as he is evil, so the cards could just be his way of amusing himself, thinking he's dropping a hint and the lowly humans are too stupid to pick up on it. Who knows?"

Despite the excitement of finally somewhat knowing what we were up against, my eyelids drooped as full sunlight spilled through the open front door and Kutya trotted in, sped over to the pork chop Daniel had slapped out of Rome's hand earlier, and curled up on the floor before setting to work on it. With his head still propped up on his fist, Rome let out a snore.

"You're tired, I'm tired, and Rome's out," Grey said. "Let's all get some rest. We're going to need all our energy and wits about us on this one. I'd love to have some of Rider's people with us for this, but I understand he's got a lot going on right now, so although you were given total access, I wouldn't call any more troops in. I can take some wolves in as backup. We'll do all right as long as we're rested, powered up, and smart."

"Wait. What about the K-Pop group? Were they demons? How were—"

"We'll talk some more later. We have to recap this all for Ginger anyway." Grey stood. "Rest. Get as much day sleep as you can, grab a bag of blood when you wake up, hopefully not until the sun is on its way down. Don't even think about leaving without me."

Daniel stood and picked Rome up, packing him over one shoulder, and headed toward the stairs. Rome shifted, and mumbled, "Don't get any ideas, Puff."

"No worries. You're not my type, big guy."

Grey shook his head as he watched them go up the stairs, then gave me his hand. I allowed him to help me up off the couch. "Get some sleep. I need you at your best because if something happens to you, I'll have to face off with Rider. I'd rather not battle my friend."

I nodded, but couldn't help asking, "Did your research tell you what Cupid does to his food supply during the daylight hours?"

"No, but he feeds at night and rests during the day, according to a lot of it, so I think she'll be all right if she's there. We'll talk more later. I'm going to drop soon and so are you." He grabbed my shoulders, turned me toward the staircase, and gave a light push. "Sleep well, Danni."

Then he was gone, the front door closing behind him. I wavered a little, but caught myself. He was right. The sun had fully risen, and I was going to drop. I headed up the stairs, to be met halfway by Daniel.

"Need any help getting to bed?"

I sucked in a breath, his words affecting me in a way they really shouldn't. He continued down, not stopping until we shared the same step. His pupils dilated as he stood a breath away from me. I knew I should move, run up the stairs, but my feet weren't getting the message.

The front door opened. "Hey, I need to grab…" Grey looked up at us and thanks to the look in his eyes, my feet suddenly got the message loud and clear.

"Sure, grab whatever you need," I said quickly, nerves causing my voice to shake and come out sounding all kinds of guilty. "It's your place. I'm off to rest now." I waved and made my way up the stairs.

"Son, do I need to tell you how dangerous you're living right now?" I heard Grey ask as I reached the bedroom. I stood inside the doorway and listened.

"I'm not—"

"I'm not blind, boy, and I'm sure as hell not stupid. I'm a wolf. I smell what's brewing between you two and let me make this perfectly clear right now: She's *his*."

"I know. We're just friends."

"Daniel, think of who you're talking to."

"We're friends. I care about her, but I know where the line is, Grey."

"You'd damn better. He'll kill you, son, and he won't make it quick."

I heard noises followed by the front door closing, then Daniel's feet moving up the stairs. I eased the door closed and tip-toed over to the bed, but Angel and Ginger were both spread out, taking up half the mattress each.

I grabbed a pillow and a blanket, and made a bed on the floor, only to stare up at the ceiling. Funny. I was so tired a moment ago.

CHAPTER TWENTY-ONE

Someone was with me. I opened my eyes to see a shadow looming above me. My mouth opened to scream, but a wave of serenity washed over me. I was safe. The presence wouldn't hurt me, and as the shadows fell away, I saw why. He was a friend. At least, I was pretty sure he was.

"Jon."

The almost ridiculously handsome man kneeled on one knee beside me, dressed in a black sleeveless shirt and drawstring pants. His golden skin was absolutely flawless, and his silky black hair was still shaved close to the skull on the sides, the middle section allowed to grow long so he could braid it down the center.

"This is no place for the lady of the house to sleep." He held out his hand, and I took it, allowing him to pull me to my feet.

"Gosh, you're pretty," I said without thinking as I was brought up to stand right in front of him.

He smiled. "You're still drowsy, and I'm not surprised, sleeping on the floor. That can't be very restful."

I looked around. The curtains had been drawn when Ginger had gone to bed, and she still rested there in her

Grumpy Bear pajamas. Angel was missing, and I wasn't surprised given the clock on the nightstand read noon. "So I'm dreaming?"

"You're not dreaming."

I looked down, noting his bare feet. "Really? You aren't wearing shoes."

"I was asleep when I got the call."

I frowned. "I didn't call you. I wanted to, but Rider said I couldn't." I poked his chest. "You're a hard person to track down, bucko."

"Bucko?" His smile widened. "I answered a different kind of call, but it still led me here."

I looked around again. "At least there aren't any Dementors this time."

"Those weren't Dementors. They were something much worse."

I shivered. "Why are you here? Is it because of Shana? Tell me she's safe."

"Your sister is safe. She's been suspended since the moment I last saw you. Nothing can get to her."

"How long does she have to stay like that?"

He angled his head to the side and stared up as if listening to voices from above before returning his soft brown gaze to mine. "It's hard to say, but remember what I told you that night, Danni. The sister you knew died during the turning."

I realized I was still holding his hand and dropped it. I stepped away and faced the window, even though the curtains were drawn and I couldn't see anything beyond. "You're not here because of Shana."

"No." He shook his head. "Shana has been handled. She is carrying the Bloom for you and will continue to do so."

"I still have issues with that. It's not the actual Bloom, but…" I continued to stare straight ahead at the curtain, happy to stare anywhere but at Jon in that moment. "She's carrying the Bloom, but there's still plenty of succubus left in me."

"Succubus is half of what you are now. You can't give that away, not even to a blood relative."

I nodded, more to myself than to him. "So she's really safe from Trixell? Rider wasn't lying about that just to make me feel better?"

Jon was silent, so I turned my head to look at him. His head was tilted down and to the side, his brow furrowed. He could have just been thinking, but for some reason, strange as it was, I got the feeling he was … *downloading* information or something. Before I could ponder it much longer, he looked up at me, and I thought I saw a sliver of anger there. "The witch cannot harm Shana. You can be at peace with that."

"You word things a little funny sometimes."

"I guess I do."

All right. So Shana was safe, Trixell couldn't harm her, and Rider hadn't lied to me. I turned to face Jon fully and folded my arms over my chest. "Why are you here, then? Why am I seeing you here at The Cloud Top?" Alarm settled in my chest as a sudden realization hit me. Jon transported souls to the afterlife. I'd seen him do it. I'd kind of been with him while he did it. "Is Rider safe? Did you take him somewhere?"

"Rider is safe." Jon held his hands up and motioned for me to calm down. "He's alive. I'm not here because of Rider. I'm here for you."

My hand went to my throat, and I backed up a step. "Are you taking me to the afterlife?"

"No, and I hope I'm not taking anyone here to the afterlife anytime soon." He sighed and gave me a very serious look. "You're about to fight a very powerful demon. An archdemon, to be exact."

"How did you …" I waved my hand, waving away the question. Jon was always so cryptic and evasive with his answers anyway. He'd only tell me he was called, but not say by who or how, and I didn't want to waste time with a man who could simply disappear at will any second he chose to. "Yes. According to Grey, we're fighting Cupid. Was he right?"

Jon nodded.

"I suppose you won't tell me how you know that, but can you tell me anything? Better yet, can you brighten my day and tell me you're here to join us? I imagine you can just poof yourself right in there and gut the big, red, horned demon-baby."

"He's not a big, red, horned demon-baby, and this isn't my fight. I can't kill him."

"Of course."

"Even if I went in with you, Danni, I *couldn't* kill him."

I blinked as I processed this. A ball of dread started spinning in my stomach. "If a guy like you can't kill him, things aren't looking too good for me. I'm just a cranky hybrid with a thing for slicing testicles. Tell me he has testicles and is just as sensitive about them as the rest of you guys seem to be."

"Danni, you need to be very careful," he warned me, completely Mr. Serious. No fun and jokes with him. "Listen to your heart and listen to your gut. If you have visions, believe them. They're there to help you."

I lowered my arms and gaped at him. "Was Grey right about me? Am I some kind of psychic now?"

"You have a gift, Danni. If you trust in it, your gut will always guide you to where you need to be, but fear will mess with your head and throw you off course. You can't panic."

"Right." I nodded. "Face off with an archdemon without panicking. Easy as pie."

"You won't be alone."

"Yeah, but I'm worried about who I'll be with too. Promise me you're not here to take me or my friends."

He stared at me for a moment. "I can promise you I didn't come here to take any spirits, but I can't promise I never will. At this time, I don't see any. Stay alert, stay calm, and stay smart and hopefully that'll remain the truth. You need to get some rest."

I raised an eyebrow. "Really? You woke me to tell me I needed to rest?"

I managed to pull a fraction of a smile out of him. "I woke you to give you a warning, and to give you strength. Lie down, Danni."

I allowed him to walk me to the bed, and I settled onto the side of the mattress Angel had vacated. "How do I know this isn't all just a dream?"

"Listen to your gut," he said as he draped the cover over my legs and sat along the edge of the bed, his thigh touching mine, spreading heat into my body. He opened his left hand and a golden dagger appeared. "Drink from my vein, Danni."

"Uh, I don't know how you just did that with the dagger out of thin air trick, but whatever you are, you're still a man and my bite can have a bad effect on men."

"It won't on me." He stared into my eyes, and I noticed golden flecks amid the brown in his. "Grey will try to feed you. He shouldn't do that before going into battle with an archdemon. Rome isn't powerful enough to give you much more than you'd get from a bag, and I think you know the danger of drinking from Daniel's blood."

I looked down, feeling heat spread into my cheeks. Geez, did everyone in the universe know there was something happening between us? Jon raised my chin with the tip of his index finger and raised his forearm. "Bite, or do I need to start the bleeding for you?"

I winced at the thought of him slicing into his skin with the golden dagger in his other hand and sighed. "All right, but if something happens—"

"It won't."

I stared into his eyes and even though I didn't know how he could know that, I trusted him, so I took his warm forearm in mine before he decided to cut that flawless golden brown skin and lowered my elongated fangs to his wrist.

When his blood hit my tongue, my body became completely weightless. Every thought, every fear, and every worry left my mind. I was flying, and I was free, and I reveled in the taste of him. He tasted like strength and power, with a hint of pure sunlight, but it didn't burn at all. It just radiated warmth, and I wanted to curl up in the sensation and stay there.

"That's good, Danni."

His voice and gentle grip on the nape of my neck brought me out of the lazy haze his blood had pulled me under. I realized I'd been drinking deeply for longer than I normally would drink from anyone else and pulled back, savoring the last drops of blood as I lapped my tongue over his wounds to seal the damage I'd caused, although it looked as if his skin was sealing on its own. I felt drunk as he lowered my upper body down to the bed.

"Now I know this is a dream," I murmured. "You taste too good to be real."

He brushed my hair out of my face as my head settled on the pillow. "Sleep well and remember this visit."

"What are you?"

"I am a man who walks between worlds."

"But what *are* you?"

"A friend, someone who'll watch out for you."

"Why?" I fought to keep my eyes open, and his fingertips gently moving over my brow as he continued brushing my hair away from my face didn't help me fight the pull of sleep. Just before sleep completely took me under, I felt him bend over me and heard his voice in my ear.

"He can only be weakened by the one he desires most."

I came awake without the slightest bit of grogginess and sat up to see Ginger sitting up next to me. She pushed a button on the remote in her hand and the curtains slid open, revealing the sun on its way down. "Rise and shine, puddin.' Better get up out of bed before I get ideas."

I laughed as I stretched. "Man, I feel good."

She gave me a look. "Well, you certainly look bright-eyed and bushy-tailed. Did you guys discover anything good after I clocked out for the day?"

"Oh, we did!" I filled her in on what we'd learned as we dressed. I'd gone to bed in my clothes from the day before, so I just kept the same jeans on and traded my shirt out for a black long-sleeved Henley and pulled on black hiking boots. Ginger opted for ripped skinny jeans, a black T-shirt from the Hard Rock Cafe and her black shit-kickers. She grabbed her black leather jacket off the floor to complete the look and did a quick finger-comb of her dark pixie cut, we brushed our teeth and made our way downstairs where Angel and Grey waited at the table, both working their way through thick stacks of pancakes and sausage links.

"Where's Rome and Daniel?" I asked.

"Daniel's salt-firing the blades with the coven," Grey answered. "One guess where Rome is."

"Bathroom," Ginger and I guessed at the same time.

Grey nodded. "We might need to leave that one here, which sucks because we could use a guy his size."

"He'll get it together," I said. "Have you been awake long?"

"Long enough to do some more research and reach out to my contacts, which I know is what you're really wanting to know," he answered, "and the kid here has been up researching since early this morning."

"I'm not a kid," Angel reminded him, her gaze tracking me as I walked over to the table and looked at the guns and holsters sitting there next to boxes of ammo.

"Salt bullets," Grey explained, nodding toward the boxes. "I hear you haven't been trained to shoot yet, so you'll go in with blades only. There are thigh holsters there for your use so you have quick access to them. They'll be long enough to allow you a little distance, but make sure you jab and slice fast and get out of the way. You don't want any nalkrims biting you."

"They're poisonous," Angel said, sliding an open book over to me. I saw another image of a snake-demon on the page. "I saw this was open this morning, and Grey left me a note of what to look into. Nalkrim serve more powerful demons and are kind of like guard dogs. They have an alpha, so that's probably Gregori. The leaders are smarter and better at blending in with humans. The rest are pretty much just fangs and muscle."

"The type of fangs you don't want to come into contact with," Grey cut in. "Their bite is pretty much a guaranteed death and I can't find anything to suggest any beings with immunity or any type of anecdotes to the poison. The wiccans don't know of any anecdote or any type of protection spells to ward against it, so we need to all be careful and avoid getting bit, especially Rome. Are you two sure he can handle a fight like this?"

"I've fought with him before," Ginger replied as she grabbed two bags of blood out of the refrigerator and popped them into the microwave. "Despite his size, the man can move when necessary, and he's great with a gun, even better with his fists. He's human, but he's strong as hell. Just make sure he has enough bullets to last him so he doesn't have to get close."

Grey nodded. "Got that covered."

"Did you find out anything else about that K-Pop group?" I took the warm mug of blood Ginger offered me as she walked over and joined me where I stood by the table, but didn't feel very thirsty. "Any better idea of what those lyrics were about?"

"You mean the D-Pop group?" Angel said.

I thought about it. "Ah. Demon-Pop?"

"Demon, douche, dickwad, whichever works," she said. "Anything but K-Pop. They've blasphemed the genre enough. Yes, I think I figured that out. It took a lot of digging around, but I think I matched screen names from some questionable sites to some of the members so best guess… they're random devil-worshipping jackasses who somehow worked their way into the festival to do their demon-summoning crap amid the huge crowd of unsuspecting hippie wannabes." Angel got up from the table and walked over to where my laptop rested on the desk. She ran her finger over the touchpad to wake it up and pointed to an open tab. "I dug into the festival and saw that they replaced this group, The Rolling Moonstones, right about the time your friend would have first been at the festival. According to what I found in some really skeevy forums, those lyrics are an incantation that calls forth an archdemon, and now that the archdemon has been called aboveground, their continued reciting of the incantation among the masses, or in this case, the Lovefest crowd, fertilizes the tree from which it draws its strength and keeps the portal open so he doesn't have to return to Hell."

I ran everything Angel had said through my brain and looked over at Ginger, who appeared to be doing the same. "This all sounds absolutely insane, even for us."

"Yup," she said, "but, I mean, we've fought zombies and a spider-woman. How much weirder are evil boy bands?"

"A little bit weirder."

She shrugged. "It's a modern day hippie festival. Shit was bound to get weird."

A flush came from the bathroom and we waited until Rome emerged, decked out in black pants and T-shirt, his usual fighting attire. He nodded at us and rolled his shoulders as his heavy boots clomped over the floorboards. His eyes went to the guns on the table. "Nice."

"How's your stomach?" Grey asked as Rome picked up one of the guns to inspect.

"All good. I'm ready to go."

The front door opened and Kutya shot in, pausing in front of me long enough for a scratch between the ears before he beelined for his food dish to gobble up the kibble someone had poured out for him. Daniel stepped in behind him, dressed in his usual attire of jeans and T-shirt. This time it was a Pink Floyd T-shirt. He carried several swords in his hands. He dropped them on the table and gave me a quick glance before returning his focus to the blades. "Salted and ready. Danni gets two. The rest of us get one and a gun."

"Rome, you get two guns," Grey said, pushing his plate away. He and Daniel dispersed holsters.

Daniel carefully avoided my gaze as he showed me how to put on the thigh holsters and gave me a sword to put in each. The blades started at my upper thigh and reached to just above my knee. They were worn on the sides of my thighs for easy access.

"Practice pulling them a few times and see how they feel," he said, keeping his eyes trained on the swords.

I set my mug on the table and did as asked. The metal slid free of the holsters easily and were just as easy to return. "Perfect."

"Good. So everyone's caught up?" Daniel asked, looking at Grey for direction. The pack leader gave a quick, firm nod.

"I still don't get how Eliza returned home, then seemed to just be snatched," I said. "Any explanations for that?"

"You'll have to ask her when we find her," Grey told me. "That part's still a mystery, but we have enough information to go in and hopefully find her. Even if we're wrong about the particular archdemon, I'm still confident it's an archdemon. Archdemons are powerful, but we can kill the fucker. It'll just take a lot of bullets and slicing. Danni, you need to drink that blood you haven't touched, or actually, my blood should be stronger than—"

"I've already had fresh blood," I said as every head in the room turned to look at me. My dream flooded back to me in a rush, and I realized it wasn't a dream. I remembered Jon's blood far too clearly and still felt the energy of it zinging through my veins. I looked at Daniel. "Jon let me drink from him."

His eyes widened for a quick second before narrowing. "Jon? The …" He looked over at Grey and I knew he was trying to decide how much he could share. "The guy that helped Seta and Rider out with the…"

I nodded.

"When did you see him?"

"He woke me up around noon. He let me drink from him. I drank very deeply, actually. I'm full."

"Wait, there was a man in the room with us?" Ginger asked the exact moment Angel asked how a man walked past her without her seeing.

"Jon's… special," I said, frowning at the hard glare coming from Daniel. "He can just pop in and out of wherever he wants. He popped in to the room, had me drink from him, and I guess popped back out after he tucked me in."

"He tucked you in?" Daniel's voice held a bit of a growl.

"Yo, does Rider know this dude's popping into your bedroom, tucking you in?" Rome asked. "That don't sound right."

"It was innocent," I said, more to Daniel than Rome. Daniel looked way more peeved.

"Why did he pop in at all?" he asked.

"He knew we were about to go after Cupid." I turned toward Grey. "And it's definitely Cupid. He said we were right about that, and he told me to be careful, and he had me drink from him because he knew you would try to give me blood. He said you shouldn't before going into battle. We all need to be strong. No giving blood."

"Who the hell is Jon?" Grey asked, looking at Daniel for an answer.

Daniel stared at me a moment longer, nostrils flaring,

before he answered. "I don't know, but he's supposed to be one of the good guys. I guess he couldn't be bothered to stay and help us actually fight."

"Hey, as long as he's not here to take anyone's spirit to the afterworld, I wouldn't be complaining," I said, then looked at Grey, "because that's what he does. He said he wasn't here for that, though, but we need to be careful."

"Well, fuck, that's not ominous at all," Ginger said. "Still, in all this bunch of crazy, no one's mentioned spiders yet, so I'm ready to roll."

Grey stared at me a moment, then checked over everyone, making sure we all had weapons strapped on. The sun went down all the way, and my already pretty energetic body filled to the brim, my heart beating faster than normal, but I wasn't afraid.

"All right then," the werewolf said. "Let's go kill Cupid."

CHAPTER TWENTY-TWO

Four women in long, dark robes stood outside the cabin, waiting for us. One redhead with bright green eyes, one raven-haired pale-skinned woman, one African-American woman with natural curls falling to her shoulders, and one Asian woman with short blue hair and multiple facial piercings.

"Shall we begin?" The redhead asked.

"Go," Grey ordered with a firm nod and the women clasped hands, then disappeared in a flash.

"Were those the wiccans?" I asked.

"Yes," Grey answered.

"I didn't know they could do that."

"They can't, generally, but one is an actual born witch. They're going to mark the corners and help with a spell to keep out demon reinforcements so we only have to deal with whatever is already aboveground with Cupid. Also, they'll try to exorcise him while we're fighting him, weakening him enough to make our weapons more useful against him." He nodded at Daniel, and Daniel gripped my shoulder.

"Be careful," he said before he took to the sky in his dragon form, which was a silvery purple this time.

"Daniel's not going with us?"

"Aerial view," Grey explained. "He'll keep an eye out until we arrive. He can reach the area a lot quicker and keep an eye out for that tree, hopefully before the red fog blocks his line of sight. Either way, he should be able to see where the thickest part of the fog is, and that's where we'll go, regardless if we can see the tree or not. Let's go."

Grey took the lead, and we followed along, listening to his directions as we walked. Once in the parking area, Rome and Ginger split off to leave in her Mustang. Grey directed me over to a sleek black Escalade and opened the passenger door. I slid inside and was quickly joined by Grey. As we pulled out and headed down the mountain, I noted a compact car zipping up toward The Cloud Top.

"Crap," I muttered, peering close enough to recognize the rodent-like face behind the wheel. "That's Pacitti headed toward The Cloud Top."

"The detective?" Grey cut a glance my way as I nodded, then shot a look in the rear-view mirror. His eyes flashed golden yellow. "I just notified the pack. He won't find out anything."

"They won't eat him, will they?"

Grey barked out a laugh. "That's a little insulting."

"I'm sorry."

"Don't be. A little humor is always appreciated when shit gets tense like this. He'll be all right. He'll just be strongly encouraged to turn back down the mountain."

"He might have seen me. He'll be back. He's a pain in the ass."

"We'll deal with him later. We have more than enough to focus on right now."

"My wolves found a back way in," Grey said as we neared the festival and split off from the road we'd taken in the day before. "Admission is still being taken, so there's a line if we go in the main way. We're going to skip that and go in through a part of the woods."

"I was wondering how we were going to get in with these weapons," I said. "Security is lax if not nonexistent, but I imagine even at a place like this, people will notice a group armed with guns and swords."

"Another part of having wiccans involved," Grey said, "is their ability to blur a few things. I imagine Cupid and his lackeys are doing some blurring too. Otherwise, there's no way an event like this wouldn't have security."

"Wait. Your wolves found a back way in? They're here?"

He nodded. "I sent a group out when the festival opened. They've been observing, trying to sense any demonic entities, searching for the tree, looking for places Cupid would be resting. He won't be out in the open."

"I take it they didn't find the tree if you sent Daniel ahead to search for it."

"They did not," He said. "You said this Gregori character told you to meet him at the tree at sundown though, so I'm thinking that wasn't just a random time he gave. Demons are not restricted to darkness, but like many other entities, they are at their strongest during the night. I'm thinking the tree blooms at nightfall. It might even be the source of the red haze Daniel saw."

"Makes sense," I said. "Has Bias Wrecker been onstage yet?"

He shook his head as he navigated a twisty bend in the road. "Not yet, which is another thing. If whatever the hell it is they're singing fertilizes the tree, that could be another reason it hasn't been found yet."

Grey took the Escalade off-road and onto what looked like little more than a dirt trail. It was bumpy and rough, jarring both of us, but he continued on. I looked behind us, saw Ginger's Mustang still tailing him, and grimaced. I knew Ginger was cussing up a storm. She loved that Mustang.

Before my organs could shift and tumble around any

further, Grey came upon a small clearing and parked next to a trio of SUVs.

"These belong to your guys?" I asked.

"Yep," he answered as Ginger pulled in next to us, a deep scowl on her face.

Remember, he's not just any wolf before you go ape-shit on him, I warned her through our telepathic link.

She flicked a dark look my way and clamped her jaw tight as we all stepped out of our vehicles, but she closed her door with extra oomph, as close to a slam as she'd risk with her baby. I turned my face away as she brushed away some dirt that had coated the side window so she wouldn't see me grin, then felt a tug of familiarity. I looked up just as a large shape flew overhead, far enough away to make anyone who saw it wonder what the heck type of impossibly large bird they'd just seen, circled, then dove, disappearing into rainbow sparkles before reaching the ground.

Daniel appeared before us just as two men stepped out of the trees. "Still no big tree with purple flowers," he said as he stepped out of the sparkles and stopped in the center of the clearing as we walked over to him, "and no red haze either."

"That demon boy-band hasn't gone on stage yet," Grey said, looking over at the approaching men. They shared nods before he turned his head to address Daniel again. "If it's not nightfall causing the tree to appear, it's got to be the incantation."

"They did perform prior to full night yesterday," Daniel said, "so if Danni had gone searching for the tree at nightfall, she would have found it. Will whatever the wiccans are doing block their incantation? If that tree is the key to finding this damn thing, we have to let that demonic group of dipshits do their thing with no blocking."

Grey closed his eyes and breathed deep. They glowed a little when he reopened them. "One of my wolves on the field is notifying them so they won't interfere with anything having to do with the tree."

"What about the red haze?" I asked. "We didn't see anything resembling that yesterday. Daniel didn't see it until he came back later."

Grey frowned and looked over at the pair of men who stood silently near him. Both were Caucasian with short brown hair and could definitely pass for brothers. One wore a dark blue T-shirt over faded jeans, the other wore a burgundy one over jeans ripped at the knees. "You covered the area where Danni was told to find the tree?"

The one in the blue shirt nodded. "Several times. We covered the entire area left of the stage. There are some big trees but none with purple flowers and none that stick out in any way."

Grey frowned. "The incantation is supposed to fertilize the tree. If it makes it bloom, the red haze doesn't necessarily have to be at the same time."

An image of the card Gregori had handed me flashed through my mind. "Have you seen anyone handing out black foil cards or seen anyone carrying a card like that?" I asked, not sure if I was breaking any kind of etiquette, but it was already nightfall and I didn't want to risk missing our window of opportunity with the tree.

"We were watching for that," the one in the burgundy shirt answered after looking at Grey as if seeking approval to answer me directly. "We haven't seen any."

"Danni, do you still have the card you were given?" Grey asked.

"I have it," Daniel said, and reached into his back pocket. "I shoved it into my pocket yesterday and forgot about it until I showered, then I just transferred everything into these jeans."

"You said you felt something when you touched it yesterday," Grey said. "Maybe you should try now."

I looked at the card as Daniel removed it from his pocket and held it toward me, noting a halo of light around it, but no one else seemed to acknowledge it. "Uh, does anyone else notice the card is kind of glowing?"

Everyone looked at the card, then back at me. Grey took the card and flipped it over in his fingers. "This is glowing to you?"

"Uh huh."

He shared a look with Daniel and held it out to me. "Touch it and see what happens. Everyone, be ready for anything."

I felt a little hesitant at first, but then a calm fell over me. I reached out and took the card from Grey's hand. The moment my fingers touched the foil, the smell hit me. Roses and spice, but this time I smelled the sulfur underneath too. I also saw it as the glowing light rose from the card, twisted in the air, and caught the wind to be carried into the woods, raining drops of white light along the ground in its wake. I pointed after it. "Uh, I think we go that way."

"Yeah, that's the way we were going to lead you to the festival," the shifter in the blue shirt said.

"Danni, do you see something?"

I looked over at Grey and nodded before pointing to the trail of light droplets starting to fade. "There's a trail of light, but I don't think it will last long. We need to follow it."

"Anybody else creeped out right now?" Rome asked.

"She has a gift," Grey said. "She's had a hunch about this festival from the start."

The droplets closest to where we stood faded. "We have to go now," I said and started walking, cutting ahead of the two wolves when they protested.

"Let Danni lead," Grey said, falling into step. "Her gift is allowing her to see what we can't."

I stared down at my arms, feeling something different running through me as I followed the glowing drops sticking to the forest floor and noted the glowing wings on the card. My heart continued to race as it had been doing since I'd awakened, but I wasn't nervous or afraid. It hit me. My heart wasn't racing. I was detecting a second heartbeat beating in tune with mine. I flexed my hands, feeling the foreign energy inside my veins. "This isn't just me," I said, realizing what I was feeling. "This is Jon. This is why he had me drink from him. Jon is inside me."

"Oh shit, she's possessed," Rome said. "If her head starts spinning, I'm out, man."

"No." I laughed and continued to lead them through the forest. "It's just his energy, or his … *something* … I must have gotten from his blood when I drank from him. It's like his blood is strengthening an ability in me. I kept picking up on that smell yesterday, but now I can track it. It looks like droplets of light, but they're disappearing, telling me whatever we're moving toward, we have to move now before time runs out. Jon said I wouldn't be alone, and I thought he was talking about all of you, but I think he was telling me he'd be with me in this way."

"Who the hell is this guy again?" Grey asked.

"A friend," I answered, recalling what he'd told me and everything I'd been told about him before. "Someone who finds you when he's needed."

"Sounds like a guardian angel," Ginger said.

"Sounds like something," Daniel said, moving in closer to me.

Music filtered through the trees and I recognized a Jimi Hendrix song being sung by a woman with a deep voice full of soul. "That must be The Jimis," I said.

The droplets turned sharp right, and I followed. They started disappearing faster, so I started to run. "Quicker!"

"Daniel, maybe you should take to the sky again," Grey suggested. "One of my scouts just relayed the K-Pop demons are behind the stage, about to go on."

"Watch her, Grey." Daniel's request came out sounding like an order and I hoped it wouldn't cost him later. Grey was fairly lenient with me when it came to my tone. I wasn't sure whether it was because he was amused by me or showing slack because he knew I was concerned about Eliza. I didn't think his leniency stretched to Daniel.

The droplets were disappearing so I couldn't stop, but I sensed Daniel falling behind and heard a loud crack. I cringed, knowing some trees had just been destroyed to accommodate his size as he took dragon form. I felt a gust of air overhead and looked up just in time to see his orange underbelly as he soared over us.

The droplets took a diagonal left and so did I, narrowly missing a tree. I heard someone grunt behind me, pretty sure it was Rome, and knew he'd connected with it. We continued running and soon broke out of the tree line behind the vendors lining the right side of the field. I saw a few look over at us, but they didn't seem to pay much attention to the group of people barreling out of the forest armed with guns and swords before returning to what they were doing. Most, I noticed, were packing up. I glanced over to where Hugh had been the day before and noted he was already gone. I was relieved, and realized I knew in my gut Hugh was not involved. Whether that knowledge came from my own instinct or whatever extra juju I'd received from Jon's blood, I had no idea.

I stepped out onto the field and instantly became in tune with everything. The field was full of people in various stages of dress and intoxication, dancing and frolicking, but I could pinpoint where Grey's wolves and the wiccans were by gut alone. I could also tell which of the festival participants were in trouble. Every person was wrapped in an aura, the colors so bright and different, the field looked like one giant psychedelic painting.

"Danni." Grey stepped close to me, and I realized I'd stopped moving.

I held my hand up to quiet him before I lost my way. I knew the colors were showing me something. I only had to recognize… *There.* In the middle of that sea of bright color, light beams moved toward the left side of the field. I looked down at the card in my hand and saw a halo of light in the same neon purple around it. The people haloed in the same color were moving left, but not toward the stage. I ran to the closest one, shouldering and elbowing my way through the crowd until I reached one, a young brunette with alabaster skin and bright green eyes. I clamped my hand on her shoulder and nearly spun her right off her feet as I turned her. "Do you have a card?"

"What?" She blinked, then looked up at Rome as my group caught up to me.

I looked down at her hand and saw it clenched around the same card Gregori had given me the day before. "Where are you supposed to meet the man who gave you that card?"

She frowned at me, then turned and pointed in the direction I saw the other purple-haloed people moving, confirming what I'd thought. I gripped both of her shoulders and forced her to hold my gaze. "That man is dangerous. Stay away from there, and him. Go home now."

I pushed the woman in the direction of the parking lot and she was quickly swallowed up in the crowd. A quick glance at the stage showed The Jimis exiting. I measured the distance between the people moving toward the center left side of the field and looked up. *Daniel, can you see me?*

Yes, he replied in my head.

I raised my arm and pointed toward the other side of the field directly in front of me. *Back there in the trees. Head off the people headed that way.*

On it.

"I don't think the tree stays in the same place every night," I announced to the others. "I just sent Daniel to block the people who were invited tonight. Let's go."

"Grab them on my signal," Grey ordered the two wolves before taking off at a run alongside me. "The K-Pop group," he explained when I glanced at him with my eyebrows raised.

As I ran along, I noticed more werewolves moving toward the stage and knew they were all tapped in to

Grey's mind-link, awaiting the mental order to snatch the performers. I shoved Gregori's card into my back pocket as we ran, wanting my hands free for whatever we were about to find behind that tree line and moved around people in my way, forcefully shoving the ones who didn't have the sense to move when a group of armed people were sprinting in their direction.

A few feet from the tree line, we were met with a stream of panicked people running away from the direction we'd been headed. The other people draped in purple auras heading that way stopped and either turned around or got bowled over. I managed not to get knocked down, and sensed my crew right behind me.

"I just put two wolves in place to block anyone else from entering this area," Grey told me as we reached the narrow path and followed it.

I heard a man's voice announcing Bias Wrecker and the sound of their intro music, and pumped my legs harder, hoping like hell I hadn't screwed up pulling Daniel out of the sky to head off the people who'd been given cards. The path was winding far deeper into the woods than I'd expected.

I heard scuffling and turned around a bend in the path to see Daniel in his human form standing over Gregori, or at least I thought it was Gregori. The man under him's head had contorted into a snake-like shape, his eyes had turned red, and a hood had grown out of the flesh around his face and neck. Daniel already had a boot planted in the man's chest, and by the time we skidded to a stop by him, he'd kneeled down and planted his sword up to the hilt in the center of the man's throat.

Bright red light zapped through the snake-man's body like streaks of lightning as it convulsed, then blackened and curled up into a tangle of tightly clumped ash, similar to a spent firecracker. Daniel yanked his sword out and the charred remnants of the snake-man crumbled.

"Was that Gregori?"

He looked at me and nodded. "I saw him walking toward the people, so I dove down and he started attacking. I don't know if he knew what I was yesterday. I'd think he would, but when he saw me in dragon form, he didn't hesitate. The people closest this way saw us fighting and took off running."

I looked around, noting there weren't any fallen trees. "They didn't see you in dragon form, did they?"

"No, but they saw this bastard's snake eyes and his giant fucking fangs." Daniel shook charred flesh off his sword and shoved it back into the holster on his thigh. "Danni, I hate to tell you this, but there're no purple flowers on any of these trees."

"And you just killed the man who could have given us answers," Grey said.

"I'm sorry, was I supposed to let the poisonous demon-dude bite me?" Daniel snapped. "Speaking as someone who's actually been to Hell before, you don't give these fuckers time to make a move!"

"Could you have given him time to clue us in on where his boss is?" Grey growled back.

"Both of you, be quiet!" All eyes turned on me and I couldn't tell if Grey's were more surprised or pissed off, but I'd deal with the fact I'd basically just told the local wolf pack's pack leader to shut up later. Bias Wrecker had started singing, and the ground vibrated. "Do any of you feel the ground shaking?"

Before they could answer, I looked past Daniel and saw one of the trees a few feet behind him growing before my eyes. "Guys. Tell me you're seeing this."

"The big, growing tree sprouting purple, somewhat pornographic-looking flowers?" Ginger asked as she stared at it. "Yep, I see that."

"Gregori was headed this way when I swooped down on him," Daniel said. "He must have intended to meet the group ahead then bring them back here after Bias Wrecker did their incantation to get this thing growing."

"Okay, so this is the tree," Grey said. "Where's Cupid? We still don't know where he's at. We need to find him."

"Man, why don't we just kill the tree?" Rome said. "If fertilizing or whatever y'all said those guys are doing to this tree with their jacked up lyrics is giving this archdemon strength, let's kill the damn tree. Maybe it'll kill him too."

"Then how will we find Eliza?" I asked.

"Archdemon goes poof, his prey goes free?" Rome shrugged. "Unless we're going to get another demon-snake-tour guide rolling through here, I say we kill the tree."

The large purple buds bloomed fully and emitted a red smoke that reeked of spice and sulfur. Ginger stepped back, covering her nose. "Well, now we know the source of the smoke and the smell. I think the purple coochie tree needs some Monistat."

"What do you say, Danni?" Daniel looked at me. "You led us here. You smelled this way before this tree even bloomed yesterday. Do we kill it, or are you picking up something else?"

I stared at the tree, spellbound, as purple and red light seemed to run from the flowers, down the trunk, and into the dirt below. The ground trembled underneath my feet, a steady buzz of energy, but I had no trouble balancing as I walked to the tree and placed my palm against the bark and swore a thousand heartbeats fluttered under my hand.

"Danni?"

"You said there was an area of red smoke so thick you couldn't see through it last night." I looked up at the cloud of red fog accumulated directly overhead, and noted how branches of it stretched out farther, but not quite as thick. "It makes sense it would be thickest where it starts, and that would be the source of power."

I closed my eyes and opened my senses as I pressed my palm harder against the tree. My head filled with an image of the pinkish red smoke stretching out over the field, and I saw as it blurred the minds of the people below, turning them a whole lot friendlier as clothes started coming off, but not all. Grey's wolves were unfazed, as well as a few other people I saw turning away from some of the randier people on the field. I watched as red and purple streaks of light ran through the smoke, flooding back into the tree, down its trunk, and into the ground, then the tree started to twist and split apart…

I caught a quick flash of a winged man sitting on a throne made of skulls. His hair was golden and curled down to his shoulders. His eyes were two different colors, one purple, one red. I sensed his hunger despite the fact he seemed to be drawing power from the energy returning to him through the smoke. Eliza sat at his feet, only a white sheet of silk worn as a toga to cover her. She cringed as the man reached down and clamped his hand on her bare shoulder. Suddenly, she looked up, startled, her gaze seeming to stare right into mine. *Run, Danni. Stay away!*

I rocked back on my heels as I felt myself pushed out of the vision I'd been sucked into, positive what I'd seen had been very real. I moved back to the tree and placed my palms over the bark, over the streaks of red and purple light energy I saw running like blood into the ground below, and felt the heartbeats, one of which I knew belonged to Eliza. "She's here. I connected with her. The smoke does something to people in the surrounding area, messes with their perceptions and their emotions, but not everyone. It doesn't seem to affect any shifters." I looked over at Rome. "How are you feeling?"

The big guy shrugged. "I could grab a burger, but I'm good."

I fought against the urge to roll my eyes. In the grand scheme of things, Rome being hungry at a time like this was far better than him being horny and fuzzy-brained. I continued to feel along the tree. "She's in here. I can feel heartbeats and I see the energy he's drawing from people running through the tree, down through its roots. It's running straight to him."

"Danni, according to everything I found, he should be aboveground," Grey said. "How can anything be running to him if it's running into the ground?"

"It's a portal." Daniel ran his hands over the tree bark, searching for a way in with me. "A demon being aboveground doesn't necessarily mean it's on the same ground we're standing on. It just means he's no longer in Hell, which is a realm itself. He's drawing energy from this realm, and collecting prey from it, but he's safely tucked elsewhere."

"Yeah, well, let's go untuck this sonofabitch and get Eliza back," I growled as I continued to search the tree, the others joining in. "We just need to figure out how to—"

A loud crack split the air, and the tree twisted, unfurling to reveal a cavernous hole, knocking us back in the process. A cloud of purplish-red smoke burst free of the space and created tendrils that reached out and wrapped around my limbs before quickly cocooning me. I heard another loud snap, an explosion of light, and opened my eyes to find myself on my ass on a damp earthen floor in what looked like the narrow tunnel of a cave system.

Daniel, Rome, Ginger, and Grey were sprawled around me. Rome straightened into a sitting position and held up his hand to reveal a tree limb with purple flowers. "Oops."

CHAPTER TWENTY-THREE

"Is this Hell?" I asked as we all scrambled to our feet. Despite what Daniel had said earlier, the strong aroma of blood and sulfur and the overall sense of dread didn't bode well.

"No," Daniel answered, unholstering his gun. "But it's probably going to get about as rough since I can sense demons and I don't see a return portal."

"Good going." Ginger slapped the back of Rome's head. "You broke the portal."

Rome grunted and rubbed the back of his head, shooting Ginger a death glare. "I got us in, didn't I?"

"Yeah, and you'd better pray we get back out," she said, "because if we get stuck wherever the hell this is with a bunch of demons and they decide they want to make sweet love to our orifices I'm gonna make sure you're the first orifice up on the offering block."

"Save it for the real enemy," Grey growled before sniffing the air. "We're in a cavern. I hear bats and I smell a shit-ton of blood, sweat, and guano."

"And sex," Daniel said, having done his own scenting.

I took their word for it, rather than smell the air myself. The sulfur, spice, and perfumy floral fragrance were overwhelming enough without purposely searching for other odors in the mix. I did open my other senses and almost wished I hadn't as I picked up several dark entities giving me the same vibe I'd gotten from Gregori, and other dark beings I knew had to be members of Cupid's demon army. I also picked up a heartbeat seeming to beat from within the walls. I noticed the flowers on the small branch Rome had broken off the tree glowed off and on, matching the pattern of the heartbeat. I picked it up and switched it out with one of the swords attached to my thigh. It fit perfectly inside the webbed holster. I unsheathed the other blade as I felt something deadly headed in our direction. "We're about to have company."

"Yeah, I picked up on that too," Daniel said, as he stepped in front of me. "Everyone behind me. Guns out. We'll shoot through as many as we can before moving to blades. I highly doubt a fucker as powerful as an archdemon doesn't know we're here already anyway."

Ginger and Rome wedged between Daniel and me, with Grey bringing up the rear as we moved down the narrow tunnel. I wanted to protest, but I was the only one without a gun and couldn't deny the logic behind shooting first, especially considering the narrow space we were in.

"Don't get bit," Grey reminded us as we continued toward the evil we felt approaching.

Light spilled into the tunnel as it opened out into a wider space. Daniel stopped there, and I felt the tension in his body as the evil I'd felt approaching us washed over the group. I looked over Ginger's shoulder and saw what looked like a small army of men and women in various styles of attire, all of them positively reeking of malevolence.

"What do we have here? Visitors with no escort," a tall, thin man in front said, his yellow eyes roaming over us. "I assume you were given cards?"

I felt warmth in my back pocket and the card lifted out on its own before flying right into the man's outstretched hand. The man's yellow eyes narrowed. "Just the one? Where is Gregori?"

"Dead," Daniel answered. "My pleasure."

The man hissed, revealing a forked tongue as his face changed shape and a hood grew from his flesh. Several others with him morphed the same way, their shirts ripping in the process. "Pity," he said. "I would have liked to kill him myself. I'll have to sssssssettle for dining on you."

"Not on the menu, bitch." Daniel raised his arm and opened fire. Ginger and Rome quickly backed him up, picking off the demons he missed as we moved out into the open space.

I heard slithering and looked up to see some of the nalkrims had taken full snake form and slithered along the walls and ceiling. One reached a point above me and dropped.

"Look out above you!" Grey yelled as he shouldered me out of the way and shot a salt bullet into the dropping demon.

With blades in hand, I took a stance, and started slicing at anything near me, careful not to hit any of my friends who I noticed maintained a perimeter around me as they fought. A barrage of bats flew into the room, temporarily blocking our view as they barreled over us. We swatted at the small creatures, carefully avoiding hitting each other, and as they cleared us, I found myself face to face with something pitch black and ugly as hell. It had black eyes, two slits for a nose and a gaping hole with tiny, sharp teeth.

My eardrum felt as if it would burst as a muzzle appeared beside my face and salt was shot into what passed for the thing's face. It exploded, resembling an inkblot, as its ass was blown away and an arm snaked around my waist.

I tried to protest but couldn't even hear myself over the ringing in my ear as Daniel lifted me off my feet and turned, shoving me back into the inner circle as Ginger, Rome, and Grey closed in around me, guns blazing, shooting at everything that leaped for us.

On instinct, I turned and buried my sword hilt-deep into the chest of a nalkrim about to clamp its mouth closed over Daniel's shoulder. Daniel's eyes widened as he looked down, realizing he'd almost been bit while moving me out of the way.

"Appreciate the help, but watch out for yourself," I said as heat spread out over my thigh. I looked down at the branch and saw it pulsating, its color an angry red. I opened my senses again, focusing on the heartbeat, and suddenly the beat became a call I had to follow.

I pushed past Daniel as he quickly reloaded and took off down a corridor where the source of the heartbeat seemed to come from.

"Danni! Fuck! Wait, damn it!"

I heard Daniel's heavy footfalls behind me as I ran down the corridor, sensing Eliza and the source of the heartbeat beyond. I heard something slithering and had barely looked up before the heavy weight had fallen on top of me, knocked me onto my back and sank its venomous teeth into my stomach. Pain exploded through my body as hot fire raced through my veins, then just as quickly seemed to back out, disappearing as it hit the air.

I heard a rage-filled roar, and the nalkrim was wrenched off of me. I scooted back against the opposite wall and untucked my torn shirt to see my broken skin knitting together as Daniel lifted the demon over his head and brought it down onto a jagged formation protruding from the cavern wall. The sharpened edge of the jutting structure popped through the demon's neck, nearly beheading it. Daniel lifted the nalkrim up again, slammed it to the cavern floor and dropped to a knee before he unsheathed his blade and buried it into the creature's chest.

The rest of our group caught up to us and skidded to a

stop, releasing a storm of curse words as they took in the scene.

Daniel was bent over me within the blink of an eye, his fingers moving over the skin I'd exposed. "It bit you. I saw it."

"I know," I said, prodding my stomach with my fingers as I worked through the overwhelming confusion and relief. I didn't feel any poison in my body, only the energy I'd awakened with. "It has to be because of Jon's blood. The poison was forced out, and my skin… It just healed automatically."

"If I ever meet this Jon guy, I'm going to kiss him," Daniel said as he pulled me to my feet. A breath later, he smashed me against his chest and held me just short of tight enough to crush bone as his heart raced a thousand miles a minute. "Don't you ever fucking do that again!"

"Guys," Ginger said, and Daniel eased up enough to allow me room to see her pluck his sword out of the charred remains of the nalkrim's body and hand it to him. "It's not time to celebrate yet."

I untangled myself from Daniel's hold and picked up the blades that had fallen from my hands when I'd been tackled by the nalkrim. The branch felt warm against my thigh, pulsating in time with the heartbeat, reminding me why I'd run. "I can't explain what is happening, but I sense a heartbeat and it's connected with this branch. It's calling me and I know in my gut that we have to follow it to free Eliza and whoever else that demon has filled his pantry with."

"Oh shit. This *is* the pantry," Ginger said, catching on.

I nodded, my stomach taking a dip as I looked down the dark corridor and realized something else deep in my gut. "Cupid knows we're here, and the bastard is playing with us. Those demons back there were just the first wave of his defense. Brace yourselves."

I tightened my grip on the blades in my hands and started walking, only to be yanked back, Daniel's grip tight around my bicep. "Wait."

I shrugged him off. "He's feeding from people, Daniel. He's getting some power or something from the red smoke, but why do you think he has captives at all? Why ones with sweet blood? He's drinking from them and I can only imagine what he's doing to Eliza. If you don't want to go with me—"

"I go where you go, always," he said, and grabbed my arm again before moving in front of me, "but I go first."

I swallowed down my knee-jerk response to tell him to can the macho shit and allowed him to lead. He had a gun, after all, and he held it, ready to fire, as we crept down the corridor. Grey and Ginger quickly took positions on either side of me, and Rome brought up the rear this time, I assumed because we'd sliced and shot through everything behind us already and as the only human in the group, the man was the most vulnerable, even if he was built like a tank.

We continued on until the corridor forked in three directions. Daniel looked back at me and I closed my eyes, sensing, and picked up multiple heartbeats just ahead. "Go straight," I told him and we continued to move in that direction.

About twelve feet deeper into the corridor, dread crawled up my spine, warning me something was wrong. I looked around but didn't see anything ahead or behind us in the darkness. Rome was a trained guard and his head stayed on a swivel. What the big guy lacked in paranormal ability, he made up for in skill, so I knew he could handle himself, but my gut was gnawing at me. Goosebumps broke out over my flesh as the feeling of unease continued to slither up my spine.

There was a rumble, and we all looked behind to see Rome covering his belly with his free hand a moment before he released a thundercloud of noxious air, which was immediately followed by a symphony of screeches and hisses, revealing shiny white teeth as shadow demons that had been creeping up on us unseen were blown backward.

"Get down!" Daniel ordered as he shoved me to the ground. Working in perfect synchronization, Rome and Ginger dropped to a knee to shoot blindly behind us while Daniel and Grey remained standing, shooting toward the top of the corridor.

I covered my ears against the screeching and sounds of pain and swallowed down the bile caused by the smell of acrid blood and charred flesh as their bullets found purchase, not to mention the smell Rome had released into the narrow space. The moment Daniel's gun clicked without discharging a bullet, he grabbed me by the back of my collar and pulled me up. "Let's go!"

We sped ahead down the corridor, and Daniel tossed his gun away, the weapon useless without bullets, and replaced it with his sword. He swung the blade side to side in front of him as we ran, in case there were other shadow demons that even our eyes couldn't pick up hiding in the darkness, not stopping until we spilled out from the mouth of the corridor, into a wider section with light available from a crack in the ceiling above us showing an arched doorway several feet ahead of us.

Four nalkrims ran toward us and using the speed I'd already accumulated to my advantage I dropped to my knees and slid across the slick cavern floor with both swords stretched out, taking down two at the knees while Daniel made quick work of beheading the other two. The demons who lost their heads burst into black ash while mine just writhed as their stumps appeared to burn, the blackened flesh spreading up their bodies. I rose to my feet and stabbed one in the chest as Daniel chopped the head off the other one, finishing them.

Daniel turned toward the tunnel as our three teammates arrived. "Everyone all right?"

"Thanks to Rome's ass pollution," Ginger said, holstering her gun before she replaced it with a blade. "I never thought I'd be thankful for the smell that comes out of him."

"Well, Rider did once say it could be used as a powerful weapon," I said.

"You're welcome." Rome curled his lip up at the inky black blood covering his arm and wiped it on his pant leg. "Y'all might have been getting eaten right now if I hadn't flushed those demons out."

"Well, at least you were finally able to flush something," Daniel said, never one to miss the opportunity to crack a joke at Rome's expense, before turning toward the door. "I'm guessing you want to go through there now?"

I sensed the heartbeats beyond the arch and started walking. Daniel quickly slid into step at my side. Maybe something in my walk told him not to try the placing me behind him crap again, but he still wasn't going to let me lead. Walking alongside me was a compromise. I noticed the way he seemed to scan every direction at once, watching out for me, but I could sense our only threat came from within the space beyond the arch made out of cavern wall and stalactites.

We stepped through into a cool, wide open space littered in bones and ahead of us on a dais of limestone sat a throne of skulls, and on that throne sat a large, muscular man with long golden hair, golden leather-like skin, shiny red satin pants, red boots, and a black vest hanging open to expose his bare chest.

"Oh look, it's Demon-David Lee Roth," Daniel muttered.

My gaze slid over to Eliza. She sat at the foot of the throne, the toga draped over her just as I'd seen in the vision. She looked up at us with tear-filled eyes as Cupid ran his finger down the side of her face gingerly. He slouched, completely comfortable, although his mismatched eyes burned with ire.

"So you are the food who entered my domain without an escort and slaughtered my guard dogs," the archdemon said, sounding like an even deeper-voiced Thanos.

Eliza, are you all right? I asked through our mental link, able to connect now that we were close to each other.

You shouldn't have come, she replied, sounding absolutely broken. *You'll be caged with them, and I can't help you. I can't help any of you.*

I followed the path of her gaze to see what looked like jail cell doors to the side of the room. Dirt-streaked, frightened faces peered out as thin fingers wrapped around bars. I recognized Alexis from her painting and knew the other naked women in the cell with her would match red dots in Rider's tracking program. The inhabitants of the other cells gave off different vibes though, and I knew the demon had been collecting paranormal beings along with human women with sweet blood. I was surprised there weren't more. From the sound of the many heartbeats I'd been sensing, and still sensed, I'd expected Cupid's pantry to hold a lot more people inside.

I followed the call of the heartbeats and realized they weren't the heartbeats of the people in the cells, or of Eliza. The heartbeats all came from Cupid. Either he had thousands of hearts or… He'd absorbed the souls of thousands and I was hearing their heartbeats inside him. I frowned, detecting one heart that beat louder, as if it were beating for… *Holy shit.*

The demon started clapping, pulling me out of my head before I could fully piece together the entire picture, but I had enough to know why Eliza was at the demon's side instead of in the cells with the others, and why she'd been given something to cover herself.

"Congratulations on getting this far," Cupid said, staring at me with those strange eyes that seemed to see a lot more than just what was right in front of him. "I can sense the succubus in you. You were given a card, no doubt for Gregori's personal enjoyment rather than my dinner. The nalkrims do enjoy their fun with succubi. It's hard to be angry though, that you not only declined but robbed me of the delivery I expected tonight, considering you brought such intriguing morsels with you this evening. A werewolf, a vampire, and an Imortian dragon shifter. Not my usual choice, but I can appreciate variety, and the worthless human looks to have sturdy bones. I can break him down for parts."

"Worthless human?" Rome looked around. "Oh, I know he ain't talking about me."

"Silence, insect."

Rome puffed his chest out. "Hey, yo, man, you're Cupid, right? So you're like that Eros dude too, right?"

"I have many names."

"Uh huh, well, I'm guessing Big Papa ain't one of them. I saw your statue at the museum, and I'd watch who you're calling worthless considering I got a pinkie bigger than your dick."

Cupid released a growl that shook my very bones as he stood from the throne, his eyes burning with rage as his lips peeled back from his teeth to reveal sharp fangs. His body expanded until he looked like an eight-foot-tall pro wrestler. Black wings unfolded from his back, and black claws sprouted from his fingertips.

"You just had to insult the size of the guy's pecker," I snapped at Rome as a mixture of hellhounds, nalkrims, and the pitch-black shadow demons that creeped me the hell out entered the room.

"Oops," he said, palming a gun in both hands.

"Kill them!" Cupid ordered, and his minions attacked.

"I still feel Jon's blood in my veins," I yelled to my friends. "Don't get dead or bitten trying to protect me!"

As the demons advanced, I hoped my friends understood what I was saying and focused on keeping themselves out of harm's way, knowing whatever Jon was, he'd gifted me with some sort of instant-healing ability as well as the psychic upgrade.

I tightened my grip on the swords in my hands and rushed forward, dropping to my knees before spinning along the slick floor, slicing as many demons as I could. I sliced, diced, kicked, and jumped out of the way of claws and fangs, all while trying to keep one eye on Cupid and the other on my friends, which included Eliza.

I noticed Cupid had advanced into the fray, but positioned himself in front of her, offering her protection as she covered her eyes, not wanting to see what was happening.

Open your fucking eyes, Eliza! I screamed through our mental link. *I know why you're here, why he's spared you what he's done to the others, but the person you sense inside him is long dead and we will be too if you don't help us!*

I can't. You don't know—

You know one of the souls inside him, and if it's who I think it is, believe me, I understand! I sliced up with my blade, catching a nalkrim along the underside of its freaky fanged head. *I'd give anything to see mine again, anything but the lives of others.*

I saw a hellhound jump on Rome's back and tried to get to him, but there were too many demons in my way. Thankfully, Grey shifted into wolf form and tore the beast off of him. I saw Ginger behead a shadow demon before it could get to Grey, and a storm of rainbow sparkles as Daniel zipped and zapped around Cupid, slicing at him with his sword before disappearing, which only seemed to piss the archdemon off. I recalled Grey saying something about the wiccans exorcising Cupid while we fought him so he would be weakened, but I didn't think they'd gotten the message from Grey that we'd found him. I didn't think the pack leader had accounted for the fact we'd find him in another realm after getting sucked into a portal.

Claws sliced down my arm, and even though my skin sizzled and burned, it instantly knitted back together. I elbowed the offending shadow demon in its freakish face, knocking it back a step and turned with my blades out, landing a double slice through its midsection. Thanks to the salt-fired blades, it went up in a puff of smoke and ash.

Rome screamed in anger as his guns clicked but

nothing shot out, and I knew I had to act. Rome was human. Without bullets, he had to get dangerously close to the remaining demons, and that was too much of a risk.

"Cover Rome!" I yelled over the grunts and shrieks and hisses as I cut a path toward Cupid. The branch burned against my thigh, the blooms shining so bright I didn't have to look down to see the glow. I felt the heartbeats pulsing against my thigh and heard them beating in a matching rhythm from within Cupid's chest, right where the demon's heart should be, and knew what needed to be done. Jon had already told me who had to be the one to do it.

Daniel caught sight of me approaching and I saw the fear in his eyes as Cupid swiped a clawed hand in his direction, but he disappeared before the nails could reach him and reappeared at Cupid's backside. Seeming to catch on to Daniel's tricks, the demon had expected the reappearance and was already swinging around. He clocked Daniel with a hefty swipe and sent the dragon shifter careening across the room.

With Cupid's attention focused on Daniel, I swerved to the right and sliced a nalkrim across the center of its torso before I kneeled by Eliza and dropped my swords long enough to yank her hands away from her eyes and remove the branch from my thigh holster. I shoved it into her hands. "I know you sense his spirit inside of that monster and his spirit senses you, but all that means is he isn't at rest and yes, his presence in the body of that evil thing is keeping you safe, but you're allowing it to kill and feed off others. Is that what he would have wanted you to do? By allowing his soul to remain in that demon, you've made him one too. Set him free!"

I heard a bellow and looked up to see Cupid barreling down on me, rage burning in his eyes. I scooped up my blades and leaped away from Eliza, preparing myself to fight him off as best I could, praying my words had gotten through to Eliza. A large wolf jumped at the demon's throat, only to be caught midair by a hellhound.

Daniel grabbed the hellhound by the tail and slammed it to the ground, causing it to release its hold on Grey, but the wolf fell to the ground in a heap, blood gushing from various wounds on his side. He shifted into his human form, but was too weak to get up.

The archdemon in front of me now, I swung my swords as I dropped to my knees and spun, my blades catching Cupid across his knees, burning him with a hiss of fire, drawing blood, but the salt was more of an irritation than the instant death it seemed to be for the others. The archdemon was too powerful.

I saw Ginger leap at his back, between his wings, with her sword raised in the air, but he grunted and bucked her off. Grey was back in the game, even if not at full strength, Rome and Daniel with him. Together we attacked as one, fighting off straggling lower-level demons as they neared us, but kept our focus on the archdemon, hoping enough slices would weaken him.

Cupid grabbed Grey and squeezed. I heard a bone break and blood squirt from an open wound and saw red. I ran straight for the demon, dropped to my knees and raised both blades over my head as I slid through the bastard's legs, slicing the crotch of his tight pants and the genitals they encased as I did.

Cupid let out a thunderous cry of pain and swung around, dropping Grey before snatching me up as if I were nothing more than a bug. He bared his fangs, and I was pretty sure he was about to literally tear my throat out and suck down my soul when a dragon appeared in the air behind him and unleashed a shower of fire on his head. The archdemon didn't catch fire, but his flesh smoked as it charred under the blaze.

Cupid roared, dropping me as he turned toward Daniel, who dove down, disappeared in a shower of sparkles before reappearing in time to shove me out of the way before the last remaining nalkrim could sink its fangs into my shoulder.

I watched in stunned horror as the snake-demon's venomous fangs punctured through the side of Daniel's throat instead. His eyes opened wide in a mixture of pain and terror as he stared at me, his mouth gaping open. His skin turned a sickly green around the location the nalkrim injected venom into him, then the veins underneath turned black and bulged like thick ropes under his flesh.

"No!" I screamed, fury snapping me out of the shock and I surged forward, slicing the nalkrim's head from its body. I dropped to my knees and had Daniel's upper body cradled in my lap before the nalkrim had finished shriveling up and rotting away. "Shift, Daniel! Heal yourself!"

His mouth moved, but no sound came out as he looked at me, eyes still coated in a sheen of fear and desperation. The black poison spread through the raised veins under his green-tinted skin.

I felt a gust of wind and looked up to see Cupid's clawed hand pulled back, ready to swipe down at me. There was a scream and the tip of the branch from the Cupid Root tree burst from the demon's chest. He released an animalistic bellow and staggered as he fell to one knee and turned to see Eliza. She backed away, her hands covering her mouth as she wept.

Red and purple streaks of light flowed from Cupid into the branch as if whatever power and strength he'd gotten from the tree were being returned to it.

"NOW!" I screamed. "He's weak. KILL HIM NOW!"

Ginger and Rome rushed forward with their salted blades and chopped away at the bastard, slicing and stabbing wherever their blades could find purchase while the archdemon struggled in vain to get to his feet. Having shifted to seal his wounds well enough to carry on, Grey joined the others, blade in hand. He raised his weapon over Cupid's kneeling body, but stopped short, catching sight of Daniel's condition.

Cupid swung a clawed hand toward Grey, only to have it sliced off at the elbow by Rome. Before the archdemon had time to react to that blow, Ginger jumped up to bury her blade in the nape of the beast's neck. She planted her feet in Cupid's lower back and yanked the blade down in a two-handed grip as she allowed her body to drop away from his, splitting the monster's back open between his wings.

Cupid threw his head back and roared in pain, exposing his throat. Rome grabbed a handful of the archdemon's hair and sliced his throat, turning the scream of pain into a strong gurgle of blood as the muscular bodyguard continued working on the wound he'd just created.

Seeing the villain was about to lose his head, and his body had already started charring like the other demons' bodies had done once killed, Grey left Cupid in Rome and Ginger's hands and dropped to his knees beside Daniel's body.

"Oh, damn it, Daniel," he whispered before looking at me with eyes filled with anguish. "He was bitten by the nalkrim and can't shift with the venom in his body. He's dying."

CHAPTER TWENTY-FOUR

Deep sobs wracked my body as I looked down to see the green tint and black veins spreading. "You overprotective jerk. Why did you push me out of the way? I was the one who was immune to—"

I still felt Jon's power flowing through my veins, the same power that had healed every cut, scrape, and venomous bite I'd received. He'd told me to stay calm, not to panic, and I'd started to panic and, in doing so, nearly missed my chance to save Daniel's life.

I dropped my mouth to the open, bubbling wound at Daniel's neck and sucked the poison out as my friends gasped around me.

"Danni, don't!"

I shoved Ginger away as she grabbed at my shoulders, spit out the poison, and turned with a hiss. "Nobody fucking touch me! I'm not letting Daniel die!"

I lowered my head again, sealed my mouth around the wound and continued the suck and spit action. Relief flooded me as I noticed how the black receded from his veins and they unpuffed more with each time I raised my head.

"Come on, Daniel. Stay with me." I repeated the

action. Suck and spit, suck and spit. Tears formed in my eyes as I felt whatever power Jon had given me with his blood starting to wane. I spit out another mouthful of venom and watched as the wound itself knitted together, but Daniel was still a little green, his breathing rough and slow. His veins no longer black and protruding, I gathered him in my arms and held his upper body close. "Fight for me, Daniel. Come on. I need you. Don't leave me. Stay. Please, please, stay with me."

His eyelids fluttered and his hand raised to wipe away the tears gliding down my cheek before he spoke in a hoarse, exhausted whisper. "I go where you go."

I heard at least a dozen exhales as my sobs turned into overjoyed laughter, and I held him closer. He still didn't shift or fully open his eyes, but the poison was gone. He'd make it.

Rome clamped a big hand on Daniel's shoulder and released another exhale before looking around. "Thank the Lord," he said. "Now that my boy is saved, how the hell are we getting out of here? Anybody know the exit or portal or whatever?"

I looked up, realizing the people who'd been caged were with us, everyone surrounding Daniel and I. They were still naked, covering themselves the best they could. Rome and Grey were missing shirts, which I could see they'd offered to two of the youngest women, who seemed very thankful for the bloody, torn garments. Spilled blood surrounded us, and Cupid's charred head and body still burned and crumbled where Rome and Ginger had chopped him down. The heartbeats of the souls the archdemon had taken beat no more.

"The only way in or out is through the smoke," Eliza said, "and I'm not sure that will come back without him. There are no doorways out. This isn't even our world."

I am a man who walks between worlds.

I smiled to myself as Jon's words replayed through my mind and flexed one of my hands. I could still feel a trace of his blood in me, and if his blood had led me to Eliza, healed me, and saved Daniel's life, I figured it might have another trick up its sleeve. I thought of what Daniel said. *I go where you go.* Hopefully, they all would this time.

"Everyone gather around me. Huddle close together and make sure you're touching someone so we're all connected." I took a deep breath as they followed my instruction and prayed I knew what I was doing, and had enough of Jon's blood left in me to do it as I pictured The Cloud Top in my mind.

Something licked my face.

"Welcome back."

I snaked an arm out and pushed the source of the familiar doggy breath away as I sat up and wiped drool from my cheek. I was in the bedroom of Grey's guest cabin and night had fallen. My body zinged with energy, as it usually did at this hour, but my mind was groggy.

Ginger sat on the edge of the bed, dressed in black jeans and a cropped black leather jacket. She smelled like wildflowers and I recognized the scent from the toiletries in the bathroom we shared. I smelled like soap that hadn't been rinsed off as well as it could have been.

I looked down, saw my ripped jeans, torn shirt, and assorted black blotches of dried demon blood, and it all came rushing back to me. My heart started racing with panic. My own heart, not the double heartbeat I'd felt earlier. Jon's blood had run its course. I slammed the brakes on my panic and sucked in air. I had to calm down unless I wanted to alert Rider to my distress, and I didn't want to disturb him if he were in trouble. Sensing my emotions, Kutya whined.

"Relax. Daniel's fine and we all made it back."

Relief flooded my chest. "How did we get here? The last thing I remember is holding Daniel. Cupid was dead, all of his minions dead. The people… the people were free, but we didn't know how to get out."

"I don't know how you did it, but you got us out. You told us to all huddle around and you closed your eyes. The next thing I know, all of us are sprawled out on the ground in front of the cabin and you were out cold." She grabbed a glass off the nightstand and held it to my lips. "Drink. We forced a little into you before sunrise, but you need more."

My thirst flared to life as the reheated blood's coppery scent filled my nose. I took the glass from Ginger and drained it, my sluggishness draining away with it. After all that remained was a red coating along the side of the glass, I set it back on the nightstand and swung my legs over the side of the bed. "Where's Daniel? Where's Eliza?"

"Daniel's handling those devil-worshiping morons who tried to pass themselves off as a K-Pop group. Grey's pack snatched them up the minute we got sucked into that other realm and their connection with him went toes up," she explained after I raised my eyebrows. "They're here at The Cloud Top wherever Grey's people do their own version of interrogation. Eliza's at another cabin, being watched over by Grey."

"How is Grey? I remember he didn't look so good."

"Yeah, he got pretty banged up, but shifters are great healers. Once he was out of the fight and could shift a few times without immediately getting injured again, get some rest and some food, he healed up fine. Rome's good, just sore, but Angel baked him a cake, so he's all happy and shit. How are you? You scared the hell out of me wiping out like that."

I ran my hand through my hair, scratching my head as I thought. "I'm good. I was sluggish, but the blood helped. I feel like me now. Just me. Jon's power, or whatever it was he gave me through his blood, must have been spent bringing everyone back here."

"How did you do that? How did you even know how?"

"I pictured the cabin and I don't know, I saw us all

here and really, really wanted to bring us all back." I shrugged. "All I knew was Jon's juju was running through me and the man can zip-zap through realms like it's nothing, so I gave it a whirl."

"You gave it a whirl?" She shook her head and laughed. "Well, I'm glad you did, because I really thought we were fucked."

"Yeah, Jon came through. I don't know how he knew we'd need his help, but he definitely delivered." I stood and stretched. "I'm going to get cleaned up."

"Take your time," she said, standing up. "I'll make sure Angel has a sandwich or something. You should drink live blood, get your strength back, and after all the stress of everything, it's probably best to drink from her and not risk your succubus side going all crazy drinking from a man."

I nodded my agreement and grabbed a pair of jeans and a gray sweatshirt before heading into the bathroom.

"Girl, I still don't really know what that red smoke did, but I think its effect wore off after we ganked that big bastard," Ginger said as I came down the stairs.

She and Rome sat on the couch, watching a live news report on the television. Kutya ran over to them and started nosing around the plate on the coffee table in front of them, but Rome quickly picked it up. "No chocolate crumbs for you, big buddy. Sorry."

We exchanged brief smiles as he passed me to take the dish to the kitchen.

"What happened?" I asked as I walked over to Angel, who was already rolling up her shirtsleeve.

"Police and fire department are out there," Ginger answered as the news program went to commercial. "It seems that Cupid's Root tree went up in a blaze. From what I gathered from the interviews, the people who were affected by the smoke were brought out from under the fog as soon as that happened. They called the fire department in, but the fire never spread from that one tree. The fire department, however, noted the lack of security and the fact they didn't seem to have any idea of the event and can't understand why they weren't notified. Police and medical personnel were called in after some of the festival-goers started reporting loss of memory, and now they're looking into the possibility of illegal drugs being given to people without consent. The Lovefest organizers are baffled because they claim they contacted authorities, got all the required permits, yada yada. Whatever dark magic Cupid worked over that area, it's gone now."

"Wait. What happened to the people we saved from his pantry?"

"Oh yeah. Grey handled that," Angel explained as I bent and started drawing blood from her wrist. "The pack got them dressed and cleaned up, then took them back to the woods outside the festival grounds. One of the women from that coven, the one with the actual witch blood, blurred their memories enough that they only remember going to the festival, so they were some of the ones reporting memory loss."

"What a mess," I said, drawing back to seal Angel's wounds. "Has anyone spoken to Eliza about what happened?"

"She wasn't very talkative after you zapped us back here," Ginger said, "and it was close to dawn. Grey was beat. We were all pretty tired and out of it. Some members from Grey's pack got us all sorted out, tended to Rome's wounds, lugged Daniel up to his bed, got you as cleaned up as they could without undressing you. I was able to grab a quick shower and then I just face-planted in the bed. I woke up maybe fifteen minutes before you did, long enough to warm your blood and get a quick update from Rome."

"Grey's talking to her now," Rome said, leaning back

against the sink with his muscular, bandaged arms folded. "I got the sense he didn't trust her enough to allow her to stay here with us. He said something about a spare room in his cabin and took her with him when he left us."

"For what? Is he interrogating her?"

Rome held his hands up. "I don't know, but it was pretty weird how she was up there next to Cupid on his throne and shit, not locked up like the others. She actually cried when he died. That crying for the enemy stuff is shady."

"She wasn't crying for him," I growled as I left the cabin, closing the door behind me before Kutya could follow me out. In case things got ugly, I didn't want the big pup trailing me.

I took a deep breath and opened my senses, pushing past the energy signature of the two werewolf guards on duty outside the cabin. I sensed Daniel, alive and well. My heart fluttered with relief to find his signature so strong. Once I picked up on Eliza and Grey, I set forth in that direction, following their signatures until I reached a small cabin set a ways back from the rest dotted along The Cloud Top. It was set back in the trees, near a cliff, and had floor to ceiling windows in front and a full wraparound deck.

I saw Grey move through the house as I approached, dressed in jeans, a light blue T-shirt, and bare feet. He stepped outside as I climbed the front steps and held his hands up. "I didn't harm her. I just questioned her."

"And?" I folded my arms. "Did you find her guilty?"

He leaned back, resting his weight along one of the windows, and shoved his hands into his pockets. "Her father's soul was inside that fucking monster?"

I nodded. "That's why I heard so many heartbeats. I thought I was hearing her and the other captives so I could find their location, but I was hearing the heartbeats of every soul that demon ever took, and thousands of them were inside that beast's chest. I heard only one beating with love and it just clicked."

"That's why she wasn't caged or naked like the rest of them."

"Cupid was still an evil bastard, but the souls of those he took over the centuries apparently held some sway over him. Her father's soul recognized her and protected her."

Grey shook his head. "If I wasn't there myself, I'd never believe any of this shit."

"Hey, you're the one who figured out we were up against Cupid in the first place."

"Yeah, still… it's nuts, especially you, with the way you teleported us all out of there. And what was up with the branch? You knew to bring that and then give it to her. How?"

I shrugged. "Jon. Drinking his blood did something. It turned my gut instincts into actual visual and audio clues. The branch glowed to the beat of the hearts calling me. The branch matched Cupid's heart, so I knew it had to go there to weaken him enough to allow our blades to actually destroy him. I knew Eliza had to be the one to do that because Jon told me Cupid could only be weakened by the one he desired most, and he desired Eliza because of the soul inside him that was emotionally attached to her. I would have never gotten close to him with that branch. He knew what it could do to him, but Eliza… he never expected her to be the one to ram it through his heart, so he didn't watch out for her."

"Shit. I wouldn't mind meeting this Jon guy. Maybe you can introduce us."

"You don't find Jon," I said, repeating what I'd been told and now understood. "Jon finds you… when he's needed."

"Nice."

I looked inside the cabin, following Eliza's energy signature. When I looked over at Grey, I saw he was watching me.

He jerked his head in the direction of the cabin's

interior. "Go on. Talk to her."

I nodded and entered the cabin, then stopped short. "Wait. I almost forgot. What about Pacitti? He was headed this way when we left for Lovefest."

"He was informed he was on private property and strongly encouraged to leave."

"Just like that?"

"*Strongly* encouraged." Grey walked over to a console table and lifted two envelopes from a tray atop it. "But he knew you were here, so he said to deliver these."

I took the two white envelopes. One had Angel's name written in feminine cursive script, and the other had my name scrawled across the top in messy block letters, underlined three times. Both envelopes were sealed. "Thanks."

Grey nodded and walked over to a bar along the other side of the room to pour himself a drink. I shoved the envelopes into my back pocket and followed Eliza's energy until I reached a closed door down the hall. I knocked and entered to find Eliza sitting in a lounge chair to the side of the freshly made bed, hugging her knees to her chest. She'd been given a set of dark blue sweats too small to be Grey's.

"Hey."

She turned glistening eyes up to me. "Danni, I'm so sorry."

"It's okay." I sat on the edge of the bed, facing her. "Tell me what happened. I figured some things out, but there's a lot of holes."

She nodded. "I know. I don't even know where to begin."

"Start from the beginning. How did your father's soul get into Cupid? How did you cross paths? Do you have any idea how Cupid was doing any of this?"

She took a deep breath and wiped away a tear. "I went to Lovefest. I go to events like that all the time and just enjoy the dancing and the music, and I was having a good time, but then I was given a card by that Gregori man. I had no idea he was a demon. My radar didn't pick him up at all, but I think that was because of the tree." She rolled her eyes. "That boy band had no idea what they were doing. They thought they were working some spell to give them power so they could gain fame and fortune. They didn't know they'd caused a tree to grow and created a portal allowing Cupid and his minions to come and go, or that they were strengthening him every night, allowing him to take more prey into his pantry."

"So you weren't the first?"

"No." She shook her head. "I was one of the first, but there were some taken the day before me."

"Why did Gregori give you a card? He gave me one, and I figured it was because of my sweet blood, but Gregori is a nalkrim and they also like succubi. What attracted him to you?"

"I don't think my being a vampire had anything to do with it. I believe Cupid had some sort of ability to blur detection of his minions and himself, but it worked both ways. On the field, Gregori couldn't detect paranormals either, other than those of the demonic type, because he himself was a demon. Although some paranormals ended up receiving and accepting invitations, and Cupid did enjoy the power kick from their blood, Gregori collected women with sweet blood and anyone he sensed a sweet disposition in. Cupid liked the taste of sweet blood, and he liked his prey timid."

I chose to ignore the hurt of being reminded I was considered a demonic type. I was half succubus and I couldn't do anything but accept it. "Okay, I can see the timid thing with you, and obviously you accepted the invitation."

"Yes, I clearly didn't have the same good sense as you because I walked blindly into the trap."

"But you were set free. You came back home after that. The only reason we knew you'd returned and been abducted out of your own house was because your mouse told us."

She frowned. "Told you?"

"Jadyn," I said, and could tell by the dawning realization in her eyes, Jadyn's name was the only word I needed to give to explain.

"How is Harry?"

"Uh, this was the girl."

"Mofo? I'm surprised she told you anything. She's not as friendly as her mate."

"Her name is Mofo?" I chuckled at Eliza's blush, never figuring her the type to name a mouse Mofo, but given the surly critter's demeanor… "That one has an attitude, but they're fine."

Eliza smiled. "Good. I was concerned about them. Mofo acts as if she doesn't need help, but they haven't had to really scavenge in quite some time."

"They're fine. Back to Cupid… You were released, weren't you?"

She dropped her gaze, unable to meet my eyes. "I was brought to him as food. He gained power from the energy his smoke drew out of the emotions filling the air at the festival, but he quenched his thirst with blood, as he'd been doing for centuries. After the blood in his pantry weakened after so many feedings, he often took the entire soul. It made him stronger, but part of those souls remained inside him. Apparently, he'd taken my father's soul many centuries ago. My father recognized me and wouldn't allow Cupid to finish drinking from me. I was released. In a sense, rejected."

"Centuries…" There was a lot to unpack in that spiel, but the time reference was what really grabbed me. "Eliza, I thought you weren't that old. I mean, no offense, but…"

"I'm weak?"

Now it was my turn to drop my gaze, but I forced myself to meet her eyes before continuing. "Timid. You're not a fighter. Rider has always said the older a vampire gets, the harder it can be to control the dark urges, but you've never come across as dark at all to me."

"I was born sick, and I never got better," Eliza said. She rubbed her hands over her knees and seemed to search for words. "This is our secret. If anyone knew my true age and thought I was a threat…"

"I get it. You're not a fighter."

"I'm not. I was almost dead when I was turned, the sickness having drained me of every ounce of life force. My father was away, having set off to retrieve the healer, but the rest of my family lined my bed, waiting for that final goodbye should he not return in time. Before I could draw my last breath, our village fell under attack by a type of monster they were not prepared for."

"Vampires."

"Yes. My sire was an evil woman. She thought I looked like a delicate little doll and she wanted me for her collection. My mother died trying to save me, even though I would have died either way. My sire killed my entire family and turned me into her very own doll, and that's all I became in the turning. A fragile doll. The vampirism saved my life, but I was born so weak, not even it could give me much strength."

"Oh, Eliza." I reached over and took one of her hands in mine. The succubus in me didn't like the connection, but I didn't give a shit.

"I never knew what happened to my father, not until I was taken before Cupid and sensed his soul inside."

I squeezed her hand. "I could sense who you felt inside Cupid, and I sensed his love for you, and yours for him. Were you able to actually communicate with him?"

"Not in words." She sighed. "But I could sense feelings, sometimes pictures. Fragments of memory. Cupid sensed everything. It was strange. The souls didn't control him, but they did have some effect on him. My father forced him to release me and I fled, distraught. I knew I should have told Rider, reported the demon's presence, but if he killed him…"

"He'd kill what was left of your father too."

She nodded. "I think part of me hoped that my father's soul would protect others, but I know now it didn't. Like I said, the souls affected Cupid but didn't completely control him. I wasn't home very long before Cupid himself opened a portal using the blood connection carried within my father's soul and yanked me back there to his pantry. He only drank from me the once, never touched me in a sexual manner, and I was given a drape to hide my nudity after my belongings were taken from me, but he wouldn't let me go again. Sometimes it seemed as if Cupid himself had feelings for me."

"I think he did," I told her. "Jon came to me, told me he had to be weakened by the one he desired most. That's how I knew you were the only one who could stab him with a branch from his own tree and weaken him so he could be destroyed."

Hey babe, Rider's voice entered my mind through our link. *I'll be home by dawn. Pack up and head back. See you soon.*

I blew out a breath. "Rider's been away, but he's headed back home now, and we need to as well."

"So many people were taken. Drank from. Used." Tears fell from Eliza's eyes and she wiped them away. "I deserve whatever punishment Rider gives me, but I hope if it's death, I'll find my father again wherever he rests now. I hope he finally rests."

"I'm sure he's resting peacefully now, for the first time in centuries," I assured her before squeezing her hand again. I stood and turned for the door. "Rest, check out the waterfalls before we head out. They're really pretty… and forgive yourself. Don't worry about Rider. He'll understand, and if he doesn't, he'll still have to get through me to kill you and I'm telling you right now, that's not happening."

CHAPTER TWENTY-FIVE

I sat on the edge of the cliff I'd noticed earlier on my way to Grey's cabin. Below me, the forest stretched on, the trees bathed in the beautiful oranges, yellows, and reds of late fall. Or was it early winter? I breathed in the cool night air, letting it chill my throat, and decided it didn't matter. It was beautiful. It was perfect. I felt a shift in the air overhead and didn't have to look up or behind me to know who had just landed a few feet away.

"You know, I'm the one who's supposed to save you," Daniel said as he stepped into my side view and lowered himself to sit alongside me, allowing his long legs to dangle over the edge next to mine.

"I don't always need saving."

"Very true."

I turned to see him staring at me, his gray, brown-rimmed eyes shining brightly in the moonlight. His mouth curved up at the corner, too soft to be a smile, but just …peaceful. Content. "But we'll always be there to save each other, won't we?"

"You know me. I go where you go." He blinked and looked down, way down into the colorful forest valley below us. "I'd rather you not go over the edge of this cliff."

I laughed. "You'd catch me."

"Always." His eyes grew very serious as he returned his gaze to me. "Don't ever do that again, Danni. Don't risk your life for me."

"I was immune to the venom."

"Did you know that for absolute certain? Did you know you'd still be immune if you drew it out of me with your mouth, or that what Jon gave you was still there? Were you one hundred percent sure?"

I looked away. "Does it matter?"

"Yes. You're loved and needed here."

I whipped my head back around toward him. "So are you."

He shook his head. "I don't—"

"I need you. I … I love you, you big dumb jerk." I took his hand in mine and stared at our intertwined fingers rather than what I was afraid I'd see in his eyes. I didn't want to break his heart or tease him, but I did love him, even if I couldn't give him what he wanted. "You're the best friend I've ever had, and when I saw that poison corroding your veins, your skin turning green around it… It was worth the risk to save you, because I don't really want to know what it would be like to live in a world without you in it. I don't think I *could* live in a world without you in it."

His hand tightened around mine and when I dared raise my eyes to look at him, he was facing the edge of the cliff, looking out, taking in the view of the beautiful valley and the waterfall in the distance. His eyes were wet, his jaw clenched, but he didn't let a single tear fall.

I rested my head on his shoulder and sometime later, he released my hand to drape his arm over my shoulders, lending me some of his warmth as the night air grew colder. "Rider is headed back to Louisville and gave us the all-clear, but he has a longer drive."

"I know." I sighed. I felt no rush to leave. "I love these

mountains."

"Maybe Rider will buy you a house here someday."

"Maybe." We continued to sit in companionable silence as I took in the scenery and enjoyed the warmth of Daniel's body spreading into my own, but as the minutes ticked into an hour and the hour stretched longer, I knew we couldn't stay. We had to go back to The Midnight Rider where all eyes were on us, watching, waiting… "He wants to kill you."

"I know."

"That's it? You know? No emotion, no concern?"

"That's it. I know, and honestly, if I was Rider, I'd want to kill me too." Daniel's lips pressed against the top of my head. "Everyone's healed up, good to go. Grey and his pack ran off Pacitti, took care of the people we sprung from Cupid's pantry and will continue monitoring that whole shitfest, and those idiots who blended the incantation into their song were just dumb-fucks trying to summon a minor demon to help them get laid and make some money." He held his free hand up when I turned toward him. "Hey, I'm not saying they're boy scouts. I'm just saying they didn't intend to open a portal for Cupid. Grey handed them over to the witch for mind-blurring after I finished making sure they were just idiots instead of evil masterminds. We've found Eliza and wrapped up our loose ends. We don't have a lot of reason to stay here."

"Except the view."

"The view is gorgeous," he agreed, but I noticed his gaze rove over my face as he said it.

"Pacitti's probably still a loose end," I said, getting up before my succubus side got ideas. I was a little surprised it hadn't gotten randy after such a long stretch of close proximity to an extremely attractive man I cared about, but I guess I'd fed it enough violence and female blood recently to keep it under control.

"Yeah," Daniel agreed, standing to join me, "but we can kick his ass back home just as easily as we can here."

"That's the craziest shit I've ever heard," Rider said as we finished our recap.

We'd beaten him back to The Midnight Rider by about twenty minutes, just long enough to get Kutya settled in before the big pup had sensed him a block away and alerted us all to his presence. It had taken the full retelling of the events of Lovefest and a lot of pets and scratches from Rider before he'd settled back into his plush doggy bed and dozed off. Sometimes I thought the dog had a closer tie to him than I did. Almost.

"I go away for a few nights, send you to Pigeon Forge, and you kill Cupid," he said with a shake of his head. "Unbelievable. And that's who was preying on the women with sweet blood."

"Yup," Ginger said with a yawn. "I don't feel so bad anymore about not being able to track down an incubus around here."

"At least we know the tracking system works," Rider said before making a shooing motion toward where she sat across from him on the other side of his desk. "Go on. It'll be daylight soon. Get some rest."

Ginger saluted him and patted Rome's head as she stood. "See you later boys, and you too, sweet cheeks."

Rider chuckled deep in his chest as she left his office. "She loves that she can get away with that."

I looked over at where Daniel sat slouched down into the couch, his gaze roaming over Rider's bookshelves, looking anywhere but where I sat perched on Rider's lap, and felt a tug of something similar to guilt in my heart. Rider was flaunting our relationship, and I didn't like it, but when he'd tugged me down onto his lap, I didn't have a lot of choice. Resisting him would have been a rejection, and a rejection in front of his people, especially in front of Daniel, wouldn't have gone over well.

Rome grabbed the arms of the chair he sat in and

pushed up. "If you don't need me for anything…"

"Go," Rider told him. "Take tomorrow off and I want you to visit Nannette just to make sure you don't have any internal damage."

"I'm human, but I'm not delicate," Rome said with a trace of indignation.

"Yeah, but demons aren't the normal type of shit I'd send you out to handle. Get checked."

"Ten-four." Rome finished hefting himself out of the chair, moved toward the door and shared what looked like some sort of special bro handshake with Daniel before leaving.

"Sometimes it's almost as if the two of you are friends," Rider said, speaking directly to Daniel for the first time since he'd arrived.

"Yeah, he's bearable when he's not wrecking the plumbing," Daniel responded, and straightened. "Is there anything else you need from—"

We all jerked a little in surprise as Jon appeared in front of the closed office door dressed in an emerald green button-down shirt, black pants, and Italian leather shoes. Kutya jumped up, yelped, and took cover under Rider's desk once he managed to push through our legs to get to the space. Unlike Daniel, Jon didn't do the rainbow sparkles. He just popped in and out of wherever he did or didn't want to be.

"I hear I should be thanking you for helping my people out," Rider said once we recovered from the surprise.

"Danni did all the work," Jon said, his gaze locked on mine. "I simply gave her a little juice. How are you dealing with Eliza?"

"I'm sending her to Nannette to be thoroughly checked out, physically and mentally," Rider replied.

Jon's gaze left mine to focus on Rider. "No punishment?"

"Do you think she requires punishment?"

"I think she's been through a lot and will punish herself

well enough on her own."

"I agree." Rider took a breath, seeming to brace himself. "You're a man of mystery, but I know you well enough to know you're not here just to check on Eliza, especially since you seem to know everything."

"Not everything, but enough." Jon glanced my way before returning his focus to Rider. "I hear you have a witch who isn't talking."

Rider stilled. "You heard right."

"Let's do something about that." Jon turned for the door and opened it.

"Stay here," Rider told me as he prodded me up and stood before motioning for Daniel to come with him.

"Danni can come," Jon said, looking back. "Trixell won't be able to hurt her. Soon enough, she won't be able to hurt anyone."

"Well, that sounds promising," I said as Jon left the office. We all followed him out, except for Kutya. The pup was sticking to his hiding place.

Jon led the way down the hall that ran along the back of The Midnight Rider, took the door on the left, passed the staircase leading up to Rider's private quarters, and pushed through the door leading down into the sublevels.

Has he been to Trixell's cell before? I asked Rider through our mental link, noticing Jon seemed to know exactly where Trixell was being held without needing to be told.

No.

Does he have access? I asked, also noticing how he was able to place his palm over the hand scanners beside each door and be allowed through.

I never gave him security clearance, but I'm pretty sure Jon has access wherever he wants to go.

It certainly seemed that way as Jon continued to lead us straight toward the back section of the sublevel my sister's body rested in. The security in place had already been switched out, so mostly shifters were on duty, the vampires always discharged to head home before daylight since they weren't as strong during those hours. They acknowledged Rider with nods, a few frowning curiously at Jon, but they didn't speak.

I felt the sun as it started to rise, but intrigue helped me fight off the pull of sleep as we continued. We reached another door with a security panel and Jon made his way through that one with no trouble either.

The first thing I saw as we stepped through was a set of cells. The room I'd never been in looked very much like a jail. Malaika sat in a chair to our left, in front of one of the cells. She quickly stood as she saw us. "Is something wrong? She's been restrained since we started with the direct injection of witch's net."

"Good," Rider said as the four of us stopped in front of the cell and looked at the woman inside.

Trixell still wore the dark gray dress she'd been in the night she'd helped my sister try to kill me. Other than a cot and toilet, it didn't appear she'd been offered anything. I wasn't sure if she'd been allowed to use the cot though. She currently appeared glued to the back wall with glittery silver web-like ropes I knew to be witch's net, the substance that blocked witches from using their power to cast spells. An IV bag hung on a hook outside the cell, holding the liquid containing witch's net currently being delivered directly into the witch's vein. Despite all that, Malaika still alternated with Rihanna to stand guard, holding their own protective spells in place.

"You can drop your spell," Jon told her. "She can't escape."

Malaika looked at Rider for confirmation. He shared a look with Jon, narrowed his eyes a little in thought, but nodded his head, giving her the okay.

I felt a change in the air as Malaika took a deep breath. Her shoulders sagged a little, as if they no longer carried a great deal of weight.

"You can head home," Rider told her. "All the way home."

Her eyebrows shot up. "You mean…?"

"You can return to your city and your family. Thank you for your help."

She blinked a few times and shot a curious look at Jon, but smiled and made her way out. Knowing she had a child she had to hate being away from, I couldn't blame her.

"I've tried a lot," Rider said. "She gets off on pain, but if you think you can get her talking, be my guest."

Jon walked straight through the steel bars and strode up to the witch. She was still unable to conjure magic due to the witch's net in her system, but without Malaika's spell in effect, she appeared more alert as Jon approached.

"You're going to tell me what Selander Ryan is up to," Jon told her.

The witch stared at him and cackled. "I will nev—"

Trixell's eyes widened as Jon's turned bright white. He closed the little remaining distance between them and as we watched, he stepped into her body. Bright beams of blinding white light shot out of Trixell's eyes, ears, mouth, nose, and probably other orifices I didn't want to think about as her back arched and she let out a scream that threatened to reduce the walls around us to rubble.

Rider pulled me against his chest as he turned away, shielding us from the light.

"What the fuck is he?" I heard Daniel ask and knew he was shielding his eyes too, hunkered down by both of us.

"Useful," Rider said, and I heard the grimace in his voice as the witch's scream reverberated around our skulls.

Suddenly, dead silence fell over the room and we squinted to see the light dimming. Once it no longer hurt our eyes, we turned to see Jon back out of Trixell's body. The witch's net was destroyed, but Trixell didn't escape. She dropped to the floor of her cell, a shivering mass of flesh and bone, her face a mask of pure horror as she stared up at Jon.

"Selander Ryan is searching for your mother. Once he

finds her, he intends to return to his body and come for Danni. His plan is to use Danni for a spell that will bring Katalinka back inside her body so he can have Katalinka and your beloved as well. Trixell doesn't know where the bones are. Your brother wanted her here so she could mess with Danni's mind, weaken her defenses, and grab her as soon as he found Katalinka. She knows nothing else useful to you, so feel free to dispose of her as you wish. Her presence on this earth will bear nothing good."

Jon straightened the sleeves of his button-down shirt as he left the cell, again walking through the bars like a ghost, and stopped in front of me. He held my gaze as he angled his head to the side. "I believe I'll see you again, Danni."

I watched him walk toward the exit, but he disappeared before he reached the door.

"Seriously, who the hell is that guy?" Daniel asked, staring after him.

"Daniel, do you have room to light it up in here?" Rider asked. I turned to see his eyes had darkened until they almost appeared black. His jaw clenched as tight as his fists as he stared at the shivering witch, his entire body thrumming with barely controlled rage.

"Yeah, I can roast her," Daniel answered.

"Good, but wait until I finish with her. Danni, go to our room. Now," he ordered, turning those fury-filled eyes toward me.

I'd seen Rider angry, and I'd seen him furious enough to remove a man's spine with his bare hands, but I'd never seen his eyes shine with the promise of not just death, but pure vengeance. I backed up without a word and turned to leave the room.

The security doors closed behind me and I'd made it halfway across the outer room before Trixell started screaming. It sounded like whatever he was doing to her, it hurt worse than what Jon had done… and Jon had left her a quivering mess.

CHAPTER TWENTY-SIX

I retrieved Kutya from Rider's office and took him upstairs, not really sure if it was for his benefit or mine, but hugging the pup while I tried to blank out what the two people I cared about most in the world did to the witch in one of the sublevels below me helped calm my nerves.

Once the tremors stopped coursing through my limbs, I kissed Kutya's head and got up from where I'd cozied up with him on the bed. I might as well get ready for bedtime, even though I no longer sensed sleep coming although the sun had risen fully.

I was too wired, an aftereffect of what Jon had done, and what Rider and Daniel were doing, and how I could share a bed with one of them knowing he'd caused someone to scream in such horrendous pain.

I'd already showered before leaving Pigeon Forge, so I just dropped my jeans and sweatshirt to the floor and slid into one of Rider's T-shirts, using it as a nightshirt. On my way back to the bed, I saw the envelopes sticking out of the back pocket of my jeans.

I'd given Angel hers before Tony had taken her to my apartment, volunteering for the task. After a few nights running the bar and Rider's operation by himself, the tiger shifter was ready to get out of the building. Whether or not Angel opened the letter that was clearly from her mother was up to her. Tony had given me another letter before they'd left, and I'd shoved it in my pocket with the one from Pacitti.

I took both envelopes out of the pocket and kicked the jeans aside before plopping down onto the bed. Kutya let out a low whine and rested his head in my lap as I sat back against the pillows stacked against the headboard. The envelope Tony had given me was from my mother. I slid my fingernail under the seal and removed the pink stationery inside.

Dearest Danni,

It has come to my attention that I have been a horrible mother. I feel the need to apologize, although I suspect you will tear this letter up and throw it into the garbage as you have done me. Yes, you tore me up and discarded me, and I cannot blame you.

I have received word Shana was seen in Nevada. Las Vegas, of all places. I didn't believe you. I accused you of something horrible. I truly thought you jealous and vengeful, and I know now I was wrong.

Shana was the child who needed me, who would love me and care for me. Shana was the one to do us proud, but I have no words for her now. To run from her wedding reception, to disappear again to Las Vegas after her husband's body was found mutilated. I don't know what to think.

You were always the strong one, the one who didn't need me, or so I thought, until you spoke so hatefully to me at your apartment. I can't blame you. I don't expect you to understand why I have always treated you and Shana so differently, but I need to try to explain, if you will allow me. Please contact me. We need to talk.

Love (Yes, Danni, I do love you),

Mom.

I stared at the pink paper in my hand, blinking, sure the words would eventually rearrange themselves to make sense. My mother hadn't apologized to me since… Ever. She'd never apologized to me and she certainly had never even slightly insinuated Shana was anything less than perfect. I was still staring at the letter when Rider entered the room.

"What's that?"

"A letter from my mother." I looked up and my breath hitched as I caught sight of Rider crossing the room, shoes in hand so as not to get blood on the floor. His steel gray shirt and dark pants were heavily covered in the coppery substance, and although it looked like he'd made an effort to wipe his skin free of it, blood smears still marred his face and arms.

He stopped, looked down at himself, and his jaw ticked. "Give me ten minutes to rinse off, then join me."

I watched him walk into the bathroom and heard his boots hit the floor before the shower started. I looked down to see the paper shaking in my trembling hand.

I shoved the paper back into the envelope and set it on the nightstand. Ten minutes. Ten minutes to get the image of Rider looking like Prom Night Carrie out of my head. What had he done to Trixell? What had he done for Seta that he claimed he couldn't tell me for my own safety?

What was he truly capable of?

Ten minutes. I took a breath and opened the other envelope, needing something to take my mind off that train of thought.

Pacitti's envelope held two pieces of paper, both with black and white images printed on them. They were grainy, but good enough quality I could deduce they were from security cameras. Daniel had taken care of the gas station's cameras, but none of us had known about the one Pacitti had clearly located, the one that had to have belonged to a private residence. From the angle, I knew it had come from one of the houses I'd seen beyond the woods where Rome had gone off to use the bathroom.

Nausea filled my stomach as I stared down at the

images of Daniel's hand being shot, followed by time-stamped images showing him there, then not, then there again and his hand perfectly fine. That could be explained as a camera glitch, surely, but I didn't know how we would explain the shots of me biting the woman's neck and Ginger sealing the wound.

Pacitti had scribbled a short message along the bottom of the last page: *I'll be in touch, and if you get any ideas... just know I'm not dumb enough not to have copies.*

"Danni."

I looked up from the pictures I'd been staring at to see Rider watching me from where he leaned against the wall, arms folded over his bare chest as he stood naked except for the towel slung around his hips catching the rivulets of water gliding down from the ends of his hair.

"I was in there for twenty minutes. Do we have a problem?"

I looked back down at the damning evidence in my hand. Boy, did we ever.

***

Rider will make an appearance in Blood Revelation Book Six: Immortal Rage *before Danni and the rest of the Midnight Rider crew return in* Twice Bitten Book Six: Merry Fangin' Christmas.

ABOUT THE AUTHOR

Crystal-Rain Love is a romance author specializing in paranormal, suspense, and contemporary subgenres. Her author career began by winning a contest to be one of Sapphire Blue Publishing's debut authors in 2008. She snagged a multi-book contract with Imajinn Books that same year, going on to be published by The Wild Rose Press and eventually venturing out into indie publishing. She resides in the South with her three children and enough pets to host a petting zoo. When she's not writing she can usually be found creating unique 3D cakes, hiking, reading, or spending way too much time on FaceBook.

Find out more about her at www.crystalrainlove.com